BLOOD & BROWN SUGAR

L.A. NOLAN

Leadstart
INKSTATE

ISBN 978-93-54581-78-6

First published in India 2021 by Leadstart Inkstate
A brand of One Point Six Technologies Pvt. Ltd.

123, Building J2, Shram Seva Premises,
Wadala Truck Terminal,
Mumbai 400022, Maharashtra, INDIA
Phone: +91 96999 33000
Email: info@leadstartcorp.com
www.leadstartcorp.com

Disclaimer: This is a work of fiction. All characters, events, and motorcycle clubs named in this book are fictional. Any resemblance to actual places, events, clubs, or persons, living or dead, is purely coincidental. The views, attitudes, and actions of the characters and clubs within this work have been conceived by me for entertainment purposes only, and in no way are meant to reflect the actual behaviours of 1% motorcycle clubs or their members. Should certain territories or names of the fictional club charters infringe on actual club boundaries, existing or past, with similar names, no disrespect was intended towards either. The genre of this work is crime fiction. Therefore, crime and criminal behaviour plays heavily within the story and it is my sincere hope despite these fictitious actions, that I have displayed the utmost respect towards 1% motorcycle clubs, their lifestyle, and their membership.

Editor: Vaibhav Pathare
Cover: Swapnil Behere
Layouts: Kshitij Dhawale

FOR MY PRINCESS BRIDE, WITHOUT WHOM, THIS NOVEL
WOULD HAVE DIED A LONELY DEATH ON A DESOLATE
HIGHWAY IN MY MIND.

L.A. Nolan is a Canadian born Brit with an insatiable lust for travel and storytelling. He immigrated to India in 2013 after removing his corporate tie and leaving Canada behind. Once in India, he joined a motorcycle club and crisscrossed the Indian sub-continent countless times. During one of these rides, he broke several bones on a desolate mountainside in the Himalayas and suffered the 1300 kilometre journey back to New Delhi, unattended and suffering. Nolan dabbled in several other pursuits, being the frontman of a rock & roll band, then tried his hand at acting in Bollywood, after which he began writing full time. Nolan still rides alongside his club brothers and has now settled in Bombay with his wife and two very naughty motorcycles, Wilhelmina and Elvira. This is his second book.

ACKNOWLEDGEMENTS

Thank you to the loyal readers of my blog, *The Wandering Hippy*. Your continued support has nurtured and encouraged me. You helped me find my voice.

The India Bull Riders Motorcycle Club. You welcomed me into the fold without question, and showed me the meaning of brotherhood and loyalty. In doing so, you laid the foundations for this novel.

My sister, Susan. You tirelessly dragged yourself through the slop of my first draft and set me on the proper path.

Vinny T, Papa Bear, and Noodles, my white shirts. You guys count. Ride on, shine on, mere bhailog.

Sandeep, countless kilometres from our rides together and many antidotes from our friendship have seeped into this novel. They have painted the backdrop of brotherhood, love, and determination on which this story is set. Without you, those experiences would not have been possible.

And my wife. Your seemingly endless supply of patience and steadying hand has kept the bike upright and pointed me north more times than I can tell.

I must mention my mother, who passed on to join my father just before publication. She would have burst with love and pride, I am sure, as it was her very nature and zest for life that gave birth to my rebellious soul.

I've seen the needle and the damage done. A little part of it in everyone. But every junkie's like a settin' sun.

-Neil Young

Brown sugar; an adulterated form of heroin, also called smack, junk, skag, dope, and chaw, is a semi-synthetic opioid derived from the morphine extracted from poppy plants.

-De-Addiction Centre, India

PROLOGUE

October 28th, 1:38 am

The sulphur tip ignited in a burst of orange and yellow as the farmer scraped his last match along the rough edge of the box. Lifting his hand to protect the flame from a slight breeze, he brought it to the end of his *bidi*. The stale tobacco caught and ignited. He inhaled deeply and tossed the matchstick into the refuse-filled culvert beside his hut, then blew a wispy stream of grey smoke towards the new moon. It was casting little illumination over his small farm in Rattoke, that suited him just fine. He coughed into the crook of his arm, his frail frame shaking beneath the thin blanket that covered him. The old man grunted as he picked up the canvas satchel at his feet and stepped forward towards the sugarcane fields that ran the length of his small property

The October crop had done well, and it concealed him as he worked his way between the rows and headed towards the fence along the backside of his land. He moved slowly, trying not to agitate the stalks of the three metre plants surrounding him. The rustling of the leaves when he did so was deafening in the silence. Not that there was anyone to hear it. His wife was asleep in their hut, his son had long since left their farm to pursue a life in Amritsar, and God willing, the Border Security Force were huddling around a campfire somewhere. His pace slowed further as he approached the edge of the field and spied the electrified fence that marked the end of his property, the barricade that represented the division between India and Pakistan.

October 28th, 1:44 am

Abha rolled over on the dirt floor of her meagre home in the slum district of Haripura, Amritsar. She shivered. Not from the chilled breeze gusting through the makeshift linen window above her, but from her aching need. Abha was sick, and she needed her medicine.

She sat up and crossed her fragile legs, rocking back and forth to ease the pain. There was little moonlight illuminating the single room dwelling. She patted the surrounding floor and found the lighter on the plate beside her. Flicking it, she lit a *ghee* candle.

Her baby stirred in a mango crate not far from her side. She shifted herself between the plate and the makeshift cradle, shielding it from the flickering light from the candle. A needle lay alongside it with a tarnished spoon and a small empty packet of tinfoil. It was of no matter. There was no need for her to cook heroin tonight. The syringe was already full.

Abha had purchased a pre-loaded needle from her normal connection earlier that evening. It had cost her 150 rupees and a sexual favour. The hit was more money than usual, but the favour was common enough.

She gagged at the memory, remembering how ruthless he had been with her, exacting his payment in an alley not too far from her home. Her eyes moistened. The 150 rupees she had given the pusher was the last of her wages. Abha had laboured on the road repair crew the previous week, carrying load after load of heavy bricks to build the curbs. But now the work finished. Now she was broke and her baby was hungry. But so was her habit.

The demon stirred inside her, making her shiver again as sour bile rose in her throat. Tears trickled down her cheeks as the sting from slapping her soft inner arm signalled Abha's fevered mind that relief was coming soon.

October 28th, 2:05 am

The damp earth was chilling the farmer to the bone. He slithered on his belly from the edge of the sugarcane field towards the border, inching forward and pausing, inching and pausing, all the while straining his ears against the night silence. He reached the desolate area of the fence used for the exchange and detected a muffled whisper.

"Bhaiya?"

"Yes, yes... I'm here," the farmer said, shifting up on one elbow. He put his hand on the end of the black 75 mm PVC pipe that came from the other side. He could hear the packages being loaded.

The packages moved along the three and a half metre long conduit. After what felt like an eternity, a pink plastic garbage bag emerged from the tube. The old man grabbed it and pulled. As it came free, another followed, and another, each package tied shut and bound to the one behind it with rough twine.

There were seventeen in all. Sixteen of them contained a one kilogram brick of pure Afghan heroin, protected by a watertight plastic bag and wrapped in brown paper. They filled one package with Pakistani sim cards and a gun, but the farmer would never know the contents. He never opened the packages.

When the last was free, the farmer fed the snake like garbage bag chain from his satchel into the pipe. Again, there were seventeen packages, each tied shut and tethered to the next. They filled the first with sim cards, this time from Indian cell phones, and each subsequent package contained a single bundle of four thousand US dollars. He pushed the final bag into the tube and forced it deeper with a bamboo stalk. He felt his counterpart on the other end take hold and pull. Another successful exchange was all but completed.

October 28th, 2:15 am

Abha lifted her right hand to her lips. A strong metallic taste from the heroin flooded her mouth as the unattended needle dangled from a vein in her left arm. Tentatively she licked her fingertips, tracing them with the tip of her tongue. The salty dirt from under her nails exploded in a riot of flavour inside her dry mouth. She savoured it. The warmth of her low was just beginning, yet something seemed wrong. She was sinking much faster than normal and the cold hard floor beckoned.

"So warm and soft. Soft like mud," she giggled. Abha was submerging into it. Her blurry eyes flicked open and tried to focus on the dancing flame of the candle. It caught her attention. She smiled at it. Another giggle caught in her throat as she toppled over to her left.

Something is wrong, the rush doesn't feel right, her mind shouted in alarm as her bliss turned to panic. Abha realised she had fallen and hit the floor hard. She couldn't reason or think. *Was there too much in the shot? Too much smack?* She giggled again.

She lay on the floor as the night wrapped its bony fingers around her. The needle slipped from her soft brown skin and fell as Abha's heartbeat slowed. The baby stirred and cooed as a soft breeze fluttered the window covering, causing the candle flame to flicker. Abha drew a sharp breath and, without ceremony, died.

✦

CHAPTER ONE

Alex Crossman closed his eyes and pinched the bridge of his nose between the thumb and index finger of his right hand. What would soon be a tremendous headache had started brewing right in the middle of his forehead.

"So, you will *not* pay us?" he asked, reopening his eyes. Alex stared at the short bar owner in front of him. The pudgy man undid the first two buttons of his white shirt, exposing the yellow stained and threadbare inside collar. A tarnished St. Christopher medallion dangled around his neck.

"*Oui*, yes. I am," he stammered, in a thick French-Canadian accent. "But I can't tonight. Not enough receipts." He held up several sheets of paper in his right hand as if to show proof of his predicament.

Alex's band, Ripe Vicar, had made the uncomfortable seven-hour journey across Highway 401 from Toronto to Montreal the previous afternoon. Alex had trailed them in his girlfriend's Honda while she snoozed in the passenger seat.

They played a gig here last night and had just finished the second of a two-show performance at this *shrine of rock-and-roll*, The Black Cauldron. Alex shook his head. It was time to go home. He fixed his steel grey eyes on the manager and stepped forward, crowding him. Alex stood at six foot two and was a solid 205 lbs, a bulk he had inherited from his father who himself had been an intimidating man. Despite Alex's threatening posture, the barman didn't flinch.

"Play Thursday and Friday night, both gigs, $1,200.00 cash. That was the deal," Alex said. His long sandy hair spilled over his shoulders as he leaned closer to him. "Now, pay up."

The owner wormed his way out from between Alex and the bar, then turned to face him. "I will not cheat you; I simply don't have the money. Tomorrow, after the Saturday night crowd, we'll be okay. I'll settle with you then. No worries, eh?" A smile broke over his lips, but his eyes kept darting nervously over Alex's shoulder towards the front door.

Alex rubbed his chin and exhaled a slow breath through his fingers. "Hey, pops, we are already skin-tight on this deal. We can't afford to spend another night in a motel, not with what you pay us. We are driving home tonight. Understand, Mr Lavoie? *Tonight*," he said, clenching his teeth.

"*Oui, oui, je comprend.* But the money, it is not there. The crowd was too thin, no? I cannot help it if no one comes, if no one drinks." He glanced around the room as his scant staff continued their cleaning. "I'm sorry for this, I am. But what can I do? Stay upstairs tonight, there's a room with a cot. I promise you full payment tomorrow after we close." With that, he spun on his heel, scurried away behind the bar and into his office.

"Just like a rat," Alex whispered to himself.

He looked over at the stage. His band was packing up what was left of their equipment, coiling wires, and casing guitars. *This news will go over like a lead zeppelin,* he thought. Alex made eye contact with his drummer, Keith, and knew that he would whine about the situation. He grinned at him and Keith smiled back, lifting his chin in a silent *what's happening* gesture.

Alex strode towards the stage, stepped up on the riser, and looked at Keith who was disassembling his cymbal stands.

"What's the scene, jellybean?" Keith asked. His jet-black hair was still matted and sweaty from the show, and it fell away from his face as he tilted his head to look up at Alex.

"Shit news, I'm afraid."

Keith scowled at him. "What happened?"

"Well." Alex paused and took his cigarettes out of his jean vest.

"There is not enough in the security box to pay us tonight."

"Jesus Christ on a pony. You're joking, right?"

Alex shook his head while he lit a smoke.

"Well, *that* is brilliant," Keith continued. "And what are we supposed to take in payment? Some lovely club Cauldron t-shirts?" He picked up a drumstick he'd broken during the gig and twirled it between his fingers.

"No, no, man," Alex soothed. He took a deep drag of his cigarette and blew the smoke at the ceiling. "Mr Lavoie will pay, just not tonight. He can't. Tomorrow night after close, he promised he'll be flush." Keith rolled his eyes. "I'll stay here with Candy and head back home tomorrow. No worries, you and the guys can take off after we pack up."

"This is bullshit, Alex," Keith spat at him, throwing the drum stick against the rear wall of the stage. It bounced off it with a crack, drawing their bandmate's attention.

"For Christ's sake, man. Don't make this worse than it is. Go home and I'll see you Sunday, to settle. We'll meet for a beer and a burger," Alex said.

The rest of the crew wandered over to join them. Alex glanced around, trying to spot his girlfriend, Candy. The last thing he needed was her high-strung opinions winding everyone up. He spied her leaning against the door to the washrooms, and true to her form, was twirling her lavender hair between two fingers while she ogled a bartender sweeping the floor nearby.

Willy joined them with his Jazz Master bass in hand. "Everything alright?" His Caribbean lilt was cool and smooth. His parents were Jamaican, and he had inherited their relaxed demeanour. Nothing rattled the boy or affected his chill. Often, Alex would jokingly grab his wrist and check him for a pulse.

"Yeah, yeah. We're good, bro," Alex answered.

"I have to hang on here till tomorrow to get our payment, but it's no problem, lads. You all take off home." There was a collective groan. Alex recalled a childhood lesson from his father. *You can lead a horse to water, but sometimes, you have to beat it with a stick to make him drink.* Alex sighed. "Guys, it'll be fine. I'll see you all at Montana's on Sunday at 2:00 o'clock, cash in hand. Beer and burgers on me, okay?" There was a muttering of reluctant agreement.

∗ ∗ ∗

As the band huddled on stage, the front entrance of the club opened, and in strode a large, dark-haired man. He paused just past the threshold, surveying the room as the door swung shut behind him. He wore a thick black leather motorcycle cut over a faded denim jacket. The man popped the snaps of his cut one by one as he paraded across the room, each one snapping loudly as he flicked them open with his thumb. His heavy boots clunked on the wooden dance floor as he approached the bar.

"*Excusé moi, Monsieur.* We are closed for the night," a young waitress called out to him from behind her mop and bucket.

His massive frame spun on her with the agility of a cat. "Do I look like I want a fucking drink?" he snarled. "Where is the rat prick owner of this dump?"

The biker turned, scanning the room with the blatant confidence of a motorcycle club enforcer, a club who had just taken control of the island's west end. It was a deliberate move, making sure the patch on the back of his cut was visible to everyone in the room.

The patch, embroidered in gold and beige, depicted a cowboy skeleton astride a powerful motorcycle with a horse skull for a headlamp. Flames spewed from its nostrils as the oilskin coat of the rider splayed out behind them. The boney fingers of his right hand gripped the throttle, while his left held aloft a battered, two tray weigh scale. It was the unmistakable patch of the Chevaux de Fer Motorcycle Club, one of the three 1% MC's in the city and victors of the recent bloody turf war on this end of the island.

The Black Cauldron is in their newly won territory, just past Rue Saint-Denis, as far east as the Chevaux dare exert authority. He ended his menacing sweep of the room by staring at the band. As he made eye contact with Alex, the waitress broke the silence.

"In there," she whispered, pointing to the office door behind the bar. He flashed Alex an unnerving grin and turned away. The thug moved to the door with purpose and after a quick glance over his shoulder, entered. The glasses hanging above the bar rattled and clinked as he slammed the door shut.

"*Bonsoir, Monsieur* Lavoie," he whispered. He let the greeting hang in the air like an ominous fog.

Mr Lavoie was sitting behind a small metal desk at the end of the narrow room. The glow of a bare overhead bulb was the only illumination, and it cast stringy shadows over the shelves, laden with cases of alcohol that lined each wall.

"Hello, Clipper," Lavoie said, rising from his seat. He bumped the cash-box on the desk as he did so, causing it to screech across the tin surface. The biker took a hasty step forward, patting him back down to a seated position with a hand gesture.

"No, no, Mr Lavoie. You keep chilling," he said.

The *silver bullet* patch on the right breast of his cut, designating him as the Club's assassin, glinted in the soft light. Lavoie eyed it as he sank back into his seat.

"I'm here to collect the rent, as we agreed last week. I know the sudden change in your"—Clipper hesitated a moment, searching for the phrase—"change in your protection services provider may have you a little rattled. Perhaps even unsure where your loyalties lay. But let me assure you, the Iron Horses are now the masters of your wellbeing and in firm control of this neighbourhood."

He smiled at the club owner. There was no warmth in it. To use the English name of the MC was a slight break of protocol, but it was late, he was tired and he didn't give a shit. Clipper wasn't French.

"I'm not, I know," Lavoie stammered, reaching into the cash-box. "I didn't pay the band. I, I have..."

"Yes, I saw them," Clipper interjected. "They don't look like they were worth much," he chuckled, then stepped forward and relieved Mr

Lavoie of the stack of crumpled bills he was offering.

✳ ✳ ✳

"What the fuck is this?" Marceau Gagnon shouted. It was late and there was a party in the other room that Clipper had just pulled him away from. Club business always came first, but collections were not a matter that needed overseeing.

His immense frame was leaning over the oak meeting table in the chapel of the Cheval de Fer's clubhouse. The heavy piece of furniture featured the MC's logo embossed in the centre. Marceau, standing at its head, glared at his Sgt. at Arms seated in one of the eight black leather chairs that surrounded it. There were no windows in this inner sanctum, so the soft amber light filling the room came from the recessed ceiling above the table.

On the wall behind Marceau was a large painting of an old school biker astride a Harley Davidson chopper. He was riding a lost desert highway and the shadow he cast was an outlaw cowboy on a galloping horse. The words *Les Cheval de Fer ne Meurent Jamais, ils Traverseront le Temps*, were scribed on a heavy brass plaque under the painting. *Iron Horses Never Die, They Ride Through Time*. The thick black carpet and the distressed russet wallpaper gave the room a somewhat sinister vibe.

"I said, what the fuck is this?" Marceau shouted again, staring at the scant stack of bills in front of him. Clipper had laid the cash on the table beside the small wooden block and gavel.

Marceau, the president of the Montreal chapter of Chevaux de Fer, lacked an understanding demeanour or friendly nature. His quick fuse temper had long ago earned him the name Tic Tock. He picked up the gavel and spun it between his fingers.

"That's all he had, Tic," Clipper shrugged.

"Oh! Well then. If that's all he had, I guess that's all we need, eh?" Sarcasm dripped from Marceau's voice as he waved the gavel in Clipper's face, then slammed it on the table. With an exasperated grunt, he pulled the green bandana off his head and threw it, exposing his close-cropped red hair. A cornfield of fire rolled over the top of his head and down his cheeks into a beard and moustache.

The rage boiled inside him. Marceau hated when Clipper, or any of them, took such a casual approach to club business. He paced around the table, looking at his inner core, his crew. The tall wiry frame of John Reeves, his Vice President, Shotgun Blu, his portly Secretary, and Tracy Simon, the club's tattooed Treasurer who stood in the rear beside Alain St. Louis.

Marceau made eye contact with each of them, then back to his bulldog, Clipper. He could see the group trading glances with each other. They didn't fear him, even though he *was* an intimidating man, but they got uneasy during his frequent outbursts. It rattled them, it *always* rattled them. He regained control of his anger.

"This is a little over half of the agreed amount, Clipper. What should we do? Accept it?" Marceau said, pointing at the cash, levelling his voice.

"I didn't know, Tic. With all the turmoil over the last few weeks, I figured some cash was better than *no* cash. Should I have just broken his arm straight away?" Clipper sounded impatient. He looked from one member to the next, as if trying to gather support.

I want to choke him, the stupid prick, Marceau thought. *Do I have to hold his hand through the simplest of decisions?* "I sent you to get the collection, you come back with half the collection. What did you tell Lavoie? You had to check with the office if payment plans were acceptable?" Tic sighed and walked back to the head of the table. He sat in his chair and spun his back to the group.

"No, I told him to get the rest and I would be back soon."

"Ahhh, soon, eh?" Marceau felt the anger building again. "Here is the thing, gentlemen. We have just fought a very hard and bloody war to win this part of the city, no? If we show any weakness, any cracks in our armour, the other interested parties may assume we can't take care of our business." He spun the chair back to face them.

"Make no mistakes, the Montreal 13 Machine is not as dead and gone as you all seem to think, we have only pushed them underground. They are still here in west Montreal," he said, as he slammed his fist on the table. "With the Fallen Angels circling both of us like goddamned shark, no? If we don't stay strong, there will be no 'soon'!" he barked.

"Okay, Tic. Okay. I hear you, I'll go back," Clipper said. "It's late, but I think he sleeps there on weekends, I saw a cot upstairs that first time we went through the place. I'll get the cash...tonight."

"I'll go with you," Alain, Clipper's top goon said, glancing at Marceau for approval, who gave a slight nod.

"We'll get it done, Prez," Clip said.

For a moment, muffled sounds of frivolity filled the room. The laughter of the Club's prospects and hang-arounds, mixed with the giggles and screams of the Horse Heads, an assorted group of strippers, party girls, and old lady wannabes that never seemed to be too far away from the MC.

"Yes, you will, my Sergeant. And if there is no cash, you take from his property. If there is no valuable property, you will take from his ass, yes?" Tic Tock said, then smiled at him.

"That doesn't mean you get to fuck him, Clip," John quipped, and the group burst into laughter.

"Fuck you, you fucking homo," Clipper spat at him, but smiled nonetheless.

"Yes, no sex for our good Mr Lavoie tonight, please, Clipper," Marceau snickered. "Now go get it done." He motioned to the door. "John, give me a minute?"

Frivolity flowed in from the main clubhouse as John opened the chapel doors and the group dispersed. He gave Clipper's ass a slap and squeeze as he passed him, then shut the doors behind them.

"Faggot!" came the muffled cry from the other side.

Marceau lit a joint and looked at John. His forehead creased. "What do you think?" he asked, taking a hit off the weed.

"About what? Clipper?" John replied, walking closer and taking Marceau's mixed package of Marlboros and marijuana from him. "He's all right, Tic. You know that. He just needs direction now and again. A little prodding." John chose a cigarette over a joint and lit it, tossing the package on the table.

"We won't be there in India to give him direction, John." Marceau exhaled a long stream of green smoke. "He has to think on his feet if there are complications, no? This is why we go, yes? To protect against unforeseen issues. It's a long way away, brother, no prodding stick long enough. We need to trust him to make correct choices."

Tic sucked deeply on the joint again, then bent and retrieved his bandana from the corner of the room where it had landed. He wrung it in his hands and turned back to face John. Marceau squinted through the smoke coming from the end of the joint dangling in his lips. "He has me worried, Johnnie."

"I know, Tic. I know," John answered, smashing out his smoke in the ashtray on the table. "Me too."

✳ ✳ ✳

Candy stirred in Alex's arms. They made the single cot work as a bed. It entwined the two of them into a vine of flesh. Alex lay on his back with Candy's head on his chest, stroking her hair. She was drunk and very amorous. Shucking her jeans and top, Candy had pounced on him as soon as the others left. Alex, however, was not feeling frisky. After Candy gyrated against him for a few minutes with no response from him, she passed out.

My God, he thought, looking at her. *What would you do without booze, drugs, and sex?* Alex chuckled. Candy was a wonderful girl. A little wild to be sure, but loyal, and with a warm heart. He cared for her. There *could* be potential for this relationship to be a long-term thing, but he didn't think so. Alex didn't give it too much time. He was only twenty-six, and she, just twenty herself.

Alex had enough on his plate for now, being on temporary layoff from the garage where he worked. A huge grease fire last week had torched the place, and Alex had little by way of savings. The situation was leaving him anxious, even though the owner promised him a position once he reopened. The garage hadn't burnt to the ground, but it would still be months before the insurance settled and they remodelled the shop.

Candy stirred again and Alex held her tighter. Her ample breasts squeezed against him. *That* gave him a stir in his loins. He should have relented to her earlier advances.

His father's voice sounded in his head. *"Son, for every action, there is an equal and opposite reaction."* Alex didn't think his dad had been speaking about refusing a shag and then wanting it later. *But you never knew with pop. He was an experience all his own.*

Dean Crossman had been a member of the Ottawa chapter of the Devil's Choice MC in the seventies. He opted out in 1986 when the chapter patched over to the Skull Riderz MC. Dean rode as an independent until he settled down in Toronto with Alex's mother in 1989.

Two years later, Alex was born, and three years after that, his younger sister, Sarah. His father had never spoken about his involvement in an MC, and Alex had no idea until the age of nine when he found his father's club cut in their bedroom closet while looking for hidden Christmas presents. The memory of him questioning his father was still vivid.

His dad was making breakfast the next morning, Sarah was watching cartoons and there was no sign of their mother. Alex thought it was a splendid time to pry.

"Say dad, where's mom? Is she all hungover from the party?" Alex was not sure what the term meant but had heard his dad say it. He knew it was from drinking booze and caused a headache.

"Watch it, you!" Dean chuckled. "Or I'll burn your eggs on purpose!"

"That means yes!" Alex exclaimed.

"Well, maybe just a little. So, be nice to her today, all right, Tiger?" Dean smiled down at his son as he slipped the eggs from the frying pan onto the plate on the table. Alex beamed back at him.

"Say, dad?" Alex asked around a mouth full of toast. "What is that blue vest in your closet?" He was spitting crumbs as he spoke.

Dean Crossman's eyebrows rose. "And what were you doing in my closet?"

"Oh, uh..." Alex stammered. "Hide and seek. We were playing with the babysitter last night."

"Is that so?" his father chuckled. Alex nodded and shoved a fork full of eggs into his mouth alongside the toast.

Dean looked out the window over the sink. He was silent for a while, just gazing into the backyard.

"Well, son, a long time before you were born, daddy was in a motorcycle club called Devil's Choice."

"Cool!" Alex sat bolt upright in his chair. "A motorcycle gang?!"

"A club," his father corrected, smiling at his son. "And it was a long, long time ago."

"So, you were a bad guy, huh? With guns and stuff?" Dean Crossman sighed and placed his hand on his son's head, tussling his hair.

"No, Alex. Not a bad guy. Just a guy who did what had to be done."

"What does *that* mean?" Alex squinted up at his dad with all the innocence of a newborn foal. Dean grabbed the back of the chair opposite them and dragged it close to his son, spun it, and sat down on it backwards.

"You may be a little too young to understand this, Tiger," he said. Alex covered his face with his hands.

"Not a birds and bees talk!" he wailed.

"No, no. God no, Alex," Dean laughed. "There are many things a man needs to do in his life, Alex. Some of them are unpleasant. Lots of times you have to do things you *don't want* to do. But that's the measure of a man, son. Doing what he needs to, regardless of how he feels about it."

"Like cleaning my room, or taking out the garbage?"

"Kind of. But I'm not talking about things you don't *enjoy* doing, Alex. I'm talking about things that make you feel bad. Things you may think are wrong, but still have to be done for the good of everyone involved."

"I don't wanna do anything wrong. I don't wanna feel bad," Alex said. His face was dour, his eyes searching.

"I know, son. I know, and hopefully, you won't. All I mean is that sometimes in life, you're faced with a situation that requires action. And sometimes, that action will be defined by more important things than good and bad, or right and wrong."

"I don't get it, dad. What's more important than right and wrong?" Dean let out a slow breath. He smiled at his son.

"Respect. Loyalty. Being a man that others can count on, Alex. Those things matter, son. Those things define you."

"You're right, I *don't* get it!" Alex said and crammed what was left of his toast into his mouth.

"Don't worry about it, Tiger. Just try to be the best guy you can be and everything will be fine." Dean stood and kissed the top of his son's head.

The crack of snapping wood dragged Alex's attention back to the present. Candy shifted and moaned as he strained his ears against the silence. *Nothing!* Alex could only hear the mechanical tic of the battery-powered clock on the wall behind them. Then, a faint shuffle and a scrape. *Someone is downstairs in the bar!*

* * *

Clipper looked up at Alain perched on the garbage dumpster behind the nightclub. He was backlit from a bright security light fastened to the wall near the corner of the building. Alain slouched forward, jimmying a screwdriver under the window in front of him. The snap of splintering wood echoed through the alley like a gunshot.

"You're sure there is no security?" Alain asked as he froze in place.

"It's a shitty little nightclub, brother, not a fuckin' bank," Clip chuckled. "We re-conned it when we shook him down, I'm sure. Now, hurry before my balls freeze."

"What balls?" Alain quipped back.

"Was that a joke? Well done, Alain. Who knew you were capable?

Now, back to chewing your way through the window frame."

Alain grunted and returned to prying the frame. With one last definitive *snap*, the window popped open and swung inward.

"*Ah, voilà*," Alain muttered. With a glance at Clipper, he stretched up to grab the window frame, did a chin up, and swung his feet into the blackness. There was a soft thud as Alain's feet hit the floor on the other side. Clipper jumped up on the dumpster and followed him through the window.

Standing in the darkness of the ladies' washroom, the two of them strained to hear if someone had detected their entrance or if there was anyone there at all. The inky black pressed in on Clipper's eyes. The only audible sound was the wheezing breath of Alain.

"You pant like a fat old man," Clip whispered.

"An old man that will kick your ass."

"Yeah, yeah..." Clip chuckled. "Have another cigarette."

The two of them eased forward, eyes adjusting. The shaft of light coming through the window was enough to make out the room's features. Alain led the way and they walked out into the bar. The glint from the exit signs and beer fridges lit the room, casting shadows in every direction. The pair paused again to listen against the silence.

"There is a cot upstairs," Clipper whispered. "I'll go, you check the office."

"I should come with you."

"No need. Lavoie is not a threat. Now go find the safe or lockbox."

Alain crept off through the dark towards the office. Clip followed, careful not to knock a table or chair. The small iron staircase that led up to the loft was behind the bar. He paused at the bottom, looking at the uniformed rows of bottles and glasses. There was a landing at the top of the steep staircase with a small entrance door.

Clipper glanced over his shoulder to Alain and drew his 9 mm Beretta. He exhaled, then began climbing the stairs, his heavy biker boots clumping on the metal surface. He tried to lighten his steps, but Clipper was not a graceful man.

Well, if that little shit, Lavoie is here, now he knows I am too, Clipper thought. He reached the top of the stairs. The landing was small, barely enough space to stand and open the door before it hit the handrail. Clipper grasped the knob, planning to fling the door open and level his gun. *If I remember the layout, the bed should be across from the entrance.*

He knew the room was sparse. *The cot, bookshelves, banker boxes, and maybe a desk,* he thought. *Not a room to get into a close quarter fist fight. No. With any luck, the fat prick is asleep and I can pin him down with no fuss.*

He turned the handle as slowly as possible, trying not to create any noise. He swore he could hear the brass on brass scrape along the faceplate as the latch withdrew into the door. It sounded deafening. The knob stopped rotating. Clipper pulled open the door with as much force as his staggered position on the stairs would allow. He stepped onto the landing and stabbed his pistol into the room towards the bed.

"*Arrête,* you prick! Stay still!" he shouted.

The cot was tussled, but empty! Clipper tensed and strained his eyes against the darkened room. There was a whisper of movement and a roundhouse kick from just inside the doorway hit him square in the chest. Clipper grunted as the air expelled from his lungs. He stumbled backwards and fired two shots from the Beretta into the ceiling as he flipped over the handrail, and with a splintering crash, slammed into the bar below them.

Clipper lay amongst the broken glass and fractured wood. He heard the shriek of a woman and then Alain shouting his name. His eyes blurred as he looked up at the landing. The ashen face of Alex looking down on him came into focus.

Clip tried to raise his pistol, still clutched in his right hand, but could not. His arm responded only with a sharp stabbing pain. He willed it to move, but it remained flaccid at his side. Crumpled, he stared up at his assailant. *I know him. I've seen him, but where?* Clipper passed out.

◆

CHAPTER TWO

Asmall white Honda coupe circled Connaught Place like a shark, sulking its way through the congested traffic. Abbreviated by the locals to CP, it is the most famous and one of the busiest commercial centres in New Delhi. Comprising three loops of businesses, the inner, middle, and outer ring radiate out from an esplanade and central park, to create a tight spiral of concentrated shopping. The British had constructed it from 1929 to 1933 and it is the unofficial centre of the bustling city.

The passenger gazed at the huge national flag and flower-filled gardens of the park where young and old alike can spend lazy afternoons, basking in the winter sun.

Local musicians gather and strum their acoustic guitars until the tan uniformed foot patrols of the Delhi Police come and chase them away.

The car made a left onto one of the short radial roads that connected the inner and outer circles and slipped past the faded alabaster buildings housing the retail outlets, restaurants, and nightclubs. After a scant distance, the car reached the one-way Connaught Circus Road and turned right. The popular shop, Fab India, displaying the latest in colourful ethnic wear, slipped by.

After crossing the little sitar shop visited by the Beatles on their way to Rishikesh, the Honda drifted across the five lanes of traffic and splintered onto Chelmsford Road, heading north to the New Delhi railway station.

Half a million people pour off of or climb onto the hundreds of daily trains across from the Paharganj Market. It was here the car pulled up tight against the curb and stopped.

Paharganj stands in stark contrast to CP's slick and modern style. It is a true Indian market. The hustle and bustle of vendors calling to consumers in Hindi and accented English create a colourful mosaic. Some may even call out in Russian, French, or German.

Merchants sell their wares from wooden carts or off of blankets laid on the side of the road. The battle to protect the trinkets from the tuk-tuks and scooters that honk their way through the morass of travellers is an ongoing effort.

The middle-aged man in the driver's seat had no interest in any of these things. He sat, smoking a cigarette, and staring into the bedlam. He wanted drugs. While there was plenty of top quality weed or hashish about, that was not at all what he was after. This man wanted brown sugar. Heroin.

Avinash Kumar was a senior agent at the Narcotics Control Bureau, and for the better part of six months, had been tracking the heroin trail from Amritsar to Mumbai with his junior partner, Sandeep Bohla.

They had been piecing together the trail and compiling the names, faces, and places. But New Delhi was a hornet's nest. This was where the two ends of the rope vanished, and he could not connect them. They knew heroin came across the border in Amritsar, and they believed it ended up in Mumbai, to ship out of the country. But this, this is where it all went dark.

Wrinkling his nose, he took a draw off his smoke. Avi's battle against leaving the evils of tobacco had not been going well. Despite the window being down, the smoke swirled around him like a shroud. The engine was running and the air conditioning was at maximum. Avinash tossed his cigarette butt out the window and closed it.

He stared at Sandy sitting in the passenger seat. Young, good looking, fit. More like a Bollywood star than an NCB agent. He himself was on the short side, balding and a little portly. He looked every inch the battle-hardened Narcotics Control Bureau officer, right down to his mirrored aviator sunglasses and cheap suit.

"What?" Sandy asked.

"I bet you can dance like Hrithik Roshan," Avinash chuckled, referencing one of India's biggest Bollywood stars. Sandy rolled his eyes.

"This again?" he sighed. "Avi, it's not my fault you have gained weight and lost your hair. Why must you torment me?"

"Really..." Avinash pressed. "Could you teach me to *lungi* dance?"

"Oh please, Avi. No more. The thought of you dancing in a *lungi* makes me feel a little ill." The two of them laughed.

They had been partners for only six months but had grown fond of each other. Avinash was a talented agent, and Sandy was an eager and intelligent man. He wanted to learn the ropes and would make the sacrifices necessary to do this job well. Avinash liked him and very much wanted to help launch what looked to be a promising career.

Without success, they were working with the Border Security Force of India and the Drug Regulatory Authority of Pakistan, to unravel the mystery of how the powder crossed the border. However, they knew the smugglers transported it to Amritsar, then packed the heroin into the spare tires of a cargo company's transport trucks. The trail then led to a warehouse in Dwarka.

A highway checkpoint inspection just outside of Delhi on one of these cargo trucks had provided this information. The terrified driver had spilled all he knew with little provocation. From the warehouse, they distributed some of the heroin to pick up points in the city, then shipped the rest to Mumbai.

What Avinash did not understand was how this happened or who was behind it all. This was why they had not shut down the shipping or warehouse operation. Avi needed to get to the head of the snake.

A month ago, they had caught a break. Sandy had been at his dentist on a Friday evening, Clove Dental, in the Safdarjung Development Area. A group of youthful men had burst in with an overdose victim while Sandy was in the chair. It was mayhem. The dentist could do nothing for the man. He knew nothing of drugs or how to deal with an overdose.

The young lad had shot some brown sugar in his car in the parking lot of Hauz Khas Village, a trendy nightclub district not too far away. When he passed out and convulsed, his friends panicked and brought him to the closest medical facility anyone in their group knew of. A dentist.

The man died. The intense questioning of his friends had uncovered a dealer in Hauz Khas, who, after the application of considerable pressure, lead them to a small time supplier in Mayapuri. He had uttered the magic words 'Iron Horses Motorcycle Club.'

"Look, look!" Sandy pointed over Avinash's shoulder at a Royal Enfield Thunderbird motorcycle weaving its way out of the market.

The rider was wearing a black leather vest, and this was an odd sight in Delhi. As the motorcycle rumbled past them, the skeleton cowboy emblem was visible on his back. The 'Iron Horses' rocker on the top and 'New Delhi NCR' rocker curved underneath were both clear as day. Sandy and Avinash exchanged glances.

"What do you think?" Sandy asked.

"A motorcycle thug shopping in a tourist market?" Avinash mused. "That's our guy." The Royal Enfield blurred by, Avinash slammed the car into gear and it stalled with a lurch.

"You will lose him!" Sandy shouted, as Avinash twisted the key and fired the car engine back to life.

"Not today," he said and pulled out into traffic amidst the honks of the other motorists.

The bike was heading down Chelmsford Rd towards CP, and he would be difficult to follow on the Connaught Circus Rd. As they reached the one-way street encompassing Connaught Place, the bike dodged and weaved through the late afternoon traffic. Avinash jammed his thumb on the horn and tried to force his way through the congestion. No one yielded. A horn blaring in Delhi was no cause for alarm. This was normal daily driving, and no one paid any attention.

In the distance, Avinash saw the bike cut between a bus and an SUV, its electric blue gas tank glinting in the sun. The rider then leaned into an erratic, sharp left-hand turn onto Minto Rd and disappeared.

"Get the plate number. The plate!" Sandy shouted.

"Shit!" Avinash screamed, slamming his hands against the steering wheel.

A three-wheeled delivery van honked at him as it came level with his door, and the driver began shouting from the open cab for him to move. Avinash considered waving his gun at him in frustration. *That would shut him up,* he thought. He exhaled a deep, deliberate breath.

"Come on, boss," Sandy whispered. "Let's go home and regroup."

✳ ✳ ✳

The slow invasion of Canada began late in 1985. The American based Fallen Angels Motorcycle Club, followed by the Skull Riderz Motorcycle Club, seeped across the border into Ontario and Quebec. Thereafter, the Canadian biker wars began.

They set Ontario aflame first. Both pervading MCs were scrambling to patch over the region's biggest MC, the Devil's Choice. Devil's Choice had a loose affiliation with the Skull Riderz in the 1970s, making it a foregone conclusion that they would patch that way.

Both the Fallen Angels and Skulls eyed the lucrative urban centres of Toronto and Ottawa, yet while the reward was great, they recruited cautiously, neither willing to jeopardise their stability by patching in unworthy chapters. By the late eighties, the Skull Riderz prevailed. They swallowed up most of the province's chapters.

In Quebec, the situation took a unique turn. A powerful French MC, the Popeyes, and the Devil's Choice shared the province equally. The Popeyes patched over to the Fallen Angels in direct response to the affiliations in Ontario. They had no wish to align with the Choice under the Skull Riderz' banner.

The crown jewel of the province, Montreal, was under the control of Devil's Choice and seemed a lock to become Skull Riderz' territory. Then the Choice inexplicably fractured from their Ontario chapters by shunning the Skull Riderz and patching over to the Fallen Angels.

The shock and outrage of the small factions of Popeye members on the island erupted. With their hopes of ruling as Fallen Angels crushed, they left their new association in droves.

The ex-Popeye members reformed and dug in on Montreal's northwest side. This collection of cast-offs became known as the Montreal Thirteen Machine.

Back in Ontario, through the late 90s and into the mid-2000s, the Canadian police relentlessly chipped away at the Skull Riderz. The upper echelon based in Chicago grew weary of the headaches and became reluctant to send resources north, leaving the Ontario chapters disillusioned and angry. A faction of Devil's Choice's heritage and Canadian born hardcore members melted away from the club and resurfaced in Kingston as the Iron Horses.

The pressure brought to bear on the fledgling club in Kingston by law enforcement pushed them east to Tois Rivier in 2010. It was around this time, the president of the Iron Horses or Les Cheval de Fer, Philippe Moreau, had courted the idea of importing Afghan heroin from India. He had his eyes firmly fixed on Montreal.

After extensive reconnaissance, the Horses aligned with a sizable riding club in India called the Bull Riders. The Horses executed a successful trial run in 2014 and swallowed the Bulls and their nine chapters, whole.

By 2015, the Iron Horses were shipping 10 kg of heroin every four months from India to Montreal. They had gained the means to reinstate the Kingston chapter and begin their war to gain control of Quebec and Ontario.

In 2016, they had formed solid chapters in Kingston and Toronto and then taken the west end of Montreal. The Horses held it with a tentative grip. A grip that relied on the seamless delivery and distribution of their Indian brown sugar.

Hiran Deol knew some of this history. Knowledge gained over the last five years during his rise to vice president of the New Delhi chapter of the Iron Horses. There were, however, facts he did not know. That two NCB agents had watched him emerge from Paharganj Market after his pickup, for example. He was also unaware he was riding alone. His wingman, the cover that should ride just out of sight behind him, was at this very moment, suffering from a hangover and still fast asleep in his bed.

Gently rolling the throttle of his Royal Enfield, he swung in and out of traffic along the congested Minto Rd. He was heading for the clubhouse in Ohkla.

Hiran, in his early 30s, was surprisingly strong for a man with such a wiry frame. His dark complexion and thick black moustache gave him a very serious look. Yet, on the rare occasions he smiled, people considered him handsome. His hair hung just over his collar and flipped in the breeze below his helmet as the speed of the bike increased.

The ride to Okhla took over an hour, and Hiran wheeled his bike into the compound of the Iron Horses clubhouse with relief. He had done many heroin runs to Mumbai over the years and felt comfortable enough, as comfortable as one can feel while transporting large amounts of narcotics. But he always felt uneasy transporting, even for short distances, through Delhi.

The clubhouse was not as grandiose as its counterpart in Montreal but was not devoid of comforts. Tucked away in the D-Block phase of the Okhla Industrial Area, it looked innocent enough. Masked behind the facade of a musician's rehearsal studio, the three-level building served its purposes well.

The ground floor was primarily bike parking, and the second floor was the clubhouse proper and the chapel. On the third floor, there were three crash pad rooms, one each for the president and vice president and a playroom for everyone. It also had one private office where Hiran, taking the stairs two at a time, arrived breathless.

Behind the enormous desk in that office sat Ramdev Kapoor, the president of the Iron Horses Delhi chapter. In the corner, on a small leather sofa, was Ipsita Chaudhary, his current sex kitten. Hiran felt a slight stir in his loins as he admired her. She was wearing a sheer white blouse and black leather pants; her long legs were crossed and a red six-inch stiletto pump dangled from her right foot.

Ramdev, comparable to his counterpart in Montreal, was a sizable man, cut like a boxer. His Sikh upbringing had furnished him with a long thick beard and moustache, and he sported an Iron Horses brown coloured turban. But unlike Marceau, he was a very attractive man and wore his looks like an athlete or actor.

Ipsita, however, was the genuine beauty in the room. Still in her early twenties, Ipsita dripped with sexuality. Her ample breasts and shapely figure had caused many a man's pulse to quicken after only catching a glimpse. Fair for an Indian woman and standing tall at 5'-9", Ipsita's near perfection was rounded out by her full lips and waist length hair of black silk. She was the stuff of legends. Hiran could not help but steal another glance at her as he crossed the room.

"*Namaskar, bhai,*" he said, smiling at Ramdev. Ramdev smiled back, but cut straight to business. He shot Ipsita a sideways glance that signalled it was time for her to leave. They both watched her sultry hips sway from the room.

"All is well?" Ramdev asked after the door had shut.

"No problems at all, brother, except the fucking traffic," Hiran answered, as he flopped down in the chair across from the desk. He pulled out four keys of heroin from the thick leather tank bag he was carrying and placed the bricks on the desk with a thump. "No problem at all," he repeated. Ramdev picked one up as he stood and walked around the desk. He smiled as he tossed it from hand to hand.

"You are an obedient soldier, Hiran. This is the last of the 16 keys for this shipment. Clipper will arrive from Montreal, Sunday, at 11:00 pm. I need you to collect him and we'll begin the run to Mumbai on Monday afternoon." Just at that moment, Ramdev's cell phone in the desk drawer chirped, the burner phone with the Pakistani sim card. He glanced at Hiran with concern.

"*Namaste*?" he answered. His face darkened as he mouthed *Marceau* to Hiran. It darkened further still as he listened. "What the fuck do you mean *complications*? What *kind* of complications?" he barked into the phone.

"Don't talk to me like that, you fucking worm!" Marceau screamed. Ramdev scowled and opened his mouth to shout back as Marceau cut him off. "You are little more than a puppet king of a satellite club, Ramdev. Don't forget that, or who you're speaking to. I'm the fucking president of the mother chapter, *oui*? There will be a civilian coming to escort the shipment. It's under control on this end, make damn sure it is on yours, and never question me again." The line went dead. Ramdev clenched his phone and shook. He tried several times to speak, but no words came. After several deep breaths, his shoulders slumped and he rubbed his temples.

"What's happened?" Hiran asked.

"They're changing the escort. Some fucking civilian... Leave me alone, brother," he whispered.

✳ ✳ ✳

"I don't know," Avinash mumbled as he peered over his brown shoe tips at Sandy. His feet were perched up on his desk at the NCB offices in the West Block of the Delhi Zonal unit like a worn leather testament to law enforcement.

One advantage of being a Superintendent at the Bureau was having a private office, albeit a humble one. Furnished with an ancient desk and a narrow bookcase overflowing with pending and unsolved case files, it had everything he needed. A credenza that housed a few shirts and reference books alongside a worn green two-seater couch where Sandy had parked himself rounded out the furnishings, aside from a suspect air conditioning unit that coughed out cool air whenever the mood struck it.

As meagre as his office was, he could at least see Dr Bhim Rao Ambedkar Park from his window, far superior to the other side of the building that afforded panoramic views of the Bureau of Energy Efficiency.

"I just don't know," he repeated, replying to Sandy's question if he thought the Iron Horses were behind the shipping of brown sugar from Pakistan, or if they were just dealing in Delhi. "What I find disturbing is we weren't even aware of them as a player. Let's be honest, we still don't know if it involves them. It's a hunch."

"Hard at work, I see!" Manoj Pandey, the Deputy Director burst into Avinash's office without warning. He had the Zonal Director in tow, and neither of them looked very pleased. Sandy stood up in a heartbeat, a gut reaction from his days in the military. Avinash removed his feet from his desk and stood along with him at a much slower pace.

"Good afternoon, sir," Avinash said.

"Is it?" The Deputy Director Pandey demanded. He was a tall, fit man in his mid-fifties, tough as nails, but respected by his subordinates.

"Yes, sir," Avinash continued. "I believe we have had another break, sir. We feel there may be a link between the heroin flow from Amritsar and a local motorcycle gang called the Iron Horses."

"It's been five weeks since your peon here caught the last break at his dentist. 'We have a significant lead, sir. We are getting close, sir.' That is what you said. *Five weeks ago.*" The Deputy Director was not shouting, but his voice was loud enough to echo down the hall outside Avi's office.

"Yes, sir," Avinash replied. "These dealers, sir, they are slippery, we..."

The Deputy Director cut him off with an impatient wave of his hand. "Superintendent, I don't care. Our Director General scolded me this morning. Consequently, the Zonal Director got a good berating from me this afternoon. He would have headed to your office to pass it along to you, but I decided to cut out the middleman! Do you understand, Superintendent? Shit runs downhill, and it gains speed on the way down!" He let the explanation sink in. "We need results! Now. Not in a month, not in a week, *now*! You give me something I can feed upstairs and do it quickly or you will be busting marijuana smoking tourists in Rishikesh before the week is out!" With that, he spun on his heel and left the room.

"Well, that just about covers our lesson on manure and gravity." Zonal Director Yadav spoke for the first time. He was a smaller man in his forties and soft-spoken. He looked at Avinash over his spectacles and smiled. "What have you got, Avi?" he prodded. Avinash glanced at Sandy, who was still frozen in his spot by the couch. Sandy shook his head.

Avinash had known Akhilesh Yadav for a long time. They had come up together, right from the academy. Family connections had propelled the Director's career along a little faster than most, but Avinash did not begrudge him that. He was a dutiful man. He couldn't simply lie outright to him.

"Not much, sir," he sighed. "These cartels are buried so deep, are so well connected. They pay off everyone. We need time and luck. We are working with the local police officers in Amritsar and the Border Security Force. Sandy here had liaisoned with the Drug Regulatory Authority of Pakistan, but sir, we just don't understand how they get the heroin over the border. How or where." Avi moved to the front of his desk and leaned against it.

"It pops up in abundance in Amritsar. We've made good inroads there, sir, having mapped out the network of dealers. We even know how it gets to Delhi and who moves it. But once it arrives, we lose complete track of the shipment until it shows up again being sold by pushers in Udaipur, Ahmedabad, or Mumbai." Avinash lit a cigarette. "Sir, we have dealers and a few transporters, but no idea who is writing the cheques."

"*Achha*. There have been some serious inquiries from the top of the mountain. You know to whom I refer. We need to inflate the situation, I'm afraid." Zonal Director Yadav made a face at Avinash's cigarette and motioned for him to put it out. "Therefore, I am assigning you another Junior Intelligence Officer to assist. Officer Shashidhar."

"Dimpi Shashidhar?" Sandy blurted out. The Zonal Director silenced him with a razor sharp glance.

"Yes, Dimpi Shashidhar, and the two of you will include her in all aspects of this investigation. *Theek hai*?"

"Yes, sir," they said in unison, as the Director left the office.

"Good. I will send her down to join you. Results, agents... now," he said over his shoulder.

Avinash picked up the butted smoke from the ashtray and re-lit it, angrily blowing smoke at the ceiling.

"I thought the Deputy Director would have a heart attack," Sandy chuckled.

"I've never liked Pandey," Avinash said absently. "He was senior to me at the academy. He was a legend. Top of his class and hard as nails. But always rumours that he was shifty, corruptible."

"Speaking of rumours, the things I have heard about Dimpi Shashidhar suggest we will soon have our hands full."

"Son of a bitch," Avi said, shaking his head.

"Yes, yes, she is," Sandy spouted, as he paced the room. "*And* the Director General's niece! A pig-headed, self-important..."

"Bitch?" Dimpi asked. She was standing in the office doorway. She had been waiting just down the hall, well within earshot of their scolding and Sandy's assessment of her.

Dimpi was wearing a light grey suit with a white blouse and holding a stack of file folders in her right hand. She was a fair-skinned and attractive woman in her early twenties, of average height and fit, her dark brown hair left loose to fall over her shoulders. The NCB preferred its female officers to wear their hair short. Dimpi did not agree with that policy.

"Why is it when a man is aggressive and headstrong, he is an outstanding Intelligence Officer, but when it's a woman who is self-confident, she's a bitch?" she asked, striding into the office, and dumping the files on Avinash's desk.

"No one said that but you, Officer Shashidhar," Avinash said, in a tone intended to remind her of her rank, and his. She backed away from his desk and looked up at him, smiling wryly.

"Yes, sir. That is true, sir. But that is the prevalent feeling shared by most male officers. No?" she asked him point blank. Without giving him a moment to respond, she continued, "Superintendent, they repute you to be an exemplary officer, tolerant, intelligent, quick to spot and help develop young talent."

Avinash looked to his partner as she spoke; Sandy rolled his eyes and smiled.

"I hope you will allow me to grow under your tutelage and I will not be offended if you address me as Dimpi, sir."

"Well, let's not rush things along too quickly now, Officer Shashidhar," Avinash chuckled. "This is Officer Sandeep Bohla. I don't much care what you call each other, but in my presence, I will be the Superintendent, and you will be the Junior Intelligence Officer. Fair?"

"Yes, sir," she said while shaking Sandy's hand.

"What's that?" Sandy asked, pointing at the files Dimpi had dumped on the desk.

"Everything I know about heroin," she replied. "Cost, effect, manufacturing, composition, everything."

"I see," Sandy said, raising an eyebrow and looking at Avinash.

"I tell you what, Officer Shashidhar. Find out everything you can on the Iron Horses Motorcycle Club. They are based here in Delhi, we believe. Get it to me as quickly as you can," Avinash said. Dimpi smiled, nodded, and almost ran from the room.

"Let's see what she digs up," Avi sighed.

✳ ✳ ✳

The drug trail from Afghanistan to India to Montreal is not as complicated as one may think. The Chevaux de Fer had long ago become an ally of one of the more prominent Afghan drug cartels and paid a premium for the transport of raw stock through Pakistan. This is where the drug is refined and packaged. Still under the cartel's protection, it crosses the border and is delivered to a tiny farming village in India called Rattoke. Each shipment comprises sixteen 1 kg bricks of pure Afghan heroin and is moved every four months.

Then the farmer carries the packages buried beneath a load of sugarcane to Amritsar by ox cart. On his way to the market, a private transport company relieves him of the packages outside city limits.

Once at the company's depot, the bricks are placed into the spare tires of moving trucks or concealed in barrels of mustard oil. For variance, they also use bushels of sugarcane to smuggle the narcotic. They execute this phase under the watchful eye of the Iron Horses.

The MC maintains its distance while still providing discreet protection and overseeing the loading. The Horses do not come in contact with the product until it is ready to leave for Delhi. They relieve two kilograms of heroin from the consignment for local distribution. From the cargo yards in Amritsar, the heroin begins its journey to the company's main warehouse in Dwarka, a large suburb of New Delhi. The MC chose this method of transportation for various reasons.

First, to distance itself from taking part in smuggling the heroin over international borders, and second, it was also a precaution against transporting the product from Amritsar. Amritsar is a well-known entry point for traffickers, making the drug business in this area even riskier.

The Horses decided it was better to pay the premium and distance themselves from transportation in such a heavily patrolled area. The MC took over in New Delhi, where the threat was not as great.

In Dwarka, the load is split up again. A delivery of 2 kg straight to the MC's dealers for distribution in Delhi, and then three separate deliveries of 4 kg to various pickup points around the city. Now, the transport company's duties were fulfilled.

The Horses then retrieve the bricks by rotating two-man teams, one man to pick up and transport, the other to trail behind and observe. They bring the freight to the clubhouse in Okhla, ensuring the consignment is not being followed. If it is, the tail man will identify the pursuers and inform the lead bike. Then they lose the followers between the pickup point and clubhouse.

From the clubhouse, three teams dispatch at different intervals, travelling by varied and changing routes to Mumbai. Each rider will transport the product in their saddlebags, hidden in plain sight, feigning the common sight of some chums on a motorcycle vacation.

The Horses handle this leg of the journey. It helps to maintain cost effective shipping fees, and the risk level is low compared to the other two ends of the operation. A member of the Montreal chapter accompanies one of the riding teams, and from this point out, sticks with the shipment all the way home to Canada.

Once all 12 kg is reunited in Mumbai, the Horses skim another 2 kg and deliver it to a network of dealers for sale in the city. They turn the remaining 10 kg over to a maintenance company, Gupta Ship Machinists Pvt. Ltd.

From Mumbai, it trucks to Goa in crates of machined ship parts. It is then stashed aboard a Montreal bound ship in the repair yards there. They stow the goods on board, along with the Canadian member of the MC, before the ship returns to Mumbai for legitimate cargo loading and customs inspection. Occasionally, the MC has run the shipment straight to Goa, but as is policy, the Horses prefer to distance themselves from any border crossing initiative, so they do this only in extreme cases. With little variance, this was the procedure three times a year. To date, it had been operating without a hitch.

✳ ✳ ✳

Ipsita lingered outside Ramdev's office door. She leaned against the wall, shoulders slumped and eyes downcast. *Leaving his presence is like walking off stage*, she mused. *If he had any idea...* She trailed her fingertips over the latest bruise on her bicep.

"I have to get out," she whispered. Ippy retrieved her cell from her purse and dialled Daya's number. The phone trilled many times until she relented and disconnected the call with a huff. "Stoned again," Ipsita muttered, shaking her head.

She paced the half a dozen steps up the narrow corridor in front of Ramdev's door, pausing, spinning, and parading back the other way. After a few passes, she resumed her sentry post against the doorjamb. Ipsita's head dropped and her eyes scanned her contacts list. She found her brother's long uncalled number. Her fingertip lingered and after a deep sigh, she stabbed the call icon.

"Hello?" a mature voice answered. Ipsita paused.

"Hi," she breathed.

"Ippy? Is that you?"

"Yes... it's me," she stammered.

"Good God. Where are you? *How* are you, *meri behen*?"

"I'm in *Dilli*. But not so good, Eshaan. I want... I want to come home." There was an unbearable silence on the line. Ipsita's grip tightened around the phone. Her knuckles turned white and her hand trembled.

"Are you injured? Pregnant?"

"No!" Ippy felt her cheeks flush. "Typical fucking response from you, big brother."

"Stay calm, Ippy," Eshaan scolded. "What do you expect? It's been years since you disappeared, vanished into the night. Not a call, not any contact. We feared you were dead, or worse."

"I'm sorry. I just want to come home," she choked. "I miss you, and Papa, and Mom." A long deliberate breath whistled through her earpiece.

"I don't think so, Ipsita. You wouldn't be welcome here now."

"Why? Eshaan, please. Talk to him." In her mind's eye, Ippy could imagine her brother scowling and shaking his head.

"It won't matter what I say, Ipsita. You're dead to him."

"Dead? Dead! For leaving to make a better life? For wanting to better our family?"

"More than that!" Eshaan blurted. "The shame you have visited on this family is too much, ya? We learnt about the Senior Constable."

Ipsita winced. She had used her powers of seduction on the Senior Constable in her village to facilitate her running away from her family.

"Father knows. *We* know you..."

"Fucked him?!" she barked.

"Laid with him," her brother corrected. "And then that television commercial. Ipsita, you were in a bathing costume. A bikini! For all to see! With so many men around you."

"It was a travel advertisement, Eshaan! For Goa, for God's sake!"

"It was too much for him," he whispered.

"That's ridiculous. I was making money, trying to find my way to Bollywood. A commercial is no reason for shame!"

"Ipsita, you *know* our father. You *know* this village. Everything changed. Whispers behind our backs, the way people looked at him, it crushed Papa. He hid away for months, so low, so depressed, we thought he would never recover. That policeman bragged about taking you on his desk, Ippy, *to everyone*. What did you think would happen?"

"I'm sorry, Eshaan. I need you and Papa; I want to come home. Please, just talk to him," she whispered.

"No, Ipsita. I won't. I won't go through it again. Weeks of every morning going to his room and expecting to find him hanging from a rope. No! What's done is done. Papa has made himself clear. He no longer has a daughter. I'm sorry, Ippy. I loved you once, but what you have done, you must live with. Stay away from us."

The call ended and hot tears spilled down Ipsita's cheeks. She rolled along the wall and placed her forehead against Ramdev's door, hunched with anguish.

There is no relief, she thought. *I'll go see Daya. I need to see her.*

Ramdev's voice suddenly raised and Ipsita heard him bark. "What the fuck do you mean *complications*? What complications?" The muffled conversation that followed lit the darkness in her heart with a spark of hope.

◆

CHAPTER THREE

Every four months, the ordeal of choosing an escort for the India shipment was an enormous pain in the ass. It left Marceau and John sweating the decision for days, agonising over which of the low-level members or prospects was dependable *and* expendable.

This month, they had exhausted all palatable options, so Clipper had volunteered. It was not an assignment that one of the inner circle would relish. High risk, lots of uncomfortable travel, and little personal reward other than the continued success and growth of Chevaux de Fer.

Marceau was leaning against the bar in the clubhouse, cell phone still in his hand after speaking with Ramdev in Delhi. The primary room of the Chevaux de Fer clubhouse was as one would expect of a motorcycle club. A massive oak bar along one wall and a pool table in the middle of the room, a black felt poker table and air hockey game on the perimeter, and the club favourite, an antique 1950s jukebox beside a huge plasma TV. Various Harley Davidson posters with topless women rounded out the decor.

Marceau stared blankly at the wall, then clenched his fists and pumped them in the air. He shook his head twice and smashed the cell phone like a package of MacIntosh Toffee on the bar. Tiny bits of plastic scattered in every direction as it splintered.

"You fucking bastard!!! *Modie tabarnak...*" He stared incredulously at Alex who they had tied, barely conscious, to a chair beside the pool table.

"We should have killed this ass clown," Alain said as he spat at Alex's feet.

"No, no. You were right to bring him to me," Marceau said, as he pushed off from the bar, leaving one stool rocking in his wake.

"But I seriously want to kill him, Tic." Alain's eyes gleamed as he stared at Alex.

"Yes, you do enjoy your job. Don't you, brother?" Alain nodded vigorously as Marceau walked to Alex and patted his cheek. "It was the right thing," he repeated while grabbing a fistful of Alex's hair. Marceau yanked his skull up off his chest, to reveal a bloody and swollen face. Marceau leaned close to Alex as he whispered, "Because you, my unknown friend, will make this right. Yes... you will." He threw Alex's head forward with a snap. Alex groaned.

The front door to the clubhouse opened and John came in, glancing around the room. "Where are Tracy and Shotgun?" he asked.

"Gone to pick up the bikes from the bar. I drove this piece of shit and his whore back in their car. How is Clipper?" Alain asked, slapping Alex in the head for good measure.

John had taken Clipper to a *doctor* friend in the east end of the city, a doctor that was more accustomed to patients with fur and cold wet noses. More than once he had dug a bullet or two out of a member and set quite a few broken bones.

"What's the word?" Marceau asked, echoing Alain's concern.

"Doc says he seems okay," John said, lighting a cigarette. "He's fractured a few ribs. Wants to keep him there until the blood clears out of his piss." He shot a look of pure disgust at the slumping figure in the chair. "So, who is this panty waste? A citizen?"

"Hard to get answers," Marceau chuckled. "He keeps passing out."

"Alain's school of interrogation," John muttered, as he walked over to Alex.

"Finest in the province, enrolment slots still available," Alain said without humour.

John placed his hand on Alex's forehead and pushed his head upright. His eyes fluttered open.

"Well hello, fucktard," John said. "Why are you pushing our friends off of stair landings?" Alex groaned again and John let his head slump forward. "Where's the girl?"

"She is resting comfortably in our guest suite," Alain sneered. "Should kill her too."

"We'll deal with her later," Tic said, giving Alain a grin. "From what she said, and from what we could get out of this whelp"—He lit a cigarette and blew the smoke at Alex—"they are nobodies. Citizens. She babbled that her boyfriend's band played at the club, and they were staying overnight to get payment. Some shit like that. He told the same tale. Swore it was an accident with Clipper, thought he was a burglar. He didn't say much. Alain had a good go at him at the club."

"Fuck them." Alain shrugged and walked behind the bar to grab a beer from the Molson Canadian fridge. The hiss from the cap as he twisted it drew glances from the other two. "What?" he asked.

"Give us a minute please, Alain. Go call Blu and Tracy," Tic said. Alain tilted his head and nodded.

"I'm just a little thirsty," he mumbled and left the room.

"A psycho alcoholic," John said after the door swung shut, then turned to Tic. "What a fucking mess this is." He ground his cigarette out in the ashtray on the poker table beside him.

"Hum," Marceau grunted. "I think what we'll do, Johnnie boy, is dispatch this one in Clipper's place, no? This little fuck will make things right for us. He can escort our product home." John's eyes widened, and Marceau chuckled.

"You don't approve?" he asked.

"No, I don't. Why in God's name would he do that for us? How can we trust him, Tic? This is an enormous responsibility, club business. You're not concerned he will fuck it up? It seems reckless to me, brother... reckless." Marceau smiled down at Alex, who had opened his eyes.

"Oh, I think he will do a fine job for us, John. He will be careful and highly motivated."

Marceau crouched in front of the chair and stared into Alex's eyes. He could see the fear through the swollen lids, but there was more. Anger. Lust for revenge. He was a tiger, this one, more than capable of the task at hand. Marceau was sure of that. He reached out to stroke his hair, but Alex pulled his head back. Marceau grabbed it instead. He affixed his icy stare into Alex's eyes. "Yes, you will perform admirably, won't you? You will go to our friends in India, you will bring our shipment home, and *then* we'll decide what we will extract as recompense for our injured brother." Marceau used his handful of hair to make Alex's head nod. "That's right, you will. If you don't, my friend, make no mistakes, we will cut your little girlfriend's tits off." Tic smiled without humour.

✳ ✳ ✳

Candy lay on the plush queen-size bed in the playroom of the Chevaux de Fer clubhouse. She drew her knees to her chest and shivered. Her body was aching from the manhandling she had received.

As yet, Candy had been unmolested but feared it was only a matter of time. She had a very limited idea of what the situation was. Only that Alex had seriously hurt a member of this bike gang and now they were making him carry out a task to make up for it. Candy hadn't seen him or heard his voice since they arrived and suspected he was no longer in the clubhouse. *I'm the insurance, the motivation for him to do whatever they are asking. If Alex doesn't comply...* Candy shivered. She didn't want to think about that.

She studied the room. *Obvious what happens in here. No doubt its only purpose is for sex.* Candy wrinkled her nose as she scanned the collage of semi-pornographic pictures on the walls.

A single 40-watt lamp illuminated the area with a soft glow. It stood atop a white three-drawer dresser that would look more at home in a child's room. There was a wooden kitchen table and chair in the corner beside a door that Candy assumed was a closet.

A small black leather ottoman stood in the centre of the suite. Candy doubted they used it to rest their feet. The predominant feature of this love nest was the swinging chair suspended from the ceiling in the far corner. It was low to the ground and featured boatswain straps for the occupant's legs. They scattered an assortment of pillows on the floor underneath it.

Candy had seen one of these in action once during a stag party hosted by a rich and influential real estate agent in Toronto. Candy was working the bar but had a very clear view of the stage. A buxom blonde girl had climbed aboard the chair and a huge black gentleman had positioned himself under it. Then the swinging began. Candy grinned sinfully at the memory.

The door opened without warning, flooding the room with a brighter, fluorescent light. She sat up on the edge of the bed. Shotgun Blu strode in with a red plastic tray.

"You like spaghetti?" he asked.

"You made this for me?" Candy enquired, smiling at him. She was grateful that the gigantic man had cooked for her, even if it was only spaghetti.

"Shit, no," Shotgun chuckled. "It's takeaway. The boys ordered a pizza and someone figured, Christ knows who, that we should feed you too." He smiled and winked at her.

Shotgun placed the tray on the bed beside her, a plate of spaghetti in a very thin sauce, one meatball in the middle and a solid looking dinner roll. A can of diet coke completed the meal. Candy laughed and tilted her head, cascading her purple hair over her shoulder.

"Fit for a queen? Well, thank you anyway... *Shotgun*?" she giggled.

"Call me Blu, darlin'," he answered, smiling at her.

"Thank you, Blu," she said. She was famished but restrained herself. "Any idea when I can go home?" she asked while picking up the can of coke. It opened with a pop. Shotgun looked at her through his shaggy bangs and pulled the kitchen chair over to the bed. He turned it backwards and straddled it like a motorcycle and studied her for a moment.

"Look darlin', it's best if you ask little and say less. Don't be noticed at all if you can help it. Your boyfriend will take care of some business. When it's done, you can go."

He lit a smoke and looked at her gravely. "Just don't create any problems in the meantime. Be a church mouse." He raised his finger to his lips. Candy pouted a little as she sipped at her soda.

"Can I get cleaned up at all?" she asked. "My overnight bag is in my Honda. I assume you have my car?" Shotgun nodded and stood. He walked to the door in the corner and unlocked it.

"I'll bring your bag in. This is a washroom; the shower is decent. There is soap and shit in there already," he said.

"I just was wondering how long I have to be here, and if I'll be okay." She quivered as her voice broke, and fixed Blu with doe eyes.

"Sweetheart," he chuckled, walking back to the middle of the room. "You seem like a pleasant girl, and yes, it's unfortunate you're caught up in this. But I am far too old a cat to be fucked by a kitten, okay? Your tits and ass have no effect on me and neither do your scared watery eyes. Be good, stay quiet, and with luck, you'll be out of here in three weeks."

"Three weeks?!?" Candy screamed. "People are gonna worry! They'll come looking, ask questions!"

"No one will worry," Shotgun said, calming her. "Alex is heading home to Toronto, he has already told your friends that you two were in a minor car accident and that you are okay. He explained they were holding you in the hospital for twenty-four hours as a precaution. As soon as you're out, the two of you will take off for a holiday to the east coast while you recuperate. You understand?" He smiled without humour. "In a couple of days, you phone whoever you need to, tell them you are fine, and back that story up. Dig it?" Shotgun spoke in a matter-of-fact voice and blew a cloud of cigarette smoke at her.

"Okay, Blu. I can do that. But all bullshit aside, I am scared," she said.

"We're not animals, Candy. No one will hurt you without cause. Just behave yourself and you'll be fine." He walked to the door to leave.

"I'm not a naïve baby girl, Blu. I know I'm the insurance," Candy called after him. "What happens to me if Alex fucks up?" Shotgun paused and looked back over his shoulder, lingering with his hand on the doorknob.

"You had best hope he doesn't, Candy," he whispered and left the room.

Fuck! Candy thought. *Fuck, shit, asshole, prick, asshole!*

"Jesus, Alex," she whispered and picked at her soggy spaghetti. *No way. I do not trust these guys.* She swallowed a mouthful of coke. *They can't keep me locked in here for three weeks. I'll flirt my way out. There will be an opportunity, someone will leave the gate open, and when they do, I am gone, girl. Gone!* She forced down the rest of her dinner.

✶ ✶ ✶

Bruised and cold, Alex was sitting on the back of a Harley Davidson Fat Bob, racing down Highway 401, east to Toronto. It was only April, not prime riding weather in Canada.

Alex was huddled behind John, who looked warm enough in his leather jacket, chaps, and wool hoodie.

"What the fuck? You wanna be my old lady?" John elbowed Alex hard in the ribs. It made him wince, as he was still tender from the many beating the Club had gifted him back in Montreal. "It's bad enough I have to let you ride bitch. Let's not get intimate." Alex shifted back in the seat. The frosty air rushed between them, and Alex shivered.

We just passed Gananoque, which means another three hours of icy cold to endure. At least the wind numbs the pain somewhat, Alex thought.

"Can we stop for a coffee?" Alex shouted. "I'm freezing here."

"Man up, fucksicle," John replied.

"My dad used to make this run," Alex said.

"What?"

"My dad, he used to make this run!"

"What run?"

"Kingston to Toronto, I think."

"Your old man was patched?" John asked, twisting in his seat a little.

"I think so," Alex shouted. *Why am I telling him this?* Alex thought. *Maybe so he'll stop elbowing me in the ribs?*

"What was his name?"

"Dean. Dean Crossman."

"No shit," John chuckled and twisted the throttle.

They had to be in Toronto by 1:00 pm, then in Brampton, at the BLS Indian Visa and Passport Application Centre on Gillingham Drive by 2:00.

Marceau had already called their contact in the Indian Embassy from Montreal. The contact had assured him that if he could get the applicant's passport in by 2:00 pm on Saturday, he would make sure they issued the visa before 3:00 pm on Monday. Marceau had threatened it better be ready, as Jet Airways Flight 9W223 left Toronto Pearson International Airport at 7:00 pm Monday evening. They booked Alex on that flight, and it would be tight enough to make the airport on time without delays.

They had saddled up at 6:00 am in Montreal, John with Alex riding pillion and Alain solo, to make the run to the Toronto chapter's clubhouse. From there they would be off to Alex's apartment and retrieve his passport, then to the visa centre. Barring any traffic issues, the trio should be fine. Fine, despite the fact there was a shit ton of cold hard pavement between them and their goal.

After 11:00 am, the duo of bikes pulled up to a mechanic shop on Albion Rd in Etobicoke. The fence gate slid open after a honk from Alain, and they pulled into the spacious black asphalt parking lot. There were half a dozen motorcycles parked in a row along the front of a two storied wooden building. It had a single door in the middle and five small windows, one on either side of the door and three larger ones on the second storey. *Like an old west saloon*, Alex thought, as he spied the maple wood sign hung from a bike chain over the door. It swayed in the chilly breeze. Burned into the softwood were the words, *Iron Horses MC Toronto. No Virgins Allowed.*

Across the parking lot, there was a line of bikes in front of the five-bay mechanic shed. There were three Fat Bobs, two Super Lows, a Softail Classic, and a Street Glide. It looked like a Harley Davidson showroom.

The young lad in greasy blue coveralls who opened the gate sauntered towards them as they dismounted. He was grinning as he approached.

"Hello, rat pricks," he laughed, looking between John and Alain. They both smiled back and embraced the lad.

"Well, look at you, Tommy!" John said. "Last time I saw you, you barely made my waist. Jesus, what have you been eating?"

"Blondes," Tom answered, and the three roared. He then turned his gaze towards Alex.

"This is him then?" he asked.

"In the battered flesh," Alain said. Tom walked up to Alex so his chest was almost in contact with him. He was a few inches shorter, and not as broad, but his eyes showed no fear as they locked with Alex's.

"Clipper is my godfather," Tom whispered. "You had best believe that I am looking to fuck you up, rock star," Tom sneered.

"Rock star?" John echoed. Tommy turned from Alex.

"Yeah, he's the frontman of a rock band here in town. Ripe Vicar, I think. I saw them at the Horseshoe a couple of months back," he explained.

"No shit," John muttered, losing interest. "Let's go see your dad."

As the foursome walked up to the front door of the clubhouse, Alex glanced around, looking for anything, anyone that may help him. *With Candy in the clutches of these goons, I simply have to do what they've asked, and pray it all goes to plan. Maybe then they'll let her go.*

As for him, he was hoping escorting their drugs back to Canada would be enough compensation for knocking their brother off the ledge.

The interior was as Alex had imagined it would be. He felt he was entering a saloon in Dodge City. An old-fashioned bar, five wooden poker table and chairs, and walls covered in strips of cedar and pine, complete with a wagon wheel chandelier. *It's like a movie set!* Only the fifty-inch plasma TV and microwave behind the bar looked out of place. The boy led them to a door at the back of the room and knocked.

"Come," came the gruff reply. Tommy motioned to John to enter, who grabbed Alex by the wrist and ushered him into the room.

"Johnnie," grumbled the absolute bear of a man behind the desk at the far end of the office. He didn't glance up from his laptop computer as he spoke.

His scalp shone through the top of his thinning silver hair. *He must weigh 125 kilos*, Alex thought as he stared at the man in disbelief. He lifted his massive head and fixed Alex with a stare over the top of his reading glasses. It was neither intimidating nor friendly. Alex's pulse quickened and a knot developed in his stomach.

"Hello, Digger. You old head gasket, you," John laughed. Digger motioned for the two of them to sit.

"So, this is your mule, eh?" Digger said, studying Alex. "Marceau filled me in. Doesn't seem like the type to do any damage to our Clipper," he said with a non-committal shrug.

"The way I understand it, he surprised him. Knocked him over a railing and he fell a good distance onto a bar." John leaned forward and slapped Alex across the back of the head as he spoke. "That's the only way a clown like this could do a lick of damage to Clip." Digger lit a cigarette and offered one to John.

"What do you need from us, brother?" he asked.

"Nothing, Digg. Just a place to crash a couple of nights and take us to some bar on Queensway this afternoon. Our new friend here has to weave a cover story for his bandmates, so he is free to conduct business for us."

"Hmm, and what story is that, son?" Digger asked, once again affixing Alex with his neutral stare.

"I uh..." Alex cleared his throat. His mouth went dry as he recited his cover story. "A car accident. I'll tell my friends we were in an accident. My girlfriend and I. I'll tell them she is in a hospital in Montreal and I came home to get some clothes and her social insurance card, and... and I have to go back to be with her."

"They won't be concerned?" Digger asked.

"They are not those kinds of friends, sir," Alex said.

"Maybe you have the wrong associates then," Digger chuckled without humour. "You see that man there?" Digger nodded towards John. "He broke my heart when he left for Montreal after Kingston. We had been riding together for years, since our old Ottawa days. Still, he went east. But he is still my brother, and I would do great harm to anyone who crosses him. Am I being clear?"

"Yes sir, you are," Alex whispered.

"Call me 'sir' one more time and I'll fucking cuff you. I am not your math teacher or your father. You want to show me respect? Look me in the fucking eyes and speak like a man when you address me." Alex lifted his head and looked into Digger's eyes.

My father would have had you for lunch, Alex thought. *Still, what the big man is saying rings a bell. "Respect is earned, son, not given," dad used to say. "Say what you mean and mean what you say."*

"All right. I will," he said.

"Good. Now get out of my office, you little puke, before I put my size fourteen boot straight up your ass." Alex stood, and Tommy led him from the room.

"What's the move, Johnnie?" Digger asked after the door had shut.

"Alain and I will run this guy to his apartment, he can get some clothes and his passport, from there we will go to Brampton, submit his visa application." Digger nodded as he listened to John. "If your guys can meet us there, say at 3:30 and take him to this Montana's on Queensway, that would be an enormous help. Oh, and tomorrow morning, can Tommy or one of the boys give this prick some riding lessons? He says he can ride, but let's make sure before we strap two hundred k worth of sugar to his ass and turn him loose in India."

Digger lifted his massive frame from his desk chair. "I thought you said you needed nothing from us," he chuckled. "Let's get at it, my boy." John stood and as he reached the door, paused and turned.

"Do you remember a Dean Crossman?" he asked. Digger thought for a moment.

"Humm, not off the top of my head. Why?"

"It's the kid's father. I'm not sure, but I may have run with him in the Choice up Ottawa, way back when I was a prospect."

"Really? Ha. Can't say I do, but I'll ask around some old-timers."

"Yeah, do that, Digg... do that."

"You gonna hang around a few days?" Digger asked. John shook his head.

"Naw, I'll leave straight from the visa office. Tic needs me in Montreal."

"You're a hard riding man, Johnnie. My ass can't handle that kinda distance all in one shot anymore," Digger chuckled.

* * *

Shotgun Blu's bedroom at the clubhouse was dim and sparsely furnished. He was seated in a wingback leather chair in the corner. One of the more attractive hang-around women known as the Horse Heads was kneeling between his legs in front of him. She was topless and her breasts were swaying as he watched her head bob up and down in his lap. He was completely disinterested.

She was sexy enough, but he had other things on his mind. Other women on his mind. Candy on his mind. It was her he wished was performing this gracious oral act. He closed his eyes and pictured her, her soft face and purple streaked hair. He placed his hands on the back of the woman's head to guide her. In his mind's eye, he focussed on Candy. His pace quickened and his hips thrust up out of the chair. There came a sharp knock on the door as he was concluding the encounter.

"Blu? You in there?" John barked as he opened the door. The Horse Head turned towards the intrusion just as Shotgun moaned and spent himself on her cheek and hair. John, surveying the scene before him, burst into laughter. "Glad I'm in time for the money shot!" he sputtered through the chuckles. The girl squealed in disgust and wiped her face as she scurried from the room. This increased John's laughter two-fold.

"Fuck off, asshole!" Shotgun bellowed, but couldn't keep the smile from his bearded face.

"You've gotta watch where you point that thing, Blu, you'll shoot someone's eye out!" The two of them roared with laughter.

"Your timing is impeccable," Shotgun said. He stood and fastened his jeans. "I thought you were in Toronto."

"I just got back. Come on, it's time for church." John motioned to the door.

The two of them walked along the main corridor of the Cheval de Fer clubhouse, past the Hall of Fame, featuring framed police mug shots of the club members.

"There has been some activity, *serious* activity in the west end," John said. "Two hang-arounds and Billy had the shit kicked out of them in some sleazy strip joint. Chateau du Sex, I think."

"Fallen Angels?" Shotgun asked, raising his eyebrows.

"They weren't wearing colours, but their ink told the tale. Billy is sure he saw a club tattoo."

"Humm," Shotgun mumbled. "If they were Fallen Angels, they would have been wearing cuts."

John held the door as they entered the chapel. The others were already seated and Marceau shot them a sour look.

"Nice of you to join us," Marceau said.

"Sorry, Tic," John apologised. "I had to get Blu from the garage. He was having his piston polished." The room broke into laughter. Despite his annoyance, Marceau smiled.

"Sit down, you assholes," he chuckled, then his tone became serious. "I am sure you all know, two jag offs hammered Guy, Pig Sty, and Billy up pretty good last night. This presents two problems. One, we cannot let acts of aggression against our boys go unanswered. And more importantly, who the fuck is it, taking shots at us?"

Marceau lit a cigarette and continued, "Billy swears he saw Fallen ink on one of these pricks, but unless we know for sure, it would be unwise to retaliate. We have just survived a nasty three-way war. Now, with our numbers depleted and funding low, we are not in a position to light a fuse on a powder keg we cannot contain." Marceau scanned the table, looking one by one at his crew. "We must move cautiously."

"Tic," Shotgun said. "Is it possible they *were* Fallen Angels, but didn't wear colours to lure us into a fight with the Machine? That would be our natural assumption and reaction, no? They let the two competing clubs scrap it out, and then they'll swoop in and clean up whoever it leaves standing?" The others around the table murmured agreement.

"*Qui*. Possible, Blu," Marceau said, nodding. "In fact, that is a very good guess as to motive. But let us be clear, gentlemen, we are far from ready for any confrontation. Let alone a war. Whoever did this is prepared to fight. The calculations are simple, we need cash, we need that shipment from India." Tic pounded the table. "In the meantime, we need to earn *as much* as we can, *as quickly* as we can. I have a feeling the next few weeks will be expensive."

✳ ✳ ✳

Alex stood over the Street 750 and sucked the blood off the knuckles of his right hand.

"Oh, just a brilliant manoeuvre, dimwit," Tommy shouted at him from the other side of the parking lot. "Pick it up!"

Alex stooped, heaved the bike upright, and swung his leg over it. The smell of fuel stung his nostrils and burnt his eyes.

It was his second drop of the afternoon, but everything considered, he wasn't doing too bad. It had been years since he rode, but the muscle memory returned to him fast enough. He was just having trouble with the slow, tight cornering. Tommy joined him and stood beside the bike.

"Stop pulling in the clutch. Trust your machine, man. You need to be light on the throttle and pull yourself out of the corner. Slow in, power out. Speed doesn't matter, dude. More figure eights, nice and tight."

Alex stamped the bike into neutral and hit the electric start. It fired up and he popped it into first and crept forward. He picked up more speed, clicked up to second gear, and started his slow serpentine. After half a dozen rotations, Alex fell into a smooth rhythm. Speed up straight, throttle back and glide, dip into the corner, then caress the throttle and pull out. Speed up, slow, corner, speed up, slow, corner... and on it went, as his mind drifted back to his first riding lesson.

"That's it, Tiger!" Alex's father had said. "See! I told you it was easy!" Alex was fourteen and his dad had bought him a 100-cc dirt bike. He was giving him lessons in a field behind his house, the one he moved into after he separated from his mother. Alex had pulled up beside his dad and smiled at him.

"Yeah, dad. It's cool," he said.

"Just be gentle on the gas. You need to finesse it, like a woman," Dean laughed.

"I'm gonna take advice about women from you?" Alex teased. Dean's face clouded as he leaned over and hit the kill switch on the bike.

"Son, it's complicated with your mother, okay?"

"How so, dad? She kicked you out. Doesn't sound complicated to me."

"No. No, Alex. We decided it was best. Look, we still love each other. But we have differing views on life, how to live it and how to raise you and Sarah."

"Dad, please. She wouldn't let you buy a bike and ride with your friends. You fought about it all the time. I'm not deaf or a kid anymore. I know what's up."

"No, son. You don't. You truly don't. They are not friends, Alex. They are brothers to me. Men I would do anything for, men I respect and love. Your mom doesn't understand that."

"Neither do I. It's like you chose them over her, over us."

"Christ no! I chose me over her! I tried it her way, Alex, I really did. The house, the job, and kids..." Alex scowled.

"Hey, hey! Don't mishear that. You and Sarah are the best things that have *ever* happened in my life. End of story. But being with your mom was not for me. No, not that. Living your mom's preferred lifestyle was not for me. I was miserable, Alex, and that was making her miserable, and *that* was not good for you guys."

"I get that, dad. But it's worse now you're gone. It's always *no this* and *no that*. She's a tyrant. I wanna come live with you."

"That's not for the best, son. Learn to live with your mother. She's a wonderful woman, Alex, she knows what's good for you."

"I fucking hate her," Alex murmured. Dean cuffed his son across the back of the head hard.

"Hey! Never disrespect your mom. What have I taught you? Respect, son. That is the most valuable currency a man possesses. Don't confuse anger with hate. Do you get that? There's a bigger picture in life, son." Dean sighed. "You're not a little boy anymore. You need to get a handle on this stuff and *listen* to what I'm telling you. It's okay to disagree, to challenge authority, and live life the way you want. But you have to be true to yourself, to *your* value system. Don't conform to rules because someone tells you to, don't *hate* something just because it doesn't suit your lifestyle. Change it. But don't give up your integrity as a man when you do. Son, one day you will realise these are the truest words you will ever hear."

"I'm sorry, dad. I don't hate her, you're right. It's just I get angry." Dean smiled.

"Figure out who you want to be, how you want to live your life and make peace with it. Okay, buddy. Go for a ride and clear your head. There's no better therapy!" Dean laughed.

Alex forced the memory from his mind, stopped the 750 beside Tommy, and flipped down the side stand. He got off the bike and flexed his fingers.

"You'll be okay," Tommy said. "The bikes over there weigh a lot less, they're a little easier to handle. Go find Alain. Your visa should be ready by now."

◆

CHAPTER FOUR

Ipsita Chaudhary sat in the rear of the white Mercedes C Class coupe as it wove its way along the Greater Noida Expressway. It was late afternoon, and the traffic was getting heavy. Shivam Sharma, or Shiv to the rest of the MC, drove the enormous car. He was the Delhi chapter's highest-ranking prospect.

Ipsita studied the back of his head. *His ears are so large,* she chuckled to herself, noting the way they poked out of his shaggy black hair. *He's the only one Ramdev trusts to drive me around. Not that Ramdev is at all worried about anyone trying to seduce me. Christ no, that's a death sentence.* But Shiv was a very skilled driver. A talent growing increasingly essential on the mean streets of Delhi. *They'll patch him in as a full member soon. I wonder who Ramdev will assign as my keeper then.*

"How much longer, Shiv?" she enquired.

"Another half-hour, ma'am," he answered with no thought to the question. She adjusted herself in the soft leather seat. *That means another hour at least.* Indian time differs from the time the rest of the world observes. Seconds were minutes, and minutes were more like hours.

Ippy was on her way to Noida, Sector 143, to see her friend and confidante, Daya Ambel. The two of them had ran away from their village in Haryana to Mumbai, with dreams of becoming Bollywood starlets. They had made their way there and dove headfirst into the underground nightlife.

Through a friend of a friend at a flashy after-hours club, they had met

Hiran. The two girls had been looking to party and make connections. Hiran happily filled both needs.

He had been there on a delivery run from Delhi and could help the want-to-be actresses with drugs and alcohol. Hiran said he could even introduce the pair to some low-level Bollywood executives. Now, two years later, Ipsita was the tarnished mistress of one of the most powerful gangsters in New Delhi, and Daya had become a heroin-addicted fuck toy for the Club.

Tears welled in her eyes. *We are trapped, the two of us.* She, by Ramdev's inescapable power and Daya, in the numbing grip of brown sugar. She wiped her tears. It was their stupid fault. She remembered the numerous scoldings from her brother and father, forbidding her to go to Mumbai. But go she did, despite her family's warnings and counsel, and left behind her a trail of shame for them.

In the dead of night, Ippy had slipped away from her tiny village in Haryana, certain she would return to her home one day, famous and rich.

Ipsita had seduced the local Constable. It had been the first occasion she had used her body to gain an advantage, to get what she wanted. It had seemed justifiable, and a one-time necessity. Arrange transport and not assist her father in finding her. That was the cost of her virginity. Lost forever on a small desk in a shabby field office.

"Shiv...," she muttered. He glanced at her in the rear-view mirror. "Hurry."

The car lurched forward as Shiv pressed the accelerator. Ipsita stared blankly out the window, watching the endless stream of traffic slip by.

Sometime later, they pulled through the rusted gates of the Shivani Apartment Complex. It was a smaller society, composed of two worn and faded apartments with only four floors each. Daya was in building B on the top floor. There was a small patch of yellow grass between the buildings and some scattered playground equipment. Two adolescent boys were shouting as they chased each other around the slide, and two older girls squealed in joy and exuberance as they swatted a badminton shuttlecock back and forth over a bench.

Ipsita smiled at them as she passed. The girls stopped playing and whispered to each other, trying to determine if Ippy was a Bollywood star. A dream that had been snuffed out after meeting Hiran. *I could have*, she thought. *I was making headway*. The sting of her father's reaction to her first commercial drove the thought from her head.

Ipsita reached the lift only to see the call buttons were dark. *No elevator today*, she thought and walked to the stairwell.

With a glance down at her high heels, she moaned, "Why the top floor?" and started her ascent. A few minutes later, she was standing outside flat 40B, ringing the bell. Her chest rose and fell, exaggerated because of the effort of the stair climb. Ippy fluttered her blouse and sighed. She swallowed hard and wiped the sweat from her brow. Ippy rang again and some muffled noises emerged from inside the flat.

"Daya?" she called. Ippy pressed the buzzer again and followed that with a harsh knock. An old woman peered out from the door across the hall, her silver hair and wrinkled face barely visible.

"Mind your business, auntie," Ipsita snapped, and the neighbour's door slammed shut. Daya's then opened and there she stood, wavering, wrapped in a thin blanket.

"Oh my God, Day... are you high?" Ippy asked, opening the screen and stepping in. The sparsely furnished apartment was stifling hot, the ceiling fans were still and the air conditioning silent.

"Daya! It's an oven in here!" Ipsita snapped as she swung the door shut. She had drawn the blinds. So, the room was dim despite the time of day.

"You live in a tomb, girl," Ippy scolded. She walked to the wall switch and flipped on a fluorescent light. She also started the living room fan.

"Is... is it?" Daya slurred. "I was sleeping."

"Come." Ipsita held out her hand. Daya reached to take it and the blanket slipped from her. She swayed, naked except for her bra. Her dishevelled and matted brown hair hung off her shoulders. Daya stared blankly at the wall in front of her as she groped slowly in the air, looking for Ippy's hand. Ippy grabbed it and with a tug, lead her towards the shower.

The stream of water was lukewarm. She guided her friend under it. Daya resisted at first, pulling away like a child. Then she relented and just stood there, letting the water cascade over her for a moment. Daya came around enough to remove her undergarment and look for the soap.

"Please pull it together, *babu*," Ipsita said, caressing Daya's cheek under the spray. "Have a wash up, I'll make some tea. I have news."

A short time later, the girls were sitting on the edge of Daya's bed, sipping strong Assam tea. Ipsita studied her. Her hair was still wet, and a thin towel wrapped her slender frame. *She has grown so gaunt. She used to rival my beauty. When we entered a room together, men's hearts would stop.*

But now, she was but a mere whisper of the woman she once was. The heroin was slowly sucking the life from her, draining her beauty and youth. Ipsita reached out and again caressed her cheek. Daya smiled, her former radiance shining through the lost eyes and weary face.

"What is this news?" Daya whispered.

"There has been some problem from Canada," Ippy said. To know club business was dangerous, to share it like this was suicide. But she felt no fear, not with Daya. "I don't know all the details, but the escort coming is not a club member. It's someone they are blackmailing for the job."

"Blackmail? How? Why?" Daya asked, after sipping more of her tea. The colour was slowly returning to her cheeks.

"I don't know," Ipsita answered. "I could only hear bits of the conversation while waiting in the hall outside the office. Ramdev received a call from Montreal, and he sent me out. I only heard what he shouted to Hiran afterwards."

"What? What did you hear?" Daya pressed.

"Only that the replacement would come one day late, which messes up the schedule, that they would have to ride hard to make the ship and that this escort was a civilian, not a club member. They are forcing him to do it."

"This is news, why? Who cares?" Daya sighed, losing interest. She eyed the needle on her bedside table, and her lips twitched. Ipsita clasped her face in both hands and turned her head so they were looking eye to eye.

"It's news because, if he is an outsider, if he is being blackmailed... perhaps he can help us," she said.

"Help us how, Ippy?" Daya snapped.

"I don't know," Ipsita sighed, letting her hands drop to her lap. "If I can approach him, maybe we can help each other, to get away, to escape,"

"We can help each other get killed, you mean," Daya quipped.

"Better to die fighting to get out of hell than killing yourself with the poison keeping you there!" Ippy shouted louder than she intended.

Shock and hurt filled Daya's face as her eyes moistened. "I'm sorry, baby... I'm sorry," Ippy said, taking her teacup and putting it on the dresser. She turned to Daya and cradled her in her arms. "We want out, *na*? To get away, for you to get clean? To go home?"

"There is no going home," Daya said, pulling away. "That bridge has burned."

"Yes, that bridge has burned," Ippy softened her voice. "But there is still hope, still us. We could start again, fresh, the two of us." Ipsita pulled Daya close. "This *firangi* will mean nothing to us. I can use him... I don't know... to cause a distraction, help us get away, give us money, buy us tickets?"

"To where, Ippy? Where will we go?"

"Your cousin in Nepal, maybe. Or Hong Kong. Remember that casting agent? He said if we ever went there, he would help us out. I still have his number."

"I'm not like you, Ipsita. I didn't sex my way into a passport." Daya scoffed.

"Okay, Nepal then, for now. We can do it, Daya. Please trust me. You know I would never hurt you." Ipsita lifted Daya's chin from her chest and their eyes locked, twinkling, and Daya grinned. She leaned forward, tilting her head.

They pressed their lips together and Ippy's tongue probed, tracing the outline of Daya's mouth. She flicked playfully with the tip until Daya's mouth opened, allowing her access. Their tongues met and swirled with each other. Daya let her towel fall away and guided Ippy's hands to her breasts. Ippy grasped them, rolling each nipple between her thumb and forefinger. Daya moaned as their kiss deepened and became more passionate.

The women fell back on the bed and Ippy straddled her lover, peeling off her blouse and unclasping her bra, her breasts swinging free. Daya pulled her down on top of her. Ippy ground her sex against Daya's bare leg, and Daya responded by grasping Ipsita's hips and squeezing.

Lust took hold of them as they became lost in each other's desire. Ipsita shucked her jeans and panties and stood in front of her. Daya drew her legs back and slid to the edge of the bed, offering herself to her lover. Ipsita knew what Daya wanted and smiled wickedly.

"Please, baby," Daya whispered. Ipsita sank to her knees and fed both their wanton desires.

✳ ✳ ✳

"Turn that air conditioning off. The sun went down an hour ago!" Avinash scolded Sandy. The two of them were sitting at the end of the Iron Horses clubhouse road.

"Were you born on the sun?" Sandy retorted as he twisted the AC knob to its lowest setting. This was a common argument between the two of them.

"Close. Rajasthan," Avinash chuckled. "But you know that." They laughed. Sandy lifted a pair of binoculars out of his lap and peered into the dark. He stared at the entrance gates of the Iron Horses' lair. The MC chose a sound studio as their cover for a base of operations.

Agent Shashidhar came back quickly with the information Avi requested of her that afternoon. The Iron Horses were larger and more organised than they had been expecting. The likelihood of them being involved in the heroin trade increased threefold after reading the file Dimpi prepared.

The New Delhi chapter was the largest of the nine throughout the country and seemed the place to start digging. Their clubhouse was easy to locate once they knew who they were looking for.

After losing the biker coming out of Paharganj Market, they regrouped and went to the source of the ache, the clubhouse. Every once in a while, you could get a mango by shaking the tree. So Avinash had two Delhi Police spot checks set up on Ma Anandmayee Marg, one in each direction from the exit of Okhla Phase One.

Avi instructed both spot checks to pull over and search any Iron Horses MC members that passed through. Any Royal Enfield motorcycle, in fact. As a precaution, each point also had two police motorcycle units at the ready. Should the searches come up empty, they would tail them. Maybe, just maybe, they could catch a break.

✳ ✳ ✳

Ramdev had his eyes closed and was leaning back on one of the gloomy grey faux leather sofas that adorned the waiting room of the sound studio. A joint was burning in the ashtray on the black stone table in front of him.

Through the soundproof walls of studio one, he was listening to the muffled beats of *Aando,* a Sufi Rock fusion band the Club used to peddle drugs in Delhi and Gurugram bars. They were working on their cover version of a hit song *Zinda Hoon Yaar, Kaafi Hai.*

He could make out the lyrics as the frontman crooned, *Mujhe chhod do mere haal pe, Mujhe chhod do mere haal pe, Zinda hoon yaar, kaafi hai! Zinda hoon yaar, kaafi hai! Leave me on my own, leave me on my own, I am alive, that's enough, I am alive, that's enough.*

His eyes popped open and Ramdev picked up his weed. The song stirred up some ghosts for him. Moments when the mantle of leadership or responsibility was not his burden. A time of youthful innocence, a time of love and brotherhood, a time he would rather not remember right now.

Ramdev took the last drag off his spliff and ground out the roach in the ashtray. He rubbed his eyes and refocussed on the colourful Bob Marley poster hanging on the wall. Taking a sharp breath, he stood and paced the room. Ramdev slumped his shoulders and rubbed his temples. A slow, deliberate sigh escaped his lips.

This plan from Montreal of using a blackmailed shipment escort made him very, *very* uneasy. He sat on the reception desk. His weight caused the lamp to wobble. Ramdev steadied it as Hiran and Shiv came in. The Club's Sergeant at Arms, Rajatt, who everyone simply called Ratt, followed them into the small foyer.

After he scanned the trio, Ramdev scowled to himself. Aside from their clothing, jeans with black t-shirts and leather vests, they could not be more different. Hiran looked like a drug-crazed wild man, fresh from some street brawl, while Ratt was a balding and dusty old father figure, sporting a scar on his left cheek. Shiv looked more like a schoolboy than a biker. It would not surprise Ramdev if he still pissed in his bed.

"You three look like those old American movie jokers. The"—He struggled to recall, then snapped his fingers in recollection—"Stooges. Yes, yes. The Three fucking Stooges," he quipped.

"Well boss, it would appear Stooges are all you get today!" Ratt laughed as the other two grinned.

"Am I laughing? I can find no good help in this city," Ramdev barked. "Sit." He motioned to the sofa. Ratt and Shiv sat down, and Hiran lingered at Ramdev's side.

"We have a change of pick-up plan," he started. The two on the couch swapped uneasy glances, then looked to Hiran who made a palm down patting motion, reassuring them. Ramdev lit a Gold Flake cigarette.

"There's been a minor complication in Montreal. It seems the escort of this shipment has fallen down some stairs and injured himself."

"What the fuck?!" Shiv blurted out. "Who?"

"Clipper. No worries, my brothers. He is okay," Ramdev assured them.

"*Accha*. Who will they send in his place?" Ratt asked.

"They have arranged that already. They have a man who is deeply indebted to the Club," Ramdev explained.

"He's not a brother?" Ratt scowled.

"No. I had my concerns as well. But they assured me that his commitment to the matter is deep. Also, our brothers in Montreal have taken a hefty insurance policy. A young lady who means a lot to this"—Ramdev took a piece of paper from his vest pocket and squinted at it—"Alex. Alex Crossman."

Ramdev levelled them with a distant stare. "Nothing changes other than we will ship straight to Goa as we are two days behind schedule. This Alex Crossman will ride with Hiran and me. Ratt, you will lead the second transport crew, and Shiv, you will go in the third, with the other prospect."

"It will be business as usual," Hiran chimed in. "No problems."

"I don't like it, boss. *Woh bhai nahi hai*. How do we trust this sister fucker?" Ratt asked.

"You don't," Ramdev snapped. "You watch him like a goddamn hawk. Stop fucking questioning me. Now go pick this bastard up from the airport. He lands in an hour and a half." The pair of them stood.

"He's riding with you," Shiv said to Ratt.

"Fuck you, prospect. Do as you're told," Ratt replied.

"Just get him and bring him here. Without fail. No mistakes," Ramdev said, and dismissed them with a nod.

"Everyone questions me," he said after they had left. Ramdev slumped back down on the couch.

"They are not questioning you, *bhai*. Just the decision. We know you didn't make it," Hiran said. Ramdev sprang to his feet and rushed Hiran.

"Why? You think I can't?" His face was less than an inch from Hiran's. "You think I can't lead? That I can't make the tough call?" Ramdev screamed. Hiran stepped back, his face neutral.

"I'm sorry," Ramdev said. "I just... *koi baat nahi*. Just go, go get us some food, ya?"

"Okay, *bhai*. Okay," Hiran said and left Ramdev alone with his mood.

✳ ✳ ✳

A short time later, Ratt, on his squadron blue Classic 500, led Shiv astride his bright red Continental cafe racer out of the front gates of the studio. He was oblivious to the fact that a white Honda started as they passed and did a quick U-turn to follow them. The tandem turned left onto Ma Anandmayee Marg amidst the endless honking and headed to the airport. The Honda City joined the flow 10 metres behind them. Just another set of headlights.

The bikes wove through the late evening traffic until they came upon the police spot check. Two attending officers waved the motorcycles over as soon as they approached. Ratt pulled up into the breakdown lane on the far side of the yellow Delhi Police barricades with Shiv behind him and they shut down the bikes.

The officer who had flagged them over, lingered a while, chatting with another attending cop, and then sauntered towards them. Ratt chuffed and rolled his eyes at his white uniform shinning in the headlights. *A beacon of hope and integrity*, he scoffed. *He's young, most likely a rookie.*

"Have you been drinking tonight?" the officer asked, scanning their jeans and leather cuts with distaste. Ratt slouched in his seat and decided to not acknowledge the cop's presence and lit a Gold Flake.

"No, sir. We haven't. Not at all," Shiv answered.

He circled the Enfields, shining a small flashlight over them. Ratt chuckled. *No tank bags, no saddlebags, nothing to search, na?* The cop shifted his weight from foot to foot and glanced back and forth between the two.

"Empty your pockets," the cop said.

"Fuck you," Ratt whispered.

"What was that?" the officer snapped. He stepped towards him and waved over a senior officer from the barricade.

"I asked why, sir," Ratt sneered. Shiv pulled the contents out of his cut pockets and laid them on the tank. Cigarette pack, lighter, cell phone, and sunglasses.

"There were reports of gunfire in the area. We are looking for concealed weapons," the rookie answered. *They are not here to play,* Ratt mused to himself. *Too much attitude, even for a Delhi cop. He must be under specific orders. This is no spot check, we're a target and they will search us. Either willingly or in handcuffs.* Ratt relented and pulled out his wallet and phone.

"Inside pockets?" The senior police officer had arrived and was looming over Shiv.

"Empty," Shiv said.

"Are they now? Show me," he growled. Shiv looked to Ratt for guidance. He nodded at him.

"Now, little boy," the officer barked. Shiv opened his vest and the cop shone his flashlight on him. For a moment, Ratt thought he saw the outline of Shiv's 9 mm in the left side weapon pocket of his cut. His heart leapt. *No! Ramdev had told us not to carry a piece to the airport.*

"What is that?" The cop waved the flashlight beam over the bulge.

"Nothing," Shiv said.

"Take this 'nothing' out, please. Slowly," the officer grunted. The one beside Ratt moved back a step and dropped his hand to his baton. Ratt tensed, preparing to spring. Shiv sighed and reached inside his cut.

"Slowly," the senior reminded him. Shiv fished into the weapon pocket and withdrew a small wooden pipe. *Thank God,* Ratt thought and released his held breath.

"A hashish pipe," he said, and snatched it from Shiv's grip. "Not nothing, after all, hum?"

"For tobacco only, officer," Shiv sneered.

"And you?" the young cop said, returning his attention to Ratt. Ratt scowled and opened his vest to show the empty inside pockets.

"Where are you two headed this evening?"

"The airp...," Shiv blurted and Ratt cut him off.

"To see my sister in Lajpat Nagar," he shouted. Both cops turned to him and shared a suspicious glance.

"You're facing the wrong direction for Lajpat Nagar," the senior officer said, pointing over his shoulder.

"You're a fucking tour guide?" Ratt asked. He did not conceal the contempt in his remark. The cop backed away from Shiv and crowded into Ratt.

"Yes, I am. We have a lovely tour about to start. One showing some very nice New Delhi jail cells, where all of your gang belong," he growled, poking at Ratt's Iron Horses patch with his flashlight.

"We are just two motorcycle enthusiasts, sir, who belong to a club of people who also enjoy motorcycles. Tonight, we're taking a long way around to my sister's, with it being such a pleasant evening, *sir*." Ratt's tone was level and calm, but you could smell the hatred underneath it.

"Be on your way," the second cop said, slipping the hash pipe into his pocket and waving them forward. Ratt and Shiv refilled their pockets and fired up the bikes. Ratt shot one last sneer at the police and the pair rolled back out into traffic.

A moment later, the white Honda City that had been observing unnoticed from the other side of the road pulled up to the scene. The window lowered and Sandy, flashing his identification card, barked at the two traffic cops.

"NCB. What did you find on those two? Why did you let them go?" he snapped. The senior officer glanced at the younger cop and wiped his brow.

"Nothing, sir. They had nothing on them," he stammered, fidgeting with the hash pipe in his pocket through his uniform pants. "We had no reason to..."

"They are heading to the airport, sir. One of them let it slip out," the rookie spoke up and pointed down the road. "That way."

"I know where the fucking airport is," Sandy barked. As the window rolled up, the Honda shot out in pursuit.

✳ ✳ ✳

"Ice cream, sir?" the Jet Airways stewardess whispered, leaning across the sleeping couple seated beside Alex. She was smiling and looked fetching in her mustard yellow uniform and navy blue neck scarf.

"No. No, thank you," Alex said, rubbing the sleep from his eyes. He returned the smile. "Are we close?" he asked.

"We will land in forty minutes, sir." She was pleasant in her tone, but he could see the toll of a twenty-hour flight in her eyes. The stewardess wheeled the trolley to the next trio of seats as Alex brought his own back to the full upright position.

He lifted the window shade. It was dark, nothing to see. Alex grasped his hips and arched his back as far as he could in the cramped seat, trying in vain to relieve the softball-sized knot that had formed between his shoulder blades. He slept throughout most of the flight, not surprising considering the experiences of the last few days. Alex emerged into consciousness in Brussels for the flight's two-hour layover to refuel but had fallen asleep again after re-boarding.

As they were picking up some new passengers and dropping a few off, Alex considered jumping ship in Belgium. Go straight to the authorities. But Marceau had assured him in Montreal that if he didn't show up in New Delhi, Candy would be dead and buried, along with all evidence of their interactions, long gone before any RCMP showed up. Then the Club would begin looking for him.

"Until I am old and grey. I'll not cease looking, and when I have found you, Alex, I will remove your fingernails, teeth, and eyes," Marceau had said. As if that wasn't motivation enough, Alain reminded him while checking in at Pearson International, *"Do your job well, Alex, because, for every one of your missteps, we'll tie your little girlfriend to the pool table in the clubhouse and leave her there until every club member has had their fill. Understand?"*

Alex shook his head hard to remove that thought from his mind. A soft chime filled the cabin.

"Good evening, ladies, and gentlemen. This is your Captain. We will start our final approach into New Delhi in a few minutes. The local time is 8:45 pm and the current temperature is 35 degrees Celsius. We would like to thank you for flying Jet Airways and hope you have enjoyed your time with us. We hope to serve you again soon. Would the crew please prepare the cabin for landing?"

The message was in English first, repeated in Hindi. The stewardesses began their rounds, waking people, asking them to lift their window shades, stow the tray table and put their seats up. Alex closed his eyes and exhaled.

The plane tires screeched as they contacted runway two, a 3,810 metre ribbon of hard tarmac cutting through the centre of Indira Gandhi International Airport's 2,066 hectares. *I'm on Indian soil. I can't believe it.*

He sucked the knuckles of his right hand. They were scuffed and scabbed from the riding lessons he received in Toronto. *Yesterday? Two days ago?* Alex had no clue. It was all blurring into one long nightmare. A rapid descent into madness.

The events of the last seventy-two hours were so completely removed from Alex's normal character. *Like I'm playing a part in a movie. Injuring that biker in Montreal and placing Candy in danger. I lied to my friends. That's not me.*

He looked out of the window at the terminal and Alex was taken aback. It was a huge modern structure. *What was I expecting? A bamboo hut?* He knew nothing of India. Just that they loved cricket, curried all the food, and cows were gods. He knew the Beatles had spent time here. Rishikesh, he believed. *The White Album*? That was the pitiful extent of his knowledge. Yet here he was, ready to plunge into a mystic land so very far from home, with so much depending on the outcome of his ability to do something illegal.

"Oh God," he whispered to himself as he ran his sore fingers through the wavy locks of his hair. He had never felt so alone and desperate.

The aircraft lurched and slowed. Then, as if by some inaudible signal heard by everyone but him, all the passengers stood. It was almost in unison! They opened the overhead compartments. Alex chuckled. The aircraft had not even stopped in its parking area yet. The stewardess began scolding them over the cabin speakers in Hindi, but it was in vain.

Many men, women, and children clamoured to elbow their way to the front of the aircraft. *In India, they trample he who hesitates,* he thought.

It was one of the most hysterical things Alex had ever seen, and one of the many lessons he was about to learn. He waited until most of the plane had disembarked, then stood to retrieve his leather backpack from the overhead bin. It was the only luggage they had allowed him to bring.

"You will travel by bike, pisshead. Travel light," Alain had told him while packing at his apartment. Two pairs of jeans, three t-shirts, five pairs of socks, his toothbrush, and an mp3 player. *No room for underwear. This is as light as it gets. Happy trails, cowboy,* Alex thought, as he slung the bag over his shoulder and walked down the aisle.

Customs and immigration passed without incident. They had designed the airport well, and everything flowed. Adorned in soft brown, yellow, and orange tones, it made Alex feel that he was in a hotel rather than an airport. An overabundance of plants and the plush carpet underfoot all added to the ambiance.

The lengthy escalator ride down into the customs area gave a panoramic view of the massive hand sculptures forming the *Om* symbol that was a feature in Delhi's international arrival terminal. Alex took it all in, a little in awe. The large brass Dancing Shiva statue before the escalator underscored once again, just how far from home he was.

Alex passed through the immigration official and as he had no bag to collect, he walked through the duty-free shops towards the exit. The arrival hall was far more like an airport than the disembarkation area, well illuminated and with generic tile floors. He made his way past the baggage carousels, whirring as they transported a varied parade of coloured luggage in an endless loop.

His heart beat a little more quickly as he neared the airport security officers on either side of the only gate from the hall. They stood in their drab khaki uniforms, eyeballing the passengers as they wandered through the sliding doors.

He was wearing Levi's, white Reebok's, and a Rolling Stones t-shirt, sporting long shaggy hair and in his mid-twenties. *Just another retroactive hippy searching for enlightenment,* he reassured himself. Alex did as the MC instructed him. *Walk through the middle of the exit, eyes front, easy pace, and don't stop.*

He took a few steps, and just like that, he was through the screening doors and into an unfamiliar world. There were throngs of men shouting and holding placards with people's names. There was a Cafe Coffee Day in front of him and he followed the flow of passengers around it to the left and the exit doors. In a whisper, he stepped through them into the New Delhi night.

✳ ✳ ✳

Delhi airport does not let anyone inside the terminal without a valid reason. Coming to see family and friends arrive isn't one in the eyes of the Airports Authority of India. Therefore, only those with a chauffeur's pass gain entrance to receive people.

There are exceptions to this rule, as there are to most rules in India. These would include handlers and assorted entourage for the connected, visiting officials, sports and Bollywood stars, and the insanely rich.

Everyone else is just one step outside the exit set of doors. Alex was breathing deeply as he walked through them. It washed over him, equivalent to being kicked in the chest by a mule. He felt disorientated and unstable. It seemed like thousands of people, all within arm's reach, were pressing in on him.

Alex stopped and grasped the railing beside the exit door. He shut his eyes and drew a steadying breath. The air scalded his throat. *I'm sitting in a sauna.* Perfumed with the musk of *chandan* and tinges of sulphur, it stung his nostrils. It was not just the temperature making him dizzy. It was the air itself.

Luggage porters dressed in red robes and turbans grabbed for his backpack and taxi drivers pulled at his elbow, urging him to follow them, as armed military guards patrolled the area. Alex stood awash among thousands of passengers being greeted by friends and family.

It was a riot of colour and noise. Multitudes of reds and yellows and greens and oranges, silk and cotton and *pashmina, sarees, salwars, kurtas,* and *dupattas.* There was an intoxicating din of excited chatter in a bizarre language. It seemed hundreds of cars were honking, dogs barking, men shouting, women laughing, and children crying.

The night air was thick with it. Thick with India, and he was smack dab in the middle of this ancient city, ready to help poison its population. What was worse, he was also ready to escort that poison home!

John and Alain had told him in Toronto to go to the last concrete pillar in the pickup area. Contacts would meet him there. His query about how he would recognise them drew a sharp blow to the ribs.

Alex smiled and shook his head *no* to the taxi driver and luggage porters. He had to tug his leather backpack away from the young lad and make his way into the crowd. They followed along beside him, relentlessly tugging at his elbow.

"Where you go sir, where you go?" This was like nothing he had ever experienced. Alex spotted the pillars at the edge of the footpath and he headed towards the last one in the row. Pale green taxis, dark green and yellow tuk-tuks, and white mini-buses were lined up along the side of the slip road, all honking and jockeying for position. It was mayhem.

He stepped between a stray dog sleeping on the ground and a policeman with a machine gun to break free from his convoy of followers. Alex scanned the crowd near the last pillar, having no idea who he was looking for. He got to the pillar with no epiphany of recognition and leaned against its cool, smooth surface. He closed his eyes and waited.

"You're Alex?" He snapped his eyes open to the question and came face to face with a battle-scarred old man and some high school sports jock.

"Yes, yes. Alex," he stammered.

"I'm Shiv," the high school kid said. "This is Rajatt. Come." He spun on his heel and walked away. They were both wearing leather cuts.

Rajatt's had the same three-part patch configuration as the boys back home, except the top rocker said *Iron Horses*, and the bottom said *New Delhi NCR* as opposed to *Chevaux de Fer* and *Montreal*. The kid, Shiv, only had the bottom *New Delhi NCR* rocker on his vest.

Alex was now realising just how big, *and* just how organised this motorcycle club was. He trailed a few steps behind and stopped at the curb, but the two of them stepped right into traffic without a moment's hesitation. Alex stepped lively to catch up with them. There were a few honks, but the cars made way. *When in Rome...*, Alex thought.

They crossed to the car park and made their way to the motorcycle parking. Alex had never seen so many bikes in one place and packed so closely together. They stood at the exit booth.

"Wait here," Shiv said as he and Ratt wandered into the endless maze of motorcycles. A few moments later, they pulled up to him. The Royal Enfield emblem on the tanks caught his eye. Alex had never heard of them. They were much smaller than the Harley Davidsons the guys in Montreal and Toronto rode, but just as loud.

Shiv nodded at him and Alex climbed on his bike pillion. It astonished Alex no one offered him a helmet. The other fellow, Ratt, wasn't wearing one either, so he accepted it as normal. The jolt as they shot out of the exit gate into the airport traffic forced Alex to grab onto Shiv's belt in fear. He was about to learn why they preferred the smaller and more manoeuvrable Royal Enfields in India.

In the amusement park thrill ride that followed, Alex feared for his life on at least four separate occasions. There were countless near misses and avoided collisions. Not the worst of which, was a huge red transport bus changing lanes to avoid an ox-drawn cart while they were beside him.

An ox-drawn cart! In the city, on a major road! Alex was aghast. Yet, Shiv had swerved over into oncoming traffic and beeped his horn. The cars racing towards them flashed their lights and honked back, but again they made way until Shiv cleared the bus and dove back onto the correct side of the road. The left side. Alex closed his eyes and held on tight. There was little else he could do.

After forty-five minutes of bobbing and weaving, Alex realised perhaps he would not die. He relaxed a bit and shouted into Shiv's ear.

"How did you know it was me? At the airport?" he asked.

"Look around, *safaide wala*, how many white people do you see?" Shiv laughed back over his shoulder. Alex looked around and scrutinised his surroundings as they made their way in and around the traffic.

"None... there aren't *any*," Alex replied.

"There's your answer, *firangi*."

Alex stared out into the night, taking in all the new and bizarre sights around him. The Royal Enfield rumbled along.

What Alex did not see was Sandeep Bohla furiously navigating the NCB's white Honda through the traffic to stay within visual distance of the two bikes.

"Who's the fucking white guy?" Sandy asked as he honked and forced his way past a tuk-tuk.

"Who indeed?" Avinash mused. He was so close to the windscreen that he almost left nose prints. "Okay, okay," he said. "They took the Savitri Flyover. They must be heading back to the clubhouse in Okhla. Try to keep up, Sandy. But head there if you lose them."

✦

CHAPTER FIVE

The tang of sheared copper filled Ipsita's mouth. She buckled to the floor from the force of Ramdev's backhand slap and yelped.

"You would rather fuck her than a man? Than me!?" he screamed, standing over her and pointing at Daya. She trembled, casting her eyes downward, and remained silent. Ipsita spat blood on the floor at Ramdev's feet.

"Funny, you used to love the fact I was bisexual," she said, glaring up at him.

"With me! You can have her *with me*!" he sneered.

"Right. With *you*," Ipsita repeated as she stood. She knew this would be Ramdev's reaction once he learnt she had been with Daya all afternoon. That little shit, Shiv, reported her every move to him. But she couldn't help herself. She needed to have Daya beside her. She needed her love like a drug.

Ipsita let the fire drain from her eyes and allowed them to moisten with tears. *Now is not the time for a fight, a fight I can't win*, she thought. Her seductive charms had their limits with Ramdev. She chose a different tack.

Because of her heels and height, she was almost eye level with Ramdev. She stepped closer to him. "I'm sorry, baby," she whispered. Ipsita reached out tentatively and brushed his cheek, snaking her fingers through his wispy beard. "You've been so busy, I was lonely." She looked slowly down to the floor and then lifted her head again to meet his eyes. "I didn't think you cared if it was Daya," she pouted.

"That little whore has been with every member of this club. At *least* twice," Ramdev said, his tone softening. "Do you want some kind of disease?" He broke eye contact with Ippy and looked to Hiran, who had been standing by the window. "Get her out of my sight," he nodded towards Daya. "She can spend the night in the playroom. Keep her clean and fucking sober," he shouted after them as Hiran led Daya out of the door.

"I need you, Ippy," he blurted. "You're coming on this delivery with us. You and Daya both." Ippy half shrugged. It was common enough they accompanied the boys down to Mumbai. It made them look more like a legitimate motorcycle club out on a ride. She pressed against him and wound her hand into his pocket, fishing out his cigarettes.

"Okay, *babu*," she purred. Separating from him, she opened the package of Gold Flakes and took two out. Ippy inserted them between her lips and smirked. With a deliberate flick of the lighter, she ignited them and handed one to Ramdev as she exhaled a long stream of grey smoke towards the ceiling. He smiled wickedly at her.

"You are a *vixen*. Pure seductress." He laughed and took the cigarette from her slender fingers. Ippy shook her head and joined in his laughter, her silky hair glimmering over her shoulders. "I need you to help me control this escort from Canada," he said, his tone turning purely business. "Get close to him. Stay close and be his friend. I require assurances he is stable and can handle the job. I don't like this arrangement," he said.

"How close do you want me to get?" she asked. Ipsita forced down her building excitement. She could scarcely believe her luck. Ramdev had *never* shared club business with her before, much less asked her to take part. *Now, out of the blue, he's asking my help to watch the very man I'm hoping to recruit in assisting our escape. It's perfect.*

"If you fuck him, Ippy, I swear I will kill you both," Ramdev barked.

"No. No, baby. That's why I'm asking. I want to do what you need of me," she soothed.

"Let him think you want him. Befriend him, seduce him, and get him under your spell. I need to know everything he is thinking. He needs to trust you, Ippy. Just get it." A soft knock broke his sentence. "Come," he said.

Normally it was Ipsita's entrance into a room that caused heart rates to spiral. But this time it was *her* heart that skipped a beat. She stood breathless as Alex walked in and approached them. His looks surprised her. Captivated her. *He is so handsome.* Ipsita felt her cheeks flush and rubbed her palms against her jeans. She couldn't drag her eyes away from his face, his beautiful face.

"Alex Crossman?" Ramdev said. It was more a statement than a question.

"Yes," Alex said. The sound of his voice snapped Ipsita from her trance. *It's so deep, and his accent is pure sex.*

"Sit, Alex." Ramdev motioned to the wooden frame chair in front of the desk. Alex sat as Ramdev walked around to the other side and sat in the black leather chair. "Do you smoke?" he asked.

"Yes."

"Help yourself then." Ramdev tossed his pack of cigarettes that Ippy had left on the desk to Alex.

"Thank you," he said, placing the cigarette between his lips and looking about the room. Ramdev produced a lighter and brought the flame to the end of Alex's smoke. He inhaled sharply and grimaced at the pungent flavour of cheap Indian tobacco. He turned his head towards Ipsita, who had settled on the sofa to his right. Ippy stifled a laugh as she saw his eyes widen and his smile broaden. *Already hooked,* she thought.

"Let's get some shit on the table, shall we?" Ramdev said, reclaiming Alex's attention. Alex nodded.

"One, we are not friends. Two, I don't like *or* trust you. Three, if you cross my club or me, I will cut out your heart. Clear so far?" Ramdev asked, levelling him with an icy stare.

"Yeah, clear," Alex said.

"Good. Now, these facts do not mean your stay here has to be unpleasant. Just do your job, do it well, and at the end of it all, we'll go our separate ways." Ramdev paused. "Show respect, and you shall receive it. But know this, you have already dug yourself a hole with that shit you pulled in Montreal. You causing injury to one of our Canadian brothers does *not* sit well with my boys here. Your leash is short, my friend. A single phone call from me... terrible things happen to your girlfriend back home. Yes?" Ramdev stared at Alex and raised his eyebrows.

"Yes," Alex whispered.

Shit! Girlfriend? How can I seduce him if he has a girlfriend? Ipsita thought. *Maybe I can use his worry to my advantage.*

"All right. It seems we have a mutual understanding. Now, here is what happens. The day after tomorrow, we leave for Mumbai. You will carry some product fitted into a false bottom of your saddlebag. Not sufficient to pass a close inspection, but adequate to fool traffic cops, ya? You will ride with Hiran and me, and two girls."

As Ramdev continued outlining their plan, Ipsita studied Alex. *He has the build of an athlete,* she thought. *Strong. Good, we may need it.* The look he had given her didn't hide the fact that he found her attractive. *Also, good,* she smiled to herself. *His girlfriend could be an issue, but perhaps the duress he is under would be enough to make him angry and my looks will help persuade him to free me and Daya.*

He was more than she had hoped. Ramdev had forbidden her to sleep with him. That was a bit of an issue. It was her greatest weapon. Ipsita was wondering how the hell she would restrain herself when there was already a smouldering want deep inside her. It was pure lust, granted. That's all men were to her, a way to scratch an itch, an unsavoury need that had to be filled once in a while. The act with men meant nothing, but it was an occasional desire she could not escape.

Yet there was something about the way Alex carried himself, something that intrigued her. That intrigue was urging her reckless mind to bed him at the earliest opportunity.

"This is Ipsita, my woman," Ramdev was saying. "She will tend to your needs for now. Be wise, Alex. There will always be eyes on you."

Ramdev stood and motioned for Alex to do the same. "Ippy, show him to his room and help him get settled."

* * *

Alex watched Ipsita's hips sway as she sauntered down the hallway. She had an impossibly sexy ass. He was jet-lagged and still swimming in a surrealistic ocean of improbable events. Alex searched for something to hold on to that was real. Anything that made sense. *Ipsita's ass fit the bill. That makes sense and is something I can grab.* He chuckled at the ramblings of his exhausted thoughts.

"Something funny?" she asked and looked over her shoulder, catching him ogling her ass.

"No. I was just thinking how crazy this all is," he said, lowering his eyes.

"It must be quite a culture shock for you," Ippy mused. "Is this your first trip to India?"

"Yeah. First time out of North America. I went to Mexico once on vacation, but this is like a different planet. I had no idea what India was about," he said. Ipsita laughed. *It's like silk,* he thought.

"And yet we know so much about American culture..." she began.

"Canadian," Alex quipped. "I'm Canadian."

"No offence intended. I just meant we know a lot about your country, and yet you know nothing of India?"

"Not really," Alex said, softening a little. "Just that the Taj Mahal is here, you curry everything and cows will wander into your house if you leave the door open." Ipsita laughed, genuine and warm. *Her face is so beautiful.*

"Well, some of that is correct," she chuckled again. "Come."

They had stopped in front of an entrance midway down the hall. Ippy opened it and stood aside for Alex to enter. It was a sparse room with a twin bed, a desk, a chair, and a small table.

"You can rest up here. The washroom's at the end of the hall if you wish to take a bath," she said.

"No. No, thank you. But a shower would be nice," Alex said. Ipsita looked at him.

"Yes, there is a shower at the end of the hall," she repeated.

"You said 'bath'," he said. Again, she giggled. Alex felt it was at his expense.

"Bath, shower. Same thing," Ipsita said. "Are you hungry? Would you like a bread omelette?" Alex didn't know what it was, but it suggested eggs, and rather than embarrass himself further, just nodded.

"Please."

"All right, freshen up and take rest. I'll be back in a little while." Ipsita left.

Alex dropped his backpack on the bed. It exhausted him to be sure, this travel. His body clock kept insisting it was early afternoon, though it was well past midnight.

Alex struggled in the shower, as there wasn't one. There was just a hot and cold water faucet, and a bucket. He made do and washed himself. Back in his room, Alex stood in only his unfastened jeans in front of the mirror. Most of the angry bruises had faded. He was fighting with the tangled mess of his hair when Ipsita returned and walked in without a knock.

"I hope you like"—Her words caught in her throat seeing his naked chest. Alex smiled. Ipsita turned her back, but not before letting her eyes roam over him—"this omelette," she finished, as Alex tugged on a t-shirt and buttoned his jeans.

"I'm sure it's fine," Alex stammered. Ipsita faced him. Their eyes met and she smirked at him.

"It's all right," she said. "I have seen a man's chest before."

"Before the first date?" Alex jibed. Ipsita's brow furrowed and she dipped her head. "I'm sorry," he said. "I joke to cover embarrassment." Ipsita raised her eyes again. *She is so intoxicating*. Alex felt awash at sea.

"No, I should have knocked. I'm sorry," she said. "Sorry, but not disappointed," she added.

Alex was a flirt. A low level flirt to be sure, but he *could* hold his own. Even with aggressive women. But Ipsita was so beautiful, it disrupted his thoughts. It seemed to Alex the only way to end this uncomfortable moment was to move past it.

"Please," he said, motioning to the table. Ipsita set the small plate down and Alex fell on it like a dog on a bone. He hadn't realised he was famished.

"I would ask if you required tomato sauce. But I think you will have finished before I could fetch it."

Alex smiled an impish grin. Ipsita's eyes were full. *Is there an attraction in them? Or is it my exhaustion?*

"I'll leave you be," she purred. "Try to sleep and I will collect you in the morning." With that, she left.

Alex lay on the bed and let his mind fill with Ipsita's image. Alex had not paid attention to the Asian women back home. Not that he was racist, not by any stretch. It had just never occurred to him to date one. *Date? Date Ipsita? What the hell am I thinking? What made me think that?*

"Perhaps that playful twinkle in her eyes," he whispered to himself. Alex refocussed his thoughts on reality. *I'm not here to find a girlfriend. I'm here to do what has to be done and get back home to Candy in one piece.*

✳ ✳ ✳

On the other side of the door, Ipsita leaned against the wall and took a deep breath. Her heart fluttered. *He is a handsome one.* She smirked to herself.

"Get a grip, girl," she chuckled, shaking her head. This was uncharted territory for her. Men don't affect her, don't break through her protective veneer. Ipsita knew nothing about this Alex! Other than he was boyishly charming.

"No matter," she whispered. "The landscape is Nepal." Once Ramdev got comfortable with Alex's behaviour, she would fleece him of his cash and pry him away from the Club's sight long enough to find a travel agent and buy their freedom. *Maybe in Udaipur.* With tickets in hand, it didn't matter how Alex distracted them. He could play sick, feign an escape or start a fight, as long as he bought her and Daya an hour or two to vanish.

At first, Ipsita had assumed she would rely on her talents of seduction and persuasion to sway him to help her. But now she noticed something different. Perhaps it was he that was seducing her. *That's fine too,* she thought. *I'll let that happen, even encourage it.*

Ippy pushed off from the wall and headed to Ramdev's room. The thought of climbing into his bed made her feel sickly.

* * *

New Delhi is a city-state. That is to say, not too far outside the city in any direction, is a border. The territory is surrounded by the state of Haryana to the north, south, and west and the state of Uttar Pradesh to the east.

Not to say New Delhi is small. The city, or National Capital Territory, covers an area of 1,484 square kilometres and is home to eleven million people in the city. There are another fifteen million in the suburbs. Any time of day, on any day of the week, the road congestion is horrible.

Delhi is notorious for bad traffic. The sheer magnitude of enforcing laws by the city's traffic cops and the obvious lack of interest in driving rules by its inhabitants compounded the issue. For these reasons, Ramdev decided that Alex must gain ride experience in Delhi, to acclimatise him to Indian driving *before* they left on a 1900 km heroin run.

Alex had a sampling of the traffic chaos on the back of Shiv's bike returning from the airport, and now he was facing his first road test. Tentatively he slung his leg over the 350-cc marine blue Royal Enfield Thunderbird that was to be his ride for the duration. Alex's heart pounded in his chest like a bass drum. Ramdev, with Ippy pillion and Hiran solo, were lined up beside him in the small parking lot of the sound studio.

They both had 500 cc bikes. Ramdev, a tan and maroon coloured Classic, and Hiran, the original Bullet model. The Thunderbird was far lighter than the Harley he had trained on back in Toronto. It gave Alex a small measure of confidence.

Alex *had* been riding dirt bikes on and off his entire life and had owned a Honda CB 360 just after high school. He just didn't have a motorcycle at the moment. It had been a few years since he had done any serious riding, but riding a bike *was* like *riding a bike.* You just had to knock the rust off. He was thankful now for Tommy's lesson in Toronto.

The single stroke 350 was a wee bit touchy, and she hopped like a rabbit as Alex let the clutch out. He pulled it in quickly and settled his feet back on the ground. Ramdev and Hiran exchanged malicious smiles.

"Don't fall down, Alex," Hiran shouted over the *dug dug dug* of the three bikes. "That would break my fucking heart!"

The security guard drew open the iron gate and Ramdev roared off. Hiran nodded to Alex to follow. He stuttered and swayed a little, but got the machine going and geared up to second. Hiran fell in behind him and they started on their way to Haryana's closest city, Gurugram.

As they approached the end of the street, Shiv came around the corner, heading towards them. Alex squeezed the front brake and the Enfield came to a halt. Ramdev spoke with him, and then they continued on their way.

It was early evening, and the traffic was thick. People returning to their homes after work clogged the roads like maple syrup through a needle. The sun still bright, Alex could at least see what was coming at him. The trio rode on the Outer Ring Road, heading for the Gurugram / Delhi Expressway, one of Delhi's major commuter arteries.

He stayed focussed on Ramdev. Well, Ipsita. She had wrapped her long shapely legs around the body of the motorcycle, and every once in a while, her sky blue cotton tunic would flutter up in the breeze and afford him a glance of the black thong peeking out her low-rise jeans.

"Goddamn!" he muttered, as he spied it again. "Stay focussed, man." He couldn't lie to himself. He was attracted to her, but he had Candy at home and there was one hell of a task to do before getting back to her and keeping her safe.

Alex felt certain he sensed a vibe coming from Ipsita the first time they met in Ramdev's office. The hours they had just spent together had confirmed those suspicions. Her soft laugh and flirtatious demeanour were prevalent throughout the day. More than once, he had caught her looking at him with serious intent. He knew she had an interest. *She may be a useful ally*, he thought.

Alex started gaining confidence by the minute. Ramdev's bike cut through the congestion like a spear. He mimicked his moves and followed him through the melee. After forty minutes, they swept up onto the expressway and the traffic eased somewhat. Hiran pulled up beside him.

"You okay?" he shouted. Alex nodded in reply. The driving here was nothing like home. In fact, if you drove this way in Canada, he didn't think they would even bother with a court trial. The MTO would just take your licence and the police would throw you in jail for life.

But there was a mad symmetry to it, and if you looked closely enough, you could grasp the way the cars, carts, buses, and trucks all flowed together. One thing for certain, you could never stop paying attention.

As the trio roared in and out of traffic, Alex began to notice the stares. At first, he misconstrued that it was because of his white skin, but the more he looked for it, the more he understood that it wasn't because of his colour. It was the bikes. In one instance, as they came to a halt for a red light, Alex spied two teen boys in the back of a compact car, grinning and jabbering excitedly while pointing at Ramdev. When they saw him, their jaws dropped and their eyes widened. His ego chuffed just a little. *I could get used to this*, he thought.

Alex never drew stares at home. He was a nameless, faceless mechanic. One of a million guys dredging their way through life. The only time he had felt anything similar was on stage with his band. But even then, it wasn't respect. It was drunken college girls, groupies, just doing what they do. Ogle wannabe rock stars. This was more than that.

A truck driver glanced over to him and smiled, and at another congested point, Hiran had wormed his way in front of him and Alex saw a woman in a passenger seat, checking him out. That in itself wasn't too unusual, but the fact that her husband was too, was astonishing. The minute

Hiran turned his head, they looked away and chattered to each other.

It was getting dark as they approached Cyber City, the IT central zone, where all the major players such as Hewlett Packard, Mitsubishi Electric India, Emerson Electric Co. had their head offices. And right smack dab in the middle of this office jungle was Cyber Hub, an exotic playland of chic clubs, bars, and restaurants. From North American cuisine at the Hard Rock Cafe and Wendy's Burger joint, to a taste of the Caribbean at Raasta's. There is no lack of choice.

The Farzi Cafe is a modern Indian bistro, where they were heading tonight. The cover band, *Aando*, that the Iron Horses used to sell drugs for them were performing and Ramdev decided to visit them. It was just as good as any destination for Alex to cut his Indian riding teeth.

* * *

The car door slammed shut and ripped Avinash from his uncomfortable sleep. He and Sandy had spent the last eighteen hours curled up in the pleather seats of the Honda after following the Horses back to the clubhouse.

"They are on the move," Sandy said. They had parked the car at the far entrance of the lane but were still in sight of the gates. Sandy had been outside having a smoke when he detected the roar of Enfields firing. As he slipped into the passenger seat, the two of them watched the three bikes emerge from the iron gates and speed towards them.

From the corner behind them, another Enfield appeared and honked, and the rumbling string of bikes came to a halt. Avinash and Sandy slid down into their seats and tried to hide from the view of the lead bike. Ramdev had come to a stop alongside them.

Sandy jammed into the footwell of the passenger side and peeked out of the window. "I think that's Ramdev Kapoor," he whispered. "And the *firangi* is there. I can't make out who's at the back." Avinash slowly turned the key in the ignition. Sandy's face paled. Avi continued to turn it. One click, two clicks. The air conditioning fan came to life. Sandy understood. He snaked his hand up and found the window button. "Easy," Avinash cautioned. Sandy glanced at him and nodded.

He pressed and released the button as quickly as he could. The growling of the bikes masked the whine of the electric window motor. It lowered a few centimetres. "Again," Avi whispered. Sandy repeated the process, and Ramdev's voice spilled through the opening.

"... to Cyber Hub to check if this fuckhead can ride," Ramdev was shouting. "We have some business. We'll be back, you sit tight."

With that, the bikes roared off down the lane. Sandy and Avinash stayed crouched until they could no longer hear them and then sat upright. "Cyber Hub," Sandy repeated. "Who was that woman on the back of the bike? My God, did you see her?"

"Yes, I saw her. Ramdev's mistress, I believe. Ipsita something or other. There was mention of her in Dimpi's file. It gives me an idea, Sandy. She may be a weak link, our way in. Call Dimpi, tell her to meet us at Cyber Hub, then call security there. I want to know what restaurant they go to."

✳ ✳ ✳

"Do you like it?" Ipsita asked as she watched Alex chew his *Galouti Kebab*. "It's mutton."

"Lamb?" Alex queried, taking another large mouthful of Kingfisher beer. Ipsita looked at him, creasing her brow.

"Goat," she replied. "Mutton is goat."

"Nah, mutton is lamb," Alex said and smiled after swallowing his beer. "And it's on the spicy side."

My God, his smile is intoxicating, she mused. "Not in India," she assured him. "It's definitely goat." With a smirk, she continued, "And I'm sure you may find everything a little spicy."

Right from the moment they sat down, Ipsita felt the sparks from him. He was stealing glances at her and every time he did, despite herself, she squirmed in her seat. The animal attraction to him filled her with guilt, as it always did. Try as she may, Ipsita could never explain to Daya her occasional need for a man to fill her. Daya nourished her soul, but men, they extinguished her wanton lust. Two separate issues, in her opinion. An opinion Daya did not share. She would forgive her seducing Alex once they were safe. Of this, Ipsita was sure.

They sat in the centre of the horseshoe shaped booth of the restaurant's prime seating area, right in front of the stage. The dark brown leather of the bench seats and wooden adornments of the room gave it a warm, rustic ambiance. Ramdev had gone to speak with the band during their set break, and Hiran was hovering around the bar behind them, acting as overseer.

Ippy felt this was her chance. They had descended into a comfortable ease last night and today. The fabricated friendship she was forming with him was clear. Ippy had created a rocky rapport between them. She decided to roll the dice.

"I understand you are not a club member?" she asked.

"What do you know of it?" Alex demanded, dropping his voice.

"Not much. Just that you may not want to be here." She watched him closely for any negative reaction. "Or assist in this shipment," she added. The word caused Alex to sputter on his beer.

"*Shipment*?" he choked. "Is that what you fucking call it? No, I don't want to smuggle heroin." Ipsita frowned and looked at the floor.

"I'm not a willing participant either," she said. "I'm trapped here like you."

"Is that right?" Alex said, his voice dripping with sarcasm.

"Yes. Yes, it is. What do you think Ramdev would do if he was aware I was speaking to you about this?" she urged, raising her eyebrows. "He would not be pleased. When I overheard you were being, well, forced to serve the Club, I thought maybe..." She leaned across the table. "Maybe we could help each other." She studied him as he took another fork full of *kebab* and chewed.

"Help how?" he asked. Alex gave up on his food. He swallowed hard and dropped the fork on the plate.

"I help you with the Club, give you options, inside information, and you help me with a distraction," she whispered.

"What kind of distraction?"

"Nothing life threatening," she chuckled. "Just something to buy me a little time to..."

"Getting along famously, I see?" Ramdev appeared at the edge of the table and slid in beside Ipsita. He looked slowly from her to Alex and back again. Ipsita's eyes dropped to her lap and Alex picked up his beer. The silence was excruciating.

"Well, that's good. As we will work together in close quarters. Just because I don't like or trust you, doesn't mean it has to be unpleasant." Ramdev smiled at Alex.

Ramdev chuckled and tore off a piece of *tandoori roti* sticking out of the basket and popped it in his mouth. The tension was unbearable. Ipsita had no way of knowing if he had overheard her. She needed to regroup.

"Excuse me, please," Ipsita said. "I need to use the loo." Ramdev stood, and she slipped out of the booth. With a smile at them both, she left and walked towards the rear of the restaurant. Ippy swung her hips more than necessary and could feel their eyes burning into her. *At least my most powerful weapon is still on point,* she thought.

The washroom was small, with only two stalls and a sable coloured laminated counter with one sink. Both stalls were unoccupied, so she slipped into the first one and closed the door. Ippy screwed her eyes shut and willed her heart to stop pounding. *There is no way he heard me,* she convinced herself. *Ramdev is not good at hiding emotion. If he had any inkling about that conversation, I would be in the parking lot, being beaten.* Deep in thought, Ippy didn't hear the door open and as she exited the stall, found herself face to face with Dimpi Shashidhar.

"Oh!" Ippy chirped in surprise.

"I will make this quick, Ipsita," Dimpi said.

"How do you..." The words caught in Ipsita's throat as Dimpi flashed her NCB badge.

"Narcotics Control Bureau, Intelligence Officer, Dimpi Shashidhar," she said and with a flick of her wrist, snapped the leather wallet shut and slipped it back in the pocket of her suit. "We know you. Ramdev Kapoor,

Shivam Sharma, and others. It's not as if your little *horses* gallop around in secret," she hissed at Ipsita.

Ipsita's mouth went dry as her innards crystallised with fear. *The NCB? How in God's name had this happened*? Now, Ramdev's anger seemed a trivial worry.

"We are aware you ship heroin from Amritsar to Delhi, and that you distribute it and live a splendid life from the deaths of the less fortunate and junkies."

"I don't know..." Ippy began quickly but yelped in pain as Dimpi grabbed her hair and pushed her back against the washroom stall with a thud.

"I don't care what you do or don't know. Or what you *think* you know. To me you are little more than a biker's whore," Dimpi growled. "Listen. This is a one-time offer to save yourself. You have five days, *samjhi*?" She shook Ippy's head for emphasis. "Five days to gather as much intel about the shipping operation as you can or you get to watch this beautiful face of yours wither away to nothing in a prison cell."

Dimpi slammed her against the stall partition again before releasing her. "I have eyes on you always, Ipsita. If anything seems amiss with your behaviour or I believe you are sharing this conversation with anyone, I'll pick you up and lock you in a dark hole so fast, your head will spin! Understand?" Dimpi backed away from her and glared.

"I will be in touch." She tossed her card at the cowering Ipsita and walked out. Dimpi paused, her hand on the door.

"You are not a stupid girl, I hope," she said over her shoulder. "If you try to run, I'll be there. Make no mistake. If you do as I ask, you can be free of this mess with no scars." Dimpi pulled open the door and vanished.

Ippy sunk to her knees on the floor and picked up the card Dimpi had flung at her. The tears came. Desperation swallowed her like a thick grey fog. There was no escape from the NCB! But if she gave information on the Horses, the Club would kill her, no matter where the NCB hid her. She was a dead woman either way.

The NCB did not understand with whom they were dealing. If she told Ramdev, he would tighten security so much, she would never get away. It would carve off her plans to escape like a surgeon's scalpel through tender flesh.

Now, with the NCB watching me, would fleeing to Nepal be possible at all? Could I inform? she wondered. *Give them enough to put Ramdev and the rest of the Club away forever. Then we'll be free,* she reasoned.

"No," she whispered. It was far too great a risk. Just six months ago, Ipsita had joined Ramdev on a trip to Hyderabad to *'deal with some club business.'*

The *club business* had been to deal with a suspected rat in that chapter. A young hang-around with the Club had been peddling heroin in Kismet: The Park, which was not a park at all, but a trendy downtown disco. He was gunned down during transport in what was media labelled as a 'Daring Indian Mafia Hit.'

As he was not a full patch member, the Horses hadn't waited to see if he was loyal or not and ended their worry of betrayal with a single sniper shot to the head, outside the police station. He was dead before he hit the ground.

Can't inform, can't run, can't go home. What was there to do? Every choice was horrible. Ippy could not survive in jail and had no wish for her life to end at the hands of a biker. *No, my only chance is to stick with the plan. Seduce Alex into helping me escape and pray we elude the NCB and the Horses.*

She stood, and steadying herself on the counter, fixed her makeup and brushed her hair. She looked at her reflection in the smokey mirror and took a deliberate breath.

"You can do this," she whispered. "You *have* to do this."

Ipsita hurried back to the table, realising her timeline had just been drastically accelerated.

✷ ✷ ✷

Alex drained what was left of his third beer and glanced around the restaurant, assessing his situation. It was busy for a midweek night. He looked at Hiran, who was still standing at the bar. It was on a raised floor, four or five steps above the dining area, and afforded Hiran a good overall view of the bistro. He was chatting with the bartender at the moment.

Ramdev was with the band that were preparing to go back on stage for their second set. He hadn't bothered to sit down again after Ippy had left for the washroom. Alex was glad. He had developed a serious dislike for Ramdev. It paled compared to the full-out hatred he felt for Marceau, but it still smouldered in him every time Ramdev spoke. *"Don't confuse anger with hate,"* his father's voice whispered in his head. Alex took a steadying breath.

"I'm supposed to respect them?" he whispered.

Ipsita had not yet returned. They had left him alone with his thoughts. Alex rolled over the quick conversation with Ippy in his mind. *Was she being genuine? God knows there was an air of desperation about her.* Something about her voice had nestled inside him and made him jittery. He allowed himself to entertain the fantasy for a moment. *Rescue her from Ramdev, the two of us escape and... and what? Bring her to Canada?*

"Jesus," he whispered.

The fact was, as much as he wanted to help, he just didn't trust her. It made more sense that she was on her own agenda and using him. *Idiot!* he thought. *She is using me. Swinging her hips and pouting her lips. It was the oldest game in the book. What did Frank Sinatra call it? The velvet trap. She wants to run away from this monster, Ramdev and wants me to facilitate that. Even if I die in the process. Not to mention, Candy's back home.*

He shivered at the thought of Candy. *God knows how she's being treated.* It made him ill. *No! I have to focus on the landscape. Complete this job and get home. At any cost.*

"Damn it," he whispered as he closed his eyes and rubbed them. His mind filled with an image of Ipsita, her soft lips smiling at him, leaning forward, parting them. He opened his eyes. "This is insane," he scoffed to himself.

Alex shifted in his seat and looked at the front door. *What is stopping me from just walking the fuck right out of here? What would they do? Shoot me in public?* He doubted that. Once outside, he could find a cop quickly enough. There was a ton of security roaming around the area. Alex could tell them everything, or at least enough for them to be interested. The police could make a call to the RCMP before Chevaux de Fer could hurt Candy.

That was the right thing to do. Not indulge in this twisted game of international drug smuggling. *This is a bike gang, for fuck sakes! Real gangsters. There was no way they'll let me and Candy walk away clean. Not, knowing what we do about their operation. Should I try to get out? Maybe I should try to save Ipsita? She could help me. But can I trust her?* Alex continued the silent argument with himself until his father's voice spoke again. *"It's not always about right and wrong, son, it's about what's right for you."*

"No, dad. No way," he whispered.

An act of pure instinct, Alex stood. He checked quickly to make sure neither Ramdev nor Hiran had eyes on him. They didn't. He moved towards the exit and formed a hasty plan. Make it to the door and get outside, turn left and mix in with the public heading to the gates. It was only 250 metres away from the bistro. Alex could sprint that if left no choice. He would tell his tale to the security guards at the gates and *make* them act, call the police.

He was almost to the restaurant exit. Alex fished his cigarettes out of his pocket. He looked down at the maroon Du Maurier package. It looked like home. The smoke would be his cover should Ramdev discover him before he made a clean break. He flashed the package at the doorman and gave him a half shrug. He smiled ear to ear and opened the door for him.

"Thank you, sir!" he chimed as Alex breezed past him. He was out.

"What the fuck am I doing?" he whispered, quickly scanning the crowd. He started to his left towards the primary entrance gate and halted. Something in the other direction caught his attention and Alex turned to look. Not too far from the bistro were two men and a woman staring at him in astonishment. *They are cops!* Alex thought.

There was no doubt. The portly older man was wearing a cheap blue suit, tie, and white shirt. The younger man beside him was athletic, wearing jeans and a tan blazer. But the woman! She was the most obvious! She *stood* like a cop, authoritative, hands on the hips of her grey business suit and hair pulled back in a ponytail. It all screamed cop. The look on their faces was one of surprise. He took one step towards the trio and the woman raised her hand.

"Stop!" she shouted as her hand dipped inside her suit jacket to her hip. The surrounding crowd turned to the sound of her voice. Alex froze, unsure what to do.

The front entrance of Farzi Cafe burst open as Ramdev and Hiran spilled out onto the sidewalk, scattering the curious civilians.

They stood in between Alex and the NCB agents. Ramdev was looking back and forth. He locked eyes with Alex, then followed his gaze and spotted Dimpi, Sandy, and Avinash. There was a collective scream from the throng as Ramdev drew a Glock from the inside pocket of his cut.

"Find Ippy! And make *the* call!" he commanded Hiran.

Hiran nodded and disappeared back into the cafe. Ramdev fired two shots in the air and the bystanders scattered like fire ants, some diving to the ground, but most running for cover towards the NCB agents.

Alex, frozen with shock, saw Ramdev lunging towards him. He tried to move his feet, but they were mired in concrete. As if in a child's nightmare, fleeing from a monster and the stairs you are climbing turn to oatmeal. Ramdev collided with him hard, almost toppling him.

"Move! Or I will shoot you where you fucking stand!" he shouted. He was so close; Alex could smell the beer on his breath.

"Freeze! NCB!" came the call from behind them. By pure instinct, Alex ran with Ramdev. A scared rabbit escaping a fox. He skirted and dodged, weaving in and out of bodies, women screaming, people pushing and running in every direction. Ramdev was ahead of him by several metres. Alex kept pace. A shot echoed off the tall office towers that walled in the Hub. *It must have been in the air,* he thought. *The police would never shoot into a crowd!*

Everything seemed to slow down and go quiet. He saw Ramdev duck his head, then spin his torso, still at a full run. As he faced back behind them, his arm extended, firing his gun. Alex saw two flashes from the muzzle and puffs of smoke. He heard a muffled *pop, pop*, followed by screams, as Ramdev completed his pirouette and continued running, knocking over an older man in his path. Alex followed as closely as he could.

Behind them, one slug smashed into a waist-high clay planter housing a palm tree and a few ferns. The bullet shattered the pottery and came to a halt deep in the moist earth inside. Startled by the crack of the pot and dark soil spilling out, the woman who was hiding behind it ran for cover across the sidewalk. The second shot from Ramdev's 9 mm clipped the left side of her neck, opening the carotid artery. A thick spray of crimson jetted out into the crowd surrounding her. The woman's scream turned to a gurgle as she grasped at her wound and fell to the ground.

"Freeze, *behenchod*!!" a woman's voice shouted after them. Alex put his head down and willed his legs to move faster. The blood was pounding in his ears. He could see the entrance gates. The security guards had abandoned their post at the sound of gunshots and they stood empty.

Ramdev had reached the turnstiles first. Alex saw him look back to make sure he was still in tow. Ramdev leapt and vaulted over the turnstile. Another two sharp retorts rang out from behind and Alex felt a bullet whizz past him. The lamp on the side of the security station exploded into a million shimmering fragments. It showered him with tiny shards of glass as he tried to copy Ramdev's move and leap over the barricade.

He reached out and his right hand contacted the icy steel of the turnstile gate. Alex mustered all his strength and shoved hard while jumping and swinging his legs up and over it.

There was a ripping sound, like the tearing of a denim shirt and then an immediate deep burn in his arm. As if someone had pushed coals from a campfire under his skin. His elbow buckled, and he came smashing down into the barricade. Sheer momentum carried him over the turnstile. The glass from the security light cut him as he hit the cold, hard concrete.

Alex could feel his warm, sticky blood pooling on the sidewalk.

They've shot me! He squeezed his eyes closed. With that knowledge came a wave of pain like he had never experienced. He heard someone screaming. Alex realised it was his voice.

"Get up! Get up, you asshole!" Alex opened his eyes. Ramdev was standing over him. He grabbed Alex's wounded arm, causing him to scream out in agony again. "It's just a scratch. She only clipped you! Come on!" he screamed. Alex felt nauseous and weak. He stood and tried to follow Ramdev. His shaking legs would not support him as he watched Ramdev run up to a black BMW waiting in the valet parking queue. He used the butt of his gun to smash through the driver's window and shoved the barrel in the occupant's face.

"*Bahaar jao*! Get out!" Ramdev ordered as he opened the door with his other hand. The valet tumbled out onto the pavement and crawled away on his hands and knees. "Alex!" Ramdev screamed as he slid into the driver's seat. The engine gunned as he ground the gears. Alex stumbled forward and grasped the rear door handle. Metal shards pierced his hand as bullets punched holes in the thin door.

Alex flung it open and dove in headfirst. He howled in agony as his shoulder slammed against the back seat. The beamer lurched forward with squealing tires and the door swung shut with a slam. Two more bullets punctured the car's trunk with a hollow thud as it fishtailed forward. Both headlights disintegrated as they smashed through the parking gate barrier and the car disappeared into the Gurugram traffic.

✳ ✳ ✳

Hiran sifted through the crowd in the Farzi Cafe. The panicked occupants of the restaurant were stooping in their booths, some pressing to the rear of the dining area and others wedging themselves behind the bar. The surrounding chaos did not break his focus and he spotted Ipsita standing near the stage.

Hiran grabbed her by the wrist and dragged her towards the *Employees Only* door beside the washroom entrance. Ipsita yelped in pain but followed. He twisted the knob. They had locked it. He pounded on the door with his free hand.

"Only employees!" someone called.

"Iron Horses!" Hiran shouted and a moment later, the door opened. The two of them slipped through into a small corridor that fed an office, a break/storage room, a walk-in freezer, and an exit. Hiran forced his path through the huddled waiters and cooks until they pushed out into the service corridor that ran the length of the promenade behind all the establishments. He fell back against the wall and gathered himself.

"Don't move," he growled at Ipsita.

"Where would I go?" she snapped. Hiran fixed her with a look suggesting he would rather hit her than listen to her backtalk. Ipsita shied away from him. Hiran pulled his phone from his pocket and hit one of the speed dial buttons. It rang three times before a deep voice answered.

"Yes?"

"Hiran here. Time to call in a favour," he said.

"I'm just getting reports now. How in God's name do I shield you from this?" came the reply.

Hiran scowled and his voice became menacing.

"I don't care *how* you do it. Just do it. Or the country will find out your daughter is a junkie whore *and* you have been on our payroll for over a year," he said.

"All right, all right. I will work it out. But you and your gang had best lie low for a while. I can delay the search, but believe me, they will watch you."

Hiran's lips curled into a vicious sneer.

"Just see that you do. Don't worry about how we handle our end of things. If you were doing your job, we would have known they would be here! Sharpen up or the consequences will be dire...*Deputy Director, Pandey*!" Hiran snapped the phone shut and dragged Ipsita down the hall.

✦

CHAPTER SIX

The Deputy Director, Pandey, was sitting in his darkened room on the edge of the bed. He placed his hand on his wife's hip and squeezed. She stirred.

"You're okay?" she asked.

"Hush," he whispered. "There has been a shooting. I must go to the office." His wife grunted and tugged the blanket up around her neck. Pandey stood and walked to the closet, pulled a suit off the hanger, and dressed.

It's the middle of the night, and I'm called by those hoodlums to clean up another one of their entanglements. How can I stop an investigation into a public shooting? he thought.

The pressure being exerted on him by the Horses to bury their involvement in the incident or at least buy them time was unbearable. He rubbed his temples.

"Something must be done," he whispered. *I can't keep travelling this road. The risk is too great.*

His options were few. To expose the Club was to expose his daughter, and to keep peddling the Horses' influence within the Bureau was to endanger his involvement with them coming to light. *It may be time for drastic measures.*

At one point, Pandey *had* considered whisking his daughter away to relatives in Canada for rehabilitation. Then he could order a SWAT strike on the Horses' clubhouse. The problem was, he had to kill the lot of them to ensure silence, and a police raid could not guarantee that result.

There was another choice. Hire a contract kill of each of the members. There were enough sinister types in New Delhi's mafia to facilitate that. *But it will be costly and mire me even deeper into the criminal underworld.* Pandey tugged on his clothes and went downstairs to wait for his driver.

"First things first," he murmured. *Slow Avinash Kumar's progress, give the Horses time, then I will find a permanent solution to silencing them for good.*

The headlights from his black SUV splashed through the front window of his living room. Pandey drew a deep breath and left the house. *The Horses must die.*

* * *

"Suspended? Sir, granted the situation at Cyber Hub was unfortunate, but suspension?" Dimpi blinked in disbelief.

"Unfortunate?!" Deputy Director Pandey barked. "You withdrew and discharged your firearm in a public place! There is one dead civilian and three others wounded!" He stood from his desk and fixed Dimpi with a frosty stare. Dimpi remained at attention, her eyes fixating on a spot on the wall behind him.

"What in God's name did you think would happen? This isn't unfortunate, Agent Shashidhar. This is a shit storm!! I've dispatched a full team to the site right now to clean this up!"

The abusive language shocked Dimpi. It was rare to hear a superior officer curse, and even more rare to speak to a female agent in such a manner. This showed the extreme seriousness of the conversation.

"Kumar!" the Deputy Director bellowed.

Avinash and Sandy had been standing in the hall just outside the office. The two of them entered and joined Dimpi to face the Director.

"Would you mind explaining how one of your subordinates incited a gun battle at one of the busiest public spots in NCR?" Pandey asked.

"Sir, I tasked Agent Shashidhar with uncovering as much information as possible about the Iron Horses Motorcycle Club. We suspect they are the major distributors of heroin here and in other cities. She compiled a detailed list of the club membership and a manifest on accomplices," Avinash said.

"All this progress in a few days! Yet I am aware of none of it! How can *that* be?" Pandey asked.

"On this list, sir, was one Miss Ipsita Chaudhary." Avinash pressed on, "She is the Delhi chapter president's mistress. We, I mean, I decided that some persuasion of Miss Chaudhary may provide a break in the case. We had just concluded..."

"Enough!" the Director screamed. "I am aware *how* it happened, Agent Kumar. What I am asking, is how you *allowed* it to happen!" Avinash opened his mouth to speak and the Director silenced him with a hand gesture. "This is a public embarrassment! What have you accomplished?"

"Sir," Sandy interjected. "If we can get a warrant to search their clubhouse—"

"Based on what!?" Pandey screamed. "Can any of you positively identify who the shooter was? Can you?" The trio looked back and forth amongst themselves.

"No, sir," Avinash stammered. "In the confusion... but the probable cause, sir. We know they were at the club. We saw the foreigner; we know they picked him up at the airport. The Horses—"

"Enough!" the Director bellowed again.

"Half measures are not how we conduct investigations here. Without positive identification of the shooter, we have nothing. Henceforth, you will clear these operations with me! Understood?"

He shifted his glare to Dimpi. "As for you, full suspension pending a thorough investigation. Leave your badge and gun and *get out.*"

A short time later in Avinash's office, Dimpi felt the tears welling in her eyes. She fought against them. *I will not cry, I will not show weakness, I'll stand strong against this patriarchal profession. There is no way they would have suspended a man.* Her hand went to her hip. Her holster was empty.

"Do you understand, Agent Shashidhar?" Avinash was saying.

"Sir?" she asked.

"Nothing. No investigation. Go home and visit your family. The enquiry won't start for a week. Take the time to clear your head. Do not, I repeat, do *not* pursue this case while you are under suspension. It will end in further action against you. Am I clear?" he said.

"As glass, sir. Am I dismissed?" she said, biting her cheek. Avinash nodded at her and shot Sandy a concerned look. Dimpi spun on her heel and left the office, slamming the door behind her.

"Hey!" Sandy called after her.

"Let it go," Avinash murmured. "Let her deal with it in her own way. You and I have work to do, my friend."

"If they allow us! No warrant? What is that about? If ever we had a reason..."

"Yes," Avi whispered. "Strange. I can only believe the Director needs us to be airtight on this. We have just made a huge misstep and we can't afford another. Let's see what Miss Chaudhary gives up, shall we?"

✳ ✳ ✳

Dimpi's car squealed as she left the parking lot of the NCB office complex. A young vegetable*wala* stationed outside the gates jumped back from his cart, as her rear tires bumped over the curb. She spun into traffic and sped away.

"Damn them!!" she screamed, as tears spilled from her eyes. After a kilometre, she pulled over under the shade of an enormous banyan tree on Vivekanand Marg. The early morning commuters honked and buzzed past her as she wiped her face.

Dimpi pulled her cell from her pocket and dialled her uncle, Ajit Shashidhar, the Director General. It rang several times, then a groggy voice answered.

"Dimpi?"

"Hello, uncle," her voice quivered. There was silence, then the tussling of bedsheets in the background.

"What is it, love?" he asked.

"They have suspended me. This morning, just now. Did you know?"

"Yes, Dimpi, I knew. I ordered it." Dimpi gasped at the news and felt the tears refresh in her eyes.

"How... how could you?"

"How could I not, Dimpi? You know I love you, that I would do anything for you, or any of my brother's family. But let us not forget, you have had a few indiscretions in the past. Even getting you into the academy was an exercise in humility for me. I can't keep cleaning these things up for you, Dimpi. They have killed an innocent woman. There has to be an inquest, surely you can see that?"

"But why *me*? There were two male agents present also! One of them a Superintendent! This isn't right, uncle!" she wailed.

"You know how it works, how it looks with you as my niece. I have superiors to answer to, just like you. Look, go home, take rest. I will expedite this as best as I can, but there is no way to circumvent the process. Stay away from this case, Dimpi. Understand? Do nothing. I will call you when the review has been scheduled."

Dimpi stabbed the call end button and screamed. She twisted the rear-view mirror, almost pulling it off the windscreen, and looked at her reflection.

"No... I will not let this go," she whispered to herself. "I will break this case wide open and show them I am worthy of this post. More than any man." She leaned over and opened the glove box to fish out her unregistered 9 mm Beretta. She slipped it in her holster, put the car in gear, and started towards the Iron Horses clubhouse in Okhla.

✳ ✳ ✳

Jasmine. He knew the scent. The sweet aroma was surrounding him, comforting him. The pain in his shoulder was only a dull throb but escalated to a fierce burn as he stirred.

His dry lips broke into a half-smile as he identified the angelic bouquet. It was Ipsita's perfume. Even in this brief time, he associated the fragrance with her full lips and bewitching eyes. A concussion grenade burst in his chest and his pulse quickened.

He cracked open his eyelids. The light in the room was painful, and he blinked twice to relieve the irritation. Alex had no idea how long he had been asleep, or where he was. His vision cleared, and the hazy figure over him focussed into Ramdev. Alex was in the small cot of his room at the Iron Horses clubhouse, and Ramdev was staring at him with a smirk.

"So, you're awake," he chuckled. The springs of the musty cot groaned in protest as Alex tried to sit upright, but the lightning bolt in his shoulder made him reconsider and he stayed prone. Ramdev chuckled again.

"It's just a flesh wound, brother. A little trench has been dug through the meat. You'll be fine." Alex blinked his eyes to further clear his vision.

"What happened?" he croaked.

"They shot you," Ipsita whispered. Alex realised she was sitting on the end of the cot. Her hand was on his leg, her fingers flexing, caressing him, and nurturing him. He flooded with warmth and want. The pure electric charge from her presence brought his senses to a heightened awareness. He lifted his head from the thin pillow and grinned at her. She returned it, a demure half-smile that spoke volumes in the silence. Aware of the explicit intimacy he was displaying between them, Alex averted his eyes, but slowly, he looked back into hers.

The relief on her face seemed to be of deeper concern than general well wishes. There was an unspoken exchange between them. As her eyes fell away, Alex felt cold, but the surge of affection returned as she resumed her gaze.

In his weakened state, he fought it no longer. He allowed himself to examine the facts as they were. Was he was falling for Ipsita Chaudhary? Ramdev's smirk turned to more of a grimace.

"If you two could stop eye-fucking each other for a moment, we have business to discuss," he said sharply, breaking the spell. Alex snapped back to the present tense. Ipsita stood, releasing Alex's leg and transforming the spot on his calf to a barren void, longing for her touch.

"I'll be in your office," she mumbled to Ramdev as she left the room. Ipsita shot Alex one last glance of unabashed tenderness before she left.

"All right, *bhai*," Ramdev began.

Alex was taken aback. *Bhai? Brother? What was this?*

"You surprised me, young Alex. That is a fact. You took a bullet and not just *any* bullet. A fucking NCB bullet, fired from an NCB gun by an NCB agent. She was trying to fucking end you, my friend. Yet you didn't panic. No. You manned up... in a gunfight. Not bad, Alex. Not bad at all. More than I expected of you for sure."

He chuckled and pulled a chair over to the side of the bed, the wooden legs scraping across the cool marble, echoing in the sparse room. "There is also the fact, one you are unaware of I am sure, that you ran *with* me to escape. With me, not *to* them to rat us out or surrender. I did motivate you a little with a death threat," Ramdev chuckled. "But let's be honest. Right then, you weren't hearing me, were you? It was all gut reaction."

He spun the chair and straddled it backwards, leaning it forward on two legs, resting his arms over the back. Ramdev stared at Alex hard, studying him for a moment. "You made a choice, mate, whether it was a conscious one or not. At that moment, you chose the MC over the Narcotics fucking Control Bureau. Go figure, hum?"

He reached over to a small box on the table and pulled out a Gold Flake cigarette. "There just may be a little more outlaw in you than you will admit, Alex. Although you *were* trying to get away from us, God knows what your plan was. An ill-conceived one at best. But when forced to make the choice, the pivotal choice, you ran with the Horses."

He lit a smoke and handed it to Alex. Alex reached for it and the musk of stale tobacco filled his nostrils. Ramdev lit one for himself and continued, "You'll tell me one day, Alex, just what the fuck you were trying to do." Ramdev shook his head and smiled. "But the pressing matter right now is, why was the NCB hanging around outside Farzi Cafe, to begin with? At first, I thought you had somehow alerted them. But seeing how you fled with us, I doubt that. Besides, you haven't had access to a phone, have you? Even if you did, you wouldn't know who to call."

Ramdev took a deep drag off his smoke and exhaled it towards the ceiling fan. He watched it for a moment as it swirled and dispersed. "I have to assume that there is some investigation into our business. I have to further assume that the NCB knows what we are up to. Troubling thoughts, Alex." He stood and paced around the bed, his boot heels clicking as he strode.

"This complicates matters somewhat. But the pleasant news is, you have gained a small level of respect from me. I read people well, Alex, that is why I am the president of this chapter." He spun on his heel and stared. "How do I know who to trust, who to bring into the fold? I can see through bullshit. I don't listen to *bakchod*, Alex, and I know a biker when I see one. Loyalty is plain to see where there are honour and respect. Even if you are unaware of these things, Alex, I see them in you."

Alex took a drag on his cigarette, letting Ramdev's words tumble around in his mind.

"Don't think this changes our arrangement at all," Ramdev said, and then barked out a sharp laugh. "It simply means I see you in a unique light. You have gained a small measure of respect." He dropped his smoke on the floor and stepped on it. "The schedule has sped up, Alex. We have to leave tomorrow morning. Certain insurance policies have bought us that slight amount of time. So, you need to fight through your pain and discomfort."

Ramdev walked to the door and paused after he opened it. Looking back over his shoulder at Alex, he spoke, "It's in plain sight, Alex. You and Ipsita. I warn you; she is a devious woman. What would a monkey know of the taste of ginger, Alex? Don't get too lost in her eyes, ya? So lost, that you can't find your way back... It appears the day will come when you will have to choose again. Ipsita, or us."

✳ ✳ ✳

Ipsita sat in Ramdev's chair with her back to the desk, gazing out the rear window of the clubhouse. The hazy sunrise was streaming through it.

On the branch of a nearby tree, two parrots were nuzzling each other. The male chuffed up and began bobbing his head up and down. The female kept turning her back to him, forcing him to flutter his brilliant green wings and hop over to face her once again. Their beaks would touch for a moment and she would pivot, leaving him ignored. She was playing hard to get. Ipsita smiled.

"Poor Alex," she chuckled. He had obviously lapped up all the fictitious affection she had let seep towards him. It was almost too easy for her to ensnare men. *The stupid lust driven animals they are,* she thought. Yet, her usual malice for her male victims was absent with Alex. She may even feel a little sorry for him. *He seems so innocent, and a genuinely likeable guy.*

She had met so few of them in her life, men offering unconditional friendship, or even a legitimate agenda for a relationship. Most just focused on the end game of removing her from her panties. *Was it feeling a touch uncomfortable to play him?*

She spun the chair around and picked up her purse laying on the floor beside the desk. Fishing through it, she found a small black and gold cigarette case. Ipsita paused, thumbed the small latch, and sprung it open with a flip of her wrist. She removed one of the rolled joints, dropped the bag, and tossed the case back into it.

She sparked the joint with the lighter off Ramdev's desk. Ippy inhaled the pungent vapour, closed her eyes, and leaned back into the chair, waiting for the wave of mild intoxication to come. Coughing, she expelled the smoke and took another deep hit.

"You silly girl," she scolded herself. While shaking her head, Ippy let the bluish weed smoke drift from her mouth. She pictured Alex's face, his sandy blonde hair, his endless grey eyes, and boyish grin. *Yes, he is a personable guy. Yes, he is attractive. Maybe under different circumstances...*

She was so focussed on her hatred of Ramdev, she hadn't noticed her appreciation for Alex. *My God,* she thought. *He's gentle, kind, and funny when the mood struck. He was no university scholar, but very intelligent and street smart. And the way he looks at me. Each moment is as if he's seeing me for the very first time, as if he's in awe of my beauty*. She had seen that look many times before, laced with lust and desire for her body. With Alex, it was different. It was more of a curiosity or admiration.

She wiped her palms on her jeans as her heart beat faster. It wasn't the weed. She hit the joint again and smiled. *How in God's name could I see him like this, in this light? I barely know him. He's not even Indian.*

"A *firangi*, no less," she whispered. Perhaps her fascination with him was more with what he represented. Freedom, hope, a life without drugs and emotionless sex. She pondered that. Ipsita had never thought of men in that way. She had never been afforded the opportunity. It had *always* been men for sex and gain, and women, Daya, for love and comfort. *Was an emotional relationship possible with a penis?* She giggled to herself. The weed was having the desired effect. Before she could answer herself, the door burst open and Ramdev came in like a raging bull. He snatched the joint from between her fingers and hauled on it twice.

"You stupid bitch," he shouted through the smoke. "What are you thinking? He will deliver you from evil? Is he the man of your dreams, Ippy?" The veins on Ramdev's neck were as taut as ship cables.

"You are nothing more than a Bollywood wannabe, who would rather lick a woman than satisfy a man. Your *only* commodity is your looks, Ipsita! Tits and ass, that's all you are. How do you think dear little Alex will see you when the beauty fades? When the ass is fat and the tits drop to your waist? What do you offer him then?" he sneered at her, blowing the weed smoke in her face. Ipsita did not allow the tears to come. She had suffered enough verbal and physical abuse from Ramdev to have learnt to let it wash over her.

"I have no idea what you are talking about..." He backhanded her sharply across the mouth, causing her to finish the sentence with a yelp.

"Please, Ipsita. Do you think I'm a fool?" He snuffed the joint out in the ashtray and walked away from her. She sat motionless, head lowered, licking the salty blood from her lips.

"No, Ramdev. I don't know *what* you are. A monster, perhaps?" she whispered. "I am simply doing as you asked, controlling him. The best way

I know how."

"Your eyes betray you, Ipsita. The way you look at him, the casual touches. It is as transparent as your cheap glass earrings. And just like them, it is all an illusion," he snarled.

"It's an act, Ramdev! How could I feel anything for this man? I am doing nothing more than *what you asked*!"

"Bullshit! I have eyes! There could be nothing between you two. He is a dead man walking."

Despite knowing better, Ipsita's anger flared. She stood and screamed at him, "Fuck you, Ramdev! You are evil, with no feelings or substance... and you are jealous for no reason. Like a jealous little boy who won't share his toys!" For a moment, he looked shocked, then as if he would strike her again, but he smiled instead.

"Jealous? You have never been more than a fuck to me, Ippy. Go to him, I don't give a shit. You do as I bid you to do, keep him in line until we get to Goa, then we are rid of him. That is all you are now, Ipsita. A whore babysitter." He sauntered to her until they were near touching. His sour breath assaulted her as he spoke. "Then and only then, I'll decide what to do with you. Make no mistake, Miss Chaudhary, do as I ask, or you and your little junkie girlfriend, Daya, will pay. In ways you can't even fathom." Ipsita stormed from the room, kicking over her purse on the way. In her fury, she did not bother to bend over to retrieve it.

✳ ✳ ✳

The door slammed and Ramdev found himself alone. He flopped in his chair and pounded his fists on the desk. *She is correct. I am jealous*, Ramdev thought. He had been aware for a while that Ipsita had lost interest in him. He doubted now that she *ever* felt anything of substance for him.

From the moment Hiran introduced them in Mumbai, Ramdev had fallen under her spell, just as so many men before him. He fell prey to her charms and grace. He became suspect not too long after their relationship began, that he offered nothing more than a promise of something bigger for her. An escape from whatever miserable life she had been running from then. *I pretended not to notice.*

When she focused on him, it was as if the sun shone on him, on his life, on his *soul*. But just as he told her about Alex, it was an illusion. There had been no real depth to their union. The more obvious it became, the more anger and violence he hurled towards her. It pushed Ippy farther and farther away until she transformed into another disappointment. *Another let down in a long chain of them.*

Ramdev's restlessness and discontent had been building. Feigning interest in club business and the constant charade of his involvement with Ippy was exhausting. It was becoming a daily affair to support the motivation to take part in either. When he first joined the Iron Horses as a prospect, it was exciting. It was everything he had been chasing in his youth. There were so few hardcore motorcycle clubs in India. Admittance into one was a lofty achievement.

As he slogged his way through the ranks, the harsh realisation that this MC was not about riding motorcycles, but was about money, violence, and drugs became plain. He lost sight of his genuine passion.

All I ever wanted was to belong to something bigger, like Ipsita, I guess. To embrace the brotherhood, to count in my community, and mean something. He longed to be a man that others relied upon, and above all, ride his motorcycle, bearing the patch with pride.

His presidency in the Iron Horses had not helped him achieve these lofty ideals. The Horses were not composed of dreams. This was a business. All those ambitions left him long ago. The tension and unrest in his guts festered further each day, leaving him filled with desperation and want. His phone chirped and broke his train of thought.

"Yeah?" he answered.

"My captain," Ratt said. "We have been watching the bikes for an hour. There doesn't seem to be any interest in them." Ramdev had sent Shiv and Ratt back to Cyber Hub to retrieve the bikes left behind after last night's debacle.

"It looks as if our Deputy Director is keeping up his end. Give it thirty more minutes. If it still looks clear, bring them home," he said and ended the call without waiting for an answer.

Ramdev stood and gazed out the window. The parrots were long gone. There was nothing other than another smoggy Delhi morning staring back at him. The potent scent of marijuana still hung in the air. It prompted him.

"If I can't flee, I can still fly," he mumbled, spying Ippy's purse on the floor. Ramdev picked it up and rummaged through it to find her black and gold *magic box*. On the bottom of the bag, amongst the lipsticks and candy wrappers, he spotted a business card. Ramdev took it out, read it, and flopped back in his chair.

Narcotics Control Bureau. Special Agent - Dimpi Shashidhar. "Well, well," he whispered. "What the fuck do we have here?"

✳ ✳ ✳

Ipsita rushed to the washroom from Ramdev's office, only now allowing the salty tears to flow over her satin cheeks. She yanked the door open and slammed it. She covered her face with her hands and propped herself back against the wall. Her jaw ached from the smack he had given her, and her pride was stinging even worse. What Ramdev had said struck a very tender nerve. She had always relied on her radiance to open doors, to get what she wanted. Ipsita sobbed.

"Goddamn you!" she shouted through the tears. "I am *not* just a sex toy. I am not!"

At that moment, she gave way to a crashing wave of emotions. Her heart and head filled with only one thing. *Daya! I need to be with her, need to be in her arms*. But Daya was not there. She was locked away in her flat in Noida. Ipsita sobbed, desperate and separated from the one person who could console her. She wrestled down her pain and replaced it with anger.

"Fine, Ramdev," she whispered. "A whore you see, a whore I'll be." The time had come to sink her claws into Alex. She needed him as an ally, and her battered psyche needed comfort.

Ipsita flung the door open and ran to the stairwell, and taking them two at a time, she climbed to the top floor. Her stiletto heels were clacking on the marble steps. Ipsita was slipping and skidding. She didn't care. She was fleeing with reckless abandon, fleeing Ramdev, fleeing the Horses, and escaping her nightmare.

She twisted the knob to Alex's room and flung open the door, stopping as Alex sat bolt upright on the cot. He winced in pain. Ipsita stood in the doorway, hair dishevelled and makeup streaked with tears. She forced her cheeks to warm as she whispered his name and conjured her best impression of a distressed damsel in need. "Alex."

"Oh my God, Ippy!" he exclaimed. "What's happened? Are you okay? Did Ramdev..."

Upon hearing the genuine concern in his voice, something inside her twinged. The earlier guilt? There was no lust in his eyes, only caring and worry. She was about to crush a hapless man's emotions again, all to fill her own needs. Ipsita forced down her empathy and sprinted to him, diving into his arms and toppling him back onto the cot. Ipsita buried herself in him. Again, she was puzzled. Her stomach was not filled with icy determination. Nor was it filled with wanton desire. These were the mental states in which she hid during such encounters. She felt neither.

"Alex, oh Alex. Please... I'm sorry, I, I..." she whimpered, nuzzling her head against his chest.

"Hush," Alex soothed. He stroked her hair and held her as tight as he could with his injured arm. "It's okay, Ipsita. It's all right."

She looked up at him, forcing her soft doe-eyes to brim with tears and shadows of pain. It came easy, far too easy. Ipsita was confused, scared. *Why am I not in control of my manipulation of him? What is that intrusive tingle in my guts?*

"I need you, Alex. I, I... Protect me, Alex. Help me escape..."

Now, with the task at hand in focus, the lust came. In a moment of erupting passion, she kissed him. Their tongues twisted around each other's, their hands caressing and searching, her whimpers lost in the pure ecstasy of this inevitable consummation. Alex drew her to him, their bodies grinding against each other. Regaining her master craft of seduction, she pushed away with her palms on his chest, breaking the kiss.

"Ippy, no... please," he stammered, but she only stood and walked to the door. Ipsita closed it and twisted the deadbolt shut. She spun back to him and gave a pained but wicked smile.

She tore her blouse over her head, not bothering with the buttons. Two of them popped, then fell, bouncing and clicking across the floor. With a flip of her head, her flaxen hair shimmered around her. Ippy crossed the room while licking her lips and with an expert flick of her thumb and forefinger, undid her jeans. Her black bra clad breasts heaved as she wiggled them over her hips and sat on the edge of the cot.

"Do you want me, Alex?" she breathed in a well-polished purr.

"More than I have ever wanted anyone," he whispered. Ipsita smiled and put a finger over his lips.

"No, Alex. Do you want *me*? Not just my body." Ipsita surprised herself with the question. She repeated her mantra. *A means to an end, a means to an end. But is it? Why do I need his desire for me to be pure?*

Alex reached up and caressed her cheek. She cringed as the slap from Ramdev was still throbbing.

"Yes. You, Ipsita. Just you. There is no rhyme or reason for my feelings. I can't explain them, but they are real. We don't have to..." She silenced him with another kiss.

"Yes, we do, Alex. Oh God, yes we do," she groaned and meant it. *There's more at play here than solidifying our escape plan and seeking carnal comfort.* Ipsita forced the thought down and allowed whatever this alien motivation was, to carry her away. *The result will be the same, just enjoy it for now.*

Alex shed his pants as Ipsita kicked off her shoes and jeans. She straddled him and began grinding with the urgency of pure passion. Ipsita filled with fiery lust, beckoning him with her eyes. Alex ripped the sheer black thong from her waist with one hand and positioned himself with the other.

As Alex found her heat, he bucked and penetrated her with one deft thrust. Ipsita rolled her head back and with her eyes screwed shut, felt him fill her. She moaned at the ceiling. "Alex! Oh yes, Alex!" They thrashed in their lovemaking, consuming each other's very essence. It ended with a blinding light of ecstasy and they collapsed into each other's arms.

✶ ✶ ✶

The warm afterglow of contentment filled Alex with comfort he hadn't known since this entire ordeal began. Ipsita stirred in his arms. Her head on his chest, she was clinging to him like a frightened child. He slipped out from under her, careful not to wake his new lover, and dressed.

Alex opened the carved wooden box on the table beside the bed. It contained a dozen Gold Flakes and a couple of joints. He picked up a joint and sparked it with a match. Sucking on the weed, he closed his eyes. Alex savoured the intoxicating bite of the sweet leaf in his throat.

The comfort from desperate sex with Ippy was fading and deeper feelings were tugging at his innards. A shadow of a thought. Was there an insinuation of hidden truth? Something Ramdev had said to him was making him uneasy. *"You made a choice, mate, whether it was a conscious one or not. At that moment, you chose the MC over the Narcotics fucking Control Bureau,"* he had said. Even more troubling, *"There just may be a little more outlaw in you than you will admit, Alex."* Then later, he had continued, *"I don't listen to bakchod, Alex, and I know a biker when I see one. Loyalty is plain to see where there are honour and respect. Even if you are unaware of these things, Alex, I see them in you."*

Honour and respect. That was my father's mantra. Could this be what he was talking about all those years ago? Could it be? he questioned. *On some level, am I engaging in this horror show? Even enjoying it? If I'm completely honest, there have been moments of pure adrenaline, and if the circumstances were different, I may even get off on this.* He looked at Ipsita. *She is a bonus. A huge fucking bonus, and despite the bullshit, I ended up in the bed of this amazing woman. It's in my genes, I guess. My father was a hardcore biker.*

From what he knew of their life together before his birth, his mom had been a legitimate ole lady. Was there outlaw blood running in his veins, like the heroin that ran through the veins of the Chevaux de Fer's junkie clientele?

The brown sugar piped from Afghanistan, into the disillusioned dreams of the downtrodden and desperate in Canada and India. Did it live in him? Was this sadistic mixture of blood and brown sugar a deeper part of his innermost being? There had always been a longing in Alex. A void, a want, an unattainable need, just out of reach. A sudden craving for carnival candyfloss on a dreary February day.

He shook his head hard and finished the joint, butting it out in the ashtray. Whatever was eating him, he was positive of one thing. Everything will come to a head in the next few days. Yet he felt none of the apprehension and fear he felt beforehand. It was as if this union with Ipsita and his brush with death had liberated him. Or at the very least, allowed him to examine the desires he had suppressed. *No, not suppressed.* "More like realising the desires I have been searching for all this time," he whispered.

◆

CHAPTER SEVEN

Marceau put down the phone, and with his elbows on the chapel table, cradled his head in his palms.

"*Sacré bleu,*" he whispered. *It's 8:30 in the morning. Too early for this shit.* He stretched in the black leather chair to arch his back and relieve the burning knot between his shoulder blades. That he was nursing a monumental hangover was not helping matters. Marceau had just been speaking with Ramdev and the news was poor, very poor. There was a light knock on the door.

"Come," he said. Tracy entered.

"A moment, Tic?" he asked. Tic rolled his fingers in the air to continue. "With Clipper out of commission the last two days, we have slipped behind on collections," Tracy said and walked over to the table. "We should send Alain out to settle up today. He is on his way here with Clip right now."

"*Bon,* good," Marceau said. *Always on top of the numbers,* Tic thought. *Thank God for Tracy.*

"Also," Tracy continued, "two new businesses have opened in the neighbourhood. A strip club..." He removed a scrap of paper from the right pocket of his cut and glanced at it, pushing his glasses further up his hawk-like nose. "Pleasure Chateau on Rue St. Cardeau. They received their liquor licence yesterday and should be ready for public entry this week. Then a novelty shop called Bong-A-Diggy, where the restaurant with the shitty coffee used to be. Across from Cafe Cleopatra. They are stocked and ready to go." He tossed the note on the table. "You and I should pay them a visit, no?"

"Yes, Tracy. We should. Clear thinking, brother. Much needed these days. I have just spoken to Delhi, and the news is not so good." Marceau stood and motioned to the door. "Come, let's have a shitty coffee ourselves and I'll explain."

The two of them left the sanctity of the chapel and entered the clubhouse lounge. The activities from the night before had laden the air with weed and cigarette smoke, tinged with the sour aroma of stale beer. Marceau wrinkled his nose.

"Can we open a fucking window in here?" he barked.

John looked up at him. He was behind the bar in a cut-off jean shirt and work pants, fiddling with the beer tap. Billy was lingering beside John and hustled over to open a window.

"Go deep!" John called, referring to Billy's football experience. Billy had a promising future cut short by a career-ending knee injury in his senior bowl game. Billy juked around a chair and fanned out his hands in a typical wide receiver pose. John tossed a beer can at him from the bar. It flew over his head and clattered as it bounced across the floor.

"You suck!" Shotgun bellowed. He and Candy were relaxing at one of the cramped wooden tables, talking. Marceau glanced at them. She was twisting her hair between two fingers and laughing at Shotgun, who was sporting a schoolboy grin. The antics angered him.

"Disappear, bitch!" Marceau shouted at her. Candy jolted with surprise and the gaiety dropped from her face like a stone. She looked to Shotgun, who nodded his head towards the door. She stood, and with a pout, left the five of them alone.

"What the *fuck* is going on with you two?" Tic asked, lifting both palms to the ceiling.

"*Nada*, chief," Shotgun replied. "Not a goddamn thing." Tic shook his head and strode over to John.

"And this?" he asked, pointing at the draught tap.

"Can't you smell it?" John snickered. "Fucking thing popped last night. Almost drowned a Horse Head, the poor girl. Covered her titties in half a keg's worth of beer before we could stop it." He smiled as Marceau rolled his eyes.

"Okay, listen up, brothers," Marceau began. "Clipper is arriving sometime this morning. Let's get him settled, then we have club business to attend to, ya? First off, John, you get out and finish the collections. Take Alain and the superstar prospect with you." Marceau smiled. "And make sure Alain doesn't kill anyone." It was rare to see a smile from him, as moments of levity were not his forte. The others laughed. "Tracy and I..." A bellow came from the hallway.

"What is that stink?? Have you rat pricks been pissing on the carpet again!?" Clipper roared as he entered the opposite side of the room. Alain was steadying him. Clipper beamed at the five of them, and his smile turned to a wince as he held his arms open.

The room erupted into a din of mixed greetings as they rushed to his side. Marceau allowed the others to hug him first. After they had backed away, he approached him.

"Welcome home, Clip." He smiled and gingerly embraced him.

"Good to be home, Prez," Clipper said.

With a sturdy clasp of his shoulders, Marceau continued, "I'm sure you want to get some rest. As for us, we have work to do."

"Oh, *rest*," Clipper said with a grin. "Where is that new girl, Stacy?"

"Her tits are in rehab," John said, prompting another burst of laughter.

Tic reluctantly joined in and then pointed to John. "You, go. Take Alain and Billy. Tracy and I have some new customers we need to sign on to our protection and security service program." The group chuckled. "Everyone be back here by 4:00 and we will give Clip a proper welcome."

✳ ✳ ✳

Shotgun walked along the hallway towards the playroom. He could hear the small radio Candy had asked for, playing through the open door. He looked into her room. She was sitting on the edge of the bed, eyes closed, swaying back and forth to an old U2 song.

"Hey," he said. She looked up at him impishly.

"Hey yourself," she replied.

"Don't let Tic get to you. He's an asshole by nature. Since birth. He doesn't even work at it."

"No effort required?" she asked in mock surprise. "It's okay, I'm a captive here. I don't get any concessions. I'm not one of you." She shrugged.

"It's not like that," Shotgun said. "Are you okay? You need anything?"

"Do you mean that, Blu? Or are you just patronising me?"

"No, no. I mean it."

"A decent meal would be nice. I am sick of pizza and hamburgers. How about taking me out for some substantial food? Italian? Greek? Anything that doesn't come in a cardboard box with a giant Mc on it would be nice," she pleaded. Shotgun laughed.

"Don't dis the Mickie Dee. It's my life's blood! Fair enough, give me a couple of hours, okay? We'll go for lunch, weather permitting. I know a patio restaurant by the river. They have a good grilled salmon." Candy tilted her head and smiled at him.

"Just you and me?" she purred.

"What did I tell you, chickie? That doesn't work on me," he warned. "Yes though, just the two of us. We can do a little shopping too if you need anything." He headed for the door.

"*Well,*" Candy said. Shotgun paused and looked over his shoulder from the doorway.

"Humm?" he prompted.

"I need some tampons."

"Fuck sakes!" he said, making a sour face. Candy laughed outright.

"Big scary biker," she taunted Blu as he disappeared.

✸ ✸ ✸

Bong-A-Diggy was a small, recently opened head shop in the west end of Montreal's party district on Rue St. Laurent, right across the street from the notorious Cafe Cleopatra. The Montreal Pool Room, another fixture ingrained in the local nightlife, was right next door. The young proprietors thought it an ideal location to peddle their wares.

They knew that the location also brought with it added financial considerations. Considerations that they would not have to suffer at the other end of the district. On Rue St. Catherine's, in a shopping plaza such as Centre Eaton de Montréal, for example.

But paying protection money to the local gangs worked out to be less costly than rent in such a prestigious mall. Not to mention, the footfall in such a retail space may not be that interested in Bob Marley flags, Grateful Dead bongs, and Led Zeppelin t-shirts.

Gabriel Floris and his recent bride, Chloe, watched as the heavyset bearded man removed another ceiling tile in the display area of the shop. A musty odour of humid, stale air wafted in from the concealed space. It mixed with the prevalent aroma of *Nag Champa* incense in the shop. The six foot tall aluminium ladder groaned as the man shifted his weight.

With the renovations completed earlier this week, Gabriel and Chloe had only just finished arranging their stock. They had spent the best part of two days lining up the colourful red and yellow bongs, and the many books on hydroponics along the smoked glass display shelves.

They had been admiring their handiwork when this gentleman had arrived and began tapping on the front window. Gabriel unlocked the door and informed him they were not yet open for business.

"I'm aware," he had said, pushing his way past Gabriel. The stranger identified himself only as 'Griff' and explained he was a member of the *Community Protection* team for this part of town. His arrival had not been a surprise. The couple was wondering when someone like him would make an appearance.

"*Ah oui,*" Gabriel had said. "They informed us of this. You are with the Horses, *oui*? Chevaux de Fer?" He struggled with his English but tried to keep an accommodating tone. The visitor's face darkened at the mention of the Club.

"No, not the Horses, and it would serve you well not to ask too many questions," he had snarled. "I'll explain, but I need to install this first."

Griff had held up a miniature portable surveillance camera. A nanny cam. After a brief inspection of the store, he had retrieved a ladder from their backroom and began lifting tiles.

Gabriel studied Griff as he mounted the device on the tee-bar track that secured the acoustical tiles to the ceiling. The chosen location was above a tile on a right angle to the cash register.

Griff was wearing jeans and a plain black polo, but the tattoos on both his arms identified him as an MC member. *But not* with Chevaux de Fer. After replacing the tile in front of the camera, he took out his cell phone and fiddled with it, setting up a Bluetooth app.

"Pencil," he mumbled at Chloe. She knocked over the coffee mug beside the cash register, sending bright coloured pens and pencils rolling in every direction. She scooped one up and handing it to him, exchanged a curious glance with her husband. Gabriel shrugged. The intruder poked a hole through the tile in front of the camera lens, small enough that it blended in with its stipple pattern. Indistinguishable, unless you were looking for it.

Griff stared at his cell and putting his hand up through the adjacent tile, adjusted the camera's angle. He frowned and enlarged the hole, twisting the wooden pencil back and forth between his fingertips in a drill-like fashion. Griff leaned close, blew hard on the opening, and looked back at his phone.

"Stand at the register," he ordered Gabriel. "And you," he motioned to Chloe. "In front of it." The bewildered couple took their positions. Griff tossed her the pencil. "Pass that to him and say 'Good morning'," he instructed. Chloe did as she was told while Griff studied his phone screen. Satisfied, he nodded to himself and slid the phone in the front pocket of his jeans.

After replacing the missing tile, he stepped off the ladder and motioned at Chloe. She collapsed it and took it into the back room. Griff glanced around the shop, idly examining merchandise here and there. He picked up a large breast-shaped coffee mug with the nipple as a spout. After a chuckle, Griff returned it to the shelf.

He lit a cigarette and paused only long enough to blow smoke at the day glow pink and green '*No Smoking, ANYTHING*' sign on the wall. He walked to Gabriel, who was still behind the counter, and took the phone from his pocket.

"Today, or tomorrow after you open for business—"

"Tomorrow, *Monsieur*," Gabriel interjected and drew a very threatening look from Griff.

"I don't give a shit, asshole," Griff snapped and continued. "The Chevaux de Fer will come and pay you a visit." Griff paused. Gabriel only nodded. "They will be identifiable by their clothing, their vests, you know this?" Again, Gabriel nodded. "After some chitchat, they will ask you for fifteen hundred dollars. This fee shall be for their protection of your business and they will explain this collection will be a monthly occurrence." Griff paused and butted his smoke out on the counter.

"I understand," Gabriel said.

"Before the chitchat begins, you will move to the register, *sava*? Keep this phone under the counter." He waved it back and forth in front of Gabriel's face. Griff turned it so that Gabriel could see the screen. "This app here, the blue one, you press that and a red record button will appear." Griff pressed it and showed Gabriel the two of them on the phone screen. "Don't let them see you doing this. Be smooth and cool. Dig it?"

"*Oui*," Gabriel stammered.

"You must start the recording *before* he asks you for the money. Clear?" Griff asked. Again, Gabriel nodded. "Now this is the important bit," Griff said. "You will tell him that fifteen hundred is too dear, you are a new business and please, would one thousand be acceptable. You *must* try to negotiate. Speak clearly and loudly, but not so loud as to make him suspicious. They will most likely tell you to fuck off. Don't take that to heart," he chuckled. "Pay them what they ask and when they have left, stop the recording. You will then call the only number on speed dial. Here." Griff showed him, and a moment later another phone chirped inside his pocket. I will come and retrieve my goods. Then you may consider our dealings concluded. This is a simple task..."

"Gabriel," Gabriel prompted.

"Gabriel. Are you crystal clear on what will happen and how to accomplish it?" Griff looked as menacing as a horny bull.

"*Qui*, yes. Yes sir," Gabriel said.

"*Bon, tres bon.* Very fucking good."

Griff laughed and flipped the phone over the counter, hitting Gabriel in the chest. Gabriel covered it quickly with his hands and saved it from dropping to the ground. Chloe emerged from the back room and stood beside her husband, taking his arm.

With a nasty look for both of them, Griff turned and began towards the door. His heavy biker boots clumped on the floor, then fell silent as he stopped to pick up the titty coffee mug. Griff looked back over his shoulder and raised his eyebrows.

"With our compliments, *Monsieur*," he said. Griff suckled the nipple, making an exaggerated slurping sound, snorted a laugh, then left. The two of them stared at each other blankly as their hearts pounded in their chests.

✳ ✳ ✳

Tic was astride his orange Road Glide, rumbling along Rue Norman with Tracy trailing behind him. The traffic was light and the ride to Rue St. Laurent only took a brief time. The tandem pulled up in front of Bong-A-Diggy, backed into the curb and kicked down their side stands in unison. Killing the motor, they dismounted and strode to the front door.

Tracy pounded on the glass hard enough to cause the black and red *Closed* sign hanging on the opposite side to bounce. The tinkle of the small bell over the door greeted them as Chloe opened it. Marceau pushed his way past her before she could speak. Tracy followed him in and closed the door. He stood with his back to it and folded his arms across his chest.

"*Bonjour*," Marceau said. He surveyed Chloe's gaunt figure and asked, "You are the owner?"

"*Oui, Monsieur. Avec mon mari...* my husband," she stammered.

"*Tres bon.*" Marceau smiled. After removing his sunglasses,

Tic looked to the back of the shop and saw Gabriel standing at the cash register. What he did not see was Gabriel starting the recording app on the phone. With only four strides, Marceau stood in front of him, his massive frame filling Gabriel's view like an Appalachian Mountain. *"Bonjour,"* he repeated.

"Good morning," Gabriel replied.

"Do you know who we are?"

"You sir, I do not, but I know *what* you are," Gabe said. His English was wrong and, in a flash, Marceau slammed his half helmet on the counter and grabbed Gabriel by the throat. Chloe shrieked as she watched Tic draw her husband close. Tic's foul breath caused the shop owner to wrinkle his nose.

"And what would that be?" Marceau asked, raising his eyebrows. "What are *we*?"

Desperately trying to recover from his poor choice of words, Gabriel sputtered. He took several deep breaths.

"You are here to offer us protection, *oui*? From vandals and robbery? You are"—Gabriel continued to struggle for the words—"community watch!" he shouted with relief.

Marceau released him and guffawed, "Yes. Yes, my friend. We are the community watch." He glanced back at Tracy, who elected not to smile. He remained motionless with a disagreeable sneer on his face. Gabriel took several deeper breaths.

"We will provide you these services mentioned, for a nominal fee." Marceau looked back and forth between the shopkeeper and his wife, as if he was trying to determine their worth. "Two thousand collected the first week of every month." Gabriel squeaked.

"But sir, we were not expecting such a tariff!" he said.

"Is that so? Not what you were expecting, eh?" Marceau mused. "That is a shame. It is what it is, my friend."

"We know of the Chevaux de Fer through other shop owners here, sir. It was our hope our fee would be more in line with theirs. Perhaps like a thousand dollars? We are a small shop. Not a lot of customers as yet."

"Yes, well..." Marceau began. "This *is* a rough neighbourhood, no? And times are tough. People are doing desperate things. I would hate to see the front windows smashed every week, or your rear door broken, and stock go missing."

Tracy slammed his elbow against the door glass to solidify the point.

"Two thousand," Gabriel whispered.

"If that truly is out of reach, there are other ways you could compensate the Club." Marceau took a step towards Chloe, cupped her smallish breast in the palm of his hand and squeezed. "Many ways," he sneered as she pulled away from him. Marceau chuckled and turned back to Gabriel.

"Okay, okay," he said, punching a key on the register. The till rang open and Gabriel lifted the tray. He took out two crisp five hundred-dollar bills and babbled to Chloe in French. She scampered away into the back room, and after a moment, returned with two more.

"Obedient boy!" Marceau praised him and took the cash. "We will consider this your startup fee, yes? One of our associates will return next week to collect this month's payment."

"But, sir!" Gabriel sputtered. Marceau silenced him with a look that suggested any *further* utterance would end his life. With one last lascivious stare at Chloe, Marceau went to the door. Tracy had it standing open for him and the two of them disappeared into Montreal's morning sun. Gabriel slowly reached beneath the counter and switched off the camera.

"Make the call," Chloe whispered.

✷ ✷ ✷

They sat at a table near the railing on the patio of L'Auberge du Vieux Port Cafe, on Rue de la Commune Est. It offers stunning views of the old port carved into the bank of the St. Lawrence river.

Candy had begged Blu to take her to Le Fcuk to shop.

"Le what?" he had laughed.

"Le Fcuk, the French Connection. Come on, Blu," she had scolded him.

In the boutique, he had purchased the most expensive pair of jeans he had ever seen or heard about. It was outrageous. Yet, looking at her now, Blu had to admit it was money well spent.

Candy was stunning in her faded jeans with a black faux leather vest, a studded belt and white V-neck tee shirt. Her black lace bra was visible through the thin cotton fabric. Candy's streaked hair fluttered in the light breeze, exposing the large gold hoop earrings. An impulse buy at the checkout. They glinted in the afternoon sun as she turned to gaze at the water.

"This place, Blu," she said, mesmerised by the majesty of the powerful river. "It's really something." Candy sipped her wine. "One would almost think you were trying to impress this poor girl." She looked back at him, eyes twinkling.

His pulse quickened. *God, she is beautiful,* he thought. Despite his vast experience with flirtatious women, strippers, hang-arounds, and even the Horse Heads, Candy was cracking his veneer.

"Me? Naw. You said you wanted an enjoyable meal. Here you go." He motioned to her plate. Candy laughed, a singsong that lingered in his ears. She leaned across the table and kissed his cheek. The sweet bouquet of her perfume engulfed him.

"Well, thank you. It is a wonderful meal, Blu," she said, stirring the green peas around her plate with her fork. "Blu, what's your proper name?" she asked him, tilting her head and squinting against the sunlight. He studied her for a moment.

"Charles," he said. Candy gagged as a laugh forced its way past a mouthful of salmon.

"Charles?!" she repeated incredulously. "Not Chuck or Charlie? *Charles?*"

"Jesus," Blu murmured. "Charles. Yes, Charles. After my dad." Candy giggled despite herself.

"That's a hell of a stretch from Shotgun Blu, hun. How did you end up with that?"

"That's a helluva story. One I'm not willing to share with you," he said with a smirk. "How about you? Candy? Where I come from, that's a stripper's name."

"I guess we both have some history we are not proud of." Her eyes darkened. They sat in silence for a moment and Candy returned her gaze to the St. Lawrence River. "I think I'll stay, Blu," she whispered.

"Where?"

"Here, Montreal. When Alex comes back... *if* Alex comes back. I think I'll stay here." She shrugged. "There is really nothing for me in Toronto. Just a waitressing job, a crappy apartment, and a string of fair-weather friends. I've been waiting for Alex to suggest we move in together." Candy sighed. "But I don't think that's gonna happen anytime soon. It's nice here." She smiled at him. "And if I'm being completely honest, I kinda like your entire thing."

"My thing?"

"Yes." She nodded while stuffing the last forkful of salmon into her mouth. Candy chewed quickly and swallowed. "The bikes, the parties, the excitement. I could see myself involved in all of that. But seeing how you treat those other girls, the Horse Heads, I don't fancy being passed around from one guy to the next all the time." She made a face. "That's not my style."

"That's the price of admission, I'm afraid," Shotgun said.

"Is it?" Candy asked. Her come hither look made his heart skip, and Blu felt uncomfortable. He was not accustomed to feeling this way.

"Finish up, Candy. Let's go," he said and downed what was left of his beer. He thumped the mug on the table and decided to flee the situation. Whatever he was suffering, Blu chose not to confront it in a romantic setting. He settled the check and the two of them headed downstairs.

Shotgun's bike stood at the curb in front of the entrance and was drawing stares. She was a stunning 1984 Softail Heritage, a magnificent beast. Her dull copper coloured tank had the Chevaux de Fer logo emblazoned across it and the cream colour leather seats accentuated the shade. Lots of chrome made her shine and command attention. Blu swung his leg over it as Candy grinned at him.

"Like a little boy on his toy," she shouted over the rumble of the bike starting. Shotgun tried to keep his level of cum-fuck-you coolness, but the gleam in his eyes betrayed him. He nodded over his shoulder and she climbed on board.

As they roared away from the curb, Candy slid forward, gripping his hips, and squeezing her thighs, her billowy breasts compressing against his back. "Yep, I could get used to this all right," she shouted in his ear.

Ya, so could I, he thought.

They travelled Rue de la Commune E in silence, enjoying the afternoon sun. Blu wove the bike in and out of the traffic, drawing stares as they sped along the avenue. It was old hat for him, but Candy found the attention *very* exciting.

"Are you serious about staying here, Candy?" he bellowed over his shoulder. Candy slid her hands forward to his inner thighs and squeezed.

"I am, Blu. Dead serious," she replied and placed her hands back on his hips.

The girl made no bones about making her desires known. Triggered by her reply, Blu suddenly turned right onto Rue de St. Laurent.

"I have an idea," he said. "About getting you some employment." Less than five minutes later, Blu stopped the bike in front of the Cafe Cleopatra. Candy waited until he shut off the engine before she punched him somewhat seriously in the rib cage.

"Meaningful employment? As a stripper?" she squealed at him. "Just because I said I had some history? There is no way, Blu. No way!" Blu laughed, cutting her short. A genuine and good-natured belly laugh. It was infectious, and Candy joined in despite her attempt to scold him.

"Titties and beer offend you?" he asked, pushing his back against her breasts. She shook them playfully. "I know the owner," he explained. "He is always looking for hot waitresses. The pay isn't great, but the tips are good if you know how to work the room." Candy dismounted the bike and looked at him, thrusting out one hip and pouting her lips.

"Whatever do you mean?" she asked. Candy bent forward and squeezed her arms together, deepening her cleavage.

"That is the stuff of legends right there, darlin'," Blu said, staring at her chest. Candy chuckled at him as he swung his leg over the bike. They stood for a moment on the sidewalk, looking into each other's eyes. Blu struggled with his rolling emotions.

"I dunno, Candy," he said, breaking the silence. "I'm a little too seasoned for an Ole Lady. Just set in my ways."

Candy said nothing, then winked at him and headed for the front doors of the club. She was swinging her hips in an exaggerated sashay.

"No need to come in, *darlin'*," she emphasised. "I got this in spades." Blu leaned back against his bike and let the mid-afternoon sun warm him. He pulled a spliff from his cut pocket and lit it. "What a fucking handful," he whispered with a smile.

Blu took a deep drag on the joint and scanned the street again. A bike appeared right in front of him! He had been so focussed on Candy, he hadn't spotted the black Night Rod parked across the street. But he sure as hell noticed it now. They had parked the bike behind a white minivan in front of a newly opened head shop, the maroon emblem of the Fallen Angels visible on the battery cover. He flicked the roach into the gutter and pulled out his cell phone to speed dial Tic.

"Speak," Tic's ragged voice answered.

"It's me. There's a Fallen Angel in our backyard," Blu said.

"Son of a bitch! Where?"

"Out front of a head shop on St. Laurent, across from Cleopatra's," Blu replied.

"Dammit! That's *our* shop!" Tic said. "We were there this morning. Don't do shit, Blu. We are on our way." The line went dead.

Shotgun looked around the street. There was nowhere to hide his bike. Other than a mailbox, there was no cover for 20 metres in either direction. *How in God's name was I so careless? How could I not have seen a rival gang member's bike parked in plain sight? These are the fucking complications tits and ass deliver into your life. This is why I'm single.*

Just as he was considering going in after Candy, the front door of Cleopatra's opened and she stepped into the street, grinning like a well-fed Cheshire cat.

"Bartender!" she exclaimed, but the triumphant look on her face transformed to confusion, then concern, as Blu started waving for her to go back inside the strip joint. Candy took one step more, then stopped.

Blu studied the van. It hid the entrance to the head shop, but the faint tinkle of the doorbell caused him to spin around and crouch behind his bike. He waved again at Candy. Frozen solid and transfixed by the sudden change of his attitude, Candy stared blankly at him.

She doesn't know what to do. Candy looked across the street just as Griff stepped out from behind the van. Her face dropped and she sprinted towards Blu as he shouted, "Inside! Now!"

The call alerted Griff, and he looked at them. His gun was out in a flash and he discharged two rounds blindly as he ducked back behind the truck. The first round skipped off the pavement just in front of Blu's bike and ricocheted off to the left, while the second slammed into Cleopatra's facade. Candy squealed as she hit the sidewalk hard. Fragments of brick showered around her.

Blu pulled out his 9 mm and shifted his stance. He peeked out from the end of his bike. There was nothing! Blu waved again at Candy to take cover behind the bright red and white Canada Post box. She crawled on all fours until the tin container sheltered her and popped up to a squat. Blu patted the air, telling her to be still.

"*Bonjour*, cocksucker," he called. "What are you doing on our turf?" There was a moment of silence followed by a chuckle.

"Just picking up some rolling papers for your mama," came the reply.

"I tell you what, rat fuck. In less time than it will take you to start it, Horses will surround you and your bike." Another laugh echoed from behind the van.

"I highly doubt that," Griff shouted back. "Instead of me splattering you *and* your pretty girlfriend all over the sidewalk, how about I just ride on outta here?"

"Not gonna happen, *Amigo*," Blu growled and stood, firing three shots into the side of Griff's bike. The last shot sparked off the gas tank and a fireball erupted, knocking Blu to the ground. Candy screamed as the orange flames spewed upwards and a rolling wave of heat washed over them. Blu scrambled to his feet and took off at a sprint to the front side of the van, his gun thrust out like a talisman. He paused and crouched. After a moment, he rounded the van's bumper, finger tense on the trigger.

The display window of the head shop shattered and a round from Griff's gun battered into the passenger door of the truck with a tinny, hollow thud. A woman was screaming inside and a man was yelling at her to get on the floor.

Blu hit the ground, rolled off the curb, and squeezed himself under the van. It was a lousy angle, but he let two shots go into the front window. The glass shards that were still clinging to the frame fell and smashed on the sidewalk.

I hope to Christ this doesn't turn into a shootout. Blu could smell the greasy smoke from the burning Harley and realised he was hiding under a gas tank that was right next to the blaze. His position was dangerous. *What a lousy fucking day this is turning into*! With monumental effort, he slithered his massive bulk under the transmission casing and out the other side of the truck.

Candy was peering around the mailbox. He waved at her, and her head disappeared like a purple rabbit down a hole. From his crouched position, he again rounded the van. A peek through the destroyed display window showed no movement. Taking a deep breath, he duck-walked to the front door of the shop. Slowly reaching up to grasp the handle, he twisted it, flung the door wide, and rolled in with one fluid motion. Blu brought his pistol up and aimed at the forehead of Gabriel. He was white from fear.

"He has gone out the back!" Gabe sputtered.

Blu jumped up and charged into the back room. The fire exit door stood open. He crept through into the vacant lot at the rear of the store. Shotgun ran as quickly as his bulk allowed to the adjacent street. He scanned back and forth but saw no evidence of the fleeing goon. Blu returned to the shop and kicked the rear door so hard, the bottom hinge broke free, leaving it hanging odd angle.

"You know who I am?" he barked at Gabriel who was comforting his wife in the back room. Gabriel only nodded. "We'll be back to discuss this with you. You will tell the police nothing of us. *Nothing*! Am I fucking clear?" Again, Gabriel nodded.

"Say it, you fucking worm!" Blu shouted.

"Nothing. I will say nothing about you," Gabriel squeaked.

"Two men, one black, one white, they came out of the bar across the street, started fighting, and it spilled into here. One went out the back, the other chased him. They wore hoodies, no cuts, no tattoos, no colours of any kind. That is *all* you know. Clear?" he shouted, waving his pistol at them.

"Yes, yes. Clear. A fight," Gabe repeated.

"Good. I'll see you soon," Blu said and ran out of the shop. He pivoted his head as he crossed the street, then set a beeline to his bike.

"Come on, darlin'," he called out to Candy. The black smoke from the fire was still swirling as the thick stink of burning rubber filled the air. People had gathered. A sizable lunchtime crowd had spilled out of the club. Tradesmen, businessmen, and half-dressed strippers clamouring to see what was happening. Blu ignored the commotion, jumped on his bike, and started it. In a flash, Candy was behind him with her arms around his waist in a death grip. They roared away from the scene as quickly as the bike would carry them.

"Still interested in being an Ole Lady?" Blu screamed. Candy didn't answer and just tightened her hold on him.

◆

CHAPTER EIGHT

amdev heard the tandem of Royal Enfields coming up the narrow street in front of the clubhouse. He stood and trotted down to the courtyard to meet them. Hiran was swinging open the iron gate as they arrived, the worn hinges crying out in protest over the deep rumble of the bikes.

Shiv pulled in on Ramdev's Classic, followed by Ratt on Hiran's marsh grey Bullet. The earlier night, Hiran had rushed back into the club, grabbed Ipsita, and left through the service corridor after calling in their insurance. Their time was running short. The boys shut the motors off, dismounted, and drew them onto their mid stands as Hiran closed the gate and joined the two of them.

Ramdev crossed the courtyard. The late afternoon sun glinted off the gas tanks and for a moment, it reminded Ramdev why he became an Iron Horse. Freedom and brotherhood stirred in his soul. He looked at his three comrades, three loyal friends. They shared the same beliefs, the same values, and trusted one another beyond question. The bond between brothers of the open road is strong, not easily tarnished. Yet it was. His heart sank.

"All well?" Ramdev asked. Shiv nodded.

"No problems," Ratt confirmed.

"All right," Ramdev said, lighting a cigarette. "Get them loaded. We shoot for Udaipur at 4:30 am. Hiran, can I have a minute, please?"

Ratt and Shiv disappeared into the clubhouse as Hiran walked over to Ramdev. "You will ride out first by half an hour. Keep a keen eye, Hiran.

Look for any trouble. Call me if you see *anything* that looks out of place. Use the primary NH8 route. We will meet you at the Highway Express Dhaba outside Neemrana by 8:30."

"Sorted," Hiran said. "Are you all right, *bhai*? You seem unsettled." Ramdev took a long drag on his smoke and then flicked it over the fence.

"I'm okay. I just don't like this business with the Director. We are trusting this corrupt bastard far too much," he growled.

"Yes, at some point we will have to deal with him," Hiran agreed.

"And Alex," Ramdev continued. "I can't draw a read on him. I don't know what his thoughts are, to see this through and go home, or if he has other plans."

"Like Ipsita?" Hiran asked, raising his eyebrows.

"Fuck Ipsita!" Ramdev barked. "If she wants to lie with goats, so be it!" Hiran looked surprised. Ramdev knew they were close enough for Hiran to appreciate how he felt for Ippy. But he couldn't let that show. *It's more club bullshit, having to maintain the facade and be a powerful leader,* he thought and let his shoulders slump.

"*Bhai,*" Hiran said with a shrug. "It's just another delivery run. Like so many before. No stress, okay?" He clasped Ramdev's shoulder and squeezed it. Ramdev half smiled and nodded.

"Just be sharp on the road, my brother. Watchful and alert."

"Done," Hiran said and headed into the clubhouse.

"Where are your saddlebags, *bhaiya*?" Ratt called to Ramdev as he stepped back into the courtyard, two other olive coloured canvas bags over his shoulder. "They are not in your office."

"You're getting old, Ratt. Your eyes are failing," Ramdev laughed. "In the corner, beside... Never mind, I'll bring them," he said, still chuckling.

Ramdev went up the stairs but passed the floor with his office. Images of Ipsita had filled his head and were churning his innards with a jealous spoon. He continued to the top floor. With purpose, Ramdev strode along the hallway to the spare bedroom. He was going to knock when a wave of anger washed over him and replaced the jealousy. He twisted the knob and pushed. It was dead-bolted. He pounded on the door with his fist and shouted.

"Alex, open this goddamn door." There was a slight commotion from within, and after a moment, it opened. Ramdev stepped into the room with such authority, Alex stumbled backwards.

Clad only in his jeans and the bloodied dressing on his shoulder, Alex looked at Ramdev and reddened with guilt. Ipsita was standing in the corner near the window. She, also in her jeans, had draped her torn blouse over her shoulders. The swell of her breasts was visible as she clutched the front closed around them. The room stank of weed and oozed of sex.

"You've been busy, I see," Ramdev sneered. Alex said nothing, and Ippy kept her head hanging. "We shoot at 4:30. Be ready. Alex, you can carry her." He flicked a finger at Ipsita. "I have felt lately that she's too much fucking weight on my ass end. I'll take her *other* lover," he said. His wicked eyes flashed with delight as Alex snapped his head around to look at Ipsita. "Oh? You didn't know, Alex? Our little Ippy here plays for both teams." He looked at her with mock scorn. "Tsk, tsk, Ipsita, my dear. Are you keeping your deviant preferences from your new boyfriend?"

Ramdev took a step towards her, and then looked back to Alex. "Yes, I've seen it firsthand. Believe me, she fucks her with such enthusiasm, I've been wanting to take Daya for a solo ride myself. Feel free to eat my leftovers, Alex, I have no use for her anymore." Ramdev barked a bitter laugh and left.

✳ ✳ ✳

Agent Shashidhar laid across the front seat of her car as the two Enfields retrieved from Cyber Hub rolled past her. Her heart was racing. Dimpi had allowed the sting of her suspension to fuel her emotions and lead her to the gates of the Iron Horses clubhouse. Now that she had calmed, Dimpi had no choice but to admit to herself she had gone rogue.

"Shit," she whispered, as the rumble of the bikes faded, then stopped altogether. She snapped a glance over the dashboard and saw Hiran closing the enormous iron gate. Ducking back behind the dashboard, she grabbed the photocopied case file lying on the floor of her car.

Dimpi rummaged through the loose-leaf papers but could find no picture of him. Dimpi flipped on her back and pulled her cell from her pocket. She raised it over the dashboard to snap a picture and realised it was her personal phone. "Shit, shit, shit," Dimpi repeated, tossing it in the glove box and digging out the NCB issued cell from her jacket. She sat half upright again and stole a peek, but there was no sign of him. She sunk back into the seat.

"I'm just an ordinary citizen, observing suspected criminal activity. There's no law against that," she whispered.

In her heart, she knew that was a lie. *I'm not an ordinary citizen, I'm a suspended NCB agent, and this is not a suspected criminal activity. It's an ongoing case, one they tossed me off investigating.* There was no way in hell her actions here would wash with her superior officers.

Throughout her career, Dimpi had always been rash and impulsive. She never considered the consequences before acting. It was true she had relied on her uncle, the Director General, in past circumstances. He had smoothed over her more extravagant blunders. *But there's no coming back from this. This is reckless.* If the NCB discovered her activities, even her uncle would not be able to help. Any evidence she gathered here would be useless, inadmissible in court, and likely to get her outright dismissed from the agency. She screwed her eyes shut and groaned.

"Okay, think this through." Dimpi knew this was too big a case to let go. It could propel her career forward by leaps and bounds if she could close it, and her peers would grant her instant respect. A successful bust here could also erase the negative remarks regarding her performance issues from her record.

There was a very dull ache in her guts. Guilt! *I'm responsible for that woman's death last night. Any way you cut it, I caused that.* Dimpi reminded herself of something every law officer knows. Civilian deaths are a symptom of violent crime, not the cause. *I'm the shield, not the axe, and this shield wants those Iron Horse bastards to hang.*

All right, option one, she considered. *Collect as much evidence as possible, and when I'm reinstated, it will be ready to present. Or option two, collect as much evidence as possible and hand it over to Avinash.* Dimpi nodded approval to herself. She was certain Avi would get over his anger of disobedience if she handed him the Iron Horses on a platter.

Dimpi got out of the car. Feeling conspicuous in her smart blue business suit and blouse, she retrieved her gym bag from the trunk. With considerable effort, she changed into her workout clothes in the back seat. Simple black track pants and a dark green Nike t-shirt were the right attire for surveillance.

She slipped on her running shoes and curled her legs up under her. Dimpi made herself as comfortable as possible and watched the front gate of the clubhouse through the side window of the car.

She bolted up and took a moment to orient herself. Both her legs had fallen asleep and were alive with pins and needles as she swung into a sitting position. *I must have drifted off to sleep.*

"Dammit." Dimpi picked up her cell phone from where it had fallen on the floor and peered at the dim glow. *After eight!* The events and stress over the last few days had caught up with her. *I'm positive the rumble of the bikes would have woken me if the Horses left, but I'd best be sure.*

Dimpi popped the magazine from her gun and seeing it full, replaced the clip and flipped the safety. She slipped her cell under her t-shirt and into her bra beside her left breast. A concealment trick Dimpi had learnt in her teens to hide her phone from her father.

She got out of the car and crouched. The sun was fading from the sky, and it crisscrossed the narrow street with shadows. It was less than twenty-five metres from her car to the gate, but there was very little cover.

To the south end of the clubhouse compound was a private residence. There were no lights illuminating the windows of the dwelling, and after a few moments of study, she determined the house was still.

Dimpi sprinted across the street, maintaining her crouch, to the waist-high stone wall around the property and climbed over it. She tumbled into the flower bed in the front garden. A dog barked in the distance. She held her breath and listened for any other sound. Nothing.

Surrounded by the sweet smell of hibiscus, Dimpi crawled on her hands and knees to the north end. The moist soil was soaking her pants and squishing through her fingers. She reached the wall, lifted herself to a crouch, and looked over the top.

There were five bikes lined up side by side on their mid stands. Only the one closest to her, the Classic 500 was absent any saddlebags. They had loaded the others and were ready for departure. Dimpi placed her gun on the ground and reached under her t-shirt to free her phone.

Dimpi clicked half a dozen pictures, zooming in on each bike, and then the entire group. She tucked the phone back into its hiding place, picked up her gun, and tried to decide her next move. Footsteps echoed from the far side and Dimpi crouched as low as she could. There was a rattle of keys followed by the metallic tick of a lock. *They're leaving!* Dimpi peaked over the wall and spied an adolescent boy near the bikes. The lad looked more student than gangster.

He was standing beside the red bike. He had a five-litre petrol can in his left hand and was opening the gas cap with his right. As Dimpi watched, he unscrewed the jerry can lid and topped off the tank with fuel.

Dimpi grabbed her phone, and masked by the sound of the pouring fuel, she snapped more pictures. Another man entered the courtyard from the side stairwell of the clubhouse. The same one who had opened the front gates earlier. She ducked and listened.

"Ready?" Hiran asked.

"All set," Shiv answered.

"When you're finished, get a rag, soak it in petrol, and rub the bottom of the saddlebags with it, all right?" Hiran said.

"Okay, boss," Shiv replied. "To mask the brown sugar, right? But do you think we will come across any police dogs?"

"Shut the fuck up, prospect!" Hiran hissed at him. "Do as you're told." Dimpi heard his footsteps fade back into the stairwell.

"Do this, do that, shut the fuck up," Shiv mimicked as his footsteps also faded away.

The heroin is in the saddlebags! It's right there! she realised.

As many times before in her career, the adrenaline rush and enthusiasm overtook Agent Shashidhar's common sense, and without hesitation, she vaulted the wall.

She ran past the Continental and Classic and wedged herself in between them. As she slipped the gun into her waistband, Dimpi's shaking hands fumbled with the straps of the luggage. She freed the thick leather bindings and tugged at the interior zipper. The sound of its opening tore through the silence. She paused, ensuring that her presence was still undetected. There was no noise other than her ragged breathing and the thump of her heart. She dug into the bag.

Dimpi felt her way to the bottom, and her fingertips came to rest on the prize. A solid one kilogram brick of pure Afghan heroin. She pulled the contraband from its concealment as t-shirts and jeans spewed out onto the courtyard stones around her. Her firearm slipped from her waistband and clattered to the ground, freezing her motionless.

Slack-jawed, Dimpi stared at the heroin in disbelief. For the many times she had examined pictures of it and studied the narcotic, she had never seen such a sizable quantity up close.

She gathered up the clothes lying around her and stuffed them back inside the saddle, flipping the outside flap closed. Dimpi retrieved her gun and the heroin and then moved back towards the wall. The faint tap of footsteps from the stairs caused her to freeze and retreat. *Someone is coming.* In a panic, she looked for a place to hide, but the courtyard was barren. The sun had set, and it was dark, but the security floodlights were on and offered no shadows. Dimpi took a chance and darted across the length of bikes, away from the stairs, and squatted behind the last one.

With a look around the rear tire, she saw an older man with more bike luggage slung over his shoulder. He stopped at the first motorcycle in the row and flopped the saddles on the pillion seat. He stood panting. She remained crouched and watched as he busied himself fastening the saddle straps to the machine. Her heart was racing. *Surely, he will see me.*

Ratt placed his hands on his hips and arched his back. Dimpi held her breath, willing him to walk away. She clutched the brick of heroin to her chest. After a deep sigh, he did just that. He headed towards the clubhouse entrance.

She let herself relax. Her nerve endings were tingling. *Just a few more moments, a few more steps, and I'll make a break for the wall.* Then her phone rang.

* * *

While Dimpi had been siting in her car, Ramdev stood in the hallway outside Alex and Ipsita's room, listening to their muffled conversation through the door, and smirked. *It doesn't matter,* he thought. His messing with Alex's emotions was a knee-jerk reaction to Ipsita's final and obvious rejection. It brought him no real satisfaction, and the betrayal still burned. He went to his office.

The saddlebags were laying in plain sight, right where he said they would be. *Ratt is like a ten-year-old boy sometimes.* Ramdev picked them up and dropped them on the desk. He undid the leather straps on one side and flipped the satchel open. He fished his hand into the compact luggage, and past the t-shirts and jeans, he felt the smooth surface of the heroin brick.

Ramdev refastened the bag and repeated the procedure on the other one. This was at least the fifth time he had checked that the precious cargo was secure. Ramdev just couldn't shake the sense of impending doom for this delivery. Sheer dread, a spectre lingering on his shoulder, a wisp of black smoke swirling over his head.

Ipsita was never far from his thoughts. Ipsita and the hordes of malignant spirits she carried with her. They spent him, these demon sentiments of jealousy and deception.

Her purse was lying where he had dropped it after finding the NCB card. He still didn't believe she could double cross him. It was apparent he underestimated the potency of her desire to leave him. His head was spinning, bewildered by the unknown. *Did she sell them out? Did she make a deal, and when did this happen?* There was no way to know.

He had written off her recent skittish behaviour as a byproduct of Alex, whatever the hell *that* situation was between them. The anguish of her fucking him flooded his bowels. *But worse,* he thought. *On this run, we might ride into a setup.*

The more he pondered it, the more he believed a sell-out to be the truth. *It would explain the sudden defiance from her. She'd always been pig-headed, but never like this. Her confidence has strengthened somehow!* he thought. *A deal with the NCB would do that. No doubt they had given her assurances of protection. How else did they end up outside the Farzi Cafe last night? They were keeping watch, keeping tabs on her movements. She must feed them information. She's fucking turned, there's no other explanation.* The facts added up and equalled betrayal.

Ramdev dug his phone out of his pocket to call Montreal and relay his suspicions to Marceau, when there was a soft rap.

"Come!" he called with impatience. It was Ippy. She slid through the door, eyes downcast, and shoulders slumped. Her makeup was fresh and hair brushed, she had also discarded her torn blouse and was wearing a black Beatles t-shirt. *Alex's,* he thought. She had knotted it at her right hip, exposing her soft midriff. His heart skipped, and jealousy welled deep inside him. *She is so captivating.*

"Let It Be," Ramdev whispered.

"I don't understand," she said. "Let what be?"

"Your shirt, Ippy. The album cover. Let It Be." Ramdev tried to swallow the anger building within him. "So much you two have in common. What do you want?"

"My purse," she breathed. Ramdev snapped his fingers.

"Take it," he said and watched as she approached the desk. His heart ached. *I wonder if there's any possibility of mending the damage. Could I salvage any relationship with her*? As she reached for her handbag, he whispered her name and tried to take her hand.

"Ippy."

Ipsita snapped back as if a mad dog had lunged at her. In her haste, her fingers only hooked one of the bag handles. It gaped open between them, yawning like a cavern. She skipped backwards.

"Don't you fucking touch me!" she said, her voice tainted with disgust. Her reaction shocked Ramdev, but he recovered.

"Calm yourself," he said. Crushed, he realised it was over between them. Ipsita peered into her purse.

"What is it you're looking for?" he asked, bemused.

"No, no, I..." Ipsita stammered. "I wanted my cigarettes."

"Hum," Ramdev mused. "See you at 4:30," he said flatly, waving her out.

Ipsita rushed from the room, her usual seductive sway absent from her gait. Ramdev chuckled. He had saved the NCB number in his phone and left the card in her bag. *My tormenting Ipsita and Alex is one thing, but tipping my hand to them was another.*

He lit a smoke and leaned as far back in the chair as he could. *This is a royal mess.* Ramdev picked his cell up from the desk and twirled it between his fingers. He tried to ignore the nagging solution that was presenting itself but could not.

The fastest way out of this wreckage is to turn the tables. Pull the rug from under Ippy and protect myself. Ramdev's brewing unrest and discontentment with his life, his woman, *and* his club, suggested that.

Deep in conflict, he weighed the pros and cons of becoming the most despised creature in biker culture. A rat! The long diminished loyalty he once felt for his MC reared its ugly head. It gnawed at him, asking him the tough questions. *Can I betray my family?*

It was useless to ponder. There was no fight left in the top dog. The love for his club and brothers was dead. It's not that he didn't share the same values he once did, but it was the MC who had betrayed him! They had lied! The Club was not what they said they were. The very thing he thought represented freedom had cheated him of a promised life of brotherhood and loyalty and replaced it with greed and violence.

In part, it had also been ground out under Ipsita's black stiletto heel. She had been a cobra in this pit of snakes, injecting him with her poison. *I want out. Away from the Horses, away from Ipsita, and away from the NCB threat. I know what I must do.*

"Enough!" he barked to himself. Ramdev stood and walked over to the couch against the far wall. He glanced at the clock. He needed rest. The vinyl cushions squeaked as Ramdev laid on it. He had to empty his head before they left.

He drifted into a troubled sleep. His distress caused thoughts of betrayal to flood his dreams. Ipsita holding Alex, kissing Alex, lying with him! Then he tumbled into a darker nightmare. Someone caged him on a ship, deep below decks. The ship careened, spilling him from his bunk. Caught in a savage storm of despair, he was bone cold and alone, shivering. Ramdev tossed and groaned on the small sofa.

He woke from his torment hours later knowing an unmistakable truth. Ramdev was clear-headed and of a single mind. He was certain now that he had to get out. It was a simple matter of self-preservation. His lifestyle brought him no joy, and if an NCB bust was imminent, he needed to scoot out from under it. Like a cockroach from under a shoe. There was a knock.

"Come," he said. Ratt entered and took the bags from the desk.

"I swear I didn't see them..." he mumbled, eyes downcast.

"I'm surprised you can ride at all." Ramdev smiled at him. "Go on now, saddle up, and get some sleep." Ratt left and Ramdev flopped into his chair.

Ramdev retrieved his phone from his pocket and thumbed through the contacts until he found Agent Shashidhar's number. Even as he was scrolling, indecision crept into his mind, raising the acidic bile of treason in his throat. After a moment's hesitation, he stabbed the call button.

He swallowed hard and closed his eyes. There was only silence, and then he heard the first ring. Ramdev's eyes snapped open and his sour guts flooded with guilt. In a panicked act of long-gone loyalty and brotherhood, he ended the call.

✱ ✱ ✱

Dimpi cursed. She felt the vibration a fraction of a second before the ring was audible. She dropped the heroin brick and grabbed her breast, but was too slow to stop the muffled chime. It shattered the silence and Ratt turned towards her. The ring was cut short. The caller must have cancelled it, but the damage was done.

Ratt drew his pistol and crept along the queue of motorcycles, staying parallel, crossing his feet, and passing in and out of the shadows. He paused between each set of bikes and thrust his firearm into the darkness.

"Shiv?" he whispered. Dimpi drew a deep breath and her knuckle whitened on the trigger. Trapped in this predicament, Dimpi realised it could be the end of her career, but more likely, her life. Her finger released the tension on the cool metal trigger. *Unless I get away*, she reasoned.

Her NCB training took over her actions. She crouched on all fours, weight on the balls of her feet, fingertips placed on the ground in front of her, and holding her pistol in her right hand. Her head rolled back, looking up and compacting her neck. Dimpi's legs tensed, her muscles coiled and taut. She was a tigress ready to pounce on unsuspecting prey as blood pounded in her ears and the itch of anticipation tickled her mouth. As a thin layer of cold sweat coated Dimpi's forehead, she drew a deep, but silent breath.

Ratt reached the end of the row. His pistol came into view around the rear of the bike she was using as cover. The gun first, his hand, and then his forearm. Her target revealed itself. He was close enough now that she could smell his Fogg deodorant. Dimpi's calves twitched, urging her on, but she commanded herself to wait for another heartbeat.

She sprung with all the power her legs could produce. Like a missile, she shot up and forward, hitting Ratt in the stomach with her shoulder. Ratt expelled a mass of oxygen and grunted like a bear. Dimpi's momentum slid her body up his, forcing both his arms upward. Ratt's gun discharged once into the air, shattering a window behind them. The recoil and Ratt's unbalanced position caused him to drop it. As the Glock clattered to the ground, it fired again.

The bullet burned its way through Dimpi's Adidas trainers and shattered her left pinkie toe. She strangled the scream in her throat and continued her assault. The top of her head contacted his jaw and Ratt's mouth snapped shut, chipping a tooth, and muffling a painful yelp. Dimpi drove her right knee into his crotch. She felt the soft orbs compress and the two of them hit the ground hard. Ratt howled in agony as fire exploded in his testicles and his skull smacked the concrete. It was Dimpi's hope to stun him enough to separate herself and sprint over the wall. She hadn't.

Ratt wrapped his mammoth appendages around her and squeezed. He was crushing her in a python hold, forcing the breath from her. Dimpi felt as if her ribs were about to break as he pinned her arms to her sides. She struggled to free them as the last of the air left her lungs and her vision blurred. She was blacking out. The excruciating pain in her left foot was keeping her conscious.

"You fucking cunt!" Ratt bellowed. "Ramdev!"

His call for help fuelled Dimpi's attempts to wrestle herself from the vice-like grip of his arms. She had held on to her weapon. She twisted her right wrist as far as possible and squeezed the trigger. The muffled shot rang out as the round tore through Ratt and shattered his left hip.

He released her, screeching in agony, his howl echoing off the neighbouring buildings. Dimpi drove the gun into his ribs and fired again. His body lurched under her. Ratt's screech turned into a horrifying gurgle and he went limp. With no time to think, Dimpi rolled off him and sprang up in one swift motion.

The pain in her foot caused her to stumble, but she gathered herself and broke for freedom like an Olympic sprinter. Each footfall was pure agony. Yet within three strides, she was at full tilt, her eyes fixed on the half wall bobbing up and down in front of her. Dimpi's mind was travelling at the speed of light. *I'll vault the wall. If the shots have alerted the neighbours, I can take refuge in their home. If not, I'll continue to the car.*

Her training was working in her subconscious as she changed her direction every few steps, darting left, and juking right. She would make it. *Almost there, girl,* she thought.

Shiv emerged from the shadow of the stairwell and she caught the flick of a red blur in her left eye. The petrol can met her full in the face, breaking her nose and smashing out her front teeth. Her entire head exploded with pain. Dimpi's upper body stopped dead with the impact as her legs flung out in front of her. The back of her skull hit the ground with a dull *thwack*, causing her already blurry vision to dim.

Through the blood in her eyes, she saw the young lad standing over her, jerry can still in hand. Her panicked mind registered the look on his face. Pure shock and utter dismay! His expression changed to horror as she willed herself to raise the pistol to his chest. She had time to wonder if he was only acting out of instinct, or if this budding outlaw was also a killer.

Dimpi was losing consciousness. Through the haze, she could see her arm, her hand... She was gripping her gun. There was no muzzle flash. *Why was there no muzzle flash?* The boy seemed to be descending towards her, coming closer... closer. *Did I fire? Is he dead?* Her body riddled with agony and then consumed by absolute fear as she realised he was dropping to his knees. Dimpi felt one of them crush her breast. She was vaguely aware of the cell phone pressing into her ribs. A millisecond later, she felt the other knee contacting her throat.

Her mind registered the sound of a dry tree branch snapping in monsoon wind. Then Dimpi Shashidhar's world faded to black.

✳ ✳ ✳

Alex was sitting on the edge of the small cot in the guest room on the top floor of the clubhouse. Even at this time of night, it was hot. The air was thick and uncomfortable, and he could taste its sulphuric tang on his tongue.

Ratt had just collected the saddlebags Ramdev had given them to store what little clothes they needed for the trip. Ipsita stood with her back to him, sorting through her purse. *Something is distracting her. Ever since she came back from Ramdev's office, she's been unsettled, as if she wants to tell me something,* he thought. Yet when he pressed her on it, she had just smiled and said she was fine.

They had made love again upon her return. Slowly this time, kissing and caressing each other, staring into each other's eyes as they climaxed. Entangled, they had both fallen into a deep sleep on the modest bed until Ratt's knock on the door a few minutes ago.

"Babe?" Alex said. Ipsita turned and gave him a warm, but bemused smile.

"Babe?" she asked. Alex laughed.

"I dunno what lovers call each other in India," he stammered. Her grin widened as she moved towards him.

"Lovers, are we?" she teased.

"Aren't we?"

"Hmmm, try *Priya*," she chuckled, brushing his sandy locks from his eyes. With a kiss, she pushed him back on the cot and straddled him. Her smile warmed his entire body. "Or *Mere Dil Ka Pyaar*," she said, leaning forward while pinning his arms above his head and kissing him again.

"Mia dill car pyre," Alex mumbled around the kiss. Ippy laughed. It filled him with love for her.

"We'll work on it, darling," she said, crinkling her nose.

A shot rang out, shattering the moment and the small window in their room. It disintegrated into a thousand shards of glass that cascaded to the floor. Ippy squealed as Alex pulled her down and rolled on top of her. The commotion downstairs spilled through the smashed pane in a concert of noise and activity. There was another shot.

"Ramdev!"

Alex slid off the bed, pulling Ippy with him. The two of them crawled across the floor, the glass shards from the window puncturing their palms. As they reached the door, the panic outside increased. They spilled out into the hallway and Alex slammed it shut behind them. The couple huddled and listened as there were more shots, more shouting, and then silence. They could hear Ramdev's footsteps pounding down the stairwell as they slid along the corridor.

"*Behenchod*!" Ramdev's thundered up the stairwell. "Hiran! Get down here! Alex!" Alex and Ippy exchanged tentative glances.

"Wait here," he cautioned and started down the stairs.

"Let me go to Daya," Ippy said and disappeared down the hallway, her bare feet padding on the marble tile.

Alex continued his descent and heard Hiran's voice mixed with Ramdev's. As he came to the bottom of the last flight of steps, he stopped. Alex stared out into the courtyard in amazement. It took a moment for his brain to process the information his eyes were sending it. He crept forward, still unsure what he was seeing.

A woman was lying on the ground and Shiv was kneeling on her with a gas can in his hand. She wasn't moving, and a pool of blood was slowly expanding around her head. Shiv was weeping to the heavens. His soft sobs mingled with a chorus of dogs barking in the distance. Ramdev moved to Shiv and placed his hands on his shoulders.

"Come on, *bhai*. Come on now," he whispered.

"I guess you're all in now. Aren't you, prospect?" Hiran said. Ramdev shot him a nasty glance. It was at that moment, Alex spotted Ratt laying at the end of the bikes.

"Look!" he called, pointing.

"Ratt!" Hiran shouted and sprinted towards the body. Ramdev turned and saw him too.

"Fuck!" He ran to his fallen comrade's side. Alex walked to Shiv and helped him to his feet. The lad was shaking.

"What the hell happened?" Alex asked. "Who is she?"

"I don't know," Shiv stammered. "She shh... shot, shot Ratt... I hit her," he said, looking at his hand. As if becoming aware he was still holding the makeshift weapon, he dropped the jerry can in disgust. It bounced off the ground with a metallic ring and settled beside Dimpi's body.

Okhla is an industrial area with not too many permanent residents. There were a few, but not a high concentration. The gunshots may or may not have been reported. The prevailing mentality of an average Delhite was to mind their own business and not cause trouble. A call to the police for *any reason* was never palatable.

Had it been Diwali, the likelihood of anyone taking notice of gunfire would have been zero. Far too many crackers and fireworks. But it wasn't. They had no idea if someone called in the disturbance or not, or how much time they had to work with before the police arrived.

"Here! All of you," Ramdev commanded. He took two steps away from Ratt's corpse as they gathered around him. "This is a terrible situation and we need to rectify it. You..." he said, pointing at a zombie-like Shiv. "You just killed an NCB agent, the one leading the charge at Cyber Hub last night. We have very little time. I doubt she arrived here by metro. Get out on the street and find her car." Shiv seemed to wake up and sprinted towards the gate.

"Hiran, get the sugar from Ratt's bike and double it up in the other luggage, then call that prospect in Dwarka and tell him to be here in thirty minutes. Alex, upstairs. Organise the girls and get back down here, *fast*." Ramdev clapped his hands together.

"Go, go!" he urged, and the group set about their tasks.

Alex sprinted up the stairs and down the hall of the top floor. His mind was spinning. He had witnessed more gunplay and death in the last twenty-four hours than he had seen his entire life. Alex had never even *seen* a gun until all this had started. He came to the end of the corridor. Daya's door was open, and she was sitting on a faded yellow love seat in her bra and jeans. Crouched in front of her, Ipsita was shaking her shoulders.

"Daya, do you understand me!?" she was screaming. Ippy looked up at Alex as he entered, panting. "Fucking stoned!" she said. Her voice was cracking with despair.

Alex's heart twinged at the sight of Ipsita's distress. He had no way to foresee it would double once Ippy realise that the death of an NCB agent had crumbled her plans of escape in Udaipur to dust.

Ippy turned back to Daya. "Where did you get it? Where??" She continued shaking her, then slapped her hard across the cheek. Daya yelped and seemed to focus.

"Get her dressed. Get her coherent," Alex said. Ipsita was not listening. All her attention was on Daya.

"Ippy!" he snapped. Ipsita spun her head around and looked at him. "Get her sorted. There is a problem, and we need to get out of here fast." Ipsita nodded. He walked to her and crouching, took her face in his hands.

"Five minutes, okay?" Alex asked.

"Okay," Ippy answered. Alex stood, hurried out, and back down to the courtyard.

Hiran was opening the gate and Shiv was driving Dimpi's car into the compound. He came to a halt just in front of the bikes. After he killed the motor, Ramdev looked at Alex and knocked on the hood.

"Search the car, search her, then get her in the trunk." He turned and started walking towards Ratt's body. "And put on some fucking gloves! Hiran, with me," he shouted over his shoulder.

Alex stood in confusion. Shiv got out of the car and handed him a pair of surgical gloves from his pocket.

"You, her. Me, the car," he breathed.

"You okay?" Alex asked him. Shiv shrugged and got to work.

Alex went to Dimpi and squatted down over her. His stomach rolled as the sticky sweet stench of death filled his nostrils. Alex held his breath, fighting down the bile rising in his throat.

He opened his eyes and looked down at the body. She had been beautiful. But now the blood and sweat glued Dimpi's long silky hair to her forehead, her gaping mouth frozen and twisted into a silent scream, exposing the shattered enamel stumps of her teeth. Shiv had snapped her nose at an odd angle across her face and her blank eyes were milky and staring up at him. Alex turned away as he dry heaved and again fought to keep the contents of his belly from spewing out over the cobblestones.

He took the gun from her hand and laid it aside. Blood had splattered Dimpi's exposed midriff, so Alex tugged at her t-shirt and tried to cover her stomach. He patted her hips, then down either side of her legs. He had no idea what he was doing. Alex mimicked what he had seen bodyguards do in movies.

He shifted his weight, turned towards her head, and beginning at the waist, patted upwards. She was soft. He half expected her to jump or giggle as he felt up under her arms. His thumb brushed over her breast, supple and warm. He snapped his hand back in revulsion.

"Anything?" Ramdev asked. Alex had not noticed he was standing over him.

"Just the gun," he answered. Alex stood and handed it to him. Ramdev tucked it in the waistband of his jeans.

"Okay, let's get her in the boot," he said. Ramdev grabbed both her arms at the elbow as Alex moved to her feet. They lifted her and the body came off the ground with a disgusting squelch. The duo shuffle stepped around the rear of the car and hoisted what was left of Dimpi Shashidhar into the trunk. She hit the floor of it with a hollow thump.

Alex looked down on her, a lifeless body lying on its side with arms splayed out and legs tangled. The stench of blood and evacuated bowels floated up and assaulted them. They had tossed her without ceremony into the back of a car like a sack of potatoes. He felt desperate, lost. Ramdev slammed the trunk shut, removing the scene from view. But that image would burn into his mind's eye forever.

"It's not right or wrong, it's just what had to be done," he whispered.

"Here, boss," Shiv said, joining them. In his hands, he had a cell phone and a file folder. "This was it. Some clothes and a gym bag in the back. That's all."

Ramdev snatched the cell phone and smashed it on the ground with an urgency that shocked Alex. Both he and Shiv jumped. Ramdev looked back and forth between the two of them. *What is that on his face?* Alex thought. *Shame? Guilt?*

"It's traceable," Ramdev stammered. They nodded and Alex glanced at Shiv. It was clear he had seen Ramdev's expression. The boy looked puzzled. Hiran walked up to them.

"Prospect en route," he said.

"Okay, brothers, this is the situation she has given us," Ramdev began. "We need to sort it and get on the road ASAP." Hiran had Ratt's cut in his hand. He passed it to Ramdev as he spoke. Ramdev looked down at it and paused. He took a deep breath and glanced at his watch. "I will take care of Ratt's body at a landfill site," he said.

"Shiv, move Hiran's and your bike to the back of the welder's place at the end of the street. Get Daya down there too. Then come back up here and wash the courtyard. Use bleach, clean it well, but don't take too much time. Stay watchful and be listening. Hiran, take Ratt's bike to our friendly mechanic in Karol Bagh. Tell him to hide it deep. Do it quickly and come back to the welding shop, pick up Daya and Shiv, and head out to Highway Express Dhaba." Ramdev lit a cigarette, then continued.

"The prospect will be here soon. Alex, take Ipsita and help him dispose of the car. The two of you follow him on your bike, not too close, ya? After you dump it, he will guide you to NH8. Then I will have him come here. If it's still clear, he can clean out anything nasty we have left behind. You head west to Neemrana, wait at the same *dhaba* there. Ipsita knows it." He looked at his watch again.

He is trusting me with this? Why in God's name would he leave this to me? Was it what he said earlier? Does he see me as one of their own? Alex thought.

"It's been fifteen minutes since the shots. If the police were coming, they would have been here by now. So far, luck is on our side but still, hurry. Be ready to run at the first sign of trouble."

They stared at each other in dazed silence, processing their orders. Hiran broke the circle first, followed by Shiv. Alex spun to leave when Ramdev grabbed his arm.

"Wait," he said and drew his eight inch long hunting knife from the sheath on his hip. He cut Ratt's nametag from the leathers. He looked down in silence at the patch for a moment, twisting it between his fingers. "Look around you, Alex," he whispered. "You are neck-deep in this. Murdered agents, dead club members, illegal narcotics. All of it. It would be very hard to explain your innocence now, hmm? Even *if* anyone would believe you, Indian police are reluctant to hear pleas of denial when dealing with their fallen officers. I'll be damned if I allow a brother's life to end like this, while you walk around above it all. Guilty of nothing." He handed Ratt's cut to him. "Put it on."

Alex stepped back from the garment even though somewhere deep down inside, there was a dull ache to put it on, to gain the respect from Ramdev, and others, that came with wearing it.

"Tsk, tsk, Alex. Don't forget our arrangement. I'll call Montreal now. What do I tell them? You're behaving? Or does your *other* girlfriend need to pay for your attitude?"

Alex took the cut and slipped it over his shoulders.

"For now, I need to bind you to us. You'll look *and* play the part. An outlaw, understand? In time, perhaps you will earn the honour of wearing that cut with pride, not just posing in it as a disguise."

✳ ✳ ✳

The next morning, just as the Horses were shaking off the night's chill and arriving in Udaipur, Avinash Kumar was poring through Dimpi's case file. Sandy came in carrying a cup of *chai* and stopped dead in his tracks.

"Wow, why so early, boss?" he asked, putting his tea down and hanging up his jacket. Avinash looked at the junior agent over his bifocals.

"You were in the same room as I was yesterday, no?" he said, sitting back in his chair and studying a sheet of paper from the file. "The Deputy Director's position was clear. We need to make some advances in this case. I'm hoping Ms Shashidhar has uncovered some valuable information here. Perhaps to get us moving, perhaps to help with her reinstatement."

"Anything?" Sandy asked, sitting on the couch.

"She is bloody thorough, I'll give her that. The Iron Horses first showed on our radar in 2015. They swallowed up an existing MC in Delhi. The..." Avinash scanned the paper.

"The Bull Riders. They had chapters in eight other cities and they labelled themselves a Motorcycle Club. As far as I can see, there doesn't appear to be any criminal activity. A few drunken brawls, some arrests for low level possession, hashish, and marijuana. I guess enough to put them in the cross-hairs of the Chevaux de Fer, a true one percent club in Montreal, Canada."

"Chevaux de Fer?" Sandy asked.

"Iron Horses."

"Oh, shit... and *Canada*?" Sandy mused. "The final destination for the heroin?"

"It would make sense. From what Dimpi has found, the Chevaux de Fer are large enough to dabble in the narcotics trade. Nine chapters in India, four in Canada. That's a well-funded organisation. It wouldn't come cheap, Sandy. That takes North American cash, drug money."

"A stack," Sandy agreed.

"Make an official request to the RCMP for information. See what they have on these guys. Be vague, Sandy. We have no solid connection yet. There is no reason to involve the Canadians too deep at this point. We don't want to look like we are chasing ghosts." Sandy nodded and stood just as the phone on Avinash's desk rang.

"Yes?" Avinash answered. There was a flurry of communication on the other end of the line. Sandy stopped and watched as Avi's face turned pale. "I understand. Sector 13 Dwarka. Yes, yes. Okay, we are on our way." He placed the phone down in its cradle and looked at Sandy, his eyes wide and disbelieving.

"What, boss?" Sandy whispered.

"Agent Shashidhar... Dimpi... she's dead."

✳ ✳ ✳

They had remained in silence for most of the last sixty minutes, navigating through the rush hour traffic from downtown Delhi to the south-west suburb of Dwarka. Avinash was driving, and Sandy sat with his head down, hands in his lap. There wasn't much to say between them. As they came off the Dwarka flyover, Sandy pounded the dashboard with both fists.

"If those fuckers are responsible, Avi, I will gut every one of them! I swear it!" he shouted.

"I know, son. I know," was all Avinash could say. As they approached the roundabout on route 201 beside the Radisson Blu, Sandy again looked up and out the window.

"Third exit," he mumbled. It was rhetorical information as they were heading for Sector 13's metro station, and the elevated tracks cut the roundabout in half. Avi said nothing as he piloted the car to the gravel parking lot, seven hundred metres farther up the road.

It was almost empty, but in the corner farthest from the entrance, a sizable crowd had gathered. Avi pulled up and honked the horn, and the mob split as he forced the nose of the Honda forward. The local police had taped off an area fifty square metres around a single vehicle at the back of the lot. Dimpi's car.

"Shit," Avi whispered. He and Sandy exchanged glances as they got out. The entire area was a din of chatter and cell phones, people snapping pictures and making videos. A Times Now news van had parked off to one side of the caution tape. A cameraman rushed the two of them, pushing onlookers out of the way. He had a young female reporter in tow. She shoved a microphone in Avinash's face as soon as she reached them.

"Sir, why did the NCB come here? Who is the victim? Is this a murder investigation?" She fired the questions at him. To keep his restraint, Avi took a deep breath before replying.

"Perhaps if you allow me to do my job, we can discover some answers to these queries," he barked. The young woman pressed in on him, disregarding his obvious agitation.

"Is this a drug related incident, sir? Is that why the Narcotics Control Bureau is here? Who is in the car, sir?" she persisted. Sandy pushed her away with his forearm.

"Back off!" he shouted. The two of them ducked under the caution tape while flashing their badges at the many attending officers trying to keep the crowd at bay.

The area was alive with activity. Both doors and the trunk of the car were open and there was a forensic team buzzing around it like honeybees, one sitting in the driver seat, one at each door, and three hovering over the trunk. They were taking photos of the car and dusting it for prints. At least a dozen officers were milling around the scene.

A single traffic cop and two plain-clothes detectives stood removed from the hub of the action. Avinash strode towards them with purpose. They were speaking to a security guard from the metro station. He flashed his badge.

"Avinash Kumar, NCB. What do we have here, gentlemen?" he asked in a sombre, yet official tone.

"Good morning, sir," the older of the two detectives answered. "This guard spotted the car, sir. It has been here since some time last night." Avinash looked at the guard, an old man, upset and shaken.

"Noticed it how? Did you see who left it?"

"No, sir," he answered, his voice timid and unsure. "I just heard the dogs, sir." Avinash glanced at Sandy who mirrored his puzzled expression.

"Dogs?"

"Yes, sir. There are many strays around here. There was a group of them, five, maybe six, all barking and scratching this car," he said, pointing to Dimpi's vehicle. "So, I came to chase them away. It was the odour, sir. I thought I should call..."

"A uniformed officer responded," the detective resumed for the security guard. "It was his initiative to open the trunk, sir. He discovered the corpse."

"What is the status so far, Detective?" Sandy asked.

"We have searched the car. We found nothing but the victim's personal items. Now, Forensics is doing their thing. We haven't touched the body. As soon as we discovered her NCB ID in a gym bag, we put the call into your office."

"Okay, let him go," Avi said, nodding at the security guard. He looked relieved at the order and scurried away.

"We will pick it up from here. Give me your card. I'll contact you later today for anything else you have." The two detectives exchanged a glance that said they were not happy being dismissed from the investigation. The senior one passed his business card to him. Avinash and Sandy turned and walked towards Dimpi's car.

"Avi," Sandy began, but Avinash just held up his hand and walked to the back end of the vehicle. He paused at the forensics kit lying beside the rear tire.

Crouching, he took a pair of surgical gloves out of the case and studied them for a moment. He handed them to Sandy and got a pair for himself. The latex cracked as he snapped it tight over his fingers.

The forensics team had moved back and began speaking in hushed tones at the sight of the two approaching NCB officers. Avi stood and rounded the rear of the car and peered into the trunk.

"God above," he whispered. Sandy put his hand on Avi's shoulder, but he pulled away. "The poor girl." Avi tried to brush Dimpi's hair from her face, but it had matted there with clotted gore. He felt the anger welling up inside his guts like a volcano. "I'm sorry, Dimpi," he choked.

He probed around her body, lifting her legs, and then moving her head. As he lifted Dimpi's arm, he noticed the bulge under her blood-soaked t-shirt. Avi peeled up the shirt gingerly and exposed Dimpi's cell phone concealed within her bra. He snapped his fingers at Sandy, who retrieved a plastic bag from the forensics kit. He dropped it in and handed the bag to the closest officer.

"Do what you do and do it fucking well," Avi barked at him. "I want results on my desk today!"

＊＊＊

Back at the office, the two of them spent the rest of the morning fielding phone calls and having discussions with the Zonal Director Yadav and Deputy Director Pandey. Both had turned the heat up on them. The press was all over the murder, having a field day by linking it to the gunplay at Cyber Hub. There was no end to the speculation and theories.

To make matters far worse, they had leaked who the victim was, thus casting a bright light on the Narcotics Control Bureau. This didn't play well with the Director General, as it was his niece's name that was being sensationalised all over the news. He had issued a critical statement to the press, assuring them the culprits would be found. That had been followed up with a searing phone call to Pandey *and* Yadav. Results were no longer expected, but demanded. If they were not produced, Avi feared serious repercussions.

He studied the photos on his desk. The ones taken on Dimpi's phone at the Horses' Okhla clubhouse. The light and angle were poor, and even with the largest enhancement, the licence plates on the bikes were unreadable. It didn't matter. He knew who owned them. Sandy burst into his office with a sheet of paper in his hand.

"Call logs, boss," he said.

They had run traces on all the recent incoming and outgoing numbers on her phone. "Standard stuff, a call to you, three to our records department and one to the Ministry of Road Transport & Highways. Nothing strange, except the last entry." Avinash looked up from the photos. "A call from a Pakistani sim card, sir. It was a missed call, only two seconds. I have reached out to my contacts in the Drug Regulatory Authority of Pakistan, but that will take some time. DRAP doesn't see us as a priority."

"It won't matter," Avi said, shaking his head. "It will come back empty, a false name."

"I thought as much," Sandy agreed. "Think it was that Ipsita woman?"

"We can only hope," Avinash said, holding out his hand for the sheet. Sandy passed it to him.

"I highlighted the last number in yellow."

Avi stood, digging his cell from his pocket, and headed for the door. "Let's try our luck."

A brief time later, the two of them were standing on the top floor of the NCB, the Communications department. Avi had his cell phone in his hand and was fidgeting with it. Sandy was leaning against a bench littered with call tracking and recording equipment.

Avinash looked at the technician sitting behind the counter. The tech nodded. He glanced to Sandy who shrugged at him, answering the unasked question.

Avi took his reading spectacles from the top pocket of his shirt, put them on, and studied the highlighted number on the log sheet. With a sigh, he dialled it. The phone rang a half dozen times. Avi's heart sank. He knew it was a long shot to begin with, too much to hope. Then someone answered. They didn't speak. They just picked up the call and said nothing.

"Hello?" Avinash said. Sandy stood and came to him, leaning his head close to the phone. There was silence, but there *was* someone. *Possibly the last person to contact Dimpi.* Avi rolled the dice.

"This is Avinash Kumar, Senior Agent, Narcotics Control Bureau. Who is this?" he said.

"I know who you are," the voice on the other end of the line said.

"You called Agent Shashidhar just before her death. Do you have any information regarding that?" Avinash prompted. The silence was deafening. After what seemed a lifetime, the voice replied.

"I had no part in that. It was an accident."

"Someone smashed her face in with a blunt object and crushed her windpipe. It doesn't seem accidental," Avi said. His anger was building. He willed himself to stay calm. The communications tech rolled his fingers at him in a gesture to keep the call active. "Can you explain that?"

"No." The reply was quick and pointed. "I didn't want that."

"Neither did Agent Shashidhar," Avi said with a wry sneer.

"Look, I didn't want, I don't want this. Any of it."

"Fair enough," Avinash soothed. "So, let's meet. Tell me about it and let me help you sort this mess out. I'm sure we can—"

"No!" the man interrupted. "I can't talk, not now. I need to think. Maybe I will call you back... if... when I can talk." The line went dead.

"Shit!" Avinash screamed. He looked at the technician who gave him a half nod.

"Udaipur," he whispered.

◆

CHAPTER NINE

"Okay. Ratt? Anyone else? All right. How long until you and the product reach Mumbai? Goa? Yes, yes... Call me when you arrive there then." Marceau put his phone on the boardroom table in the chapel. After a deep breath, he looked around, making eye contact with each of his inner circle.

"There are serious complications," he muttered. A collective moan followed. "A gun battle at the Horses clubhouse in Delhi last night."

"Another one?!" John burst out in surprise.

"Yes," Marceau continued. "We lost a brother. Ratt. You remember, he came two years ago to help us with that hit on the 13 Machine courier in Laval?" The group mumbled assent. "But this is bad, gentlemen. A prospect killed an NCB agent in the scuffle."

"Oh, fuck," Blu said. "This is *not* good."

"The shipment?" John asked.

"En route," Marceau continued. "The Delhi chapter cleaned up the scene and are on the road. But the NCB is now aware of the Club's involvement and will have sunk its teeth into them. They are behind schedule and with this recent development, will head straight to Goa. Ramdev believes they can still make the ship. It's tight but doable. As far as shaking loose from this investigation, I don't share in his optimism."

"What's the play, what do we do, Tic?" Alain asked, lighting a cigarette.

"We may lose Delhi for a while, as they must go underground. Udaipur and Jaipur chapters are too inexperienced to deal with co-ordinating these shipments and the Mumbai chapter is too far from our source to make it possible. We are facing some trouble." Marceau rubbed his temples.

"We can't afford that," Tracy said, tapping a pencil on the table.

"I know, Tracy. I know. The actual problem is, we don't know what information the NCB has collected. Have they been watching us for a while? Or were they just fishing and got lucky?"

"We have to assume the worst, Tic," John said. "They show up out of the blue at that nightclub and the next day a shootout at the clubhouse? It looks like they are operating on credible intelligence."

"Yes," Marceau agreed. "But is the situation salvageable? To date, we've not had any tangles in Delhi, not a single one. Why are we on the NCB's radar?" He shook his head. "A dead agent. They won't let that go. The NCB may have been observing the Horses at the nightclub. Ramdev can be a hothead, so it must have gone sour. Gunplay in public would definitely prompt them to dig up information on the clubhouse location. They investigate there and again it goes wrong. As bad as this is, they may not know what we are doing or about the sugar."

"We need eyes on it, captain," Tracy said. "We need to assess this for ourselves."

"Yes, we do. Volunteers?" Marceau asked.

"Me. I'm on it, Tic," Clipper said. They met his suggestion with a chorus of denial.

"Recover first, my friend," Marceau pointed out the obvious. "You can barely walk, much less, ride."

"Look," Clipper began. "It's my fault. If I hadn't fucked up with this Alex kid, maybe none of this would have happened. Let me go, skipper. Allow me to make it right."

"Me," John spoke. "I'll fly into Delhi and assess the situation there, then down to Mumbai. I'll meet up with the shipment as they pass through on their way to the Pune stop."

Clipper slammed his hand on the table and objected further. But Marceau wouldn't hear of it.

"*Bon.* And Johnny, you will do whatever is necessary to keep us clear of the NCB. Repair any damage that they have done, ya? We will cut our losses with the clubhouse. Investigate the situation when you get there, find out what the problems are, and fucking fix them. Locate a street rat to take the fall for the murder. That is an option. Ramdev just packed up and ran. I have little confidence in how well he has *cleaned this up.*"

John nodded as Marceau continued, "Ramdev reports our boy, Alex, has come into the fold. It seems our new friend has embraced his task. You need to determine the truth of that. Alex is expendable and may prove to be a convenient scapegoat if required. I fear there is much work to set right this listing ship. If there is a change in management needed in Delhi, and I believe that is the case, facilitate that."

"With prejudice?" John asked.

"No, no. No need to dispatch of Ramdev. We don't kill our own, John, not without reason," Marceau said with a humourless smile. "It just may be time for a fresh perspective of that chapter's business. When you land, contact Hiran first. Get his take on things. Hiran is a straight shooter. He will cut through the shit." John nodded again and stood. He walked away from the table and got on his phone.

"Let's deal with our gun battles now." Marceau turned to Blu.

"He was a Fallen Angel, Tic. His bike told the tale," Blu said.

"The shopkeeper? How was it left?" Marceau asked.

"I told him to say it was a street brawl that ended up in his store and we would be in touch with him."

Marceau's chair creaked as he leaned back and stared at the ceiling for a moment. "Why was he there then? This Fallen Angel. Quite a coincidence, no?"

"They are shaking down our clients, Tic. They are trying to create confusion on the streets by misleading our clientele. They are pitting us against the Machine, like we thought, to bleed us dry and cause enough unrest so we fracture. Then they sweep in and take all of Montreal," Tracy said.

"Perhaps," Alain mused. Marceau turned to him and raised his eyebrows. "They may have something else in mind. Perhaps they are setting us up with the Montreal Police by manipulating the shopkeeper to squeal?"

"No," Marceau said. "Angels take care of their own business. Besides, why would they set up an extortion bust? While inconvenient, it doesn't cause a *fracture*. I think they are baiting us into a war with the Machine, as we've said. Now we are aware who is setting the fires." Marceau stood and paced the room, gathering his thoughts. "This very well could be the vanishing point, the endgame for all concerned," he reasoned. "To handle this situation correctly is to see the Horses get complete victory on this island."

"What's the mindset of the store owner?" John asked, rejoining the group at the table.

"A timid little mouse," Marceau replied, turning to him.

"Can we use that to our advantage and force him to retract his first statement? I'm assuming he has already spoken with the cops. Get him to say it was a Fallen Angel and a 13 Machine brawl? Take the heat off us for a while?"

"There's enough evidence to support that," Blu said. "I fucked up his bike, but I'm sure Montreal's finest will tie it to the Angels."

"Hum. Well, yes," Marceau said. "I will speak to the little mouse. In the meantime, John, call Toronto and ask Digger to send some bodies and weapons. I think this situation will get worse before it gets better and we need support."

Marceau banged the wooden gavel, and the group stood and dispersed.

✳ ✳ ✳

Shotgun headed straight for Candy's room. She had been distant after they returned from the head shop. He had seen her to her room and told her to rest. Candy had not spoken a single word on the trip back to the clubhouse or after their arrival. He knocked. After a little scuffling inside, the door opened a crack and Candy's face appeared.

"Hey you," Shotgun whispered. Candy let the door swing open and crossed the sparse room to sit on the edge of the bed.

"Hey," she replied. Her head was slumped and her hands folded in her lap. Blu went in.

He felt for the girl. This shit was more than Candy bargained for. She was just a kid, terrified by the entire ballgame.

Years of treating women as little more than overnight companions hadn't hardened his heart to the point of not having any empathy, and despite himself, he liked her. He sat on the bed.

"You all right?" he asked, placing his hand on her shoulder. Candy nodded, but didn't raise her head.

"Yeah, I'm okay. I've never had to hide from bullets before," she said. Her matter-of-fact tone surprised him.

"Darlin', it happens all too often for me," he chuckled. Candy tilted her head and looked up at him through her bangs.

"One hell of a life you lead, Charles," she said with a teasing smile. Shotgun chuckled again and caressed her back. Candy responded to his touch by leaning into him and putting her head on his chest. Blu wrapped his arms around her and rocked her tiny frame.

"It will be okay, Candy. It will. You are safe here with us," he soothed.

"With you," she corrected. Shotgun put his hands on her shoulders and eased her back. He placed his fingers under her chin and lifted her head until their eyes met.

"Yes, darlin'. With me," he said. Her wry smile turned genuine, and she kissed him.

"Promise?" she asked. Blu responded with a smile and pulled her close again. He knew full well that any relationship with this girl was a mistake. Yet he caved in to his desires and let his guarded emotions free.

"Promise," he whispered.

✳ ✳ ✳

What the Chevaux de Fer didn't know was that the Fallen had an agenda, and it was far more sinister than a simple extortion bust. *That* was only setting the plan in motion. The Angel's modus operandi had long since been to cure *any* problem by cutting off its head. That is what they were planning to do.

Griff sat in the Cleopatra Cafe, watching the young nubile women undulate to music and shed their clothes. He had waited until the detective had left Bong-A-Diggy and the mobile glass repairmen had replaced the shop window, and Gabriel and his wife, Chloe, had rearranged their shelves.

Griff was leaning up against the mailbox Candy had used for cover earlier that day, observing them through the front window of their little store. He flicked his cigarette into the gutter and strolled across the roadway.

In his pocket, he had the phone with the video of the Chevaux de Fer shakedown. The original idea was to pass it on to a colleague in the RCMP's Outlaw Motorcycle Gang Unit, but today's incident threatened to involve Griff's club. This development forced the Club's management to amend the plot. The Fallen needed a smokescreen to veil their intent and speed up the dismantling of the Horses. They had decided on a fresh angle. They trusted that their intimidation of the owners would be enough to see the plan through to its end. Griff rapped on the front window of the boutique.

Chloe peeked through the glass. The look on her face expressed she needed no more visits from unsavoury bikers.

"Bonsoir," he said. Chloe did not reply, but opened the door and allowed him inside. Her husband emerged from the storage room.

"I've done all you asked," he muttered. "I thought our business was through."

"Change of plan, my friend," Griff chuckled and patted him on the head. "I'm afraid I need some further help. You have spoken to the police, yes?"

"Oui," Gabriel affirmed.

"Just leave us be!" Chloe shouted, her voice quivering. *"Retourne là d'où tu viens.* Go back to your hole."

"Hush!" Gabriel blurted, but too late. Without hesitation, Griff backhanded her and Chloe fell to the floor with a squeal.

"Shut... the fuck... up," he said, shaking his fist. He glanced to Gabriel and sneered. "You chill that bitch out and do what I say, or I'll snap her in two. Understood?"

"Yes, yes," Gabriel said in a panic, dropping to his knees beside his sobbing wife. Griff retrieved the phone from his jacket pocket and handed it to him. Gabriel peered up in dismay as he took it.

"Call the police and tell them you have a video of the people involved in this afternoon's shooting."

"I've given my statement already. Two men, one black, one white, came in fighting from the bar across the street. The Horses told me to say that," Gabriel whimpered. Griff crouched beside him and raised his fist. Gabriel cowered.

"You will retract *that* statement, Gabriel. Quiver when you speak of the man on the video. Tell them he returned after the police left and did this to your wife." Griff pointed to her darkening bruise and cut lip.

"You tell them it was the same man that bruised her, the same man that threatened you, and the same man involved in the gunfight today." Griff stood.

"All the same man, Gabriel. The man who has been extorting protection money from you. Tell them you can stand it no longer and the truth is the best way for you now."

"I understand," Gabriel whispered.

"Do it quick. Not in an hour, not tomorrow... now. One last thing, the other man involved in the fight was wearing biker leathers. Be vague in his description, but be positive you saw the number thirteen stitched on his vest."

Griff walked to the door. He turned and added, "Do we have an issue with this, Gabriel?"

"No. No issues."

"Good," Griff chuckled. "Do this and all your problems vanish like smoke, my friend. Don't, and your problems have just begun." Griff left.

Gabriel stood and helped his wife to her feet. He wandered to the cash register and found the card Detective Dubois had given him earlier that day. He tentatively dialled the number.

* * *

Marceau wove his bike through the meagre traffic on his way to Bong-A-Diggy. He was a little high. He and John had a power meeting over the plan for India and smoked a joint.

The late evening air caressed his forearms, chilling him. It was threatening rain, and Tic cursed himself for leaving the clubhouse without a coat. He rolled the throttle, and the Harley leapt in response, her twin-engine growling in the night.

The entanglements in India were plaguing him. He knew John could handle it, but the threat of their heroin mule train collapsing was a tremendous concern. It could effectively spell the end of the Chevaux de Fer as a legitimate controlling club in Montreal or Toronto. It could be their demise.

A thin sprinkle began and caused the highway lamps to shimmer on the slick pavement. His vision blurred and he slowed the bike. His mind was wandering. *After this business with Gabriel, I'll take a break across the street in Cleopatra's. That little blonde cutie is dancing this week. A few icy beers and a lap dance is the right prescription to relieve this stress.*

Marceau pulled up in front of the strip club and put the Harley on its side stand. He stood on the sidewalk, peering through the drizzle at Bong-A-Diggy. The main lights were off, but there was illumination. *Most likely from the office*, he reasoned.

He glanced along Rue Du St. Laurent and took off his half helmet. Marceau strode across the street. It may have been the rain, or it may have been the hash, but while Marceau *saw* the bleak grey Chevy Impala parked up the avenue, it didn't register any alarm. He didn't notice that someone in the passenger seat followed his movements.

He stepped through the front door of the tiny shop with authority. Why wouldn't he? He was the badass president of the most feared bike gang in Montreal. *This should take very little time. A quick but threatening conversation with that weasel of an owner, then on to more pleasurable pursuits.*

Tic froze. It took only a second for him to understand the scene in front of him, and his entire body flooded with anger.

The scant light was not from the office, but from a desk lamp beside the cash register. Gabriel was leaning over it with a cell phone in his hand, speaking with the as yet unknown Detective Dubois.

The detective had a small spiral notebook and was listening as Gabriel spoke. The stranger was erect, legs parted, shoulders back and chest out. A notebook and his horrible suit meant only one thing. *A cop*! Chloe was standing beside Gabriel and as her face registered a mixture of surprise and fear, she screamed.

"That's him!" Her arm stabbed forward at Marceau. He could see the deep rouge nail polish on her index finger as it pointed at his chest.

The cop spun towards him, flicking open his jacket and retrieving the gun on his hip in one fluid motion. Like a cat, Marceau dropped to his knee and thrust his hand into the weapons pocket of his cut.

Tic was faster. He knew it and knew he had the drop on the detective. He grasped the cold metal butt of his Beretta and drew. His mind acknowledged with fear that he was going to kill a peace officer. While he reconciled that fact, the tinkle of the doorbell and the click of a .38 revolver being cocked rang in his ear.

"Go ahead, cowboy. Make a move," the icy voice from behind him said.

✳ ✳ ✳

Blu was standing on the curb of the passenger drop-off outside the departure terminal of Montreal's Pierre Elliott Trudeau International Airport.

"Fuckin' rain," he muttered. John pulled his bag from the side door of the Club's van and offered him a cigarette. With a glance at the *Défense de Fumer* sign stencilled on the column beside them, Shotgun chuckled and took it.

"You rebel, you," he jibed.

"Fuck you, Shotgun," John said as he lit the smoke for him. "Keep a handle on Tic, brother. I worry when I'm not here. You know what he's like. Don't let him start a full-scale war, we can't deal with the action right now. Or the attention." He lit his cigarette.

"Yeah, yeah. This could get hideous. But you recognise he doesn't listen to me, Johnny. Just you. It's only ever been you," Blu said while nodding.

"Bullshit. He respects you. Your opinions count, my friend. Advise him well, and with any luck, I'll be back in a week. We have no love in the NCB, man. Zero support other than that bastard Director Pandey. I will assess his worth as well, Blu. He is turning into a serious liability. I don't think he can bury an agent's murder, it's gonna be tricky. We'll give them a perp body and evidence, but I doubt that will be the end, bro. Just tread soft, keep this Fallen Angels shit contained, and we'll sort it when I get back."

John paused for a moment and looked over Blu's shoulder at the twinkling city lights. "Digger is coming with his kid and a few prospects up from TO just in case, but keep it smooth, brother." He flicked his half-smoked cigarette into the stream of traffic that was honking through the morass of departing passengers. They embraced.

"Smooth as a baby's ass, brother," Blu said.

John grabbed his bag and picked his path through the crowd towards the entrance. "Smooth as Candy's ass, you mean? Ohhh, that is *tight*, bro!" John tossed over his shoulder.

"Asshole," Blu whispered with a smile. He rounded the truck and hauled his hefty body into the driver's seat. Blu pulled out into traffic, turned on the radio and Bob Dylan was wailing what it felt like to be a Rolling Stone. He sang along, letting the lyrics distract him.

A taxi cut in front of him just as he reached the end of the drop-off zone, causing him to slam the brakes.

"Rat prick!" he shouted at the cab and sounded the horn. He hated driving a cage. His cell phone rang and he fished it from his pocket.

"Ya?" Blu answered.

"Brother, I'm fourteen-forty one," Marceau said.

"Fuuuck!"

Fourteen-forty one was slang for *Service de police de la Ville de Montréal*. Their headquarters address was 1441 Saint Urbain Street.

"What happened?"

"Best not say. Too many ears about. Do what needs to be done, get me out of this hole."

"On it," Blu said. He hit the end button and then punched the accelerator. The rear of the van fishtailed on the damp pavement as he sped onto Autoroute Twenty.

Shotgun flipped on the intermittent wipers. They squeaked across the windscreen, smearing the coating of road dust into arches of muddied streaks. As he shifted glances between the highway and his cell, Blu scrolled his contacts for Michelle Duchamp. She was the attorney the Horses kept on retainer, who had often represented them at bail hearings.

To date, Michelle had navigated three assault charges, one illegal weapons seizure, a handful of possession busts, and a nuisance charge, without a prison sentence for them. In fact, the only jail time served in the last twenty-four months was ninety days for public exposure. A very drunken Clipper had waved his manhood at two horrified Toronto Maple Leafs' hockey fans after a Montreal Canadiens win.

He found the number and dialled. A sleepy voice answered on the second ring. "*Bonjour*, Blu. *Qu'est-il arrivé*? What happened?"

"*Bonsoir*, Michelle. Call display?" Blu asked.

"I have your motley crew on speed dial," she said gruffly.

"Tic's arrested, he wouldn't say why." Blu heard the rustling of bedsheets in the background. "Sorry to wake you," he added.

"If he won't explain, that means it's bad. All right, he's at 1441 I assume?"

"Yes."

"I'll be over there in thirty minutes. No need for you to come. I'll call you after I've seen him." She hung up without waiting for a response.

Blu made the left-hand turn on to Rue Norman, then a right into the rear parking lot of the clubhouse on Clair Crescent.

He sat in the darkness, letting the day's events run through his mind. *How in God's name am I supposed to keep a lid on this shit? I'm third in command... third. I've never had any designs on running this club.* Blu recalled a Shakespeare quote buried deep in his high school memories.

'Some men are born great, some men achieve greatness, and others have greatness thrust upon them.'

"Bullshit," he whispered to himself. He retrieved his Du Maurier cigarette package from his pocket, sorted through it, and found the joint he had tucked away. Blu flicked his zippo and brought the tip of the flame to the twisted end of the spliff. He pulled on it hard and the pungent smoke filled his mouth. Blu inhaled it deep into his lungs.

Candy was another issue. Why he was struggling with that, he didn't understand. *If the little tart wants to roll in my bed, why shouldn't I indulge her? She's no different from any of the other nameless, faceless women who have tumbled in and out over the years. But she is, isn't she? That's the problem,* he thought.

"Aw, Jesus. Stay focussed," he mumbled. The landscape at the moment was Marceau and this impending war. The Fallen held the all cards right now. *How could they think we would blame the 13 Machine? The Machine is all but wiped out.*

There were a handful of faithful 13 members still lurking, enough to be a nuisance to the Horses, but they could do no actual damage to their hold on Montreal's west end.

Blu took another long draw on the joint and as he exhaled, a seed of an idea sprouted. *The 13 Machine. The war has left them depleted and desperate. Now we share a common enemy.* He would have to think about this.

With a last hit, he got out, flicking the roach across the parking lot. He slammed the door and walked to the back entrance of the clubhouse.

✳ ✳ ✳

Eight kilometres away from the Chevaux de Fer's clubhouse, Griff was in the side lot of the strip club, Cabaret Les Amazones. He was leaning against the brick wall, smoking a cigarette and listening to the voice on the other end of his phone.

"The parking garage on Rue St. Antoine," it was saying. "I will pull around back at 7:30 tomorrow morning, through the alley. Be waiting, because I won't."

"Mind how you speak to me, boy," Griff grumbled.

"No disrespect, but this is an enormous thing you're asking. There is more at risk here than losing my job. I could end up in prison for a very long time."

"Job? You're a driver for the Canadian Court Services. Sounds to me like you already *are* in prison," Griff asserted. "Do I need to remind you what you owe our club, you *and* your junkie brother? How far is it from the garage to Palais de Justice?"

"If I take it slow, five to seven minutes," the driver said.

"Good. That's enough time. There is no one else in the back of the transport?"

"No, just the prisoner. We will cuff him to the bench before we leave the station."

"All right. And your partner? You have persuaded him?" Griff asked.

"Yes, yes. For two grand, he'll take a *nap* until we reach the courthouse."

"Good," Griff said. "Stay focussed. This will be over soon enough and you can consider yourself debt-free. I'll see you in the morning."

Griff snapped his cell phone shut and strode over to the Harley 750 Street the Club had loaned him after Blu had obliterated his Night Rod. He took the key from the ignition and slipped it in the pocket of his faded jeans. His hatred for the Horses swelled inside him. Griff walked to the front entrance of the establishment and pulled open the heavy wooden door.

Blue and purple lights washed over him as Bad Company's 1975 hit, *Feel Like Making Love,* screamed out through the club's sound system. Griff could feel the patrons' eyes upon him as he made his way through the small tables, towards the back of the room.

He was wearing his recognisable MC colours and he felt good to be back in his cut. Griff didn't like this sneaking around shit. He was a Fallen Angel and everything he did or said revolved around being just that. He spotted the Montreal chapter president, Alfredo Guzzi, seated in a booth in the rear corner. Beside him was an enormous man, an enforcer from the Boston chapter. He slid in beside them.

"All set?" Guzzi asked, leaning forward over the table.

"Yes, the driver is relieved to work off his debt and the guy riding shotgun is for sale. Two grand and we get an open window," Griff said, over the pounding music. The larger man nodded as Guzzi waved his finger in the air at the waitress.

Griff leaned back and studied the dancer on stage. She worked part-time for the Club as a whore and Griff had sampled her wares on more than one occasion. The girl was only twenty-five years old and was just the way he liked his women. Brunette, beautiful and on her knees. She began thrusting up and down, impaling herself on an invisible lover, her heavy breasts bouncing as she shook her head from side to side in time to the music. The stripper's lengthy hair flicked out around her as she built tempo and reached her simulated climax.

"Here you go, boys," a sexy blonde waitress said as she placed three bottles of Molson Canadian on the table.

"I do love your Canadian beer. It goes down just right," the enforcer said. She flashed him a flirtatious grin.

"That's not the only thing we have up here that is wet and goes down smooth." She winked at him and walked away, swinging her hips. The trio laughed.

"We have the boys coming up from Boston. Last I spoke with them, they were finishing up some business in Vermont. They'll arrive here within two days if there is no border hassle," Guzzi said.

"Okay, captain," Griff replied, taking a swig from his bottle.

"The Horses will be at the courthouse tomorrow. So, while they are engaged there, you'll have time to case out their clubhouse. The day after next, we pick up our Boston brothers and proceed with the plan."

"Boom!" the second biker said, smiling.

"Done deal," Griff said and drained his beer.

"This should spell the end for these fucking ponies," Guzzi said and shook with laughter. The enforcer joined him. Griff did not. He just didn't believe it would be all that easy.

✳ ✳ ✳

There was a chill in the morning air. Marceau didn't know what time it was, but the sun had not yet come over the top of the Service de Police de la Ville de Montréal. With his feet shackled and wrists cuffed, he shuffled along the back alley of the building. Two Court Services officers and Detective Dubois escorted him through the narrow-fenced enclosure towards the transport wagon.

A fresh breeze blew and the bright orange nylon jumpsuit he was wearing did little to protect him from it. Tic Tock shivered. The group arrived at the rear of the truck. The back door stood open, beckoning him into the icy, desolate box.

One guard went to his knee to remove the leg shackles so that Marceau could navigate the welded step. The metal chains that bound his wrists clinked as he reached out for the support bar on the side of the truck. He climbed into the van and sat on the left-hand bench. It was solid and uncomfortable. The same guard followed him in to refasten his ankle bindings and attach his wrist cuffs to a block between his legs.

"Enjoy the ride." The detective grinned at him and slammed the door, leaving him in silence and solitude. He had done this trip many times. Within an hour, he would stand before the judge and they would set his bail. Then he could get back to his club, back to business.

Marceau had spoken at length with Michelle Duchamp the previous night and it was clear there was considerable work to do. The true intent of the Fallen was now unmistakable. This frame job made it obvious. They wanted to dispose of him as president of the Chevaux de Fer, and while the

Club was in disarray, break their backbone and destroy them. Tic scoffed.

"They do not know us at all," he hissed. The rumble of the truck's motor vibrated through the seat as it sprung to life and they lurched forward.

Marceau sat with his head hung, playing over recent events in his mind. *Since that little punk, Alex, had knocked Clipper off the stairwell landing, everything had gone from shit to extra deep shit. That pain in the ass had caused more trouble in the last week than he was worth. Sending him to India may have been a terrible call.*

Tic was craving a cigarette, something fierce, and it made him irritable. More irritable than his usual state of annoyance with the world.

The transport van is moving too slow for this time of the day. There shouldn't be any traffic issues. He cocked his head and listened to the motor, the rhythmic hum of the vehicle. *Our speed is little more than a crawl.*

The truck slowed further and made a left-hand turn. Marceau sat upright and spread his feet as they bounced over the curb. *There's no way we have reached Rue Notre-Dame. Something isn't right.* The hair on the back of his neck bristled as the van lurched to a halt and the diesel motor quietened to a slow idle. Marceau heard the driver's door slam. There was a faint conversation, but he couldn't make out who was speaking or what was being said. The rear door opened with a groan.

"Two minutes," the driver said, as a large bearded man climbed into the compartment with him. He was in civilian clothes, but Tic knew who and what he was. The door swung shut, but not closed.

"Hello, Marceau," Griff whispered. "Tic... tock... tick... tock... tic...," he taunted as he took two steps towards him. Still out of reach from Marceau's shackled hands and feet, Griff crouched and glared into his eyes. "Tock."

"Who the fuck are you supposed to be?" Marceau asked.

Griff chuckled, "Me? Oh, I'm no one important."

"That's obvious," Marceau said. "Yet, judging by the amateur ink job on your neck, it's clear you're a Fallen Angel. Who did that? Your whore of a mother? Looks like she did it with a crochet needle and food colouring."

Griff smiled at the insult. He stood and slipped two fingers into the front pocket of his Levi's. Never taking his eyes from Marceau's, he produced a single white gelatine capsule. He secured it between his thumb and forefinger and held it out for his inspection.

"Meth?" Marceau asked. "I hear most of you Fallen Angels are tweakers," he sneered.

"You arrogant prick. All you and your band of frail little ponies had to do was *fuck off*. That was *all*. Just disappear. But no, you thought you had the balls and knowhow to tangle with the best." Griff flipped the capsule into his palm. "Now you will pay, my friend." He stared at Marceau hard. Tic's expression twisted with loathing and hatred.

"I won't beg," he growled through gritted teeth.

"I don't care," said Griff with a nonchalant shrug, and then like lightning, lashed out with his left hand, snapping the butt across Marceau's Adam's apple. Marceau yowled in pain and his mouth gaped, gasping for air. Griff flipped the capsule in and covered it with his right hand. Griff leaned forward, using his weight to keep him pinned to the bench, and massaged Marceau's throat.

"If you swallow it, it will be much worse," Griff panted. "Just bite the fucking thing." Marceau thrashed under him, kicking out with his legs and trying to raise his hands. He pulled at the chains binding his arms. The veins in Tic's neck were as taut as ship mooring lines and his face was becoming a deep shade of purple. Griff widened his stance to avoid Marceau's kicks and kept the pressure on him.

Marceau lurched, and with a gurgled cough, spit out a mouthful of white froth. It oozed between Griff's fingers. He pulled his hand away. Tic hissed like a snake and convulsed, and his eyes rolled back in his head, exposing the eerie whites.

Contorting and writhing, Marceau gagged as the spittle continued to spill over his beard and pool on his lap. He raised his hands, fingers clawing, grasping at his inaccessible assailant. Then they fell. Marceau's body went limp and slumped over on the bench. He twitched and a stream of urine ran down the floor. Griff nodded once.

"*Au revoir*, cocksucker," he whispered and exited the compartment, sealing the door behind him.

✳ ✳ ✳

Shotgun Blu, Alain, and Tracy were standing on the top steps of the Palais de Justice. It was humming with activity as dozens of prosecutors and defence attorneys scurried around the entrance. Clad in their sharp navy blue or grey business suits, they gibbered on cell phones, carrying file folders and expensive black attaché cases. No one paid any notice to the trio of scruffy bikers, other than the odd sideways glance.

The group was chatting while returning the foul looks as Michelle Duchamp descended the stairs from the courthouse. She was a portly but attractive woman, dressed in a cream-coloured blouse and a dark brown blazer. She had tied her hair up in a bun and had a file folder in her hand. Michelle squinted at them through the morning sun.

"The transport is due shortly, and the list is up," she said. "They've posted Marceau to appear in courtroom six." The group stood in silence for a moment.

"Good morning, Michelle," Tracy said with a smirk.

"Boys, this is serious. They have him on a weapons charge, extortion, threatening a police officer..." She shook her head. "I don't know what I can do here. I apologise if my mood is less than jovial, but the Crown Attorney won't speak to me. It will be a challenge to even *get* bail. So, good fucking morning," she said. "Wait outside the courtroom. You look like a band of outlaws and that makes my job harder. I'll see you soon." She reached out and touched Blu's elbow, then spun and trotted back up the steps.

"All business, that one," Alain said with a shrug. "What do you think, Blu?" he asked.

"Jesus. I don't know, brothers. This may be a little more than we bargained for. I didn't see the *'held without bail'* thing coming," he said.

"She will get him out," Tracy said. "No worries, Blu. Marceau will handle this." He climbed the steps to the doors of the courthouse.

"You all right, brother?" Alain asked. Blu sighed.

"Yeah, yeah. It's just... If Tic's inside and John's in India..." Alain put his hands on Blu's chest.

"We've got your back, brother. Some of us believe you've been the right man for the president's chair for a while now." Alain winked and started up the steps. Blu smiled and followed him. He glanced over his shoulder and spotted the court services van passing the front of the building. His heart skipped.

The inside foyer was spacious and smelled like a library. The musk of old books and bite of vinegar floor cleaner hung in the air. They strolled the corridors until they found court six and sat in a group on the single wooden bench outside the double doors. Blu folded his hands in his lap and closed his eyes. *How will I handle this if Tic doesn't get released? Digger and a handful of the Toronto crew are arriving this afternoon. But then, what?*

The courtroom door swung open and Michelle came out. She stood in front of them, dazed and ashen. Blu glanced at the others. They shared the same puzzled expressions.

"What?" he asked her.

"He's dead," Michelle breathed. The three of them shot up from the bench in unison. Alain grabbed her shoulders.

"What?" he shouted, causing several passers-by to jolt in surprise and stare at them. Michelle freed herself from his grip.

"Dead... suicide, they told me. A pill... cyanide, they think," she whispered.

"How? What?..." Tracy stammered.

"When?" Blu demanded.

"Just now. The Crown Attorney said... on the ride over from the police station, he had a pill." Her eyes teared and she gasped a breath.

"No," the three of them chorused.

"Impossible," Blu said and slumped on the bench. The anger welled inside him. It was ripping at his innards like a caged animal. He felt no fear, he felt no indecision, and he knew what they must do. He lifted his head and locked eyes with Tracy. His scowl deepened, and he clenched his teeth.

"Get me the president of the 13 Machine on the phone."

◆

CHAPTER TEN

Before 2010, NH8 was the designation for the major highway from Delhi to Mumbai, then in the south, the name changed to NH4 from Mumbai to Chennai. Old-timers still refer to it in these increments.

But now the entire route, re-designated as NH48, is the principal conduit for thousands of motorists to travel through India, north to south. The highway winds its way through six states and provides access to many of India's largest cities. It is *not* the preferred route for drug smugglers, but the Horses were at a full gallop and needed to reach Goa as quickly as possible.

Alex squirmed in his seat, his eyelids drooping. They had set out from Udaipur at 4:30 that morning, and ten hours later, they continued to push forward. *Still*, he thought, *travelling through the landscapes of Rajasthan, Gujarat and now Maharashtra, has been exhilarating.*

The rugged desert had stirred a deep-seated wanderlust in his soul. It had struck fast and without warning, like a wave of intoxication. The twisted rock formations had brought a numbing sense of serenity. With each bend in the road, a new dreamscape would appear in front of them. It took Alex a few hours to name the emotion. It was something he had never felt. With Ipsita close to him, wrapping her arms around him and holding him tight, he could almost forget the malevolent cloud hanging overhead. The true and sinister nature of this ride.

He reached down with his left hand and grasped Ippy's thigh just above her knee and squeezed. She responded by putting her hands on his hips and returning the gesture.

As Alex seriously weighed the pros and cons between his previous life and the one he has just been thrust into, he realised it was one hell of a tradeoff to consider switching. To live his life by his own rules and fuel this emerging sense of freedom and respect, he would need to cross some considerable moral boundaries. *Could I do that? Be an outlaw, be a biker?*

Alex focussed on Ramdev in front of him. Daya was riding pillion, her long brown hair flowing out from her helmet. She sat motionless, like a sack of rice. There were no loving or playful interactions between the two of *them.*

Ramdev held fast on the right-hand side of the lane and Alex, as they had told him to do, staggered to the left. He caught the glint of Shiv's headlight in his mirror and he knew Hiran was twenty metres behind them, riding tail. The four bikes wound like a snake down this ribbon of black tarmac, a rhythmic mechanical dance through the wild and unpolished landscape surrounding them.

Despite the desperate situation, or perhaps because of it, Alex tasted a freedom he had never experienced. The simple sight of the sun faded asphalt slipping under his front tire gave him wings.

It seemed the more kilometres of open highway the group ate up, the more untouchable he felt, impervious to the pressures of his everyday life and cleansed from the expectations of an unforgiving society.

It just doesn't matter here. On the road, nothing does. The genuine nature of being a biker flowed within him, carrying with it an inescapable sense of exemption. *This must be the drug that they crave, the reason they shun cultured civilisation and live by their own rules.* Alex had tapped into the deep-rooted psyche of every biker. *This is the soul of it. This is why my father had left my mother. This is the justification they used to transport drugs, to kill, to do whatever needed to be done to preserve their brotherhood. And nothing could touch them, not as long as they had each other.*

Ipsita's hand slipped forward and caressed his crotch. He felt her chest heave against his back as she laughed. Alex released her leg and slapped at her. He could picture her girl-like pout and a smile broke over his lips. The bike leapt as he rolled the throttle, anxious and willing. He wove within the lane for a while, letting the wind caress his face and the late afternoon sun warm him.

Ramdev raised his right hand and made a fist, then slowed and pulled off to the side of the road. Alex followed, and when they came to a stop in single file, he hit the kill switch. Dust swirled around them as the bikes unsettled the gravel on the soft shoulder. Alex wiped his visor clean. He shook his head to clear the dull ringing in his ears, lingering after the continuous thump from his bike engine.

Ippy groaned and slipped off the seat. Alex kicked down the side stand and followed her, peeling off his helmet. He lit a smoke as Hiran joined them and Shiv scampered down the slight incline to relieve himself behind a tree. Ramdev walked over and shot a disdainful glance at Ipsita. Taking the hint, she went to stand with Daya.

"We are making excellent time, brother," Hiran said. Ramdev nodded while lighting a joint. He took two long hits on it and passed it to Hiran.

"You're doing all right, Alex?" Ramdev said. Alex looked at him through his windswept bangs.

"Yeah, I'm okay. Surprised you give a shit," he answered. Ramdev shrugged.

"I do, in a way. But it's your cargo I'm worried about and I don't mean her," he said, glancing at Ippy. He took the joint back from Hiran. "We'll stop in Thane. I haven't been able to get a hold of Marceau all day, and it's making me a little uneasy. We'll tell Mumbai to collect from us there instead of going all the way into the city."

"I'll call them," Hiran said and walked away, fishing out his phone.

"You did well, Alex. Back in Delhi." Ramdev took another long pull on the joint and then offered it to Alex. Alex shook his head, but inexplicably, his pride swelled with Ramdev's praise.

"I meant what I said to you before we left. Despite the... unusual circumstances, you have proven yourself to me, Alex. Your character, at least. I will stress it to Marceau. There may be a place for you with the Chevaux de Fer. You would need to want it though."

"How do you live with it?" Alex asked.

"Live with what?"

"Living outside the law. Running drugs, shooting at police, killing people." Ramdev raised his eyebrows and chuckled.

"You think we run around killing people daily? No one enjoys taking a life, Alex. Well, there are some true psychotics, I suppose. But I don't. Hiran doesn't. To say I chose this life would be to mislead you. This life chose me, and once I tasted it, I couldn't live any other way. I am talking about the purity of it, Alex, real biker freedom. Not the bullshit that gets tangled up with it. Once you feel it, it sets you free and you find others who feel this way as well. Brothers. As in all things, Alex, there comes a time when you must choose, and once you do, protect that choice. Being in a motorcycle club isn't about drugs or killing. At least it shouldn't be. It's a lifestyle. One that you don't consider without giving it much thought."

"No shit?" Alex laughed. Ramdev smiled and flicked the roach into the dirt.

"No shit. That thing inside you are trying to keep alive, it will kill you, Alex," he said. Ramdev's phone chirped and he pulled it from his cut.

"Hello?" he asked. Alex walked towards his bike.

"Sumit? Calm the fuck down!" Ramdev barked. Alex stopped. He watched as Ramdev twitched, listening to whoever was yelling on the other end of the line.

"Yes, I told him to call. It's not an issue, just come to Thane and pick up..." The yelling was audible from the receiver. "You question my leadership? I've got years on you!" Ramdev's shoulders slumped. "Yes, but..." The line obviously went dead.

"Everything okay?" Alex asked him

"Saddle up!" Ramdev called, ignoring Alex's question, and they returned to their bikes. The group pulled back out onto the highway and sped towards Thane.

✳ ✳ ✳

Over Alex's shoulder, Ipsita could see Thane's skyline. It was much larger now, silhouetted in the comforting haze of a low sun. She swayed in unison with the bike as Alex wove it in and out of the multitude of vehicles that had increased with every passing minute once the city was in view. She felt him slouch forward and let his arms go limp, in stark contrast to his rigid spine and chuffed out chest posture on the open highway. Ipsita squeezed him. *It must exhaust him*, she thought and drove her thumbs into his spine. Alex forced his shoulder blades together in response. Sweat moistened her brow as Ippy continued to massage him. Twisting his hips, he took one hand off the handlebar to flex his fingers. Then he repeated the process with the other.

Please God, let us stop soon, she prayed in silence as her thighs were sore and raw.

The murder of the NCB agent seemed to have freed her from one obstacle but created another. There was no doubt Dimpi's superiors would eventually come calling, demanding the same from her that Agent Shashidhar had. But after a sleepless night in Udaipur, Ippy concluded the unfortunate demise of Dimpi may have bought her some time. The problem now was freeing Alex from Ramdev's gaze long enough to find a travel agent. There was to be no advancement of that tonight, stuck in a highway motel. But perhaps in Pune or Goa, an opportunity would arise. *I will just have to make sure it does*, she encouraged herself.

After an additional forty minutes of heavy congestion, Ramdev led them into a small roadside hotel. The group came to a halt.

"Stay put," he said to Alex after dismounting. "If they see a *safaide wala*, they will charge me double." He walked past him and into the lobby. Ippy climbed off her pillion seat first, then Alex followed. She lit a cigarette as Daya wandered up to them.

"*Safaide wala*?" Alex asked.

"Your pale ass," Daya said before Ipsita could answer. "*Safaide wala,* a white guy," she confirmed and chuckled. Ippy smiled at Daya and gave her a wink, a non-verbal communication telling her that everything was all right. The two of them had grown skilled at speaking without speaking over the years, and Daya answered back with a coy grin. Unaware of their exchange, Alex smiled as well, then busied himself unstrapping the saddlebags.

A few minutes later, Ramdev appeared from the hotel reception. He tossed Alex a key.

"108, first floor. Eat when you want. Don't leave the hotel. We saddle up at 6:00 tomorrow morning. Load your bike and be ready." He grabbed Daya's wrist and pulled her away with him. "Shiv, unpack the bikes. Give me an hour, then come to my room. Hiran, find us some rum." He strode with Daya in tow towards the exterior stairwell. Daya glanced back over her shoulder and Ippy furrowed her brow. *It's okay,* she mouthed at her. Daya rolled her eyes.

Gujarat is a dry state. But now that they were in Maharashtra, wine shops were available. There was one opposite the hotel. Hiran started walking towards it. Ipsita smirked at Alex and raised her eyebrows. Alex laughed and nodded.

"Sure," he said.

She chased after Hiran and paused at the roadside, waiting for a gap in traffic. When it came, Ipsita trotted across the tarmac to the shop and took her place among the half dozen bodies milling around the counter.

Despite her road weariness, Ipsita focussed on the immediate task at hand. She had no concerns that by this point, Alex was under her spell. *Wouldn't hurt to shore that up a little further,* she mused. *I'll give him another earth-shattering shag tonight.* Her lips peeled into a wicked grin. *I'll enjoy that myself.* Ippy quickly dismissed the creeping scorpion of guilt that stung her guts at the thought. She shook her head. *This is an unexpected thing,* she admitted as the twinge faded. *Focus, girl. You need to get this sorted. Time is running short.* The man behind the counter spoke.

"You?"

"Canadian whiskey *hai*?" Ippy asked. The proprietor of the small shop looked at her in utter confusion. She may as well have asked for an electric kettle.

"Old Monk rum," she said. The man nodded and grabbed a bottle from the shelf. *Tomorrow in Pune, we'll make our break, with or without tickets*, she decided.

* * *

"We know of them, yes. But if they don't break any laws, what are we to do?" The Superintendent of Udaipur Police was saying in answer to Avinash's enquiry about the Iron Horses.

"They do, in fact," Avinash said as he studied the Superintendent. "Frequently."

"None of which we are aware of, sir," the Superintendent answered. "If the NCB were more forthcoming with intelligence on their current investigations, we may be of more help. I will arrange for a constable to give you all we have on them. But it is little more than the location they meet and a few traffic violations."

"Very well," Avinash said, irritated. "Please send all the information you can find over to the rest house." He spun sharply on his heel and left the Superintendent's office. Sandy was waiting for him in the hall.

"Anything?" he asked. Avinash furrowed his brow and shook his head. The two of them proceeded to the Innova SUV parked in front of the station and told the driver to take them to the government rest house. Avi stared out of the rear window as the tourist-laden streets of downtown Udaipur slipped past them. He held Dimpi's cell phone in his hand, absently twirling it between his fingers. Sandy was watching him.

"He'll call, boss. These guys are in over their heads. They know it, they're scared," he said.

"We'll see," Avi replied. "While we are spinning our wheels waiting for the RCMP to get back to us, there's little else to go on."

"The Club is an ongoing investigation in the RCMP, so my casual enquiry didn't carry much weight," Sandy explained. "The Canadians are looking to build a joint task force. They want us to join their Outlaw Motorcycle Gang unit. An alliance. They've collected a massive amount of information. There are so many procedures to follow, Avi. We opened a Pandora's box in Canada, I think."

"We may have, yes. But what were the options?" Avinash sighed. "The raid on the moving company in Amritsar... nothing. The search of the clubhouse in Delhi... nothing. And Dimpi... no murder weapon, no prints, and no witnesses. These Horses are like ghosts. If we don't get a break soon, we could lose them altogether."

They rode in silence, weaving their way through the heavy traffic until they pulled up into a private compound with a scant three storeyed building. The two of them went to their assigned room. Avi sat at the small desk and Sandy flopped on one of the twin beds.

"We can question the Udaipur chapter tonight," Sandy suggested. "It's unlikely they will give us anything substantial, but maybe a clue where the Delhi boys are heading? At the very least, it will let the Horses know we are on their tail."

"Yes," Avi said, rubbing his eyes. "Okay, maybe they will slip up if we shake them hard enough. We'll take a few local constables with us, impound a bike or two on some manufactured violations." Sandy nodded in agreement.

"I'll make the call."

Avinash watched the junior agent walk to the wooden screen door and step out onto the second-floor balcony. *He's a good kid,* Avi thought. *Worth having in this fight.* He followed him pacing back and forth across the terrace, speaking on the phone. Avi suddenly wished he had a drink. He closed his eyes and rolled his head. The tension in his neck felt like a steel band. Sandy entered the room and was about to speak when Dimpi's phone chirped. He froze in his tracks. Avi looked at him and held his finger to his lips. Sandy nodded.

"Hello?" Avinash said into her cell. There was only silence. "The Iron Horses, I presume?" he prompted.

"Yes," Ramdev replied. Avi gave thumbs up to Sandy.

"I further presume you are looking for a way clear of this mess you've created?"

"I didn't kill her," Ramdev said. His voice was barely a whisper.

"Well, let's start there, shall we? Who is I?" Avi questioned.

"I'm a member of the Iron Horses."

"A name would be better to address you with. Last we spoke, you expressed an interest in working with us to end this predicament?" Avi waited. There was a lengthy pause on the other end and he could hear unsteady breathing.

"Can you assure me I walk away, free?" Ramdev asked.

"That depends on the information you give us, and your role in the murder. If you have taken part in the demise of Agent Shashidhar, then no. The NCB is not in the habit of allowing murderers to go unpunished. However, if you assist us to apprehend the people who killed her, we can speak about it. Tell me about the heroin," Avinash said sharply, deciding to force his hand. There was silence on the other end of the line. "You weren't aware we knew of your heroin shipping?" Avi chuckled.

"No," Ramdev stammered.

"I see. I would recommend you don't contact your moving company in Amritsar," Avi pressed. "Seems they are having some legal issues. I think you may face trouble reaching your Udaipur chapter as well."

"Shit," was Ramdev's only response.

"Look. Let's meet and discuss this. All we want is to bring the killers to justice and stop the Horses' heroin flow through India. If you can help facilitate that, you could walk away from this mess. Clean. What's your name?" Avi softened his voice a little.

"Ramdev. I just want out of this. The drugs, the Club, all of it."

"So, let's make that happen, Ramdev. Where are you?" Avi said, cradling the phone between his chin and shoulder. He pulled a notepad from his inner jacket pocket and snapped his fingers at Sandy, who passed him a pen.

"Doesn't matter. We won't be there when you arrive," Ramdev said.

"All right, Ramdev. Where *will* you be and what is your position in the Club?"

"Delhi chapter president."

"Well hell! That's grand news, Ramdev. That means you have all the information we need! This increases your likelihood of a clean exit from this entire predicament." There was another extended silence.

"I'm not fucking around, Agent Kumar. I can give you everything, but I need your assurance. In writing."

"What is 'everything'?"

"The killers, the sugar, the players involved... everything. But I want out and they can never know I flipped. They will fucking kill me, understand? These are my conditions."

"Who are they?" Avi asked. "The rest of the Horses?"

"Do you *understand*?" Ramdev shouted.

"Oh, I understand, Ramdev. Dangle a carrot for me."

"Twelve keys of H, the murderer, and a list of all Delhi Horses," Ramdev whispered.

"More," Avi said simply.

"What more?" Ramdev exploded.

"Your suppliers, your mule train, and destination contacts."

"No fucking way! That's a death sentence!"

"You've already got one, son, because we already have you. You just didn't know it!" Avi said and hung up the phone. He slumped back in the chair and lit a cigarette.

"Oh boss, was that the right move?" Sandy asked. "We could lose it all here. If he spooks and runs, or worse, if the Horses close shop, they could leave us empty-handed!"

"We can get it all too. They won't close shop, it's their income. You were correct, he's scared. He won't run." Avi exhaled a stream of smoke. "This is bigger than we thought, Sandy. 'Twelve kilos,' he said. 'They will kill me,' he said. It's huge, and he wants out. This isn't just heroin peddling in India, they are shipping to Canada. They must be. I could smell the fear on him. At first, I thought Dimpi got unlucky, forced their hand, made them do something they didn't want to do. But no, killing is nothing to this club. They are big, they are strong, and very well connected. We have our teeth into a massive heroin distribution network here. International smuggling, Sandy. The proverbial brass ring." Dimpi's phone chirped again. Avi smiled at Sandy and let it sound a second time, then a third. He answered.

"Well?" he asked nonchalantly.

"Okay, I'll give you all I can, but they handle the suppliers out of country. I don't have that kind of access. I am only told where to pick up and where to drop off. That's all." Ramdev said.

"Fair enough," Avi said. "Put it all on paper and we will have a look. Where and when do we meet?" he asked.

"I want my guarantee on paper as well, Agent Kumar. Freedom in plain English. Understand this, after I meet you, I can't go back to the Club. We need to do a deal there and then. I need to walk away from that meeting a free man with an unblemished record. Then I will disappear," Ramdev said.

"We can make that happen. However, you will not disappear from the NCB. You may need to testify; your statement will not be enough. If we require you on the stand, you come. Do you agree?" Avi and Sandy exchanged anxious glances. The pause was excruciating.

"Hotel Wilsha, Carambolim, Goa. Be there in two days, alone, Agent Kumar. It's near Karmali railway station, Carambolim Lake road. Take a room there and I will contact you. I'll see you long before you see me. If I sense any kind of trap, I'll vanish along with the drugs." The line disconnected. Avinash put the phone down and closed his eyes. He released a held breath.

"We have the bastards, Sandy." Avinash drawled. "And we will make them pay."

✳ ✳ ✳

Hiran stood at the bottom of the hotel stairwell watching Ipsita climb the steps. Dressed in baggy camouflage cargo pants and a tight black t-shirt, Ipsita looked every inch a biker bitch siren.

"That ass looks superb in *everything*," he whispered. He put the bottle of Old Monk rum he had just bought on the ground and lit a Gold Flake. Hiran knew better than to crowd Ramdev after they first got to a hotel.

Normally it was Ipsita he would have given a quick ride, but times have changed. Hiran knew he was relieving his stress with Daya. It should have bothered him, but it didn't. Daya had been Hiran's lover after they met in Mumbai. When she started with the brown sugar, he turned away from her and when he found out she had a deeper relationship with Ipsita, he left her alone completely.

Hiran finished his smoke and climbed the stairs. He arrived at his room to see Shiv had already carried up the bags and was in the shower. He rapped on the restroom door.

"Ya?" Shiv called.

"All good, brother?" Hiran asked.

"All good. Will be out in a minute." Hiran sat on the edge of the small armchair and opened the rum, pouring two stiff shots into the plain glasses on the table and topping them off with water. He sipped his drink. Ramdev's muffled shouts filtered through the wall. They provided little in the way of privacy. Hiran could tell it was in anger, not ecstasy.

He stood, and draining his glass, headed out into the hallway and approached Ramdev's room. The door was ajar, just a crack as if the latch hadn't caught when they entered. Hiran grasped the handle and opened it further. He strained his ears against the patter of water splashing onto bare tiles in the shower and tried to tune into Ramdev's hushed mumbling on the phone. *It must be Montreal,* he thought. Hiran, with his foot hanging in the air mid-step, turned, and retreated from the room. Ramdev's whispers became agitated, freezing him. His eyes widened as Ramdev said, "Okay,

I'll give you all I know, but they handle the suppliers out of the country. I don't have that kind of access."

"What the *fuck*?" Hiran whispered and pushed the door further. Ramdev was on the bed, blocked from his view. Sweat rolled down Hiran's paling face and nausea churned in his stomach as he listened to the rest of the conversation.

He shivered as he reached the inescapable conclusion that his closest brother was a rat. Hiran clenched his fist, then reached for his gun, but the part of him that loved Ramdev forced him to slip it back into his cut. *There must be an explanation!*

He heard Ramdev end the call and get up off the bed. Hiran backed out of the room and, holding his breath, eased the door shut. He took three steps and fell against the railing. Hiran filled his lungs, clearing the dizziness.

"Okay, okay," he whispered. "I need to be sure."

Hiran crept back to the door and listened. There was no sound. *I'm acting like a fool,* he thought. At any other time, he would enter Ramdev's room with little more than a cursory knock. Hiran opened the door.

He wormed around the half-opened door and padded into the room. Ramdev's clothes were lying haphazardly on the bed. Hiran snatched his leathers and riffled the pockets. He took his cell and scrolling through, located the last number called. He laid the phone down on the bed, took a picture of the screen, and put it back in Ramdev's cut.

Hiran slipped back out into the hall and staggered to the end of the hallway. He turned the corner into the stairwell, leant back against the wall, and lit a smoke. He looked at the photo of Ramdev's phone and quickly dialled the captured number.

"Hello?" came the voice on the other end after only one ring. Hiran remained silent. "Hello? This is Special Agent Kumar of the NCB. Who is this?" Hiran stabbed the end call button and snapped his burner phone in two. As sorrow filled his belly, he pulled the sim card out and ground it under his heel.

Ramdev, my closest friend, is a rat. For years we fought our way through the ranks of this fucking club together! Every promotion, I was proud of him! Every single one! As if it had been my achievement. That cheap fuck. Now he has betrayed it all, our trust, our bond, our brotherhood. His eyes moistened. *Through our probation and every shit task we endured together, I never faltered. Even in matters of the heart and of the family, I was always there. What the fuck is he thinking?*

Now, unabated tears flowed. He wasn't sure how but was certain Ipsita had created this mess. *That cold-hearted witch had placed him under a spell, manoeuvred him into a position where to rat seemed his only choice.*

Hiran squinted his eyes shut and cursed. *No matter what the situation, to rat was never the answer. To betray the Club was never acceptable. No matter how deep the shit, the Club would pull you out.* He flicked the cigarette butt over the railing. The evidence was obvious. Hiran knew what he had to do. He hurried back to his room to fetch his spare burner to call Montreal.

* * *

As Ipsita crossed the road to the wine shop, Alex slung the saddlebags over his left shoulder and pulled the magnetic tank bag free. He slumped under the weight of the bags as he started for the stairs. *God, they look steep.*

The first floor hallway ran the length of the building on the highway side like an open veranda. Alex trudged along it, watching the southbound traffic honk its way towards Thane. *We must be on the outskirts,* he thought. Alex strode through the door of room 108 and dropped the luggage on the ceramic floor with a thud.

He sighed at the twin bed with two thin pillows and sat at the desk. They had painted the room in faded pastel green and the only wall adornment was a small tv. The semi-sheer orange curtains tied it all together.

Alex picked up the air conditioning control from the counter, turned it on, and went to the washroom. They had tiled the entire room, bar the ceiling, in a light yellow and mildew combination. The shower was a rusty odd angle pipe, protruding from the far wall. It had a single cold water tap, as did the tiny rust-stained sink.

At least there was a western-style toilet, he mused. Alex twisted the knob and a trickle of lukewarm water spilled from the bare pipe. Alex returned to the bedroom and stripped, dumping his dusty jeans, t-shirt and Ratt's cut on the bed.

Returning to the washroom, he stood under the stream of water. The pressure had increased, but it was getting colder. As Alex scrubbed the road grime from his face, he heard the exterior door open and close.

"Alex?" Ippy's voice called.

"In here," he answered. She opened the bathroom door and beamed as she scanned his naked body.

"What have we here?" she asked, playfully. Alex laughed.

"What did you get?"

"Rum and a bottle of coke from the restaurant. I remember you saying that's how you mix it in Canada. I think I will try that."

"Then pour us a drink and come clean off with me," he invited, grinning. A moment later, she entered the washroom, wrapped in a towel, with a glass in each hand. Alex backed out from under the spray and kissed her. Ippy arched up on her tiptoes and moaned as their lips met. He took the cocktail from her and gulped half of it down in one go, letting the sweet warmth fill his stomach. Ippy put hers down on the sink and handed him her towel. She stepped into the shower and began soaping herself.

"Jesus," Alex muttered as he felt himself swell. Ipsita tittered, spying his condition.

"My God, Alex. You are a virile one. Go, relax, and let me freshen up. Then we can talk, okay?" Alex nodded and left.

Alex flopped on the bed, his hair wet and tangled. He semi wrapped himself in the thin sheet under him after tugging it free. He downed what was left of his drink, closed his eyes, and felt sleep overtaking him. *Let it come.* Alex was bone-weary as there was little last night.

They had sequestered the two of them to a compact room in Udaipur's clubhouse as soon as they had arrived. It had been early afternoon, and they had left them isolated until later that evening. One of the Udaipur Horses had brought them a pizza and a couple of bottles of water and did not disturb them until the next morning.

They had made love, but it lacked the searing passion of their earlier union. Alex had tried to rest, but his dreams were filled with the grotesque scenes from Dimpi's murder. He tossed and turned until Ippy had coddled him to sleep.

Ipsita crawling onto the bed shook him back to reality. She lay on her belly, wrapped in a towel, and propped herself up on her elbows.

"Alex?" she frowned.

"Humm?"

"What happens after Goa? After the drop?"

"With what?" he asked.

"With you." Ippy rolled over and stared at the ceiling. "Do you simply go back to Canada? What happens then? Will I be able to just walk away from all this? Or will they kill me? Ramdev has no use for me anymore and I am a witness to a murder."

"I don't know, babe," he said. Ipsita smiled at his use of the endearment. "What do you want?"

Ipsita popped up and straddled him, her wet hair dripping on his bare chest.

"I want out, Alex, you know that. I don't know how, but this thing that has happened with the agent, it's dangerous for me," she said, reaching out and brushing his cheek. "I'm a simple girl and I need your help."

"You want to come to Canada?" he laughed. Ippy thought for a moment, pondering what he had said and shrugged.

"I don't see them allowing that, Alex," she breathed. "But it's a lovely thought." The two of them stared at each other in silence. Not an uncomfortable silence, just a shared one. The simple honesty of her words cut through him like a serrated blade. His heart hammered.

"Ippy, I'm feeling..." Alex whispered. He could think of nothing else to say. She placed her finger across his lips.

"Hush, don't say anything silly now," Ippy cooed. "Just be there when I need you, okay? At some point, Daya and I will have to run. You know this. Promise you'll help."

"I do. I promise," he whispered.

* * *

"What the fuck are you doing?" John screamed at the taxi driver as the cab swerved, just missing an old man on a scooter. "Chill out, or I will rip you a new one." The eyes in the rear-view mirror squinted, and then the eyebrows raised. "Take it easy; your driving," John hissed.

"Yes, sir. Sorry, sir," the driver muttered.

John hated India. This was his third trip, and he never understood the mindset of the others who came back after a run, grinning from ear to ear and singing praises of the mystic east. Most babbled on about how much they enjoyed the country, the culture. In John's estimation, it was too hot, too loud, and contained far too many people. *And forget about the food, you couldn't get a decent hamburger or pizza. What the hell was there to like about India?*

The pace of the cab slowed a little. John leaned his head against the door and slid forward in his seat. His unfocused eyes flicked over the blurs of white and red and yellow traffic passing the window. He'd had no proper sleep since Toronto.

After landing, John had wandered through the duty-free shops in the arrival terminal and tried to call Hiran, but a canned voice kept telling him the number was not in service. He called Montreal and received the developments about Ramdev from Blu, along with Hiran's replacement number.

"There's something else," Blu had said. John groaned.

"No more, Blu. Please, man. This shit is too deep already." John leaned against one of the massive concrete pillars in the arrival hall.

"John," Blu whispered. "Tic is dead."

"What?" John barked. "How? When?" He pushed off the pillar and began pacing through the crowded terminal, the throngs of scurrying passengers parting like the Red.

"Cyanide. He was on his way to an arraignment, in the police van. It had to be the Fallen, John. Had to be."

John sank down into one of the plastic bench seats and held his head in his hands. His anger boiled up and threatened to explode, causing some very serious damage to the innocent passers-by. He took several deep breaths and swallowed his rage.

"You have to make this right, Blu," he said after a while. "Those rat fucks have to pay. I mean the ultimate price. I am so sick of this shit, Blu."

"I've got a plan. It may take some doing, but if I pull it off, we can sort this mess. Done, free and clear to run Montreal clean."

John took a deep breath and looked up at the television screen in the terminal. It was still littered with news coverage about the Cyber Hub shoot out and Dimpi's murder. Manoj Pandey's face appeared on the screen and John winced at the sight of him.

"Too many fires, brother. But I can't leave until I clean up the mess here," John sighed.

"I know, I know. I've got this. Trust me, Johnnie. I loved him too, we all did. I'll fix it."

"Tall order, brother. You gonna just snap your fingers at The Fallen? Make them disappear?" John scoffed.

There was a long pause. John could hear Blu scratching his beard and then a long sigh whistled through the receiver.

"Tell you what, let me think on this. End to end. Call me when you get to Mumbai and I'll fill you in on the plan. We need to discuss Billy and the hang-a-rounds too."

"Okay, Blu. Do what you need to. Don't hang on for me, bury Tic." It was a sour pill, but John had to swallow it. The situation here had to be rectified, and Blu had enough troubles to deal with. It was best to get Tic in the ground quickly so he could focus.

The loss of a brother dug deep at a biker's soul, but the club always came first. Even when that brother was a president. To that end, they could exact their revenge and balm their wounded psyche by lashing out, and in one fell swoop, right the wrong against the club, as well as satisfy their individual needs for recompense.

"Alright, Johnnie," Blu whispered. "The plans and arrangements are already happening. Oh! I almost forgot."

"What now?"

"Digger called. Found out about a guy you asked him about. Dean Crossman. He said you may know him as Mad Dog, or Mad Dog Dean. You know him?"

"Jesus! Yes, brother. That was our little Alex's dad. I rode with him in Ottawa and Toronto." John fell silent for a moment and read the headlines scrolling across the bottom of one of the random television monitors scattered about... *Police are still searching for Cyber Hub shoot-out culprits... NCB Agent Dimpi Shashidhar found murdered in Dwarka...*

"Fan-fucking-tastic," Blu muttered. "Now what?"

"I dunno, Blu. I have to think about it. Too many other pressing matters at the moment. We are splashed all over the news here."

"I feel you. But at the very least, it should buy the kid his life, no?"

"Yeah, I suppose. Lemme call Hiran," John said and hung up.

He called and confirmed the news of Ramdev's betrayal. John had stood in the arrival hall at Indira Gandhi International Airport and planned out a course of action.

Their corrupt NCB Director, Pandey, had called Hiran a few moments before, informing him about the security footage of the Farzi Cafe shootout. One of Udaipur chapter's members was en route to pick it up later today. But now that John had arrived, he could retrieve it. It was a much more secure plan. John instructed Hiran to call the Director back and move up the meeting time.

Next, he contacted Sumit, the president of the Mumbai chapter, and asked him to arrange a ticket for the first available flight to Mumbai. John warned him that under any circumstances, no one was to know he was in the country. He had a coffee and Sumit called him back. There was a Delhi / Mumbai flight in three-and-a-half hours, giving him enough time to deal with the Director. John caught a taxi and gave the driver the location he got from Hiran, a small food stall in Kashmiri Gate.

Forty minutes later, he was sitting across from the Director in a cramped city *dhaba*. He had retrieved the security video from Farzi. The manager there, a friend of the Horses, had kept it away from the police and turned it over to the Director's peon at their instruction.

"So... Manoj Pandey. At last, we meet face to face," John stated. He studied the man in front of him and formed an immediate dislike of him. He was wiry, shifty, and despite his value to the Club, John detested the fact that he was so corrupt.

"Yes, we do," he replied with a thin smile. "How are things in Montreal?"

"Oh, just peachy keen," John drawled. He hated making small talk with ass clowns.

"My daughter would have attended a University in Montreal. McGill. A fine school. That was before—"

"Before she started shooting brown sugar and taking it up the ass from bikers?" John interrupted.

"Yes. Before her addiction," he scowled. "We retrieved this from the security footage from Farzi Cafe the night of the incident." He handed John a silver pen drive.

"It's an interior shot of the club, from behind the stage, looking out over the restaurant. There is a ten second clip that shows Ramdev speaking with the band. Then in the background, walking towards the washroom appears our Agent Shashidhar."

"All right," John said, raising his eyebrows.

"Yes. Just before entering the lavatory, she turns and looks over her shoulder. At that moment, Ramdev also turns to return to his table. From the angle of the camera, they appear to make eye contact and acknowledge each other with a nod."

"Oh, very, very good." John smiled. "This is what we need. A fictitious tie between our Delhi president, whom we shall now label as rogue, and your dead agent who tried to help him out."

"Exactly. After receiving the details from Agent Kumar that your president had contacted him, I assumed this would be the road you would take. One rotten apple in an otherwise law-abiding club." Pandey flashed a snake-like smile.

"Humm," John murmured.

"Very fortuitous! It was pure luck the footage existed, and nothing more than chance Ramdev nodded when he did. Most likely he had made eye contact with someone else."

"Yeah. Fucking *fortuitous*," John sneered.

Pandey ignored the jibe and continued, "But it doesn't matter. It appears he is looking at Agent Shashidhar. More than enough to convince my NCB agents they knew each other and were working in tandem."

"So, a key of sugar and a brief conversation with your Agent Kumar should seal the deal that Ramdev Kapoor was rogue," John added. Director Pandey nodded and stood to leave.

"If there is nothing else."

"Yes, there is," John muttered. He stood and motioned to the Director. "Come." John led them out of the small restaurant and headed towards the alley beside it. Pandey stopped and his face clouded.

"Come. Come, Director," John chuckled, noting his concern. "Nothing sinister will happen to our biggest asset in India. I have a big ole bag of compensation for you, just here." John pointed down the alley. A weak smile broke on Pandey's lips.

The two of them entered the corridor behind the building. John picked his way through the soggy cardboard boxes and piles of rotting vegetables.

Rats scurried about as they disturbed the overstuffed nylon bags of refuse. The Director pinched his nose and squinted his eyes as they pressed deeper into the narrowing alley. Inky shadows enveloped them, shielding the pair from public view.

John spun on Pandey. The afternoon stubble from Pandey's neck bristled against John's palm as he grabbed his throat. The Director's face contorted as a scream gurgled from his gaping mouth. John's knuckles whitened as he twisted the raw flesh. Pandey's feet lashed out at him. John extended his arms and dug his fingertips deeper until Pandey dropped to his knees, and suffered all his direction-less rage. John needed to purge the fury that had built since he spoke to Blu. He wasn't in Montreal, and there was no way to help with that. Someone had to pay for Tic's death, and as he couldn't reach The Fallen, Pandey would do. John maintained the grip. Pandey's arms fell limp to his side and his body became dead weight. John tossed him into a sludge pile of rancid foodstuffs.

"Just takin' out the trash," John whispered as he stepped over the body and trotted towards the street corner where he had left the taxi waiting. He slid in the back seat.

"Airport," he said, and pondered the story he was about to tell. The taxi lurched out into traffic and John cursed. It was a thin tale to be sure, but it seemed the situation here was far worse than he feared. John had to hustle. He dialled the number Hiran had given him and took a deep breath.

"Hello?" a voice answered after several rings.

"Am I speaking with the Narcotics Control Bureau?" John asked.

"You are. Senior Agent, Avinash Kumar. To whom am I speaking?" Avi answered. John cleared his throat.

"Let's just say I am of upper management in the Iron Horses. I would like to discuss this developing situation."

"Situation?" Avinash asked.

"Yes, the situation in which you have a dead agent and we have a rogue president."

"I see," Avinash said. "Well, please do elaborate. What should I call you?" John ignored his question.

"The Horses have a very strict no drug policy. We don't deal, Agent Kumar. Simple as that. Whatever has happened between your agent and Ramdev Kapoor has nothing to do with us."

"Is that so?" Avi chuckled.

"Yes, that is so," John replied, his voice ringing with annoyance. "We are a law-abiding club." John winced as he used the term Pandey had uttered.

"We do not indulge in illegal activity. Ramdev was operating well outside the parameters of the MC. We were not aware of his activities, and whatever has happened was of his own doing. In over his head perhaps, I don't know. I hear that the drug dealing world is unsavoury, filled with disagreeable sorts."

"Humm, you think Ramdev got in trouble and came to the NCB to save himself? For what purpose would he implicate your entire *law-abiding* organisation, I wonder?"

"I imagine offering you an international drug ring would make you salivate, Agent Kumar. Isn't that what you guys do? Drool at the prospect of a big syndicate bust? A single foolhardy Indian that ensnared himself with an Afghan drug pusher isn't as appealing, is it?" John reasoned.

"I'm curious what the RCMP has to say about you, Mr...?" Avi left the question hanging. John winced, realizing they had already connected the dots to Canada; although deep down in his guts he knew they would have.

"Your accent betrays you, my friend. Did you think we were unaware of you?" Avi prompted.

"I would hope they tell you the same as I. Canadian Motorcycle Clubs don't deal in heroin."

"I'm *sure* that is what they will tell me. In the meantime, it would be tragic if any ill fate befell Ramdev. That would look suspicious. Don't you agree?" John stayed silent for a moment. He knew he should hang up, but his hatred of authority got the better of him.

"Accidents do happen though, don't they, Agent Kumar?" John disconnected the call without waiting for a reply.

The taxi wove its way along NH8 towards the airport. John had just enough time to catch his Mumbai flight and meet Sumit. There was much to decide. Ramdev must die.

* * *

Sandy watched Avinash as he was having his phone conversation with John. They were sitting in the back of the white SUV, heading towards Udaipur airport to catch a flight to Delhi, then another down to Goa several hours later. The Deputy Director had not seen this as an opportunity worth warranting one of NCB's private jets, nor had he felt like requisitioning military transport. It was a frustrating position for the two of them.

"The Canadians have landed," Avi said as he put down the phone.

"Shit," Sandy said. "So, all the cards are on the table?"

"That is the situation," Avi replied. He turned his head and peered out the window as he absently picked up the phone and spun it between his thumb and forefinger.

"They'll kill him, Avi. They will get rid of him and we will have nothing solid, nothing but a Motorcycle Club to sit and watch for weeks on end until they make a mistake," Sandy reasoned. "You know the Horses will be air tight after murdering Dimpi. How long before we catch another break on these guys? How long before they do something stupid?"

"Perhaps. But do we risk warning Ramdev? *Can we?*"

"Hell yeah!" Sandy blurted. "Why *wouldn't* we?"

Avi considered the question for a long time before answering. Sandy fidgeted in his seat. It was obvious he wanted to light a cigarette. Avinash also felt the urge to smoke. He put two fingers to his lips, motioning Sandy to give him one. Sandy drew his package from his pocket, removed the cigarettes and handed one to Avi.

Avi took it and drew deeply as Sandy brought the flame of his lighter to the tip. He savoured the smoke in his lungs and released a slow and deliberate exhale. Avinash knew this decision he was about to make could ruin his case. Dash it against the rocks like a fishing boat on high seas.

In all my years at the Narcotics Control Bureau, I have been a good agent. Good, not outstanding. I've never made a huge arrest, never closed the big case. This was the reason! he thought.

In every investigation, there comes a moment, a tipping point, where, if you make the right decision... glory. If you don't, you lose it all or end up with a partial bust. *I always make that one wrong decision, the crucial one.*

He took another long drag on the cigarette, coughing. Every fibre of his being, all his instincts as an officer, was telling him to warn Ramdev. That was the obvious move. *His club now knows he has come to us. If Ramdev realises that, he will run. Go so far underground, we will never hear from him again. But also, a chance he will come in for protection.* Procedure dictated that he tell him the truth and offer that protection.

That was what Avi's gut was telling him to do. But the nagging burn of his past mistakes and the knowledge that these bikers held no respect for the law caused him to think twice. *Would Ramdev trust me with his life?*

"We do nothing," he said. Sandy groaned in disapproval. "We'll get to him first, son. Without fail. We will bring him in." Avi resisted his instinct and made the opposite choice.

"Get on the phone to the airport authority. I want the name of every white male who has entered the country from Canada in the last forty-eight hours," Avi whispered.

"That is a huge ask, boss," Sandy said.

"I don't give a shit, Sandy. This time we will not settle for second best. This time we nail them all."

✦

CHAPTER ELEVEN

Candy sat cross-legged on her bed in the playroom of the Chevaux de Fer clubhouse. She rocked back and forth, pondering the events of the last several days. The gun fight, the death of Marceau, and her hasty decision to stay in Montreal as a bartender at a strip club, becoming the ole lady of a biker, surrounded by violence and drugs. *Is this what I want?* She wondered. *Back in a strip club, too. At least I can keep my clothes on this time.* Candy wrinkled her nose at the memory of a six-month stint served as a stripper in a sleazy bar in Mississauga. It had made her some quick cash, and that *was* where she met Alex. But there was no way in heaven or hell she would ever go back to being some prancing, pornographic pony for men to leer at and dream of riding. Bartending was a monumental step up from that.

"Better tips for my tits," she chuckled. *Far more lucrative than my last three jobs. And there's Charles to consider.*

She couldn't deny what she felt for Blu. *Wasn't there a name for that condition? Stockholm syndrome?* She shook her head no. She wasn't in love and she knew her mind. Blu was the level-headed gentle bear of a man that had always attracted her. Very unlike Alex.

Alex. Such a sweet guy, just not the guy. The two of them had always known their relationship would end one day. They were great in bed together and the laughs were plentiful, but he wasn't the man she envisioned waking up with every morning for the rest of her life. *He doesn't make me feel safe, grounded. Blu does. Sometimes, to get the man, you must accept the circumstances*, she thought. *Look how he managed that situation outside the club. He protected me, saved my life.*

This was Blu's lifestyle and if she wanted him, she would have to learn to live with it. She loved the concept of being a biker's woman. The freedom, excitement, the allure of living outside the law pulled at her wild nature. *What do I have waiting for me back in Toronto, anyway?*

"A few fair-weather friends and a dead-end job as a check-out girl," she whispered.

She looked at the floor and knew she had to talk with Alex. There was a soft knock.

"Darlin'? You decent?" Shotgun asked through the door.

"Not for years now," Candy giggled. "Come in." His bulky frame entered the room. The springs of the mattress depressed as he slumped on the bed beside her, absently placing his hand on her knee. Candy reached out and caressed his cheek.

"Are you okay?" she asked.

"Yeah, yeah. I'm fine, darlin'. Just a lot to do. Setting up the meet with the 13 Machine, planning for Tic, and the India situation is boiling over." He hung his head and sighed. "I've called for church tomorrow after the Toronto boys arrive. I'll be at the head of the table, Candy."

Candy concealed her shock at him discussing these things with her. She hadn't been privy to this lifestyle for long, but she knew that club business was club business and not shared with girlfriends or hang-arounds.

Candy slipped around behind him and popped up onto her knees. She caressed his back, squeezing his shoulders and driving her thumbs into the base of his neck. Shotgun groaned.

"Charles," she whispered.

"Hmmm?" he said, closing his eyes and lolling his head from side to side.

"I want to speak to Alex. Can I, can you call him?" Blu opened his eyes.

"Why, Candy?" He turned to face her. She dropped her gaze from his.

"I should tell him that..." She halted and gathered her thoughts. It had been obvious where this attraction was heading, but neither of them had said or acted on anything to make it real.

"I'm not a slut, Charles, I won't betray him, I can't. I just need to explain to him we are through." Her eyes misted.

"Do you think now is the best time to give him that kind of news? Your boyfriend is swimming in a deep pool of Indian dog shit." Candy nodded.

"It's time," she said. Shotgun glanced at his watch.

"Yeah, I can call Ramdev." He stood and fished his phone from his pocket. Candy returned to her cross-legged position, watched him dial and pace the room as it rang. He halted and smiled at her. It was as warm as a campfire. They both understood this was their tipping point. He motioned to her to give him a cigarette. Candy leaned forward and took the package off the bedside table.

"Hello, *bhai*," he said. Candy lit two cigarettes and handed him one.

What she didn't know was that Blu had spoken with John before coming to her room. John had filled him in on the ugly goings on in India and Blu was having a tough time using a cordial tone with Ramdev. To Candy, the conversation seemed natural enough.

"Yes, it's been a long time... Yes... No, No. Tic is out doing collections," he said.

Candy lilted her head and raised her eyebrows. *A lie!* she thought. Blu scowled and shook his head at her. "Listen, brother. I have to talk with Alex. Is he close by?" A half-smirk crossed Blu's face as he listened to the reply. "I don't care if he's got her hanging upside down from the ceiling," he said with a chuckle. "I need a word... okay, okay." Blu covered the phone with his hand.

"This may not be as painful as you feared, darlin'. Looks like your sweetheart has a little stress relief partner of his own."

Candy recoiled. *Alex is fucking another woman?* She didn't love him, true. But she disliked the idea of being disregarded so quick for another lover.

"Alex is *what*? Is he now? No, Tic didn't say a word about his performance. That surprises the shit outta me, *bhai*," Blu continued. "So, we should patch Alex in then? Full member?" he said, still chuckling and again covering the phone. "It seems little Alex has taken to the biker lifestyle well. Ramdev thinks we should consider him for membership," he told her, raising his eyebrows in exaggerated surprise.

"Yes, okay, thanks." Blu took a drag on his smoke while he waited. He gave Candy a quick wink. "Alex? It's Shotgun Blu. Candy wants to speak with you... I don't have a clue, fuckwad. Ask her yourself," he said and handed her the phone.

"Alex?" Candy whispered.

"Hey you," Alex stammered.

"Are you with someone?" she asked. Alex's exhale whistled through the receiver.

"Look, Candy, there's a girl." There was an audible slap of a hand on bare flesh through the receiver. "A woman, I mean... here... I, I mean, we..." Candy smiled despite herself.

"It's okay, Alex," she whispered. "That's why I wanted to talk to you. Things have changed here too." She flashed Blu a soft smile. "I have done some thinking and decided I want to stay in Montreal when you come back. You *are* coming back, right? You're okay?"

"I'm fine, Candy, I'm fine. Stay there? You mean, live there?"

"Yes, Alex. I'm sure that's what I want."

"If that's what will make you happy, Candy. We all need to find happiness, right? Don't stress, it will be fine. Just do what you need to do, okay?"

"Okay, Alex. Be safe, and thank you." The phone hissed with the static of an overseas connection for a moment.

"For what?" Alex asked. Candy paused as she tried to find the right words. The absurdity of how this relationship was ending struck her. It was laughable.

"For the last two years, I guess. Just thank you, Alex. Please take care, come back in one piece. We can talk more when you're here," she whispered.

"It's okay," he said. "I think we understand each other."

"Goodbye, Alex," she said and ended the call.

Candy handed the phone back to Blu. He took her hand and squeezed. He looked at her in a way that made her fearful and unsure.

"I can't promise you a goddamn thing, darlin'," he drawled.

"I know. Don't need a *goddamn thing*. Just you, Charles, if you'll have me." He smiled at her.

"Please stop calling me that," he chuckled. Candy stood and leapt into his arms, pressing her lips to his. Blu enveloped her and kissed her deeply as he carried her to the bed.

He tossed her onto the mattress. She squealed playfully, bouncing straight back up and clawing at his belt buckle. Candy peered up with a devilish grin as she freed him from his jeans.

"I will call you whatever I want, mister," she said as she massaged him to full rigidity. "And you will *like* it," she said, dipping her head. Shotgun moaned.

"Yes, I believe I will," he whispered.

✳ ✳ ✳

Blu sat in the clubhouse, awaiting Digger and the rest of the Toronto chapter. He lit a joint and watched as the smoke swirled in the sunlight streaming through the rear window. He had left Candy sleeping after an interminable session of lovemaking in his room.

The deal was closed with her. *Damn, she's barely over half my age.* He tried not to analyse it too much. He had been with plenty of women younger than him, but this was different. She wanted more, the full patch, to be his Ole Lady. He smiled to himself. *Why not?* Led Zeppelin erupted from his cell on the table, demanding he needed a *Whole Lotta Love.*

"Yeah?" he answered. There was a considerable amount of static. He knew who it was.

"Hello, brother. How's the weather?" John asked.

"No change since we spoke a few hours ago. Stormy, and it's not looking to clear up soon," he mused.

"I'm feeling you. What's the present situation?" John asked. Blu sighed, took a last hit on the joint, and snuffed it out in the ashtray.

"I'm waiting for Digger. We will vote on whether to patch over what's left of the 13 Machine. There is only one way this thing can go, so I reached out to Taz Richards. He is acting president of the 13."

"I know him," John said.

"I've invited him to Tic's cremation. Before the ceremony, I'll take him aside and make the pitch. Like I said, we don't have too many options. It's a fucking nightmare, bro. I wish you were here."

"Look, speaking of Tic, you need to step up, take the big chair until I get back. You're next in line according to bye-laws. We will do a proper vote when I get my feet back on Canadian soil. Two days at most, brother."

"Shit," Shotgun muttered.

"Easy, big fella, you'll be fine. Lean on Digger if needed. You've got this," John soothed.

"I'm waiting to fly down to Mumbai at the moment. I spoke with our asset; seems our number two here was correct about our number one. We have a cavity, bro, so I'm gonna pull the tooth." There was a pause. "We need to discuss our top-level friend."

"Okay," Shotgun said. "The thoughts you were having on the way to the airport? The ones regarding Pandey and his continued use to us?"

"Yeah, I made the call on the spot, Blu. Like we considered. If we play with snakes, we're gonna get bit. The whole vibe, brother. We needed distance from that. The rewards ain't worth the risk at this point."

"Agreed. This crap keeps getting deeper."

"You may need wings to stay above it before this is over," John chuckled.

The rumble of a half dozen bikes split the silence of the room.

"The boys are here, John. Gotta go. Keep in touch, brother. Let me know when the deed is complete and stay whole, okay?" Blu said.

"All right. You too, big man. Stay watchful. I have a nasty feeling, *comprende*? With Tic removed, it won't be long before the Fallen Angels come knocking."

"I'm on it. *Ciao*, brother," Blu said and hung up the phone.

"Look at the size of you!" Digger's voice boomed out. "You know gravy is a condiment, not a beverage, right?" he roared.

"Fuck you, Digg," Shotgun laughed. "You aren't the poster boy for Lean Cuisine yourself!" Blu stood, and the two embraced.

"It's been too long, my friend," Digger said, smiling.

"It has," he said, lighting a cigarette. Blu smiled as Digger's son, Tommy, made his way over and embraced him. One by one Blu welcomed each of the Toronto chapter brothers who had made the ride through the night.

Riley the VP, Shiny the Sergeant at Arms, Ricky T their secretary, and a couple of prospects Blu had never met. As they greeted each other and chatted, the rest of the Montreal crew filtered into the chamber. Alain, Tracy, and Clipper, who was still limping. Clipper made his way over to Blu and Digger.

"So, you ain't dead after all!" Digger said and embraced him with care.

"Me?" Clipper laughed. "Not a chance, brother. I'm too fuckin' ugly to die!" The group chatted and laughed for a while, then Blu called for their attention.

"Welcome, brothers. It's very comforting to see you all, but if you would,"—Blu motioned to the chapel—"there is club business to attend to." The group moved towards the door. Blu caught Tracy's eyes and called him over to join him.

"Call those three hang-arounds we were discussing; we will vote on their prospect patch. And speaking of prospect, where the fuck is Billy?"

"I don't know, captain," Tracy said with a scowl.

"Call him, get him in here too. Do it quick, Tracy, I need you in there." Blu nodded towards the chapel. Tracy grasped his shoulder hard.

"No worries," he whispered.

"Quick like a bunny," Blu said.

The group walked into the chapel and Blu closed the door behind them. They packed the place, the Toronto executives taking up the vacant seats left by John and Tracy, with the prospects sitting on the stools brought in from the bar. Tic's seat was open and everyone's eyes turned to Blu as he strode towards it. He stood at the head of the table and cleared his throat. The chamber went silent.

"Gentlemen, I included the prospects for the first bit of this meeting as it is a grave situation and I want all of us on the same page. First off,"— Blu paused, taking a breath—"I will act as interim president until John's return as per our line of succession bye-laws. I hope there are no issues here?" There was a small round of applause and Blu smiled.

"It's all good, brother," Clipper shouted, and the claps became more vigorous.

"Okay, okay, guys," Blu said, trying to keep the smile from his face.

"As you are all aware, this is because of Tic's... "—Blu clouded as his voice reduced to a whisper—"Tic's murder."

There was a soft murmur throughout the room and the mood sobered. Blu paused a moment and steadied himself on the back of the chair.

"Just to update our Toronto brothers, we think this results from a chain of events over the last few days. We have every reason to believe that the Fallen Angels are behind these occurrences and his murder." Shotgun sank into the chair.

"They've been trying to gaslight us into believing the 13 Machine is making a comeback in the west end. We think their hope is we will go off half-cocked and retaliate. A revenge effort to wipe them out." He let them absorb that.

"Then with our numbers depleted and exhausted, they'll try to gain control of Montreal, and stamp out the Chevaux de Fer forever. When we didn't take the bait, they moved on Tic. My guess is, with our president gone, they'll attempt to do the job themselves."

The room bubbled over with condemnations and profanity. Blu waved his hands for silence and after a few moments, a hush fell back over them. "So, we've called our Toronto brothers here for support."

"Bring those rat pricks on, Blu!" one of the Toronto prospects shouted and Digger shot him a stern look.

"I know we are all hurting over the loss of Marceau. He was an honourable man, a solid leader, and our trusted brother. We will cremate him today at Crématorium Mont-Royal, at 3 o'clock."

Tracy entered with Billy in tow and gave a nod to Blu. They took up positions at the back of the crowd. Blu continued, "It's on Chemin de la Forêt Outremont, close to here. Don't be late. You can see Tracy for directions." A ripple of acknowledgement flowed around the table.

"All right, with all that said, prospects... fuck off." Blu smiled. There were a few chuckles as the junior members stood and left the room, ushered out by Billy.

"Off we fuck!" he shouted as he closed the door behind them. The group chuckled.

"Okay, gentlemen," Blu continued. "We need to talk about Billy. He's been with us, what? Eighteen months?" There was a murmur of agreement. "Does anyone have any reason we shouldn't consider him for a full patch? Any concerns at all?"

"Other than his ugly fucking face?" Clipper asked and everyone laughed.

"He's an obedient kid, Blu," Tracy said. "It's been overdue, I would say."

"No worries here, Blu. I like him, despite myself," Alain added.

"Christ on a pony, that settles it then. Alain doesn't like anyone!" Clipper said, and they erupted in laughter again.

"Fair enough, all in favour?" Blu asked. The Montreal crew's hands rose. "I spoke with John earlier. His proxy vote was in favour. No opposition? Passed." Shotgun Blu dropped the gavel on the hardwood table for the first time. His heart skipped as he did it.

"All right, next, the hang-arounds. I understand we are putting the bum's rush on this, but we are heading for some stormy waters and we need the troops. We can't ask a man to protect a club he is not a member of," Blu explained.

"So, Pig Sty, Glenn, and Stephan. What's the feel' on them?"

"Pig Sty is golden. I'll be honest, I don't know Stephan all that well. For me, Glenn is out. He's a shifty prick and we shouldn't trust him with all that Bolivian marching powder that he hoovers up his nose," Tracy said.

"Let me assure you about Stephan, brothers," Clipper said. "He's solid. I wouldn't have vouched for him if I weren't sure. He's been with us six months now, and rocky ones to boot. He has been at every event we allowed him to attend and has raised no red flags. As for Glenn, I agree, it's too soon. He's odd. Seems he's brother potential, but there are too many unknowns."

"Let's not be hasty because we need more bodies, boys. Pig Sty, no doubt. Stephan, I'll go for it. I trust Clip's judgement. I haven't spent enough time with Glenn to comment." Alain added.

"Okay, all in favour of a prospect patch for Pig Sty and Stephan?" Blu asked. Again, it was unanimous, and he banged the gavel. "Digg, any business you want to address with your crew?" Blu turned to him. Digger was lighting a cigarette and smiled at him through the exhale.

"No, we decided before we rode up, brother. Our two prospects are ready to be patched," he said.

"Good, good. We will tell them after the cremation. That leads to the next piece of business. The Montreal 13 Machine. I've asked Taz Richards to meet me before the cremation. I will propose we patch over the remaining members of their club."

"We all expected this was coming, chief," Tracy said.

"Not to meddle in your business, Shotgun, but you've thought this through?" Digger asked.

"Yes, it seems pointless to carry these old hatreds. The Machine are toast, but we need what's left of them. The pockets of the island still loyal to them could come in very handy. It's a simple truth. The Fallen will start their push for control soon. I don't want to just hold them off this time. I want what *they* want, to end it once and for all," Blu explained. Shiny from Toronto raised his hand and Shotgun nodded at him.

"Do we have any intel on the Fallen's numbers, Blu? Any idea what they may plan?" he asked.

"Speculation," Blu said. "We are flying blind here. Their present Montreal strength is around eight, but they can call on their Boston chapter easily enough. It could bring them up to twenty. As far as where and when they hit us, it's anyone's guess. But I promise you this, brothers, it will be soon. Without Tic, they must feel they've depleted us and we don't associate the Fallen with the virtue of patience."

✳ ✳ ✳

Griff sat in the chapel on the second floor of 9756 Notre-Dame St. Est, the Fallen Angels' clubhouse. He was pushing cigarette butts around in the ashtray with the tip of his smoke, waiting for the impending meeting. The meet that was to decide which club gains control of Montreal. He wiped a thin film of sweat from his brow.

The two-year turf war with the Machine had left the Fallen Angels with a sizable part of east Montreal to command. It had been a merciless and bloody war that fostered his deep-seated hatred for the 13 and the Horses. The 13 were all but cleaned out, but the Horses stood fast in the west.

The Montreal 13 Machine had been the dominant force when the Fallen had arrived. Montreal was theirs. The Chevaux de Fer had been nothing but a thorn in the 13's side. During the conflict, the Chevaux de Fer began moving heroin and gained money and power. *They're just a small splinter chapter from Toronto who wormed their way onto the island by peddling prostitutes giving back alley blow-jobs,* he thought.

With the confusion caused by the war, the Horses took control of the west end by gobbling up open territory that the Fallen had won, but not yet secured. They provided protection to the business owners there, who had grown weary of the car bombs and gun battles in the streets. Soon after their infestation, a pusher popped up on every street corner and in a good number of bars and strip clubs as well, each of them peddling nickel decks or duce bags. Heroin fed the Chevaux de Fer's growth.

Griff smashed out his cigarette, spilling the ash onto the table. *I came to Montreal to climb the ranks of my MC, not to trip over that wannabe biker club*, he thought.

The Montreal chapter of the Fallen Angels was eleven members strong. Hard men, each of them up to the task of exterminating the Horses. Another fifteen brothers had ridden up from Boston, by far the strongest of the Fallen's many chapters.

They were hardcore bikers, fearless, and willing to lay down their lives for the Club. They were filtering into the room. Griff wrung his hands and pursed his lips.

I have to hard sell here. If they don't believe I've planned this last push well, there will be questions and unrest.

Alfredo Guzzi took his seat at the head of the table with a curt nod to the group. Alfie was a lifer and looked it, with long black hair and a nasty pink knife scar that popped on his left cheek against his olive leathered skin. He wore a faded jean cut. While most of the younger members and prospects favoured the leather, the old boys stuck to denim.

"Good morning, gentlemen," he began. "And welcome to our Boston brothers. Thank you for making the trip up to assist us with our local annoyances. We have been engaging in a three-way turf war in Montreal for quite some time now. We plan to close out this battle once and for all and assume control of the island." He paused.

"The Montreal 13 Machine are all but wiped out and no longer pose a significant threat to our interests here. However, the Chevaux de Fer, the Iron Horses, have secured a stronghold on the west end. The heroin, protection, and prostitution trades are very lucrative there and we intend to claim them as our own." He turned to Griff.

"I'll hand it over to my Sergeant at Arms, Griff. For those of you who don't know him, Griff was with our Tampa Bay chapter for many years, but as he has Canadian relatives, migrated up here to help found our Montreal chapter. Griff?"

"Thank you, Alfie." Griff stood. He felt the blood pounding in his ears. He scanned the room, making eye contact with each member before he began.

"Yesterday, the Chevaux de Fer's president committed suicide. This leaves the chapter in some disarray." A chuckle rolled around the table.

"We know there will be a cremation today at 3:00 for Marceau. There will be full attendance. This should leave their clubhouse empty and unprotected. We'll take this opportunity to plant a firebomb on the roof of the clubhouse." Griff stepped back and walked counterclockwise around the room, his cowboy boots clunking on the tile floor.

"The clubhouse is in a multi-unit complex, and they occupy the two north-end units. However, the other tenant is a small carpet distributor, who uses Budget Rental trucks for the bulk of their deliveries. It's not uncommon for several of them to be in the lot. At this moment, there is one of these trucks en route from Ontario. We liberated it from a Kingston garage last night and we *persuaded* the mechanic not to report the theft until tomorrow." The statement raised a few chuckles.

"Tonight, we'll be in this truck, parked across from the rear entrance of the Horses' unit. There'll be a wake to honour their fallen brother. This works to our advantage. We'll let them drink themselves stupid, then at 1:00 am, detonate the explosive and let the roof collapse on their grieving process. The blast will be large, and we won't have much time." Griff lit a cigarette while that sank in.

"We expect a response from the police in eight minutes, enough of a window for us to clean out whoever is staggering around in the rubble. After the blast, we'll rush the rear door, smash it down, and kill whatever is moving. Questions?"

One of the Boston crew raised his hand and Griff acknowledged him.

"Is the firepower sorted?" he asked. Griff nodded.

"Yes, we know you can't carry over the border. We have it looked after with a half dozen AK's, two Uzis, and a collection of Glocks." The member nodded.

"All right, gentlemen, we'll leave here at midnight. Stay chill until then."

* * *

It had been a slow procession from the clubhouse to the morgue. After retrieving the casket, Shotgun Blu had led the hearse on his bike. Behind them, a two-by-two column of rumbling Harley Davidson motorcycles followed. With their helmets off and full colours on display, the motorcade cut through the heart of Montreal, carrying their slain comrade on one last ride.

The pack had stayed in tight formation. There was a squeak from Blu's brakes as he slowed them to a halt in front of the huge double oak doors of the crematorium. His boot heel crunched in the wet gravel of the lot as he swung his leg and dismounted. The persistent drizzle popped and hissed on the engine as he left his bike rumbling.

Hoisting the white coffin from the rear of the hearse with Clipper, Tracy, Alain, Digger, and Tommy, the procession trudged up the path and into the viewing area of the chapel. After setting their brother atop the marble pedestal, Blu whispered a silent prayer, and retreated to the parking lot.

In 1901, the Mount Royal Cemetery Company had established the first crematorium in Canada and it was the right place to say goodbye to Tic. Blu stood in the parking lot. The sky was cold, wet, and grey, and the air stung his cheeks. Blu shivered as he lit a joint and strolled along the line of bikes. They had backed each of them into the curb, with headlights left on, a precise and uniform honour guard. Blu exhaled a long stream of smoke; it mixed with the mist from his breath. He blinked his damp eyes several times as a low groan passed his lips. Marceau Gagnon had been a close brother for ages. *I'm gonna miss that bastard.*

A red and white Bonjour taxi pulled in and stopped in front of him. Candy's black stocking leg extended from the door. As her stiletto boot heel came to rest on the pavement, his heart skipped. She glanced up at him through her bangs and half veil and smiled at him. Sour frustration replaced it as the other girls babbled and sobbed in the taxi behind her. A few of the Horse Heads that Tic had favoured.

"Hey, babe," she muttered, taking the joint off him and hitting it twice. "How are you doing?"

"Me?" he chuckled. "Better than you it seems." Candy rolled her eyes at the women. The distant growl of a bike overpowered their chatter. "That's Taz. Go on, darlin', get them inside. I'll be in shortly." Blu patted her ass. Candy kissed him on the cheek and then wiped her lipstick off it with her thumb.

"All right, be quick," she whispered. "Let's go, ladies." Candy barked at the other women. Blu smiled. It hadn't taken her long to assume the role of a high-ranking Ole Lady. They followed her up the sidewalk to the doors like ducklings following their mother. Shotgun turned as Taz pulled into the parking lot.

Taz Richards was a sizable man, not Blu size, but hefty enough in his own right. He peeled off his helmet, exposing his short salt and pepper hair and matching goatee. He sported two thick silver earrings in each ear and a heavy silver necklace. Blu felt the tension between them. They had been bitter rivals for many years. Taz was wearing his Montreal 13 Machine cut over a frayed jean jacket. It was a minor act of provocation. Blu ignored it.

"Hi, Taz. Thank you for coming," he said.

"Hello, Shotgun. I'm sorry about the circumstances. There was a time Marceau and I were drinking buddies," he said, clasping Blu's offered hand and firmly shaking it.

"He mentioned it often."

"I bet he did," Taz laughed. "I hate to be forward, but I have an idea why you asked me here, Blu." Taz's eyes narrowed as he spoke. "If it's what I believe it to be, then I don't think you're gonna be pleased."

"Hear me out, Taz," Blu said and motioned for them to walk. The two of them strolled towards the entrance. The awkward silence underscored the gravity of the impending conversation. Blu stopped beside a small marble bench, shy of the doors. He turned and faced Taz.

"It's not all that complicated. These fucking Fallen Angels are forcing my hand. This mess"—he nodded towards the crematorium—"is just the beginning. It will pop off again, Taz. These ass clowns won't leave it be, they want the whole fucking island. We could hold them off, that's the goddamn truth, but at what cost?"

"Humm, that *is* the question," Taz said. Blu nodded.

"Yeah, it's a mother of a question, Taz. I don't want a dozen Chevaux bodies piling up in my backyard again. I'd settle for the west end of the island, for now. But push has definitely come to shove, my friend. They murdered our president, man. We have no option but to slit their fucking throats. They knew it when they did it, but my belief is, they wanted us to think it was you."

"Blu... " Taz said, raising his hands.

"I know. I know you had nothing to do with it. Look, Taz, level with me. What are your numbers like?" Taz's face contorted. He glared at him, eyes filled with the pain of sour memories and bitter losses.

"You got brass fucking balls, man," he whispered through clenched teeth. Blu stepped back and exhaled a deliberate breath.

"We both lost, Taz. Loyal men... brothers. It was not a one-sided affair."

"And now we just shack up together? For what, Blu? The greater fucking good? Six months ago, you and I were shooting at each other in an alley behind a fucking pool hall. Do you remember that? Now you want to what? Patch me over?" Blu held his gaze firm and nodded. Taz scoffed. "Jesus H Christ," he spat.

"What's stopping you, Taz? You're the president of the only chapter. You have no one else to answer to. It makes sense. We combine forces, stomp out the Angels and take the island, all of it. We all win, Taz."

"Tell you what," Taz said.. He lit a cigarette, snapped his zippo shut, and blew the smoke at Shotgun. "You step up with the honesty, what are *your* numbers like? How about your H trade? Will we get a taste of that? The whores? Is there enough pussy for everyone? You're gonna divvy up all that cash and share?"

Blu pressed his fingertips into his eyes and then rubbed his temples. *If I have any chance of swaying him, I have to put everything on the table,* Blu thought. Taz was old school, a true biker. He lived by the code, and Blu had to believe if he could reason with him, he would understand this was the best move for both of them. *Goddamn, I wish John was here.*

"In Montreal, we have a dozen patched, two prospects, and a few a hang-arounds. Toronto is double that. The Hamilton chapter is new, with eight solid guys, as is the one in Halifax. We are looking at a couple of clubs to patch over in Winnipeg and Calgary. India is solid. We patched over an existing MC, the Bull Riders. Nine chapters over 200 strong." Taz whistled.

"It's not just the numbers, okay? When this breaks open with the Fallen, I want all my enemies in front of me. If we do go toe to toe with them, I can't have you nipping at my ass from behind." Taz nodded at the logic.

"A spot at the table for you, Sergeant at Arms, full membership. *Equal* membership for your patches, but not the prospects. They have to serve their hang-around time with us. But you tell them, Taz, if they patch, our war is over. No lingering bullshit. If they don't join, they had best lay fucking low. If any ex-Machine pokes his head up out of the weeds, we will blow it clean off. They get the pass to walk away whole, but they have to walk away."

"I have your word?" Taz asked.

"Solid as oak."

"President to Sergeant is a fuck of a pay cut, Blu."

"No one will disrespect you, Taz. They will hear your voice loud and clear at the table. Think about it." Taz shook his head. His silver earrings clinked.

"I'll take it to our table. I don't know what they will say. Hell, man, I'm not even sure how I feel about this." He glanced at his watch.

"Come inside, brother. Say goodbye, then go talk to your club. Yes, no, or maybe, whatever the decision, come to the wake tonight. We can talk more then, if needed, field any question your boys may have. We can work out logistics," Blu said.

"It's a little early to call me *brother*." They both chuckled and trudged towards the entrance. Blu pulled open the massive door and motioned for Taz to enter. Taz paused. "How in the holy hell and heaven high do you believe this will work?" he asked.

"I have faith, Taz. Miles and miles of faith."

* * *

A man was scaling up the roof access ladder on the north side of 115 Claire Crt. He was wearing a crisp pair of navy blue coveralls with *Bell Canada* embroidered in white across the back. A leather tool belt hung from his hip, and a small satchel slung over his shoulder waved from side to side as he climbed. Griff sat in the cab of the stolen rental truck with Alfredo Guzzi, across the street, watching his progress.

"I should have done it," Griff whispered.

"Why? We have a demolition expert visiting," laughed Alfie. "Fresh from the United States Marine Corps." He clasped Griff on the shoulder and shook him. "No?"

"Yes," Griff replied, never taking his eyes off their guy on the roof as he hurried towards the air conditioning unit in the centre. "No, no, you stupid prick. Not the AC unit. That's too far from the main room."

The man reached the massive unit and put his back to it. Facing due north, he paced and after ten steps, crouched and disappeared from view. Griff sighed. "Okay," he whispered.

"The first door there?" Alfredo asked, pointing to the rear of the building. Griff tore his gaze from the rooftop and followed his gesture.

"Yes, that leads to a short hallway, then into their primary room. We will park the van there, backed into the fence," he said, motioning to a spot beside a garbage dumpster, 20 metres opposite the door.

"At ten to one, three men will station themselves across the road at the front entrance in case anyone staggers out that way. Then after the blast, the rest of us will go in the back and clear out the building. By 1:08, we should all be back in the rig and out of here."

"*Tre bien*," Alfredo said. Griff glanced at the clock on the dashboard.

3:15. Plenty of time before the Horses returned. He opened the driver's door and swung his legs out of the cab. "Where you going?" Alfredo asked.

"Just taking another quick look around, make sure there is nothing to snag us up," he said and sprinted across the road.

The Horses had installed three security cameras, one each on the front and back entrance doors and one on the corner of the building. It gave an overall view of the parking lot. The tech on the roof had reappeared and Griff waved at him, then pointed to the lot camera. He nodded and moved towards it.

As Griff watched, the man knelt and leaned over the edge, fiddling with the wires behind the device. After a moment, he stood and dragged two fingers across his neck in cut-throat motion.

Griff walked into the lot towards the rear entrance and got as close as he dared. He noticed nothing that raised cause for alarm. Standard door and hinges. *A sledgehammer should make quick work of it, if it's still an issue after the blast.*

Nodding to himself, he did a loop around the twenty metres they would have to cover from the van to the entrance. He checked the spot he was planning to park, looking for nails or broken glass. *A flat tire will not play well tonight.*

Satisfied, he turned on his heel and walked back towards the stolen transport. With a glance up, he spun his finger in the air, giving the all clear to reconnect the camera. That was when the police cruiser crept around the corner.

"Perfect," Griff muttered. The driver door of the cab was still open. The officer was clearly eyeballing it. *If he spots the Ontario plates, it may intrigue him enough to run them. They may even come up stolen.* The patrol car slowed to a stop in front of him and the cop put it in park, smiling at Griff through the windshield. After a brief pause, he got out.

"*Bonjour, bonne après-midi,*" the constable said. Griff twisted his face into a plastic smile.

"Pleasant afternoon, Constable," he said. The cop nodded and switched to English.

"Have a problem?" he asked.

"No. No, sir. We just got ourselves a little turned around. We were searching for the highway."

"Humm," he muttered, noting Griff's cut and then looking to the truck. Guzzi was sitting motionless in the passenger seat. "Fallen Angels. Yes, I would say you're far from home," the cop said. His hand dropped to the butt of his revolver as he glanced over his shoulder at the Chevaux de Fer clubhouse. He clearly knew where he was and with whom he was dealing. "What's in the back?" he asked, gesturing to the rig.

"It's empty," Griff said, maintaining his facade of goodwill.

"Is that so?"

"Yes, sir." Griff let his eyes drift past him to the rooftop. No sign of their man.

"Wouldn't be full of those Native brand cigarettes your lot like to smuggle in here off the Ontario Reservations, would it?"

"No, no, sir. Empty, like I said. One of our... members had a fall in Toronto. We were just bringing his bike home. Already dropped it off, and we're heading back to Toronto now. We just missed the highway, as I said." Normally Griff's tone would drip with malice when speaking to a police constable, but now was not the time. He saw the bomb tech drop off the last rung of the access ladder and skirt across the road.

"I see. A fall, eh?" he repeated. "Let's have a look, shall we?" He took a step forward and beckoned Alfredo to get out of the cab. Alfie opened the door. "Around the front, if you please," the cop called to him.

Alfredo complied and walked around the nose of the truck to join them. The constable further slowed his pace, allowing the two of them to lead towards the rear.

"Is he all right?" the policemen asked. "Your *member*?"

"Yes, yes, Officer. A couple of broken ribs is all," Griff said and tensed as they rounded the back of the truck. He was half expecting to see their man waiting there with his gun drawn. The constable stopped as if sensing his trepidation. He circled them and stood a full five metres behind the truck.

"Open it," he said. He spread his stance and his knees flexed. The cop's hand was grasping the butt of his gun now. Griff shrugged and grabbed the handle of the roll-up door.

"Hands where I can see them, please," the cop commanded. They complied. He pulled the lever and shoved the door. It clattered, echoing off the vacant interior of the cargo van as the taut springs snapped it open. The trio stood in silence, staring into the empty compartment. Griff turned towards him.

"See?" he said.

The cop relaxed and his hand fell away from his holster. At that moment, their man appeared from the culvert behind them and crept towards the officer. Griff took a step forward and raised his hands. The policemen reacted to his panicked expression and tried to draw his pistol.

The bomb tech grabbed his forehead and folded him backwards like a matchbook cover. With one fluid motion, the nine inch long blade of his bowie knife slid through the base of the officer's neck. Blood spurted from the cop in a fountain as the shiny tip exited from his mouth. His eyes rolled back in his head as he spewed a watery gurgle. The constable crumpled to the ground; his gun still tucked away in its holster.

"You fucking moron!" Griff shouted as Alfredo sprinted forward and grabbed the falling body. "We were clear of him!"

"The fuck you were!" the tech said as he grasped hold of the fallen officer with Guzzi.

"Oh, we are fucking done! This is brilliant!" Griff screamed at him.

"Move!" Guzzi barked as the two of them dragged the body to the truck. Griff stepped aside and watched them hoist it into the back. "Close the fucking door," he said to Griff, then pointing at the tech. "You get in that cruiser and ditch it up near Mount Royal. Don't fucking speed, these cars are GPS tracked. Let's hope he had just started his shift, it's bad enough he's about to go off his patrol route."

The bomb tech sprinted towards the cruiser, picking up the officer's cap out of the dirt on his way.

"*Fils de pute!!* Make sure you rip out the dashcam," Griff shouted after him.

"If we get out of this, it will be a goddamn miracle," Alfredo whispered. "Come on, *permet de retourner au* clubhouse. Move, move."

Griff and Alfredo climbed into the cab and fired the engine. The truck pulled away in a cloud of dust as the cop's blood soaked into the gravel of the soft shoulder.

* * *

Friday night they'll be dressed to kill, down at Dino's Bar 'n' Grill. The drink will flow and the blood will spill, and if the boys want to fight, you better let'em. Thin Lizzy's classic pounded out amidst the laughter and screams in the Chevaux de Fer's clubhouse.

Marceau *Tic Tock* Gagnon's wake had begun after seven and was still going strong just shy of midnight. A few of the lads positioned Tic's orange Road Glide in the middle of the suite. They had stuck varied pictures of Marceau to it. The most predominant was his 2002 mug shot Clipper had put on the gas tank. Tracy had perched the urn with Marceau's ashes on the seat and someone had secured a blow up sex doll with a banana rammed in its mouth to ride bitch.

Shotgun stood with his back to the bar, surveying the smoke-filled room. He leaned with his elbows on the oak counter and one boot heel hooked over the foot rail. There was a pint in his left hand, a joint in the right and as he watched, Candy was slapping away Alain's hand from lifting her ridiculously short skirt. Digger approached and stood next to him. The music pounded and the smell of weed and beer wafted through the air.

"She's a fine one," Digger chuckled as Candy stuck her tongue out at Alain, then looked to Blu to flash him a wicked smile. He laughed despite himself. He hadn't announced them as a couple, but the boys didn't miss much.

"She's a bloody handful is what she is," he said. Digger patted his belly.

"She'll keep you young and fit, my brother," he laughed. "It's almost 12:00. Make the official announcements and welcomes. But wait a few minutes yet, okay? I know it's just window dressing, but this wake is about to turn into a patch over party. Marceau's funeral and the surprise amalgamation of our two clubs shouldn't be on the same day."

"Um," Blu muttered. "There's a lot of protocol and tradition we need to adhere to, bro."

"That there is. Let's have a toast." Digger called to Clipper who was standing behind the bar. "Clip, pour up some Jack!" Clipper nodded. "Tracy, Alain... come," Digger bellowed. The five of them gathered as Clipper brought the tray of whiskey. Digger lifted his shot glass.

"I fear not my final miles, I know my time has come. Lay down my bike, pack my leathers, do the things that must be done. I fear not my final miles, for in my brothers' hearts I drum, resting easy with the knowledge, forever we are one. Marceau!"

They chorused Tic's name, downed the whiskey, and in unison, smashed their glasses on the floor. The commotion drew concern from the room. Someone lowered the music and the crowd looked to the five of them. Blu glanced at Digger, who chuckled and shrugged.

"Brothers," Shotgun called out. "Can I have your attention for just a few moments?" He strode to the centre of the room and placed his beer on the seat of Tic's bike. He laid his hand on the urn and stood silent. The crowd shifted, so no one was standing behind him. Blu looked up to view those in attendance.

"I would like to thank everyone here for coming this evening and helping us remember Marceau's brotherhood and celebrate his life." The room burst into applause and shouts. Blu waited for the din to quieten down before continuing.

"All that needed to be said was said at the service and I won't dwell." He looked at the urn. "We loved you, brother. We will miss you." Aside from scattered murmurs and a few soft sobs, the room remained silent.

"I'm sure you have all noticed the members of the Montreal 13 Machine that have come tonight to pay respects." Again, there were mixed murmurs from the crowd. "Taz, will you and your crew join me, please?"

"Righto," came a call from the back of the room as Taz and seven members of the Montreal 13 Machine made their way forward.

"Taz Richards and I met this afternoon, and we have decided after much deliberation, to create some scrap of good from Tic's tragedy." He paused as the eight of them assembled in front of Tic's bike.

"We will patch over the remaining Montreal 13 and join to fight off this fucking scourge, the Fallen Angels, before they tear our beloved Montreal to pieces!" They removed their cuts and dropped them at Blu's feet. The room was silent for a heartbeat and then exploded into frivolity.

The announcement was only for the prospects, hang-arounds, and Horse Heads. After a lengthy conversation, the membership had voted on the move after the cremation. It had been a spirited argument, but Blu had won them over, except for Clipper. He had agreed, *for the good of the Club*, after much cajoling.

After the vote, Taz had called to say the remaining seven of his members accepted the patch over, but his three prospects threatened to walk if they lost their rank. After another lengthy discussion around the table, Shotgun called Taz back and told him to let them go. His crew wouldn't bend on the prospects.

"Welcome, gentlemen. Welcome to the Chevaux de Fer!!" Shotgun shouted, and again the room erupted. After a considerable amount of arm-waving, the crowd quietened again. He raised his beer high above his head.

"I would also like to announce that our own little Billy, and with Digger's permission,"—Digg gave him a quick nod—"Toronto chapter's Brandon and Chu-Too shall receive their top rocker and patch tonight!" The room melted into complete pandemonium. They lifted the prospects into the air, people came forward to hug the ex-13 members, and the music fired up again at an even higher volume and blared from the speakers. The jubilation spun to extra heights.

Blu dodged most of the spraying beer on his way back to the bar where Candy was waiting for him. She giggled and leapt into his arms and he grasped two handfuls of bare ass under her miniskirt. She kissed his neck.

"Spoken like a genuine leader," she laughed in his ear.

"Where the fuck are your panties?" Blu asked, chuckling. He kneaded her flesh for good measure.

"You ate them, remember?" Candy wiggled free and disappeared back into the party with a sultry glance over her shoulder.

"All well?" Billy had made his way over and stood in front of him.

"My dick loves *and* hates me, son," Blu laughed. Billy laughed with him.

"I wanted to thank you," Billy began, but Shotgun held up his hand.

"You deserve it, Billy. Have done for a while now." Blu smiled. "You've proven your loyalty, and you have earned our respect. Now, you're a brother for life." The two embraced. "Go grab one of those Horse Heads and celebrate with a blow job!" Blu said and slapped his ass. Billy looked at the floor sheepishly.

"But there isn't a private spot in this entire building," he said. Blu waggled his eyebrows and pointed his index finger at the ceiling.

"The roof, Billy. It's a bit of a tradition when you get patched. The access ladder is in the storeroom."

"I know where it is," he laughed. "It's a little chilly for a rooftop hummer, isn't it?" Blu shivered and rolled his eyes.

"Wear a fucking coat, Billy."

✦

CHAPTER TWELVE

This has always been my favourite part of the journey, Ipsita thought. Midway between Mumbai and Pune lies a modest tourist destination called Lonavala. Perched high in the *ghats*, surrounded by lush jungle and offering spectacular views, it was a grand getaway spot for weekenders.

She adored the speciality of the region, a sweet known as *chikki*. Her love of the peanut brittle confection bordered on obsession. Ipsita consumed as much as possible on every trip through Lonavala.

The *ghats* just south of Navi Mumbai are beautiful and riding through them had brought Ippy peace. The Mumbai/Pune Expressway was closed to motorcycle traffic, forcing bikers to twist their way along the old Highway 48 that cut through the heart of the hills. *I'll miss the simple beauty of India*, she thought.

Normally, this leg of the journey was an unhurried affair. The two cities were a mere 150 km apart, allowing for a more leisurely pace. The prevalent foliage was alive with chattering monkeys. Pastel green leaves on the gum trees were dotted with pale yellow flowers and shook as the primates leapt through the branches, disturbing the emerald doves nestled deep within them. The more adventurous romped without care, scampering along the short stone wall that was the only protection provided between the cavernous valley and the road. White backed vultures screeched overhead as the bikes wove their way through the narrow path, a faded scar that carved itself across the face of the *ghat*.

The winding roads allowed Ipsita to relax after the monotonous highway travel through Gujarat and the north end of Maharashtra.

This trip was more urgent as they were now on a tight schedule. To compound the issue, Ramdev's throttle cable had broken soon after they had set out. Even in a garage, it was a tedious affair to replace the throttle cable on a Classic, let alone huddled on the side of the highway as an endless stream of traffic roared past them. After that, Shiv's rear tire had picked up a nail, and they wasted another hour removing it and finding a nearby *puncture wala.*

Ipsita squeezed her legs tight around Alex and slid herself forward, laying her head on his back. She settled into the sway of the motorcycle, joining in the metronomic rhythm as the machine began navigating the serpentine tarmac that cut through the hillside. She hummed to herself as the apricot sun melted behind the tree-lined peaks of the *ghats.* Alex reached down with his left palm and clasped her thigh just above the knee. He caressed it, then let go to navigate through the next S-bend. Ippy flipped up her visor and inhaled the viscous aroma of the honeyed jungle-scape.

Ipsita grinned. *It's incredible how hard this firangi has fallen for me,* she mused. *And in such a scant time.* Not that he had said anything outright, but it shone from his face like a searchlight. Ipsita swore to herself that no matter what it took, tonight was the night. She would collect Daya after they all turned in and make their break.

After she had allowed Alex to ravage her in Thane, she had persuaded him to delay things as long as he could in the morning after their escape, by telling Ramdev he had overheard her and Daya discussing their plans to get to Goa first and take a train back to Delhi. A short time later, after some further oral manipulation, she also had him agree to clip all their clutch cables in the night. Ramdev would no doubt suspect her, but Ippy had no wish to commit the crime herself and risk getting caught. He had brought up the idea of her coming to Canada with him again. *He is so sweet and naive,* she had thought, but dismissed the idea. Ipsita had no desire to replace Daya, especially with a man. Yet, there was a moment of consideration.

It was perfect. As soon as Alex cut the cables, she would bid him a teary farewell, and slip out with Daya to the train station. There she would purchase two tickets to Lucknow in Uttar Pradesh and from there, on to Nepal.

Ramdev, believing she was stupid enough to flee in the same direction they were heading, would have the bikes repaired and charge after her and Daya towards Goa. They would finally be together and free of this nightmare.

Her dream-like state faded as Alex slowed the bike and the melodic dance of man, machine, and road melted away. She peeked over his shoulder to see Ramdev pulling off the road.

"Oh, no," she whispered. Another breakdown would delay them further, and she was eager to get to Pune and set the plan in motion. Alex came to a halt behind Ramdev and she dismounted. Alex put the bike on its side stand, swung his leg over, and stood beside her.

"Another problem?" Alex asked, after pulling off his helmet. Ramdev was walking back to them with Daya in tow, shaking his head.

"No, everything is fine, I just wanted a word. Let's have a quick smoke too," he said. Staying in character, Ipsita snaked her hand into Alex's cut pocket and pulled out his package of cigarettes. Squinting and wrinkling her nose, she put two in her mouth and lit them. Alex beamed at her and Daya chuckled at the couple.

"You two make me ill," Ramdev said, observing their antics. Shiv and Hiran joined the group, and the air took on a chill. Ippy couldn't put her finger on it, but there was a real tension between Ramdev and Hiran.

Ramdev continued speaking to Alex as Ipsita stepped back and took Daya's hand. She smiled at her and Daya forced a grin. *She must hurt for a fix,* Ippy thought. *That will be another hurdle.*

"You okay, *babu*?" she asked. Daya nodded and mopped the thin film of sweat from her brow.

"I've seen better days," she whispered.

"Fight this, Daya. Get through it, and a brighter morning awaits us both. Be ready to run tonight, my love. It's going to happen." A cloud crossed Daya's face and Ippy squeezed her hand hard and shook her head. Daya relaxed.

Ippy cared so deeply for this girl. She had been her only source of comfort since leaving home. But at times, she was so weak, needy, and now with this addiction, it was worse. She was almost a liability. *At one point, I may have to grapple with the possibility of leaving her,* she mused. *Could there be another?* Ippy doubted it. As hard and manipulating as her nature was, she needed Daya.

"The track gets a little tricky from here," Ramdev was saying. "Stay close, okay? Some sharper twists and turns for the next thirty minutes, then we have to take an abrupt right-hand turn to cut through Lonavala. After that, we'll be back on straight roads." Ramdev glanced at his watch. "That'll put us in Pune sometime around 8:00."

"I'll drop to tail, boss," Hiran grumbled. "Just in case we separate." Ipsita watched Hiran's eyes narrow as he spoke and noted his flat and emotionless tone. Ramdev nodded.

"Okay, saddle up," Ramdev said, flicking his smoke into the underbrush and turning back to his bike. Ipsita squeezed Daya's hand and walked to Alex as the group dispersed.

"Something is wrong," she said.

"Huh? What?" Alex asked.

"They *never* break formation and the chill around Hiran... there is *something wrong*, Alex. I can sense it." Alex shrugged and mounted the motorcycle. Ipsita pulled on her helmet and joined him. "Just be careful, okay?" Her voice was suddenly inaudible because of the rumble from the bikes starting.

Over the next ten minutes, Ipsita fidgeted. She kept stealing glances over her shoulder and saw Shiv and Hiran had fallen well back. Ippy had been on enough rides to know that they never left more than a five metre gap between them. *This isn't right.* Ramdev slowed. *He must be aware the distance was increasing.* Ipsita could see Daya looking back at her. They couldn't have been travelling over 20 kmph.

The bikes dipped into a severe left-hand hairpin. The grade of the track steepened sharply and at the apex of the corner was a small offshoot. That is where tragedy struck. Without warning, a battered green Piaggio Ape three-wheeler shot out from the slip road. The mini-truck's headlight bobbed as the vehicle bounced onto the main tarmac.

A cloud of dust swirled behind it, a one-eyed spectre emerging from a hellish smoke-filled pit. It careened to the left and threatened to tip. The worn rubber tires screeched, looking for purchase as it sought to right itself, but the speed was far too great and the vehicle was out of control.

The mini-truck slammed back onto all three tires and bounced, the rusted springs shrieking as it sped towards Ramdev. Ipsita's cry filled her helmet. She saw Ramdev snap his head around towards the runaway tri-wheeled monster. He must have instinctively twisted the throttle, as his motorcycle leapt forward, but it was not enough. The truck smashed into the rear end of the bike.

A rush of vomit climbed Ippy's throat as Daya's leg ripped away just below her right knee and spun off across the lane. Ramdev's Classic crumpled as it absorbed the impact of metal on metal, then sprung off the lorry, spinning into the culvert. Performing in a grotesque ballet, Ramdev cartwheeled high in the air and followed his bike towards the ditch.

Ipsita's eyes burned as the contents of her stomach coated her visor and dripped onto her chest. Daya's body lurched backwards, a helpless marionette set to motion by a child yanking her strings. She somersaulted from her pillion position and hit the pavement in a crumpled heap.

The pickup bounced off the impact and spun towards them. Blinded by its glaring headlight, Ippy realised she was about to die. Her stomach rolled as their bike dipped, front brake locked and howling. It filled her with an unnatural sensation of weightlessness.

Momentum flung her forward as the smell of burnt rubber and vomit stung her nostrils. Her lungs collapsed in a gush as the cold and unforgiving surface of the mountain road rushed up and slapped her in the face. The contact lit a fire along her right side as she slid across the rough tarmac, coming to rest in the middle of the bend.

There was a banshee howling. Ipsita rolled over and sat upright. *It's me!* she thought, recognising her ragged voice. She filled her lungs to capacity and held it, quietening herself. Ippy pulled off her helmet and struggled to stand. The searing hot poker in her hip caused her to stumble, but Ippy forced herself to her feet.

She stood, surveying the surrounding carnage. Alex was standing over their bike where it had slid to a stop five metres in front of her. He bent at the waist and grabbed his knees. Ippy looked behind her in the direction the truck had been heading. It was still close by, stopped on the centre line. Hiran was beside it. Shiv roared up to Alex.

"Are you whole?" he was shouting.

Ippy was expecting gunshots, but they didn't come. *Hiran isn't unloading his gun into the cab of the truck. Why? Why isn't he killing them?* She looked to Daya, who was in a tangled lump where she had landed. Ippy took a step and near tumbled as her right knee buckled under the weight. One heel had snapped from her boot. She threw her head back and screamed.

"No!" Hot tears came as she sobbed. *Not Daya. Please, no! We are so close!*

Alex looked up and started towards her. Ippy limped forward, trying to reach her lover. She could see a seeping pool of sticky crimson forming under her. Ippy wailed again. She closed her eyes and felt Alex's arms close around her.

"Shhh, hush... you're okay, baby. You're okay," he soothed. Ipsita pushed him off her.

"No! No!" was all she could manage as she limped towards the lifeless body of her childhood friend, her most trusted confidante, her lover.

Ippy fought the haze in her mind and tried to reconcile with what was happening. Ipsita saw Shiv lifting Alex's bike and wheel it to the shoulder. Upon hearing Hiran come to a stop beside them, Ipsita took Alex's hand and moved forward a few more steps, Alex in tow. She fell to her knees beside Daya and laid over her, protecting her. The warmth of Daya's lifeblood soaked into her pants as she wept. *All our plans, gone! Daya, gone!*

"Shiv," Hiran barked. "Get her off the road!" Ipsita clung to her in desperation, but relented as Alex forced her to her feet. She allowed him to lead her over to the bikes. "Alex, come!" Hiran called as he descended the embankment where Ramdev had fallen.

"Stay here, babe. Lean here," Alex said, patting the seat and rushing to where Hiran was standing.

The ringing in her ears subsided. Ipsita took several quick breaths and worked to focus her mind to reason out what had happened. *Daya is dead, I'm alive, Alex is alive, Ramdev... Where is Ramdev?*

She looked back to Daya, but Daya's body had vanished. There was just a trail of gore leading to the culvert. Shiv brushed past her, rushing towards Hiran and Alex, and she followed. The pain along her right side was tormenting her every step. Ippy stopped on the edge of the tarmac and gazed into the culvert. Alex, Shiv, and Hiran were standing over Ramdev, his shattered frame mirroring the twisted wreck of the motorcycle lying not too far away.

Two broken machines, one of metal and plastic, one of flesh and bone. Tattered and discarded, both in this nameless ditch in the *ghats* of Maharashtra. An evil satisfaction seeped through Ipsita. Its hateful warmth comforted her and a cruel delight filled her belly. She navigated her way down the embankment as a wicked smile contorted her face.

Hiran crouched beside Ramdev. "You piece of goat shit," he whispered. Ippy saw Ramdev's expression change from anguish to confusion, then to fear. It warmed her further.

"What, brother? What do you..." Ramdev gagged. Blood spewed over the front of his jean jacket and cut. *His precious cut.* Ipsita's smile widened as the sticky maroon fluid soaked into the president's patch on his left breast.

"Did you think we wouldn't find out?" Hiran pulled a brown manila envelope from his inside pocket. "You rat fuck. The NCB? How could you, Ramdev? After all we have done together, the shit we have eaten, the blood we have spilled. You betray your position? Your club? Me?" he screamed as he shoved the envelope in Ramdev's face.

"What's that?" Ipsita asked, baffled.

"Photos," Hiran said, not taking his eyes off Ramdev. "Of our president speaking with an NCB agent. The one Shiv put an end to. All the time we were wondering how she ended up at our clubhouse, why she was at Farzi Cafe. It was him all along."

"Fuck me," Alex whispered.

"No," Ramdev gurgled. He tried to speak further but couldn't. His shattered ribs had punctured his lungs and they were filling with blood.

A rigid flash of frigid understanding struck Ipsita in the back of the head. *Hiran discovered someone had been speaking to the NCB and believed it had been Ramdev. So, they murdered him. Killed him, and Daya was a byproduct, in the target's way.* The horrific epiphany splintered her heart and scorched her soul. *I killed Daya!* Ippy fell to the grass, recoiling from the ugly truth, and wrapped her arms around her knees. She screwed her eyes shut. *No, God. Please God, no.* She willed the entire scene to disappear, praying that it was a nightmare. Her self-preservation drained away. At that moment, Ipsita no longer cared what became of her. Ippy, in shock, simply surrendered to the ebb and flow of karma.

"Whatever will be, will be," she whispered.

"Shiv, grab all the sugar off of his bike except one key. Take his Glock, but leave Ratt's Beretta. Understand?" Hiran said while folding the envelope and slipping it into Ramdev's pocket.

"We need to get out of here before someone drives by. Alex, come." Shiv sprinted over to the wreck and started digging through the saddlebags. Alex moved around Ramdev's splintered legs and stood beside Hiran.

"Finish him," Hiran whispered. Ipsita snapped her eyes open and watched with dread.

"*Oh no.* Not happening. This is *not* my fight," Alex stated. Hiran drew his Glock and placed it against Alex's temple.

"I beg to differ," he growled.

"Do it, Alex," Ipsita whimpered. "Kill that fucker."

"Listen to her, Alex. It's time for you to show your hand. You're all in or you're out. What side of the fence are you on?"

Ipsita forced herself up and hobbled over to Alex. She clasped his shoulder and using what was left of her self-will to manipulate him, whispered, "My side, Alex. My side of the fence. He's a monster, you know it. He raped me, beat me, subjected me to horrors I can't even speak of." Her voice was soft, pleading. "Hiran will kill you, Alex, so just rid me and the world of this worthless piece of shit." Alex looked at her. Ippy stared back at him and nodded.

Ramdev's eyes widened with fear as Alex crouched beside him. As Ipsita watched, Ramdev transformed into a little boy, lost, alone, facing the monsters under his bed. Alex reached out and grasped Ramdev's nose between his thumb and forefinger. Ramdev bucked, gasping for breath through his blood filled mouth. He coughed and sputtered, swiping at Alex's hand.

Ippy heard Ramdev's wrist bone crack as Hiran stood on his flailing arm. Ramdev thrashed back and forth in the coarse grass, choking and heaving. He twisted as much as the tattered frame of his body allowed. Alex held his nose firm. Ipsita dropped to Alex's side and covered his hand with her own. She squeezed along with him, her nails cutting through the skin of Ramdev's nose as it snapped like a dry twig. Then, with one last spurt of blood from his gaping mouth, Ramdev went limp.

"Whore babysitter," she growled and spat in Ramdev's face. The three men stared at her in shock.

"Let's leave here now," Hiran said. "You're whole?" he asked Alex. Alex nodded. "I'll lead. Shiv, you tail. We need to get to Pune and regroup."

Ippy stood, took Alex's hand, and led him away. An eerie calm descended on her. An inner voice whispered that from this tragedy, her previous sins have been trumped and washed away. *Could it be that committing a bigger sin erased the past smaller indiscretions?* She didn't know, but she felt free of them. *I'm in shock,* she reasoned.

They mounted up in haste. Aside from a bent brake lever and the left mirror snapped away clean, Alex's bike was okay. The trio peeled onto the pavement and roared away.

Over the next hour of painful riding, Ippy withdrew into her own thoughts. Daya's death had not changed her circumstances. She would still be accountable to the NCB, and with Ramdev gone, Hiran would take the reins. Hiran had never been overly sympathetic to her, especially after Ramdev had claimed her for his own. For the first time in a very long time, Ipsita's calculating mind would not provide an answer. *I could run alone*, she thought. The very idea seemed hollow and pointless. Daya had been her measure of self-worth, and without her, was life worth living? Her deep-rooted survival instinct resolved that it was and whispered to her, *Alex. Canada. Make it work.*

They pulled into a small roadside *dhaba* on the outskirts of Pune. Ippy knew it was more than a restaurant. She had been here. It was the Horses' clubhouse. She was sore, tired and miserable, but felt a wave of relief as they came to a halt in the parking lot. The group trudged up the entrance steps as the red neon *Spicy Bite* sign blinked over them.

"You okay?" she asked Alex.

"Huh?" he murmured.

"Are you all right?" Ippy repeated. Alex was staring blankly over her shoulder, his eyes unfocussed.

"Yeah, yeah. I just did what had to be done," he whispered.

"Get the bags, Shiv," Hiran shouted, drowning out Alex's answer. Hiran pulled the latch and swung open the door. The three of them entered the smoke-filled room and Ipsita jolted at the sight of the *firangi* sitting at the table closest to them. She had met him twice before over the last few years and hated him with a passion. Ipsita's heart sank, as seeing him, she realised beyond a doubt that Daya's death was no accident. He was glaring at Alex. A sardonic grin cracked open his weathered face.

"Hello, rat prick," John chuckled.

* * *

The young stewardess of SpiceJet flight SG 1821 giggled and peeked at her feet.

"Well, that depends," she cooed. "Have you been a good boy?"

"Oh yes, I've been the model passenger," Sandy answered.

"All right, then. I'll see what I can do," she replied, flashing him a flirtatious smile and rushed off along the aisle. He leaned out and watched her tight red skirt as she sashayed her way to the front of the jet.

"Really?" Avinash sighed. "Another cookie?" Sandy chuckled. "You're too good looking, Bohla. You know that, don't you?"

"With great power comes great responsibility, boss," he japed.

Avinash looked out the window of the plane. They were sitting at the terminal in Mumbai, standing by to pick up passengers for Goa. Half the travellers from Delhi had disembarked, and the crew was doing a quick cleanup of the cabin while waiting for the new ones to board. His phone chirped.

"Agent Kumar," he answered. Avi's face darkened as he listened. "Goddammit!" he exploded.

Twenty minutes later, he and Sandy were sitting in the back of a local police van, heading towards the *ghats* outside of Lonavala. Avinash sat on the two-plank bench alongside the ghosts of a decade's worth of prisoners. They had embedded the rusty walls of the wagon with the odour of stale cigarettes and sweat.

His head was hung and he stared at the knurled floor of the paddy wagon as they lurched along NH8. There were no windows, and the small sliding panel to the cab supplied the only light. He was glad for the isolation. Avi was awash with shame, anger, and anguish. It felt right to be hiding from the view of the citizens he so desperately tried to protect. The self-loathing that churned inside him was not fit for public consumption. *How did I make such a crucial error again?*

"Boss?" Sandy murmured. "You couldn't know. No way to foresee this."

"Thank you, Sandeep, but that is untrue, I'm afraid. You expressed your concerns, and I didn't listen. In my arrogance, I was sure we could get to him first."

The two sat in silence for the next forty-five minutes. The van lurched to a stop and a uniformed officer opened the rear doors. As Avinash climbed from the van, his phone chirped, causing his heart to leap as he answered. He prayed that by some tragic mistake, it was Ramdev.

"Agent Kumar," he said.

"Avi," Zonal Director Yadav began. "We have a huge issue. Pandey is dead."

"Oh God," Avi whispered.

"We need more than God now, I'm afraid. Where are you?"

"Just outside Mumbai, at a crash scene. Ramdev is dead."

"I know, I know. Get on with this, Avinash. There are grumblings of corruption, the prevailing rumour is Pandey was feeding information to this bike gang," Yadav said.

"It adds up, sir. I received a phone call from another gang member today. A foreigner. He seemed to possess an unusual amount of information."

"A foreigner?" Yadav blew a deep sigh into the phone. "We need answers, Avi. Now."

"On it, sir," Avi said and ended the call. He looked at Sandy. His face was grim.

"Corruption. We are out of time," he said. Sandy simply nodded as Avi spun and surveyed the site.

The portable floodlights set up by the local cops bathed the crime scene in an iridescent glow. Irregular, misshapen shadows crisscrossed the officers and forensic personnel scurrying about. Small gas generators hummed and the faint aroma of petrol hung in the air. They had stretched yellow caution tape around the operation. It fluttered in the night breeze.

Avi shook his head. *Perfect*, he thought. *The set-up is ideal.* An isolated area, the chance of another vehicle or witness here was slim to none. The site was accessible for rejoining the major highway, making their escape swift and unnoticed. Any doubt he had that this was a coincidence vanished.

An unshaven detective approached him. He had the same expression on his face they always do when Avi arrived. That look of distaste, the unwillingness to hand over what they felt to be *their case* to the NCB.

"Senior Agent Kumar?" he asked. Avi nodded, then motioned to Sandy to go investigate the wreck. Sandy turned and strode towards the floodlights.

"I am Detective Patil, sir. It seemed like a standard hit-and-run, sir. Then the officers noticed his vest was from a motorcycle club and also found a weapon with some photographs. Command then ordered me to the scene, and by the time I arrived, they had uncovered the heroin. I called the NCB right away, sir."

"Very efficient of you, Patil." Avi held out his hand. The detective's face was blank.

"The photographs?" Avinash sighed.

"Oh, yes, sir," he said, snapping his fingers at a uniformed officer lurking nearby. The cop handed the envelope to Avi.

He opened the envelope and his heart skipped. *Dimpi!* It was from the night of the shooting at Cyber Hub. Avi was sure of it. The quality of the capture was not good, but it showed Dimpi and Ramdev acknowledging each other. *Must be from the security video.* Avi closed his eyes. *Another fucking blunder*, he thought. *How did we miss these, why didn't we have these?*

"His weapon?" Avi asked.

"Already on its way to the forensic lab, sir," the detective said. "You hope it is the same one from the shooting in Delhi, sir? No offence, I did a little digging into this case."

"Ambitious, aren't you?" Avi sneered. He knew there would be no such luck. Forensics had recovered no casing or fragments in Cyber Hub or Okhla. But there may be something. Any scrap would help.

"Boss!" Sandy shouted from the culvert inside the caution tape. Avi spun on his heel and walked to him.

"Nasty," Sandy said. "He drowned in his own blood. The coroner says four hours ago, tops. There's a girl as well." He pointed several metres away. "Severed leg and mangled body."

"Identification on her?"

"No," Sandy replied.

"Of course not," Avi growled. The detective had joined them. "Find out who she is, Detective. Do it now." He bolted up the embankment, leaving them with Ramdev's lifeless shell. Avi crouched and put his hand on Ramdev's chest. "I'm sorry," he whispered. Sandy shuffled from foot to foot, rustling the same dry grass that had consoled Ipsita a few hours earlier.

"Rough break, boss," Sandy said.

"The hell it is, this is my fault." Avi's fears regarding the loss of this case were being realised. The second he answered the phone on the plane, he knew the brass ring would elude him again. "I should have heeded your advice, Sandy. We should have told him. Warned him."

The Horses dropped me a nice little package. Yes, they've created a convenient fiction to absolve themselves from any wrong doings. The evidence laid out in black and white. All that's missing is subtitles. A rogue club member that was in over his head with an Afghan drug lord, a dead renegade NCB agent that got involved trying to get him out, and a single kilo of heroin left on the scene. The consolation prize for screwing up yet another major bust.

"Next move?" Sandy asked.

"Pune, then a flight to Goa," Avinash sighed and stood. "What else can we do?" Looking at his watch, he shook his head. "They are only four hours ahead of us now, Sandy. We are closing in on them, we will be in Goa before the sun rises."

"We have no idea where they are heading."

"Not the exact location, no. But we are aware of the area. I believe the hotel Ramdev suggested meeting us in won't be far from their destination. We'll get down there, Sandy, and pray for a break."

* * *

The knuckles on his left hand popped as he squeezed the clutch. Alex winced. The scab on his shoulder from the gunshot cracked every time he moved. His hips, knees, and the palms of his hands were bruised from the fall. Alex blinked twice, trying to focus on the bike in front of him. There had been little discussion before they rolled out of the small restaurant in Pune.

After arrival, the group climbed the narrow staircase to a common room above the eating hall. There was a table, a couch, and thin mattresses scattered on the floor. Other than that, it was bare. After piling in and a quick meal of *dosa* and a tea, Ipsita and he collapsed, clothed, on the mattress closest to the window. She had whispered in his ear there was no reason to proceed with her escape and rolled with her back to him and slept.

He had tried to sleep, but the hushed voices of the others' conversation and the soft whimpers of Ispista's dreams kept Alex awake. At least she was getting sleep, blissful escape. *I should take her home*, he had reasoned.

At 4:00 am, John kicked his boot. *"Saddle up,"* was all he said. That was three hours ago.

They were back on proper highway now. *John doesn't share in Ramdev's concern for drawing any unnecessary attention*, Alex thought. John was leading, followed by Sumit from Mumbai. *The prick hadn't introduced himself, but that's what his cut said.* Alex was third, then Hiran, with Shiv tailing, following the pace set by John, who had them wound out

They had been at a steady 120 kmph for the best part of the trip and it didn't look like they were going to slow down. Ippy slumped against him, limp as a sack of potatoes and scarcely hanging on to him. Her eyes had been vacant and unseeing as they mounted up in the pre-dawn light. *She's okay for now. I'll press her on Canada later. Right now, I'm dealing with my shit*, Alex thought. The shit inside his belly that began as they were winding their way through Rajasthan.

As he settled into the ride there, Alex discovered he trusted the bike along with his abilities to handle it and had relaxed. It was somewhere between Jaipur and Udaipur that the harsh realisation had come to him, that he was riding a motorcycle laden with heroin through the deserts of a foreign land. *How the fuck did I end up here?* was his first thought, but he pushed the question away and focussed more on how he felt about it.

It was an awakening of sorts. He was taking a deeper look at himself. The endless pavement and the rush of the wind had sharpened his mind. The outcrops of red and umber rock formations spoke to him as they thrust themselves into a spotless blue sky, unafraid and powerful. It transfixed Alex, forcing him into a long overdue exploration of his soul. He likened himself to the dark-winged hawks that circled above them. They were free and unabated. These were feelings Alex had never owned.

His entire life, he had felt stifled, directionless, and without purpose. Now, filled with this newfound awareness, Alex knew he belonged. To what, he didn't know. But there was an undeniable comfort in belonging to something bigger than himself.

Ipsita stirred. As had become his habit, Alex dropped his left hand and grasped her leg behind the knee. Ippy recoiled, he softened his grip.

Ipsita Chaudhary. *Another complete mind fuck,* he sighed to himself. She was, without a doubt, the most attractive woman he ever met. *But she's more than that, isn't she?* Her intelligence surprised him and her wit was razor sharp. Not that he was a misogynist, Alex just had no occasion to reconcile beauty, intellect, and humour in a woman. *I hadn't had occasion to, or just didn't bother to notice? Another one of my personality flaws spilled out onto the pavement!* Stuck inside his own helmet for hours on end, Alex probed these dark corners of his mind.

She had said no to Canada without any real consideration. Despite the outlandish position they were in, he believed it to be a solution. Even more mystifying than that, he was developing serious feelings for her. He *wanted* her to join him.

Alex let go of Ippy's leg and flipped up his visor. The wind rushed into his helmet and he inhaled the salty, sweet fragrance he now identified as India. Sulphur and honey, pepper and syrup... *blood and brown sugar.*

"Let's not forget," he whispered. *You're a murderer.* The cryptic voice in his head finished the sentence for him. He was. A murderer. He took another man's life. It was true Ramdev would have died with or without his prompting. Alex decided *that* fact absolved him of the sin of execution. He couldn't push that rationale to mercy, but at least, it relieved the moniker of a *ruthless monster* from his conscience.

Alex acknowledged the fact that there was a gun pointed at his head. But deep inside, he knew the truth of it all. *I'd have killed Ramdev without the pressure from Hiran.*

The reason was plain enough on the surface. Ramdev was the prick that had harmed the woman he was falling for, and he was the facilitator of Alex's immediate woes.

But there was more to it than that, *much more*. As Ramdev bucked and writhed, Alex had savoured not just the sweet satisfaction of revenge, but validation. The overwhelming sense of righting a wrong. Alex was an archangel dispensing justice. Ramdev sinned. Against Ipsita, against him, but above all else, against his club.

Your club!? his inner monologue screamed. Alex sighed. His head was pounding with a grisly headache. Until two weeks ago, Alex was confident in himself, but now he was unsure. Everything that happened from the moment he kicked Clipper off the stair landing had drawn his entire life into question. There was *one* thing he could settle in his nagging guts, one fact standing above the swirling dust in his mind.

Despite how hideous this entire experience had been, he didn't hate it. Quite the opposite. He felt a part of it. As much as Alex loved and missed his father, never in the years since his death had he thought back on him so much. All those cryptic pearls of wisdom his father was fond of dropping on him were beginning to make sense. The veil was lifting, and he finally understood what Dean Crossman was about.

He felt he belonged here and embraced it. Alex had never felt more alive, and if he dug just a little deeper, he would uncover the nasty realisation that the *worst* emotional knife blade he felt was a lack of respect from the Horses. He was an outsider, and he wasn't sure he wanted to be.

John pulled off the road into a small *dhaba* and the column followed. Alex missed the gearshift while climbing the broken curb into the parking lot and fell behind them. After stamping the bike into second gear, he followed them in and came to a halt between John and Sumit's bikes.

"Let's talk," John said after Alex had pulled off his helmet. Ipsita wandered away towards the restroom. "Order some food and drink," John said to Sumit, who nodded and left. Alex followed John up the worn stone steps to the main dining area. Like most *dhabas*, it wasn't elaborate. They kicked their way across the dirt floor amidst the white plastic tables and chairs scattered around the room. Alex warmed under the heat radiating from the tin roof and walls. John sat at the table farthest from the bikes. Alex followed suit, and Hiran returned from the open kitchen on the far wall and joined them. John lit a cigarette, took a deep drag, and then fixed Alex with a stony stare.

"From the moment you became involved in our club's enterprises, my life has been a complete fucking misery," John said through a veil of exhaled smoke.

"Funny," Alex quipped. "I was thinking the same thing." Hiran's chair scrapped across the dirt as he drew his fist. John put his hand on his arm and shook his head.

"How do you see this ending, Alex?" he asked. Alex considered the question and shrugged. It was something that had been nagging at him, but he had no idea. Alex lit a smoke of his own and watched the rusty ceiling fan spin for a moment.

"I don't know," he said. "Back in Montreal, I was hoping to get your shit home, then Candy and I would ride off into the sunset. But now, I'm assuming you'll dump my body in the water off the coast of Newfoundland after I deliver the heroin."

"Into the sunset? That was never in the cards, I'm afraid," John scoffed without humour.

"Why would you tell me that?" Alex asked, narrowing his eyes. He hadn't expected that degree of honesty. "What incentive do I have to do anything for you if I'm a dead man walking?"

"Candy," John said simply.

"Well, it would appear *that* situation has changed, no?" Alex asked.

"So, you're aware?" John asked, eyes popping open. Alex smirked and nodded. "Your situation has changed with her, true, but the outcome has not. You don't want her harmed, do you?"

"No. Not at all," Alex said. "But that is unlikely now, isn't it?" It hadn't taken Alex long to reason it out after the phone call with Candy. He knew her too well. She was an opportunist, a free-willed and uncaring spirit. There was no doubt Candy had aligned herself with a club member to improve her situation. John smiled at him. It troubled Alex, as the smile was genuine and warm. Laughing, John concurred.

"Yeah, I suppose it is. That leaves us in a bit of a quandary. Doesn't it, Alex? I have no control over you, no leverage, except maybe Ipsita." Alex's face darkened at the mention of her name. John's eyebrows raised. "Humm, more leverage than I realised it seems."

"I'm not a fool, John. I know she is using me," he growled. John's face clouded and he lilted his head.

"For what?"

Alex realised that in his anger, he had said too much. He had to change tack.

"To gain favour with you, with the Club! It's no mystery she has been my keeper, watching me, letting Ramdev know where my head was at. She's been a stress relief for me, John. Nothing more."

"Hum, my eyes tell me different," John chuckled. "So, you don't give a rat's ass if we leave her in a ditch outside the shipyard?"

Alex smashed out his cigarette in the wooden ashtray on the table and lit another. Panic welled up inside him, unfathomable and pure. The constant dark cloud of foreboding and fear of death that had been shrouding him burst open and doused Alex in desperation. A deluge of anguish and despair caused an emotional break.

The runaway train that had been flying headlong into obscurity hit the station bollard, and a bitter shower of truth and acceptance of his fate washed away his indecision and restraint. Alex heard a voice speaking. He knew it was his, but there was no conscious formation of words or what he was saying. The tirade spilled from him like rice from a torn sack.

"I have done everything you asked of me. They have shot me, I'm transporting illegal narcotics, I witnessed the brutal killing of an NCB agent and helped dispose of her body, I've run from the police and committed a goddamn murder. All in the name of the Chevaux de fucking Fer! Not once did I wince, not once did I hesitate! Most of this, even after I found out my girlfriend, *your leverage,* was screwing the life outta some biker back in Montreal."

Alex was panting; a light sweat formed on his brow. After a few quick breaths, he continued, "And you are sitting here trying to intimidate me? To motivate me with *threats?* I don't give a flying fuck anymore, John. I truly don't." John glanced at Hiran, who nodded.

"He has performed well," Hiran said.

"Fuck you too, Hiran," Alex barked. Hiran smiled, bemused.

"Okay, Alex, enlighten me. What gets you out of bed in the morning?" John chuckled. This was the moment of truth. Alex, without even knowing if what he was saying was the entire truth, showed his hand.

"This," he said, grasping the lapels of Ratt's cut and shaking them. "You have what I want, you are what I want. You *live* what I want," he whispered. The three of them sat for a moment, while John and Hiran exchanged expressionless glances. John whistled through his teeth.

"Jesus Christ, son. You think this is the YMCA? Fill out a form and get a membership card?"

"No, no..."

"You are living on the edge, Alex, hanging on by your goddamn fingernails." John barked out a sharp laugh. "*Are what I want, live what I want,*" he mocked. "Wow!"

"John," Alex began. John held up his hand.

"Look, I get it, kid. Okay, we have forced you into this, and now you've had a taste of being an outlaw and you want more. But Hiran's told me about you, your aversion to violence. Regardless of your stock, you're not cut out for this lifestyle."

"What stock? What the fuck does that mean?" Alex demanded. John fixed him with a cold, hard stare.

"None of your damned business," he whispered through clenched teeth.

"You're wrong, John. You know nothing about me or where I've come from. Think I can't kill a man? Run from the police and be okay with it? You're wrong. I've just never had a *reason* to before this."

"Go see to Ipsita, have something to eat, we are out of here shortly," he said. They locked eyes. Alex was searching to see if John believed him. They were as blank as a shark's. Alex stood and left.

"Holy shit! You *believe* that?" John said after Alex was out of earshot.

"To be completely honest, *bhaiya*, I've been expecting it," Hiran said. "How do you say it in Canada, a fish to water? He's changed in the brief time he has been with us." John shook his head and looked at his watch.

"Okay, we are about three hours from Goa, let's go straight to the shipyard and sort that out. Then we will decide about Alex," John chuckled.

"*Theek hai*," Hiran said. "What's funny?"

"I did a little looking into Alex Crossman before I left, then I spoke to Blu in Delhi." John stared at Alex long and hard. He was sitting across from Ipsita, caressing her cheek. "I rode with his father when I was a prospect. He was a good man. Loyal. True. Maybe the kid is all right," John chuckled again. "How's that for a big ass slice of irony?"

✳ ✳ ✳

The rusty water stung Ipsita's eyes as she splashed her face. A dingy towel hung on a nail beside her. After drying herself, she stared into the cracked mirror above the sink. A broken woman stared back. One drained of her radiance and soaked in woeful torment.

"What in the hell do I do now?" she demanded of the washed-out reflection. She spun and leaned against the sink, willing herself to banish the fog of sorrow from her mind. Her night had been a long and hideous nightmare. Unable to concentrate on anything other than her guilt and grief, Ipsita had collapsed into a restless sleep. The morning had brought no relief. She had gone through the motions of freshening up, then climbed on the back of Alex's motorcycle.

As the sun rose and warmed her, Ipsita wrestled with her options on how to escape the Club and the NCB. But try as she might, every time she tried to reason, the thought of continuing on without Daya quashed every logical thought.

"Dammit!" she cursed. "We are almost to Goa; I have to act." *Why?* her sorrow asked. *Let the Horses kill you, or let the NCB take you to prison. What's the difference? You'll never be at peace now.*

Ippy wandered from the restroom and back to the dhaba, flopping into a chair at the first table. Exhausted with the debate raging in her head, she settled on the obvious solution. Alex. She turned to see him deep in a heated conversation with John and Hiran. *Did he stand a chance to convince them to let me go? How could they be willing to let me walk away free? I know so much about their business operations, yet they never worried about me hearing or seeing those things in the past. But we've never had the ominous cloud of the NCB swirling over us either.* Ippy sighed. "And Ramdev always protected me."

Ippy lit a cigarette and leaned back in her chair. Alex's voice echoed across the room and she snapped her head around towards the shout. He was yelling at John. *What the hell is he doing? What is he saying?* Her life was a fiery mess, her future hanging by a thread.

"Fuck it," she whispered. *How tedious could it be to feign a life with Alex? At least until another choice presented itself. He's a decent enough man and displays affection for me.*

She could never trust a man, not *blindly* again, not after the abuse she had suffered. The only way she had kept her sanity to this point, was by controlling the bastards from the shadows. But with her support gone,— *Dead, you mean... with Daya dead*—could her extraordinary self-will see her through the turbulent waters ahead? *It will have to,* she conceded.

Alex sat opposite her and smiled.

"You okay?" she asked.

"Yeah, I guess. Look, Ipsita, I am reeling here. I don't know what the next twenty-four hours will bring, but I'm sure it will be bad," he sighed. "Cards on the table, okay?"

"Okay."

"At the moment, I am sifting through a lot of shit in my head here, and I know you are not the solution to any of it. I just laid an awful lot in John's lap, some truth I am grappling with. I'm certain my wanting you to join me is a minor issue compared. But... Jesus! How to say this? I like you, okay. More than I should, and I want you to come to Canada with me. My dad used to say, *I may be green, but I'm not a cabbage...*"

"What the hell does that mean?" Ippy laughed. Alex flashed his boyish grin.

"It means I'm not stupid. It's clear what your job was, but I feel something for you, Ippy, and I'm gambling you also do for me. What do you have to lose? They will kill you, Ippy, I'm sure of it. Just come with me."

Ipsita studied him for a moment. He was struggling, to be sure, but there was honesty in his eyes. She had no clue if she could handle this transformation he was going through, and she dreaded the thought of tying herself to another Ramdev to survive. But maybe Alex was different. If she told the entire truth, Ipsita had slight feelings of affection for him. The pangs of guilt while she lied to his face and the mild wave of nausea that came following her manipulations had become more prevalent. *There was also the physical want to consider.* Her body didn't betray that truth, moistening as she crawled into his bed at night. *Go on, then. Trust him, trust yourself. What is there to lose? The path of least resistance is a well-travelled route for me.*

"Okay, Alex. Ask them," she said. Alex smiled and brushed her cheek.

"I have no way of knowing what John will say. No guarantees, Ippy."

"No shit..." she whispered.

* * *

The faded periwinkle walls of the humble room in the Hotel Wilsha were the most obscene colour Avi had ever seen. It was making his head ache.

As the supply of live bodies and options was quickly diminishing, Avi decided that the best course of action was to check into the meeting place he had arranged with Ramdev. He understood the chances of the MC checking in here were zero. Ramdev may have been a rat, but he wasn't an idiot and Avinash knew that. Yet during the conversation, Ramdev *had* picked this location with no forethought. It was Avi's hope this was a regular haunt of the MC and they may pick up a lead. There was a light knock.

"Come," Sandy said. He had been sitting at the rickety table, staring out the window. The door opened and a young lad of 10 or 11 with a tray of *pakora* and two bottles of water entered. He looked at Avi with respect, and fear. Avi motioned him forward, and the youth set the tray on the table. Sandy picked up one of the battered vegetable snacks and popped it in his mouth.

"Kya aapke yahaan kabhee motorsaikil wale mehmaan aye hain?" he said around his mouthful of deep-fried cauliflower. The lad stared at him wide-eyed. "Motorcycle?" Sandy continued, holding up his hands and grasping invisible handlebars while rolling his right wrist. "Bikers? Here?"

"How did you ever graduate from the academy?" Avi asked him. He shifted his gaze to the child. *"Kya aap English ya Hindi bolte hain?"*

"Both, sir," the boy said.

"We are police officers, son. We are working on an enormous case." Avi smiled and showed the adolescent boy his badge. The boy's eyes widened as he reached out and brushed his fingertips over the gold shield. Avi slipped it back into his breast pocket and sat on the edge of the bed. "There is no need for you to worry. You are in no trouble." The boy bobbed his head from side to side. "Have you worked here long?" Avi prodded.

"Yes, sir. This my uncle's hotel." Avi continued to smile at him.

"Good, good. What we would like to know is if you ever have guests here that arrive by motorcycle. Royal Enfields." The boy's face brightened. Royal Enfields were a deep source of national pride for Indians, and every lad's dream to own one.

"Yes, sir. Sometimes, from Delhi or Mumbai, they come. Loud talking and music. They drink too much beer. My uncle is afraid of them," he said.

"A club? All dressed the same?"

"Yes, sir. I know motorcycle gang. I have seen them on Netflix." The youth beamed. Avi chuckled.

"When was the last time they were here?" The boy squinted his eyes, thinking hard.

"*Chhe maheene,*" he said and nodded.

"Six months?" Avi confirmed. The lad nodded again. "Okay, son. You have been very helpful." Avi handed him a ten-rupee note. The boy snatched it and darted from the room.

"Thank you!" he called over his shoulder.

Avi gazed out the small window into the jungles of Carambolim and sighed. A slight flicker of hope ignited in his belly. *Can I save this case?* By a stroke of luck, could he link this club to the heroin and bring it crashing down? *Only if I find them,* he thought. *We have to locate the Canadian. He's the key to this now.* Avi knew he held the answers and was sure he could extract them.

I will not come up short again, I will see this through to the end. I'll find the heroin, find the killers and collapse this entire operation around them, he thought, as his flicker of hope ignited into a flame.

"Anything back from the Airport Authority?"

"No," Sandy replied, picking up his phone. "Let me call them now."

"And that Mumbai detective, the girl at the scene, see if he's identified her." Avi stood and walked to the small window, the wooden floor creaking under his polished black shoes. He put his hands on his hips and arched his back, stretching to release the knots. Sandy was speaking on the phone and was getting agitated.

"No luck with the list," he said. "The Bureau of Immigration said there were half a million tourist entrees this month, almost twenty thousand from Canada. They are whittling it down, but it will take some time. Let me call Mumbai." Avi stood in silence and waited. He listened to Sandy's brief conversation.

"The detective is not picking up, so I called his station, and he isn't in. I left a message for him to call us as soon as he can."

A wave of exhaustion overcame Avi. It filled his eyelids with lead. Walking to the bed, he laid on the thin mattress. It did nothing to comfort his aching back. There was no action he could take right now. He needed rest, if just for a few hours. Avi's mind couldn't focus. He closed his eyes and drifted into a light sleep.

Sandy was babbling on the phone. His voice brought Avi back to consciousness. Several hours had passed, yet he felt no better. Avi blinked twice and swung his legs off the bed.

"He's right here," Sandy was saying and handed him the cell.

"Hello?" Avinash croaked.

"Sir, Detective Patil here. We have identified the girl." There was a shuffling of papers in the background. "A Daya Ambel. Her family reported her missing or abducted several years ago, sir. From Haryana, along with another woman, Ipsita Chaudhary." He paused, and there was more shuffling.

"But this is of more interest, sir," Avi grunted for him to continue. "The weapon at the scene. Forensics have linked it to a shootout eighteen months ago, in Goa."

"Goa? Where?" Avi blurted.

"Hmm, Carambolim. An exchange between a biker and a traffic cop. There were no casualties, but they recovered the slug from the officer's car. The assailant fired through the radiator and escaped."

"Where?" Avi shouted.

"There is a location in the file, sir. I will text you the pin."

"Do that, Detective Patil," Avi said and ended the call. A few moments later, Sandy's phone beeped. Avinash opened the text, and it was a Google Map pin. Avi stabbed the screen with his finger and stared at it as Google Map opened and went blank. *Goa's known for many things. Good internet is not one of them.*

"Shit!" Avi shouted.

"Wi-Fi," Sandy said, and the two of them charged from the room like bulls released from a pen. The old man at the front desk jumped and dropped his newspaper as the duo came crashing down the stairs.

"Wi-Fi password!" Sandy shouted at him.

"Hotelwilsha123," the proprietor stuttered. Avi handed the cell to Sandy and paced the small lobby as he entered the password.

"Come on, come on," Sandy murmured. "Got it!" Avi rushed to his side, and they peered at the phone. "There, right there, not twenty minutes away!" Sandy said.

"Yes, and look at that," Avi said, pointing at the screen.

"Gupta Shipyards. It happened right outside their front gates!" Sandy said.

"Let's go!" The two of them sprinted out the door.

* * *

The air was thick with the smell of diesel fuel. It hung like a fog and coated Alex's palate with every breath. A soft breeze tinged the oily aroma with seawater and rust. It had discoloured the once light grey walls and fixtures, and layers of enamel were peeling and flaking off most surfaces, as a steady advance of amber corrosion ate its way forward.

Alex let go of Ipsita's hand to cover his mouth as he navigated the narrow iron stairwell, deep into the ship's engine room. They reached the lower deck and walked between the massive Perkins two-stroke engines. Crossing to the starboard side of the ship, Alex picked his way along the elevated metal grated walkway. The group stopped in front of a bank of electrical panels.

"This is where you will come if they board us," the scruffy marine mechanic ordered. "To hide." Alex scanned the large boards covered with lights and meters and levers, none of which held any meaning for him.

"Where?" Alex asked, looking from the machinist to John, who had been trailing behind them. The mechanic chuckled and pulled down on the electrical disconnect protruding from the middle panel. The unit groaned in protest and swung open, exposing a cramped closet with a bench seat at each end. There was an overhead shelf with a cargo net strung from end to end. Alex presumed it was for the shipment.

"I see," Alex replied curtly.

"You'll sit here while we load in Mumbai and move here straight away if you hear the ship's klaxon, okay? This means we are being boarded, so you enter here to hide," the mechanic said. Alex nodded and glanced at Ipsita, who was eyeballing the dreary space. "Move," he said and shut the compartment. The mechanic led them back to the stairwell, and they climbed up to the deck.

Humid Goan air surrounded them as soon as they stepped from the murky hatchway into the sun. Hiran was leaning against the bulkhead, having a cigarette.

"Get loaded," John said to him. He nodded and walked off towards the gangplank.

Alex paused at the rail of the ship and stared out in amazement. There were at least a dozen vessels crammed together in the shipyard. Not symmetrical as in a pier, with each boat tucked away in its slip. Here the ships were snug, moored together side by side, like a parking lot. They varied in size. The one Alex was on was 350 metres, but there were ships much larger. Mechanics and engineers scurried around them like rats. There was a vast array of hammering, air ratchet noises, and arc welding flashes that created daytime shadows.

Alex looked up at the pale azure of the sky. It was odd there were no seagulls, but a plethora of crows circling overhead. *India is an unfamiliar land.* They walked aft towards the bridge and after climbing another endless set of wrought iron stairs, stood in the wheelhouse.

"Wait here," the technician instructed, and then disappeared through the hatch on the other side of the cabin. The trio remained in silence for a moment, then Alex spoke.

"John?" he began. "What's the procedure? I mean, how does it all work?"

"It's simple enough," John said, lighting a cigarette and leaning back against the navigation console. "You spend the next thirty days in a small uncomfortable cabin, then just off the coast of Newfoundland, you and our merchandise gets picked up by a lobster trawler. It will take you into Nova Scotia, where we transfer you into the back of a seafood delivery truck. Two days later, you'll be sitting in the clubhouse in Montreal. End of journey," he said and drew deeply on his smoke. Alex considered this.

"What about customs and immigration?" he asked. John laughed.

"This ain't our first rodeo, cowboy. Don't worry your pretty little head about it."

"Okay, and Ipsita?" Alex murmured.

"What about her?"

"She can come? Can she come with me?" John glared at him for a moment. He drew a last drag on his smoke and butt it out on the floor.

"I was wondering when you would ask that. Tell me, Alex, why the fuck would we smuggle this twat back into Canada for you?" Ipsita gave a short, painful gasp.

"There is nothing for me here, please, if you can," she quivered. Alex looked to John, his eyes pleading.

"I know you don't owe me anything, John. I know I am here to pay off a debt. But it was just a fucking mistake. I got caught up in this because I thought the bar I had played in was being robbed. Nothing more than protecting my payment. I have done that, paid off my debt, and more. I've told you, I will commit to you, to the Club, the Chevaux de Fer. I'll prospect, or whatever it is. Whatever it takes, John, I'll do it."

"And as I told you, Alex, you don't get to decide. I've thought about it, about you, and the only reason you will not get tossed in the ocean on arrival is because I knew your old man." Alex took a step back and steadied himself against the ship's wheel. His face went ashen.

"My father?" he stammered.

"Yeah, your father. I rode with him, Alex, and he was one hell of a guy. He was decent to me when I was nothing more than a snot-nosed kid. Helped me out more than once. So, out of respect for *him,* you won't become fish food. But beyond that..."

"I knew it," Alex whispered.

"Knew what? Your dad was a biker? Yeah, yeah, Alex. You're not the first Crossman to ride a bike and kill a guy, big fucking deal. It don't mean you're a biker. There's no legacy clause in our club and you're right, we don't owe you a goddamn thing. You or her. Do you think entrance visas come easy? Or cheap?"

"I don't believe our connection can handle a visa, anyway. An exit stamp is one thing, a Canadian visa is quite another." A tall and dignified-looking older man said as he stepped into the cabin.

"Captain fucking Ahab!" John laughed.

"Hello, John," the older man replied and smiled at him. "It's been, what? Three years?" They embraced and John spoke over his shoulder.

"Alex, this is Captain Carl Banner. A filthier fucking pirate you will never meet," John laughed. A younger Indian man flanked Carl, also in a sharp uniform and carrying himself with an air of authority.

"My First Mate, Asif Hussain," Captain Banner introduced him.

Alex was still numb from the news that John had known his father. More than know him, he had befriended him. Alex shifted his gaze to Ipsita who looked as bewildered as he was. *My father was in deep, way deeper than I ever thought. Why didn't he tell me? I loved and respected him so much, why didn't he trust me enough to tell me?* Alex realised the cabin was silent and everyone was staring at him.

"Hello," he managed. The First Mate gave him a curt nod.

"As I was saying, an entry visa is a troublesome thing. Even more so, as you are late and we sail for Mumbai in thirty minutes. However, it could be done. There is a price for everything," he laughed and gave John a scornful glance.

"Circumstances arose, Captain," John said. "I needed to deal with them."

"I'm aware," Banner said absently. He smiled as Hiran entered the cabin.

"*Namaskar*, Captain," Hiran said and smiled back, then looked to John and nodded. "All stowed."

"Give me your passport," Banner said to Alex. Alex dug into his inside pocket and produced it. With a glance at Ippy, he handed it to Banner, who at once passed it over his shoulder to his First Mate. "The girl?" he asked John. John studied her. He inhaled deeply and then looked to Alex as he let out a slow deliberate breath.

The retort of small arms fire rang out in the distance, breaking the silence. The group moved in unison to the front window of the wheelhouse, peering towards the parking area of the shipyard. Hiran's cell chirped.

"Yeah?" he answered. "Okay... *theek hai*... stay down, *bhai*. We will come." He stuffed the phone in his front pocket and pulled out his Beretta. "Shiv and Sumit, police at the gate. I guess one of your boys got trigger-happy," he said to Banner, as he drew his gun.

"All right, you get hidden," John said to Alex, then turning to Banner, "Get the fuck out of here. We will try to hold them." He turned for the door and Ipsita grabbed his arm.

"Please!" she wailed. Ippy had her passport in her hand. She thrust it out to him. She was shaking, as tears flooded her eyes. "Please," she whispered again. John stared at her in silence for a heartbeat, glanced at Alex, then snatched it from her and tossed it to Banner.

"For fuck sakes!" he shouted. "Move. All of you!" They scattered like startled mice.

◆

CHAPTER THIRTEEN

Billy pushed open the ceiling hatch with a grunt. The compression hinge hissed, then held the weight. A draught of chilly air wafted into his face as he clambered back down to the storage room and grinned at the young brunette, Sofia. She quivered from the descending breeze, causing her breasts to jiggle under her leather bodice.

"Up you go," Billy said. She giggled and set her high-heeled ankle boot on the first rung of the ladder.

"You'll catch me if I slip, right?" she asked, flashing a look of mock concern. Billy nodded at her.

"Without a doubt," he said and slapped her ass through her short jean skirt.

The Horse Head tittered again and began the ascent. Billy ogled Sofia's hips swinging as she pulled herself up the narrow metal ladder. Her soft cheeks were peeking out of their tiny black panties with each step.

Sofia reached the top and lifting her unsteady foot through the hatch, climbed to the exterior. The moment afforded Billy a quick glimpse of something even softer. He stiffened in anticipation. The girl peered through the opening at him.

"Hurry, *mon garçon* sexy. It's cold up here. I need you to warm me," she said with a seductive pout.

"I love being patched!" Billy chuckled and climbed the ladder as if she had shot him out of a cannon. In a flash, he was in the tart's arms. Billy lifted the girl from her feet and spun in tight circles, her gleeful laugh muffled against his kiss. Sofia was nipping at his bottom lip as his fingers dug into her ass. She moaned and gyrated against him.

"Congratulations, baby. Take me harsh and fast," Sofia purred in his ear. Billy put her back on her feet and waited, bemused. After stepping out of her panties and hiking up her skirt, she spun around to put both palms against the air conditioning unit and presented herself to him. "Come on, stud," she invited.

"Not just yet, sweetie. There's a little ritual we need to take care of first," he said, grabbing her wrist and pulling her away from the unit.

Billy put his back against the icy metal and smirked. He fumbled with his belt buckle with one hand and placed the other on Sofia's shoulder, pushing her to her knees. She peeked up at him and shot a wicked grin as she licked her lips.

"Such a vixen," Billy sighed as she gripped him with both hands. Sophia flicked her tongue, causing Billy's knees to weaken as a shudder passed through his soul.

"A vixen worth having as an Ole Lady?" she asked. With a wink, she engulfed him. Billy shook and uttered some kind of agreement. He closed his eyes and let Sophia work her magic. Her skills were legend within the Club, and while it was true she had been with a few senior patched members, it was no secret that she was sweet on Billy.

Being a young virile lad matched with Sofia's talent, he was reaching the peak of his excitement. As her urgency quickened and the moment of completion loomed, Billy inhaled sharply and opened his eyes.

A short red flicker in the dark farther along the rooftop caught his attention. He tilted his head like a dog that had detected his master's distant whistle. Billy gazed at the spot in the darkness. A heartbeat later, the flicker came again.

"What the..." he grumbled, pushing Sofia off him.

"Hey!" she protested, tumbling off her haunches and falling on her backside. With interest lost in his initiation ritual, Billy dragged up his jeans and plodded towards the light. "What is it, *bébé*?" she asked.

"Hush," Billy scorned her. The blink came again and Billy quickened his pace. He was no demolitions expert, but he knew an explosive device when he saw one. He squatted to inspect it.

"What the fuck?!" he yelled. Billy picked up the brick-sized IED, and turning towards the building edge, he darted the seven steps to it. As he approached, he spied the rental truck in the parking area. There were at least a dozen men in the shadows beside it. An acidic cauldron boiled in Billy's stomach as he realised what was happening.

"Tell Blu the Fallen Angels are here!" he barked at Sophia. Billy swung his arm as hard as he could, throwing the IED towards the truck. He had been a capable quarterback in high school and the rig was only forty yards away. Billy heaved with all his strength.

A muzzle flash sparked in the shadows beside the truck. The shot rang out just as the device left his fingertips and his right thumb disappeared in a torrent of pulp and splintering bones.

Billy howled in pain as he followed the IED with his eyes. It was tumbling end over end through the air and was looking to land on top of the rig. He had the distance.

"Touchdown," he whispered. But at the arc's pinnacle, the bomb's light blinked from red to green and the ensuing flash blinded him. The blast erupted high in the air, short of its target, and the concussion wave rolled past, knocking him from his feet.

The explosion shattered the still night air like a freight train in a tunnel. Through the ringing in his ears, Billy could make out Sophia's scream, and the disorganised shouts of the men from the lot. The distinct tang of motor oil and almonds burned his nostrils, confirming Billy's suspicion that it was C4.

He twisted onto his stomach and forced himself to his knees. Billy tried to draw his pistol, but his shredded thumb screamed in protest. He abandoned that idea, stood, and stumbled to the hatch.

*　*　*

John leapt down the wheelhouse stairs three at a time and hit the starboard deck at a full run. He could hear the gunshots coming from the front gate. His heart pounded in his rib cage, matching his footfalls as he charged along the gangway. *This is the last thing we need, another shitty occurrence to top off a lengthy list of shitty occurrences,* he thought.

This grouping of vessels had four ships rafted side by side. They were on the last one, farthest from the pier. Just ahead of him, near the bow, the gangplank to the adjacent ship was looming. As he reached it, his motorcycle boot slid on the damp steel deck and he almost lost his footing. John grasped the thick chain of the walkway and stopped himself from toppling over the rail. Hiran was tight on his heels as the two of them galloped over the short bridge between crafts.

Two more, he thought, as they maintained their sprint across the bow of the second ship. Mechanics and shipbuilders were scattering in every direction, seeking refuge lest a stray bullet find them.

"Move!" John screamed as they continued their charge over the next gangplank. A lad on the other side threw himself behind a bollard, avoiding their rapid advance, spanners, and a hammer spilling from his tool bag and clanging onto the deck as he fell.

There was a flurry of gunshots. John looked towards the retorts but couldn't see the shipyard parking area through the large green hoarding fence around the perimeter of the dry-dock platform entrance.

They came to the wharf, and ran headlong to the gate, their footfalls thundering on the wooden planks like horses. Vaulting the ropes and skirting tool-chests, the tandem reached the access turnstile. John crouched against the hoarding and took a cautious glimpse through the opening.

On the opposite side of them was the primary entrance gate and a modest security shack. The red and white striped barrier arm had a car wedged underneath it. Someone had smashed its windshield with several bullets. The door on the driver side stood open and also had a few holes.

A guard lay face down on the ground in front of the car, his gun in the dirt just beyond his outstretched hand. The body of another guard hung over the half-opened barricade, blood dripping from a hole in his chest.

On the far right end of the lot was the workshop. The two massive sliding doors were half open and John could see Sumit hunkered down behind a stack of oil drums, just inside the building.

Opposite the security hut were two rusted blue shipping containers stacked on top of each other. Shiv was on all fours behind them. His head was hanging, and he wasn't moving. John thought they had shot him and his spirit sank.

Without warning, Shiv leapt up and fired two rounds, one shattering the window and the other slamming into the frame of the hut. John exhaled a sigh of relief.

There was a muzzle flash from the door and the slug clanged off a shipping container, causing Shiv to duck and retreat further behind them. He made eye contact with John and nodded.

To their left, were the employees' cars and scooters parked in a haphazard maze and across from the dry-dock turnstile, were their motorcycles. It was a full thirty metre dash, with no cover. In the centre of the yard was a battered flatbed truck with the faded company logo painted on the doors.

There was a clear line of sight from the security hut to the turnstile and the shipping containers, but Sumit had no angle to fire on the shack from inside the shop. John pulled out his phone and called Shiv. He watched him answer.

"We are fucking pinned, *bhai*," he said.

"It would appear so," John said, glancing at Hiran, who had crouched on the opposite face of the turnstile. "We need to get to the bikes and make a run at the gate."

"Suicide," Shiv said.

"You have a better plan?" John shouted. "One of us needs to get to that truck and empty a clip into the shed while the rest of us try for the bikes."

As he was speaking, John saw Sumit leave the workshop and sprint for the shipping containers. He had obviously drawn the same conclusion and repositioned himself for better cover. Gunfire erupted from the shack window and door. Chunks of dirt were kicking up around Sumit's feet as he ran the ten metres.

Slugs slammed into the containers as Sumit dove to safety beside Shiv, several more shots hitting the hoarding behind them. "Crazy fucker," John whispered.

"It's an open run for us, John," Shiv said. "They don't know you're there, and you have some obstruction from the lorry. Best be one of you."

"Okay, wait for my signal, then give us cover fire," John said and put his phone back in his pocket. "Me or you, brother?" he asked Hiran.

"Give me a fucking gun," Alex said. John lurched in surprise. He hadn't noticed Alex nearing them.

"Boy, what in the hell are you doing?" John screamed.

"I'm protecting my club," Alex said. Hiran stared at him in astonishment.

"You have gone bat shit crazy! Get to the ship!" John growled.

"Right after you guys make it out." He held out his hand. "Gun," Alex repeated. John looked from Alex to Hiran and back again. "What do you care if I get clipped?" he asked. John shook his head.

"I care because you have to escort the shipment. You think I trust that filthy fucking pirate?"

"So, if you trust me, give me a gun," Alex insisted.

"Give him a piece," John said after a pause. Hiran pulled a Glock from his cut and handed it to Alex along with two extra clips. Alex took it and slipped the ammo into his pocket.

"Okay, when I tell you, run to that truck. Keep changing speed and direction, and I do mean run, kid. Like you never have before. When you get there, wait to see if they fire. If they do, hang on till it stops, then shoot a round every two seconds at the shelter. Nice and steady. Window, door, window, door. Got it?" John instructed. Alex nodded.

"When the bikes start, you empty the clip at them, reload and empty the next one too. As fast as you can pull the trigger, okay? If we make it out the gate, stop shooting. We want them to chase us, not stay here, ya?" Again, Alex nodded. "As soon as they're gone, get back on that fucking boat."

"And if they don't? Leave?" Alex asked.

"*Kill them* and get back on the fucking boat," Hiran said.

"We will give you support fire from the other side if they don't take the bait," John said, scowling at Hiran. "Okay, let's do this." John looked at Alex and smiled. "You really *do* want in, don't you?" he asked.

"Yes, I really do," Alex smirked. John waved at Shiv and as soon as he waved back, John barked.

"Go, go!"

✳ ✳ ✳

Alex blasted off. He crashed through the turnstile and cut sharply left. He sprinted like the devil himself, as shots rang out from behind the container to his right. As soon as Alex cleared the entrance, Hiran and John started firing as well. Three shots came in rapid succession from the hut window and slammed into the boarding over Alex. He heard them whizz past him. Alex forced himself to slow and cut right, adrenaline pumping through him like liquid electricity.

The truck bounced in his vision as he ran. *Twenty metres away now. I can make it,* he thought. Alex sped up again and swerved left as the gunfire from behind him and the containers assailed the shack.

A single shot from the hut kicked up stones in front of him. He changed direction again. *Ten metres!* He was close enough now to see the oil-soaked planks on the truck bed. *Another few steps, and the rig will hide the shack from view,* he thought.

His calf muscles tightened and burned, and Alex pushed his legs to their limit. *Five metres to go!* Alex didn't slow his approach and slammed into the side of the cab hard. He grunted in pain and drew half a dozen quick breaths. The cover fire stopped and bullets from the security hut began bouncing off the hood of the truck like hailstones.

Alex made himself as small as he could behind the front tire. He screwed his eyes shut and waited, trying to steady his breath. After a few moments, everything fell quiet. He heard a scooter go by on the road outside and there were several crows cawing, but no gunfire.

He counted to himself. At ten, Alex leaned around the head of the truck and squeezed off a round towards the hut window. It hit just to the right. Then the door... window... door... window... door. He tried to stay steady, to keep the rhythm. Alex had no idea how many rounds were in the clip and hoped he wasn't firing too fast. *Window... door... window... door...* click. He was empty. "Shit!"

Alex crouched as he dug the other clip from his pocket, fumbling with the release. Gunfire erupted from the shack. It was not at him but was at the others running to their bikes. They were still behind him and he had no clue how close they were to their bikes.

Sweat rolled off his forehead, stinging his eyes as he continued to flounder with the reload. His hands were shaking and his vision blurry. The clip slammed home. *Should I continue firing or wait for the bikes to start?* He didn't know. Alex squatted with the gun between his knees and banged the back of his head off the tire.

"Shit, shit, shit," he murmured. The rumble of the Enfields' straight pipes flooded the air in mechanical thunder. Alex stood and jumped out from cover, arms extended in front of him and knees flexed. He pulled the trigger as fast as he could. His wrists were alight with pain as the pistol bucked up and down in his hand. The facade of the shack disintegrated under his assault, bits of framework falling everywhere.

The bikes tore past him in a stampede. For a moment, he didn't think there was enough room between the car and gatepost for them to exit.

Hiran was in the lead, with John close behind him. Dust spewed from Hiran's rear tire as it slid and locked up in the gravel. His bike slammed broadside into the car with a crunch and leapt forward as the engine screamed, scraping along the car's side, then shot through the gap as John followed in its shadow. Sumit was next to manoeuvre through the narrow passage and Shiv was trailing them.

As the bikes roared through the gate, a face appeared in the hut window. Alex had been firing without aim but shifted his attention to the fresh target. The cop ducked as Alex assaulted the window opening.

Alex's gun clicked empty again, and he retreated behind the truck to reload. He ejected the spent clip and this time, slammed the new one home with ease.

Alex re-emerged to spy an older man spring up in the doorway. He shot at him but was too slow. The cop fired once and a chunk of Shiv's skull spun away as his head snapped back. The slug's impact flung him from the bike.

Shiv's lifeless body hit the ground, and the bike careened off to the right, running over the dead security guard before flipping end over end and crashing into the oil drums. A spark from the impact ignited the leaking fuel. The tank exploded with a roar, shooting a fireball into the sky and engulfing the front of the workshop in flames.

Alex shot again and saw the older cop lurch backwards as his bullet found its mark. Then two shots from the window forced him back to safety.

Seconds passed like minutes. Alex peeked around the bumper. There was no movement. He sprinted to the tail of the truck and lay behind the rear tire. From this angle, he had an obstructed view of the hut, and could only see the side of the car and Shiv bleeding in the dirt.

The hollow whoosh of fire extinguishers distracted him. Workmen were spraying them over the flames and the yellow chemical dust they belched out floated through the yard.

Alex's mouth dried with fear. They weren't leaving. Sour bile rose in his throat and his bowels went loose. He felt he may shit himself right here. Alex crawled back to the front of the truck to position for the coming fight. He sprung up to a squat, blood thumping in his ears as he took a deep breath. A car door slammed, breaking the silence. A moment later, the car engine fired.

"Thank Christ," Alex whispered. He peeked around the tire and saw the small sedan reverse out of the compound, the security barricade dragging across the roof, and then bouncing off the hood as it spun backwards onto the road. The rear tires spat gravel as the car shot forward and disappeared from view. Alex didn't hesitate. He stood and ran with his remaining strength back to the ship. Back to Ipsita and, he hoped, back to Canada.

✳ ✳ ✳

Back in Montreal, the explosion had shattered the back windows of the clubhouse. Bottles and glasses fell from the bar and dust swirled down from the ceiling as the acoustical tiles fell. In a din of confusion, there was shouting and bodies were flying in every direction. The lights flickered, and the music stopped.

Blu scanned the room for Candy. There was no way to see her in the pandemonium. "CLIPPER! Weapons!" he called out. Clip was already opening the gun cabinet behind the bar.

"Here, boys. Here!" Clip shouted and distributed M16s and shotguns to the rush of brothers storming the counter. Blu made eye contact with Digger and waved him to the front door. Digger nodded.

"Toronto with me!" he hollered and sprinted to the exit. His boys followed. Tracy appeared at Blu's side with an assault rifle in one hand and a shotgun in the other. True to his name, Blu took the latter. Alain sprinted up to them with a scoped rifle.

"Roof!" Blu commanded him. Alain turned and ran towards the supply room, recruiting others to follow on his way. Blu heard shots and screams from the front of the building.

Two of the ex-13 members flipped a table and crouched behind it, facing the rear entrance hallway. Others took up positions around the room and readied for the coming assault.

Blu took a sharp breath, glanced at Tracy, and moved to the rear exit. Tracy followed. They slowed as they reached the hallway. Blu crouched and stole a look. The rear door was closed. With a nod, the pair crept up the corridor. Reaching the rear door, he glanced at Tracy, who shrugged. Blu grasped the handle and flung it open.

In an instant, a score of slugs slammed into the wall opposite, showering them in chunks of drywall and splinters of concrete block. Blu pressed himself as tightly as he could against the panelling, and blindly poking the muzzle of the shotgun through the door, squeezed the trigger. The gun bucked, and he heard a pained yelp as the lead pellets shredded flesh and bone.

"Again," Tracy said, coiling up to sprint. They heard the crack of Alain's sniper rifle and the assorted pop of small arms fire raining down from the roof. Screams filtered in from the utter confusion outside. Blu fired through the door again. Tracy stood, ran around him, and dove out of the entranceway. Blu took a deep breath and launched his heavy frame in pursuit.

He did his best to tuck and roll, but Blu hit the asphalt hard. Rising to a crouch, he bolted towards the club van parked five metres away. Bullets shrieked past him as he bobbed and weaved his way to cover. He threw himself against the pavement again and popped up to a squat behind the van.

Tracy was already there, blood streaming down his face from a wound on his forehead. Whether from a slug grazing him or from the asphalt, Blu didn't know. The clang of punctured tin echoed as shells pierced the truck's thin skin and ricocheted around inside. The two of them huddled between the building and the nose of the van. Brick fragments sprayed around them as the Fallen Angels peppered the surrounding wall with gunfire.

"A hell of a party, Blu!" Tracy shouted as he peeked around the bumper of the truck and squeezed off three rounds from the M16. Blu leaned down and looked under the van. He saw someone's feet coming up the left side of the vehicle. With the shotgun levelled parallel to the pavement, he pulled the trigger.

The assailant's left foot separated from his leg at the ankle and his body hit the ground with a thud. Blu glared at him as the man lay on his side. He put his hands out in front of him and opened his mouth to speak as Blu pulled the trigger again.

The battle raged for what seemed a lifetime, Blu shooting blindly around the front of the truck, then sheltering from the return fire. Random screams and shouts filled the air, and the smell of cordite stung his throat. Tracy was cursing in French and spraying round after round out into the parking lot.

Slowly the return fire diminished. From the roof, each sharp retort of Alain's sniper rifle fell a rival and turned the odds in the Horses' favour. The endless clatter of automatics was shredding the attacking club trapped on lower ground. They were quashing the assault with malice. The faint wail of police sirens called out in the distance, followed by a command of retreat from the remaining Angels.

Blu stood and cautiously looked around the corner of the truck. Bodies littered the parking area, corpses strewn here and there in a grizzly mosaic. He saw a scant few running off into the darkness towards the empty ACS employee parking lot across the street. A last rifle shot rang out from above and one of the escaping men tumbled and fell on the road.

"Fuck you, Fallen Angel assholes... *tabarnak*!!" Alain screamed at them from the roof. Blu saw Clipper limp from the clubhouse doorway, followed by five or six others. They had won the firefight. Tracy stood next to him with his hand pressed to his wound. Clipper limped to them as quickly as he could.

"You guys whole?" he asked. Blu nodded.

"Yeah, we're good. Gather the weapons, do it quickly and get them the fuck out of here. We only have a few minutes, Clip," he said.

"Guns to the truck! Now!" Clipper bellowed as he hurried to the tail of the van and opened the doors.

"There are shell casings everywhere, Blu!" Tracy called back over his shoulder as he ran inside to get the keys. Blu knew that, but what could he do? Damage control. Without a weapon, it was hard to prove who shot it.

"Charles!" Candy screamed from the doorway. She picked her way down the three metal steps, then ran to him, her heels clicking on the ground. She collided square with his chest and clung to him like a child.

"It's okay, darlin'. We're okay," he soothed, stroking her hair. "Get back into your room and stay there. You tell the cops you were asleep. The noise woke you, but you stayed in your room. You know nothing... okay?"

"But..." she started. Blu pushed his finger across her lips.

"Go, now, I'll be there soon." He kissed her and smiled. "Go!" Candy spun and trotted off towards the door. She passed Tracy at the door who was on his way out. Tracy sprinted to the van and got in the driver's seat. He fired the engine as the last of the weapons were being thrown in the rear.

"Anymore?" Clipper shouted.

"Wait!" One more Chevaux de Fer sprinted from the door with two M16s in his arms. He tossed them in the back of the van.

"That's it," he said. Clip slammed the doors shut and pounded on the side panel of the van. Tracy backed up a bit to clear a body laying prone at the front wheels, then spun the tires as he sped out of the parking lot.

Digger emerged from the clubhouse and walked over to Blu. The two of them stood listening to the sirens approach. Digger lit a cigarette and gave it to Blu, then lit one for himself.

"Are we whole?" Blu asked.

"They were sitting out front, waiting," Digger said. "I lost Chu-Too. He opened the door and charged out like a horny bull. They nailed him hard. Tommy took a round in the leg. It's minor, he'll live, and Billy lost a thumb." Digger took a deep drag on his smoke.

"He found the bomb on the roof and tossed it at them. Pure fucking luck, my friend. Without that, this situation would have gone a very different way."

"Hum," Blu murmured. "Yeah, we got lucky. But we dealt them one hell of a blow."

The parking lot flooded red and blue as the lights from a dozen police cruisers splashed over everything. Blu and Digger sank to their knees and put their hands behind their heads.

"You have one hell of a lot of explaining to do, son," Digger chuckled.

✳ ✳ ✳

The nine millimetre slugs were hitting the rear of the decaying security hut in rapid succession. Sandy crouched beneath the shattered window, listening to the rhythmic impacts. He was praying for a pause so that he could return fire.

The dark blue curtains had fallen from the wall and were lying on the floor amid scattered papers from the desk. Sandy fired three shots at a white biker sprinting across the parking lot. Then the rest of the crew had peppered them, driving the duo deep within the small shack. At least four guns were firing. But now it slowed to a single shooter squeezing off a round every few seconds. Just enough fire, forcing them to keep their heads out of sight.

"You all right?" Avi shouted to him. He was crouching behind the door across from him. It was ajar and providing him with thin cover.

"I'm okay," Sandy called back.

He was still grappling with the events that had just transpired. They had pulled up to the gate nice and easy and the security guard had motioned for them to open the window. Sandy had shown his badge and asked for the owner of the yard. The attendant motioned towards the lot and asked him to park there and wait.

Another guard had gone to the barricade and pressed on the swing arm to lift the gate. As they pulled forward, Avi spied the row of Enfields in the parking lot. He pointed and barked an alarm. Sandy slammed the brake and at that moment, the security guard shifted to the front of the automobile and opened fire.

Avi lay across the seat as Sandy popped open the passenger door and rolled out onto the ground. He drew his Glock as he came upon one knee and put two rounds through the guard.

The barrier fell and hit the roof with a thud as Avi put a round in the second guard's chest. They looked at each other, astonished. Then the other shooting began. They had scrambled into the security hut and returned fire.

Sandy refocussed on Avi behind the door. "I guess we're in the right place," Avi shouted. "My phone is in the car." Sandy dug in his pocket and pulled his cell out. *No bars!*

"I have no network."

"Shit! Landline? On the desk?"

"Not anymore," Sandy said, spying the shattered remnants of a phone. He forced himself tighter against the wall. The firing stopped and the thunder of bikes starting echoed through the yard.

"They're making a break!" Avi shouted and peeked out of the door. "Wait, let them get close..." he said, as the surrounding air erupted. Slugs were flying past them in rapid succession, tearing into the hut and destroying everything they struck. The drone of the motorcycles grew louder, followed by the crunch of an impact. One bike had smashed into their car. Sandy tried to lift his head, but the cover fire kept him hidden from view.

There was a sudden silence. *The shooter is reloading,* he thought. Avi sprung to his feet and fired through the open door. Sandy peeked out the window and watched the tail biker hurl backwards, as Avi's slug connected with him. Avi grunted and fell to his knees as a returned shot found him. Sandy shot at the approaching column of Enfields until he clicked empty.

As he fished for a fresh clip, he crawled towards Avi. The room shook and there was a massive explosion outside the hut. The air filled with the pungent stench of burning oil.

"Avi!" he shouted. Avinash's eyes fluttered as blood seeped from his chest, his white shirt staining red.

"I'm hit," he croaked.

"No, no! Shit!" Sandy screamed and pounded the floor. He scanned the hut for a makeshift bandage to dress the wound. There was a yellow nylon scarf hanging on a peg on the door. Sandy stood and grabbed it. Dropping to his knees, he wadded the material up and pressed it to the centre of the crimson pool on Avi's chest.

"Hold this tight, Avi. Hold it," he shouted, guiding Avi's right hand to the makeshift bandage.

"Boss, we have to go," he said. He crouched behind Avi and lifted him from his armpits. Avinash bellowed in pain and Sandy laid him back on the floor. "Do you want to die here? Come on! Help me!" Again, he heaved and again Avi screamed, but struggled to his feet.

Sandy peered through the door. Other than the men trying to extinguish the fire in the garage, everything was quiet. He staggered with Avi to the rear door and guided him into the back of the car. Avi groaned as he lay across the bench seat.

Sandy slid in behind the wheel and twisted the key, while silently praying a stray slug hadn't punctured the radiator. The engine turned over twice and fired. He slammed the transmission into reverse and hit the gas. They shot backwards onto the road and Sandy spun the steering hard. He could see the cloud of dust trailing the bikes not too far ahead. Sandy stamped the accelerator and gave pursuit.

* * *

Griff heard the wail of police sirens fade with every step. *That doesn't mean I'm free and clear. It won't be long before the cops figure out what's happened at the Horses' clubhouse and begin searching the surrounding area. Then the city,* Griff thought.

There's no doubt that was Montreal's biggest fucking gun battle in history. They'll throw all available resources into finding everyone involved.

Griff had emerged unscathed from the melee and was running towards the Meadowbrook Golf Club. He crossed the railway tracks bordering the south end, the ballast stones between the ties crunching under his weight. Griff sprinted to the chain-link fence.

With minor effort, he lofted himself over and trotted across the fairway of the 17th hole, collapsing in a small stand of trees on the far side. He rolled onto his back and stared up through the budding maple tree boughs.

It was a cloudless night and there were a thousand pinpricks of light, dancing in the sky. He breathed, trying to recover and slow his heart rate. *If I can get to the other side of the golf course and make it to Westminster Avenue, I can hail a taxi and get back to the clubhouse.*

Griff had no idea how many of his brothers lay dead. *How many had escaped or were in custody?* He had heard Alfredo's call to retreat and charged from his position behind the rental truck and headed north.

Griff pounded his fists into the dirt and stifled a yell as the bitter frustration of failure took hold of him. He shook the thoughts from his mind. *Not now. Now I have to keep moving.*

Griff forced his exhausted legs to lift, stood, and loped across the manicured grass. Breathless, he reached the parking lot ten minutes later. He slowed his pace and strolled through the cars. The course was closed, but there was an event happening in the club. Griff could see the members laughing and chatting over their drinks through the windows of the enormous lounge.

Stopping behind a large Cadillac Escalade, Griff yanked up the hood of his black sweater, pulling the drawstrings to conceal as much of his face as possible. He strode towards the entrance gate. There were a few of the club members standing outside, chatting and smoking. He passed through them as a ghost. They paid no attention to him.

A few taxi-cabs stood in line at the front of the gate and Griff knocked on the window of the first one. The driver rolled it open.

"*Oui?*" he asked

"Notre-Dame Est," Griff replied, avoiding eye contact. Griff climbed in the back as he started the engine.

The moment he allowed himself to relax, a wave of pure hatred rose from his innermost core. His hands shook, and he gritted his teeth. Visions of his brothers falling around him replayed in his mind and again, Griff had to stifle a scream of frustration. He forced himself to calm and stared out the window.

"*Passez une bonne nuit?*" the driver asked. Griff ignored him. *Was he having a good night? Jesus Christ, if he only knew.* Griff stayed silent. The driver took the hint. Twenty minutes later, the taxi swung left onto Notre Dame Blvd.

"Bar Le Relais," Griff said. It was a small tavern opposite the clubhouse. The chauffeur nodded and a few minutes later, stopped at the curb. Griff tossed the driver a twenty for the fifteen-dollar fare.

"Keep it," Griff said and got out. He waited for the taxi to disappear around the corner before he jogged across the street to the Fallen's clubhouse. He pressed the buzzer on the wall and looked up at the CCTV camera. A few moments later, the door opened and one of the new prospects let him into the lobby. Griff climbed the stairs to the second floor and went straight to the chapel.

There were three of them around the table. Ziggy and Jeff, Montreal full-patch members and one Boston brother that Griff didn't know. They sat dejected. Broken. They looked up as he entered. Griff turned to the prospect that had followed him up the stairs.

"Fuck me, is this it?" he asked.

"So far," he answered.

"We jacked a car at the end of the street and came straight here. We've seen no one else," the guy from the Boston crew said.

"Alfredo is in his office," Ziggy whispered. Griff spun and started out the door. "It's bad," he called after him.

The room was narrow and long. Alfredo lay on a tattered settee at the opposite end from the entrance. The only light was coming from a small desk lamp. Griff couldn't see him well, but the scent in the air told the tale of impending death. Sour breath, like curdled milk, and the pungent tang of sweat-soaked clothing assaulted Griff as he walked towards Alfredo. He lifted the desk chair and set it closer to him.

"Hey, Alf," he said, sitting. "You got hit bad, man."

"I know, Griff. I'm not a kid. It's closing time, brother, last call," Alfredo whispered and then hacked out a liquid-filled cough. Spittle and blood dripped from his mouth. "Water," he whispered, lifting his arm and pointing at the table. Griff spun around, grabbed the glass, and held it to Alfredo's lips. He sipped the water and coughed again.

"You want whiskey?" Griff asked him.

"No, no. I want to go out sober. How's the Club? How bad?" Alfredo asked.

"It's tough, Alf. So far, only six of us have turned up here."

"Six?!" Alfredo repeated, then winced with pain. "Oh, Griff. What happened, man?"

"Don't you stress about it, Prez. I'm gonna make them pay for this. They don't get away clean," Griff assured him, but Alfredo was shaking his head.

"No, no, no, man. You need to gather up whoever remains and get across the border. Tonight. Now. The *les keufs* are coming, brother. Fallen Angels are lying all over that parking lot and whom they don't arrest, the Chevaux will finish. Time to cut bait and run, my friend." Alfredo hacked up another mouthful of mucus and blood. "Get to Boston and regroup. Tell them we have lost the island."

"No, man. No fucking way," Griff exploded, but Alfredo put his hand on his arm.

"You tell them, I lost the island," he said. A police siren droned in the distance. Alfredo paused as they listened to it, trying to decide on its direction. After a moment, it faded and Griff released the breath he hadn't realised he was holding.

"Go, *mon frère*. Gather the survivors and go. That is my last official command," he croaked. "Griff, you have been an outstanding soldier, loyal to the Club and to me. Honour me, man. Tell those Boston bitches how it *really* is up here. Fight for Le Montréal, fight hard. Then, when they re-start the chapter, tell them I said it should be yours. *Make* them understand."

Another coughing fit silenced him. Griff clasped his hand and leaned close, hugging him. He stood to leave.

"I will do it, Alfredo. I swear, brother," he muttered. "And when I return, every one of those Horses will die. You have my word."

"One more thing," Alfredo croaked. "The drawer." He lifted his chin towards the desk. Griff walked behind it and pulled open the middle compartment. The keys to Alfredo's 1936 Knucklehead EL slid from the back and hit the coin tray. Griff stared at them.

"Look after her, Griff. She is my only true love." For the first time in many years, Griff's eyes dampened with tears.

$* * *$

"Hang in there, boss," Sandy said. He knew the odds of finding a hospital and getting Avi into surgery in time to take care of him were slim. *I have a choice to make,* he thought. *Try to save my partner, or chase down the Horses.* Sandy's internal rage screamed at him to pursue the bikes and kill the bastards astride them. But Avinash was his mentor, his friend. His conscience and love of the man tore at his guts. Sandy bargained with himself. *We're on state highway 366, the major road to Cortalim. If I come across a clinic, I'll stop. Until then, we'll follow the Enfields.*

He pushed the accelerator hard, and the speedometer touched eighty. The narrow uneven blacktop was rushing towards him at breakneck speeds.

Sandy honked at the locals congesting the surface of the roadway, and they scattered. They abandoned their papaya carts and tea stalls and jumped back into the jungle.

The kaleidoscope created by the shattered windshield obscured Sandy's vision. He wished he had taken the time to kick it out. He could make out his prey. They were only three hundred metres ahead.

The lane choked further as they entered a tiny village and a local twenty-seater bus pulled out from the top of the road. Sandy heard the chorus of horns from the bikes and the bus lurched to a stop. The fleeing outlaws had slowed to avoid a collision but were now around the vehicle.

Sandy had no intention of slowing. With his thumb pressed firmly on the horn, he swerved left to skim the nose of the bus. His fender clipped a tuk-tuk parked on the side of the roadway and it bounced up onto the footpath toppling, causing panicked shrieks from the onlookers.

A scrawny brown stray dog, startled by the commotion, bolted across the road in front of him. Sandy quashed the urge to brake. The stray leapt for safety, escaping his tire, and scrambled, yelping, to the far side.

The rear end fishtailed in the loose gravel on the shoulder, sending stones flying. As the wheel tugged at his hands, Sandy wrestled for control. The tires found purchase on the hot tar surface and screeched. Their vehicle straightened and Sandy flattened the accelerator to the floor.

"I haven't got long," Avi called. Sandy glanced in the rear-view mirror to see he had pulled himself up to a semi-sitting position. His wound was mortal, and it soaked Avi in sweat and blood.

"Keep the pressure on," Sandy shouted back. "The bikes are near now." He drew his gun and stuck it out the window. The wind was shrieking through the holes in the windshield as he discharged two rounds. They sailed over the bikers' heads. He had to get closer.

A shot rang out from the trailing bike and the slug blew through the windscreen, causing the top corner to free itself from the weather stripping. It folded inward and dangled, further impairing his vision.

"Fuckers!" Sandy shouted as he grabbed it and tugged. The full force of the rushing wind hit him in the face, filled with dust and road dirt. Sandy slowed and pulled at the limp sheet of shattered glass. It relented and peeled down far enough to see through the opening.

"Come on, son. Catch them," Avi called. Sandy put the gun between his legs and grasped the wheel with both hands. They hurled forward.

"Phone!" Avi shouted. Sandy glanced at the console and saw it in the passenger cup holder. He tossed it over his shoulder and heard Avi calling for backup and an ambulance.

The bikes were pulling away. *There's no way to keep up with them in an automobile. Not on these twisty roads,* Sandy thought as he lost sight of them on a sharp right-hand bend. As he rounded it moments later, he came nose to nose with a small white compact car.

The driver had drifted out on the corner and was coming at them head to head. Sandy edged as far left as he dared. The small car lurched to its left as well and their wing mirrors contacted each other and a rainbow of shattering glass and plastic cascaded into the air.

Sandy thought he was clear of the near-miss, but his quarter panel rubbed the guard rail. The gnashing shriek of tearing metal filled the car as their sedan skipped up onto the tarmac and again, he regained control.

Dense jungle canopy blotted out the sky above as they hurled forward. The serpentine curving of the road increased and Sandy was now only catching glimpses of the Enfields at the exit of each bend. As he rounded one corner, they disappeared from the next.

Sandy pushed the car to 90 kmph. He dared not risk any more speed. They were bouncing through potholes as he navigated the broken surface. Sandy let go of the wheel to dig in his pocket for his sunglasses to ease the rush of the wind. He found them and dipped his head to put them on as they drifted through a left-hand corner. Sandy looked up and was staring down the length of a long causeway. It was littered with light traffic, but he spotted the bikes. They were midway across the land-bridge.

He slammed his foot to the floor, and they lurched forward. *This is what I need! Straight road!* He pushed the car to its absolute limit and the small white posts marking the boundary on the edge of the shoulder ticked by like a picket fence.

Sandy pulled out to round a small Honda motorcycle. His horn wailed as he roared by him and returned to his lane. He could see the bikes better now, the Iron Horses patches on their backs clearly visible.

The trio were riding in a chevron formation. Both rear riders were Indian. *Who's the one on point?* He had no helmet and his shaggy salt and pepper hair was fluttering behind him. *A white man. It must be the firangi who called Avi forewarning him of Ramdev's death!*

"We are gonna do this, boss," he hollered, glancing in the mirror. Avi's eyes had closed and his head lolled to one side. "Avi!" Sandy screamed and looked back over his shoulder. Avinash's eyelids fluttered. Sandy returned his attention to the road and cursed.

A scooter with a young woman appeared from behind an oncoming truck to overtake. The lorry driver assessed the situation and, in a panic, locked his brakes. Seeing Sandy speeding towards her, the girl panicked as well, slowing her scooter to a near halt. She looked for an escape, but couldn't duck back behind the truck. The lorry had boxed her in between itself, the oncoming car, and the road edge barricade.

Sandy slammed the brakes, and his vehicle pulled right. The tires cried out in a symphony of shredding rubber. There was a resounding crunch as his car broadsided the woman. Her terrified face peered at them as she flew across the hood.

Shattered plastic rained down around them, as the front of the car smacked the rear end of the truck. It spun them, causing a series of violent clockwise spirals along the centre of the road.

The wheel ripped from Sandy's hands as the momentum pinned him to the seat. There was a crack of snapping wood and the car lurched and slowed. He watched the landscape tilt as the automobile came up on its passenger side wheels. Sandy was sure they'd roll, but the car hit another post. The impact snapped it off ground level, halting the car, and they fell back on four tires.

The dust settled. They were teetering on the bank of the causeway. Both the rear wheels were hanging over the embankment and it raised the front off of the shoulder. The murky green waters of the Ziari river were glinting fifteen metres below them as the car see-sawed on its frame.

"Just sit tight," Avi said. "I called; help is coming." Sandy took a deep breath.

"Dammit, Avi," he whispered. "I was sure I could..."

"Hush," Avi said.

There were murmurs and gasps from the small group of onlookers that had gathered. *Will they tip us into the water?* Sandy wondered. *Indian vigilante justice was common in such cases.* He was positive he had just killed that local woman on the scootie.

"Narcotics Control Bureau," he shouted. "Stand back from the vehicle."

"Sandeep?" Avi croaked. Sandy spun to look at him. The car frame groaned and the back end dipped, lifting the front tires. He settled back in his seat, the car righted and he looked at Avinash through the rear-view mirror.

"What do you need, boss?" he whispered.

"I'm sorry, son. I screwed this case up right from the start."

"No, just some terrible breaks."

"Terrible breaks?" Avi chuckled. "A junior agent is dead. The motorcycle club we are trying to apprehend has gifted us all the evidence we have and we've lost the trail of the heroin, *again*. Now, with us being no further ahead, I fear I will die." Avi coughed and took a shallow breath. "You were right, Sandy, back in Udaipur. I should have told Ramdev, I should have warned him. I made the wrong call."

"You had to follow your gut," Sandy consoled his partner.

"That's the point, I didn't. I knew I should have told him the Club was wise. It was my arrogance, my hubris. I wanted this so *fucking* bad." He coughed again.

"Avi..."

"I've tried to mentor you. You're a talented agent, Sandeep, and an excellent friend. I hope you heed my lessons well... guess you'll never teach me to *lungi* dance," he whispered and laughed, hacking up a mouth full of scarlet froth.

"Yes, I will, Avi. You've taught me well, boss. We'll live to fight another day."

"Will you now?" A deep voice called out. Sandy looked out of the shattered windshield and saw John standing at the hood of the car. Hiran and Sumit flanked him and he had his pistol drawn.

"I have to be honest, it don't look good, Special Agent...Dip Shit?" John questioned. He stared at Sandy with complete disdain and raised his gun.

"Don't," Sandy said. "You've won, just walk away. Our backup will be here soon. You still have time to escape. They are less likely to pursue if you leave us alive."

"Bullshit!" John laughed. "Besides, fishing you out of the water should slow them down enough, I would think." He moved his pistol from Sandy to Avinash and back again, deciding whom to shoot first.

"You should have listened to me, old man," John said to Avinash. "I told you we would clean this up." Sandy looked in the mirror. Avi's face contorted with loathing.

"Fuck you," Sandy whispered.

"Nope. Fuck you, pig," John said and pulled the trigger. Sandy felt the slug rip into his chest and then another into his shoulder. The three bikers kicked the bumper in unison and Sandy felt the car tilt and slide backwards.

The car hung for a moment, groaning in protest, then the underside scrapped across the gravel as they slipped off the embankment. Sandy looked in the rear-view. He saw Avi, eyes closed tight, clutching his chest, and the green water rushing towards the rear window. There was a jolt of impact, then blackness.

✳ ✳ ✳

"All in favour?" John's voice squawked out from the Bluetooth speaker in the middle of the chapel table.

"Aye!" The room erupted.

"Then God bless King Blu, long may he rule!" John chuckled. Cheers and congratulations came from every direction. Blu smiled despite himself and patted his hands in the air for quiet.

It had been a month since the shootout and the MC was settling back into a routine. This was the first church after being dragged away in handcuffs post showdown with the Fallen. During the legal complications and clean-up, Blu, Tracy, and John took care of club business via three-way phone conversations. This had been their first proper vote, and it was to elect Blu as president.

"Thank you, brothers," Blu said. "Please, please. Let's quieten down and catch up with our associates." The room settled to a cheery silence. "What is the situation, John?" he asked, glancing at Billy who was hovering over the phone to make sure the Cellcrypt app was secure. Billy nodded that they were on a protected line.

"I've set up an initial meeting with our guy in the Foreigners Regional Registration Office tomorrow. He assures me buying a business visa will be easy enough. We just need to grease the right palms," John told them. "So, I'll stay another six or eight months. Delhi chapter voted Hiran in as president, I want to help him out and have him orientated before I leave,"

John chuckled. "Acclimatise him to life in the big chair. Job two is making sure the next couple of shipments go through without a hitch. The NCB burnt down our fucking transportation network from Amritsar and the New Delhi chapter is thin as far as bodies, but I will see that sorted. No worries."

"All right, Johnnie, and the other potential opportunity? Where does that stand?" Blu asked.

"I'm heading out to Tosh after my FRRO meeting. It's a hill station in Himachal Pradesh, about a twelve-hour ride from Delhi. I'm told they produce the best hash on the planet," John said, and a cheer came from around the desk. "We can buy *mucho* volume at *minúsculo* cost. I'll dig into it and let you know what the margins look like after I have a handle on their production times and so forth."

"Yeah, I bet you'll dig into it!" Alain shouted. There was a chorus of laughs.

"Last," John continued. "I've called for what they call a *Bulletiapa*. It's a meet of all the chapters. We will assemble over the next week in Jaipur and have this all set, boys. Full distribution of the sugar all around India and look at ways to increase our shipments home."

"Very good, John," Blu said. "On this end, we are still sweeping up the aftermath. I'm assured by our legal eagle, Ms Duchamp, that we can avoid any hard time. There will be a few weapons charges and so forth, but without the guns, they can't establish who shot who. We'll tread softly for the next little while. But for all intents and purposes, Montreal is secure and under Chevaux de Fer control. With our recent members,"—Blu gave a wink to Taz who sat on his left—"we will lock down the east side and be ready for distribution soon. Speaking of which, Clipper leaves in the morning for Halifax to pick up our product and collect our messenger boy."

"Who I shall promptly dump off the edge of the pier," Clipper growled.

"No, you will not," John and Blu said in unison.

"He has stepped up, and is worthy of a prospect patch," John said. "He wants it, and I want it too. Believe me, this entire operation would have collapsed if not for him. He is the reason this shipment is on the boat."

There were murmurs of surprise from around the room. "I'll discuss the situation with Blu in more detail later, then he can bring you all up to speed. In the meantime, get Alex and the product back to Montreal safe, okay?"

"As you say," Clipper grumbled, not happy.

"I spoke with our friend in Immigration regarding the *other* package," Blu said. "He suggested a student visa for the time being. Register her at McGill or Concordia University. As long as her entry visa is in order, he can fudge the rest."

"It's clean as a baby's ass," John said. "Straight from the Consulate General of Canada in Mumbai. Their passports are waiting in Halifax. We slipped them in the diplomatic mail. Okay, all good then?"

"Yes, brother. We are tight. I'll talk to you in a couple of days," Blu said.

"Okay, Mr President," John said, his voice dripping with sarcasm. "I'm off to Cyber Hub. Hiran assures me you can get a steak there. I swear if I eat one more piece of goddamn chicken, I'm gonna sprout fucking feathers," John laughed, and the group joined in with him.

"John, that steak you're looking forward to, it ain't beef, brother. It's buffalo," Blu coughed out between peals of laughter.

"What the fuc..." John howled, but Blu nodded at Billy who hit the call end button mid-sentence. Billy cutting him off redoubled the laughter. Blu looked around the table, making eye contact with each of them. Tracy, Alain, Clipper, Taz, and Billy were smiling back at him and the newly patched ex-Thirteen Machine members looked comfortable enough.

"All right, brothers. Let's get this ship sailing smooth," Blu said and banged the gavel. He stood with the rest of them and wandered out into the lounge. Candy was leaning against the bar, chatting with one of the new prospects and Billy's girl, Sofia. An enormous grin spread across her face when she saw him. Blu approached and loomed over her.

"What's going on here?" he asked, bemused.

"Nothing, my love," she said, wrapping her arms around him and standing on her tiptoes to kiss his cheek. "Just planning a little threesome for later." Candy grinned. Blu slapped her ass. She yelped and giggled as the two of them wandered away from the group.

"Let's get some dinner, darlin'," he said.

"Humm, I can't." Candy pouted and then looked at her watch. "I have to be at the Cleopatra in forty-five minutes. I'm a working girl, you know." Her eyes sparkled with pure affection as she stared up at Blu. "Come with me," she said. "You can sit at the bar and ogle the strippers," she giggled.

"This is my life?" Blu sighed, defeated. "Reduced to being the bartender's bitch, waiting in the shadows for her shift to end?"

"Yep, and *then* you will buy me a late dinner!" Candy chirped, dragging him towards the door by his index finger.

"Jesus!" Blu whispered as he allowed her to lead him forward. He glanced around the room as they left. It had come together after the extensive destruction from the melee with the Fallen. Everyone was smiling and laughing, drinking beer. Things were being sorted out in India and in one fell swoop, they had eliminated all the enemies of the Chevaux de Fer. For the time being at least, they were whole and out of jail.

Yes, he thought, as Bob Marley crooned in his head. *Every little thing, gonna be all right*. He glanced at Candy's leather pants. Her ass wiggled as she skipped in front of him. Blu laughed. "Yeah, everything's gonna be just fine," he whispered.

✳ ✳ ✳

The icy breeze of the North Atlantic caressed them, causing Ipsita to shiver. Alex pulled her close. She was standing at the rail of the ship, staring out over the endless expanse of the ocean. He stood behind her, wrapping her in a warm embrace, and rested his chin on the top of her head. They watched the last traces of sunlight dance across the frothy waves. Ipsita spun in his arms and smiled up at him. She raised herself and planted a kiss, nipping at his bottom lip.

"Is Canada always cold?" she asked.

"This isn't Canada yet, babe," Alex whispered, his eyes glassy and filled with longing as he peered westward. "It has its cold months, yes, but warm ones too." He smiled. "It's the most beautiful place on earth."

"And you'll keep me warm? In the cold months?"

"Every minute of every day," he assured her, pulling tighter still. "You'll want for nothing, Ippy. I swear." She laid her head on his chest.

"I believe you, Alex."

They stood in silence for a moment, rocking with the gentle roll of the ship.

"I've never been one for much planning or forethought. I'm an impulsive one, you know. But this, I have never run away from life so blindly," Ipsita said.

Alex chuckled and teased, "It's crazy, I know. You *may* be insane."

Ippy pushed off his chest and punched him on the arm.

"How romantic!" she squealed and he grinned at her.

"You're scared?" she asked. It was more of an accusation than a question.

"I am," he admitted. "Yet, I believe this is where we are meant to be. I don't understand how or why, I don't even care. But I am not the same man who left Canada. My world has changed, Ippy, and me with it."

"But you're happy?" she prompted.

"Yes." Alex lit a smoke and thought for a moment. "The things I've done, Ippy, they are so far adrift from anything I have ever experienced. There is blood on my hands. Actual blood. This beast inside me, this wanderlust, this... whatever it is, it's awake, and I'm sure it's the real me. I was living a lie. I drifted through my life, just going wherever the wind pushed me. But now, I feel I belong."

"To what, Alex? Belong to what?"

"You," he said simply. "The Club, the lifestyle." He laughed. "All of it." He took a long drag on the cigarette and flicked it over the rail. "I don't know where we end up. Toronto? Montreal? Will the MC embrace me or kill me? I don't know. If they *do* bring me into the fold, how will we live?

All I'm positive about is you *and* being a biker. Somehow, God willing, it'll all come together."

Ipsita stared at him and smiled, her eyes brimming with hope.

"Sorry to interrupt," Captain Banner said. The two of them jumped. They had been so lost in each other, they had not heard his approach.

"Hello, Captain," Alex said.

"I've received word from the Club," he began. "We will be in Canadian waters come the morning, sometime around 6:30. We'll link up with a lobster trawler and make the transfer to it. The trawler will take you into Halifax. From there, Clipper will escort you back to Montreal. A refrigerated delivery truck. *Fresh Lobster. From the coast to your kitchen,*" he chuckled.

"Shit," Alex said.

"Yes! More cold!" Ipsita whined.

"Not that," Alex corrected. "Clipper. My knocking him off a stair landing and messing him up set this nightmare in motion. I don't imagine he will be too pleased to see me."

"I wouldn't worry, Alex," Banner said. "Word around the campfire is the MC is looking to give you a prospect patch. Congratulations," he chuckled. Banner spun on his heel and walked towards the aft of the ship.

Alex looked at Ipsita in astonishment. She smiled up at him and laughed. He looked like a child.

"See? It will all work out," she said.

"I can't believe it," he stammered. "I thought they would put a bullet in me and dump me off the wharf," he laughed.

Alex quivered with anticipation. He was sure he was on the path destined for him. His father's footsteps laid out before him. A straight highway to check out of society and say *fuck you* to all the entanglements of a *normal* life.

He was now free to become the man he had been hiding, the man he didn't even know existed. The morality of it didn't faze him in the least. The thought of being an outlaw wasn't a moral issue for him, it wasn't an issue at all... it was a relief.

"Promise me one thing," Ipsita whispered.

"What's that?" he asked.

"Now that you'll be a big dangerous biker, living life on the edge and all that, make some time for me. Make some time to try and grow what we have planted. I trusted you, Alex, followed you here not knowing my own heart. I'm scared, unsure." Her eyes edged with moisture. "All those horrid memories of Ramdev," she whispered. "I don't want to be a plaything. I will commit to this Alex, I will." Alex embraced her tenderly.

"You will always be foremost. That will never change. I know you rolled the dice, know you don't feel for me as I do for you. But I'm willing to try, and I'm not him, Ippy, not by a long shot," he comforted.

"I trust that, Alex. I pray it's enough," Ipsita whispered, as silent tears rolled down her cheeks. She clung to him as the last glimmer of sunlight dipped below the watery horizon.

✳ ✳ ✳

The sun was blinding, a painful glare seeping through his closed eyelids. Sandy groaned as he flicked his eyes open and shut. He blinked hard, trying to remove the blur. It was white light.

Sandy dialled into the faint buzzing in his ears. *It's fluorescent lights, not the sun.* He blinked again, and his focus returned. Pale green curtains, an alabaster ceiling, and a metal frame bed with dingy light blue sheets drew into contrast.

Mixed with the buzz of the lights was the soft *whomp* of a ceiling fan. He turned his head with effort and saw it spinning in an endless spiral. His stomach rolled with nausea. Sandy's lips were dry and cracked. He ran his swollen tongue over them and realised there were tubes in his mouth. He coughed and tried to sit upright. The rush of pain checked that idea, and he lay on his back, trying to breathe.

"Doctor!" a woman called in the distance. A hazy outline blotted out the fluorescent sun.

"Hello, Agent Bohla," the doctor said. "Welcome back."

"Where?" Sandy croaked.

"Hush now," the doctor soothed. "You must have questions. But please try to rest. You're in Sarvodaya Hospital ICU & Trauma Care, Pune. You will be okay. It was touch and go for a while, my friend. Two gunshot wounds to the chest and you were half-drowned. You're a very lucky young man. Lucky the ambulance arrived when it did."

"How long?" Sandy croaked.

"You have been in a coma for almost a month. We didn't know if you would ever come back."

"Avi?" Sandy said. The doctor looked at the nurse beside him. She shook her head.

"Ah, your partner. I'm afraid he expired before we could even *try* to help. There was too much damage. I am sorry." Sandy screwed his eyes shut and whimpered.

"Please now, take rest. It will be a long road to recovery. But you're alive, Sandeep. A miracle. Now, slowly, we can get you well."

The pain of injuries and emotions flooded every fibre of Sandy's body as hazy memories flooded back to him. *A month! They had gotten away, clean. They killed my friend. They killed Dimpi, and they are still out there doing as they pleased.* Tears leaked past Sandy's shut eyelids.

"No," he whispered. *This will not stand. The doctor is correct, it will be a long road. A road of recovery and then of vengeance. I'll get well and find them. Then I will end this, end it my way. That white man, that fucking firangi, he will pay. They all will pay.*

Sandy felt a pinprick in his arm as the nurse injected him with a painkiller. His mind clouded. He was slipping into the comforting blackness of sleep. *With or without the NCB...I will destroy the Iron Horses... By God, I will burn them down, right to their very foundation... and then I'll murder them, and everyone they ever knew!*

◆